Karen,

Don't let this scare you away from your friendly dentist

ü

27 GAUGE LONG SHAFT

Craig M. Droskin

ISBN: 1500292125
ISBN 13: 9781500292126
Library of Congress Control Number: 2014911495
CreateSpace Independent Publishing Platform
North Charleston, South Carolina

PROLOGUE

THE ATHEIST EASTER EGG

7:00 a.m., Easter morning, about nine years ago. Denver, Colorado

Nine-year-old Robbie Cline couldn't contain his excitement any longer. He'd already been up for two hours with two failed attempts to wake his parents for the much-anticipated candy basket and Easter egg hunt. At the Cline house, Easter was the candy holiday. The Easter bunny consistently delivered enough chocolate bunnies, Cadbury eggs, and jelly beans to supply Robbie and his siblings with sweets deep into the summer if they rationed properly. The Easter bunny was the number-two holiday morning superhero, whom the Cline children ranked just under Santa.

Robbie was cunning and manipulative. He usually got his way, but his parents were hard workers who looked forward to sleeping in on weekend mornings. Mr. and Mrs. Cline didn't appreciate Robbie's first attempts to start the holiday celebration at such an early hour. He decided to change his tactics and send in little Brad, his four-year-old brother, for a final must-succeed effort to wake their parents. Brad was less calculating than Robbie but much more vocal and demanding.

In cases where Robbie would carefully tiptoe around spankings, Brad would explode into classic baby fits that were as loud as they were animated with tears, jumping, and even an occasional scream drop and roll. When Brad didn't get his way, his screechings and gyrations resembled those of someone who'd been soaked with gasoline and lit on fire. The trick for Robbie was to shrewdly plant his own agenda into the mind of his little brother, then stand back while the baby fit developed. Stiff spankings for little Brad would inevitably follow the tantrum but would ultimately lead to Robbie's desired parental behavior or action.

As a notoriously picky eater, Robbie often used similar tactics at the dinner table. Little Brad would happily eat Mom's homemade roast beef dinner that, in Robbie's view, was unfit for human consumption. When their parents looked away, Robbie would quickly point to the undesirable food and silently lip the dreaded word *onions* to his brother, signaling that the meal had been prepared with the toxic vegetable all children with any sense hated.

Robbie knew onions were an instant recipe killer, and he'd trained his brother to agree. After the idea was planted that Mom had poisoned the pot roast with onions, little Brad's customary fit would ensue. The unruly behavior consistently earned little Brad spankings. Robbie would then join in with tears, and delicious bologna sandwiches with crusts removed would promptly replace the poisoned pot roast, as their frustrated mother would try to keep the two gaunt children from starving.

Not only was the mission accomplished, but Robbie thoroughly enjoyed watching his brother's animated fits and the beatings that followed. On rare occasions the Cline parents caught Robbie in the act of corrupt dinner ingredient disclosure. These slipups were invariably costly, earning Robbie his own measure of spankings. He would also share in the punishment if his parents noticed that he was giggling while watching his little brother's beating.

Now, according to the football helmet clock on Robbie's wall, it was 7:05 a.m. It was time to move Easter forward. "Little Brad," Robbie whispered while gently nudging his brother to wake up. "Little Brad, the Easter bunny was here, but Mom and Dad said we can't get up and see our baskets yet. Don't you want to see your candy and start finding eggs?"

After Brad woke up, it wasn't difficult for Robbie to convince him to go pressure their tired parents to let the second-best holiday of the year begin.

Brad slowly stumbled toward his parents' room down the hall, while Robbie peeked around the corner from his bedroom door. The two-tiered operation was well conceived: Mom and Dad would have to get up, and little Brad would get a spanking. What a great start to Easter, Robbie thought.

Little Brad reached up and opened the door to his parents' room.

Robbie quickly ducked back into his bedroom, where he giggled uncontrollably and bounced across the floor. The excitement was just too much. He'd be enjoying a breakfast of chocolate, caramel, and jelly beans only after his annoying little brother got the spankings he always deserved.

Robbie calmed down long enough to peek back out into the hallway, but there was no crashing, no screaming, and no crying. The Cline parents slowly emerged from around the corner, guided by little Brad's hand.

"What a suck-up," Robbie whispered to himself before quickly turning his focus to the ensuing celebration. He burst from his bedroom and hopped down the hallway, shrieking, "The Easter bunny came! The Easter bunny came!"

Robbie darted past his parents toward the small living room. Little Brad let go of his parents' hands and clumsily followed.

"Aren't you going to wake up your sister?" Mr. Cline asked.

"How many hoops do we have to jump through?" Robbie murmured under his breath as he slowly turned and stomped back to his sister's bedroom. "She probably won't remember Easter anyway. She's only three years old."

"Get up Milinda, or I'm going to eat all your candy!" Robbie shouted.

Little Brad followed him into Milinda's room. "Get up Mini, or I'm going to eat your candy." Brad was unable to pronounce Milinda, so Mini had stuck as an equally acceptable title for their sister.

The three Cline children took each other by the hand in a rare moment of solidarity and bounced down the hallway to assess the treasure that the Easter bunny always delivered. Each of the children wore peculiar-looking pajamas that had once featured the ever-popular feet sewn right into the pants. The Clines were on a tight budget, so when the children outgrew their jammies, Mrs. Cline would amputate the feet with scissors, allowing perpetual use. Robbie's pajama pants were bright blue and now skintight like a leotard. They ended just below his knees. These jammies had been a Christmas present from Santa nearly five years ago.

As the kids exploded into the living room, they shouted out the names of the gifts that the Easter bunny had spread across their couch. "Balloons, candy, soccer ball, new jammies!" The Easter bunny was always nearly as generous as Santa, and the Cline parents proudly looked on at the modest things they were able to provide for their children.

"I love the Easter bunny!" Robbie exclaimed as he ran in circles through the living room, stuffing a Cadbury egg into his mouth. He immediately began collecting the hard-boiled eggs that had been decorated and hidden the night before.

"Slow down and let your brother and sister find some of the eggs, Robbie," his father said

"Then they better start looking!" Robbie shouted as he ran back to his bedroom and found a blue egg that was hidden in his shoe. It still smelled like vinegar from the dipping dye.

Robbie had already collected five of the thirty eggs, while his brother and sister were still eggless. They were more interested in the helium-filled balloons that were neatly tied to their Easter baskets.

Eventually when the egg hunt and excitement died down, the bartering for candy began. Robbie often tried to take advantage of his younger siblings with the cunning manipulation of a government secret agent. Robbie offered, "I'll give you five jelly beans for one of your Cadbury eggs, Milinda." Robbie explained once again, "I give you five, and you *only* have to give me one." This sounded like a good deal, but Milinda had learned to seek counsel from her parents when dealing with Robbie. She looked upward at her mother and father for their approval prior to consummating the deal.

"No, Mini. I think you should keep your own candy," her mom advised.

Little Brad was no scholar, but even *he* knew that five traded for one sounded like the kind of deal that would finally give him the upper hand on his older brother. "I'll trade!" Brad cried.

The bait was taken just like Robbie had intended. Little Brad was to be his barter victim from the very beginning. Despite the discouragement of the Cline parents, Brad couldn't refuse the deal of the century that would let him get the best of Robbie. The trade was executed, and Robbie promptly ate the Cadbury to seal the deal. Besides, Robbie knew Mom and Dad always kept extra Easter jelly beans hidden in the kitchen this time of year. He would easily replace the bartered jelly beans from the surplus.

Finally, just after Robbie carefully hid the spoils of Easter to prevent Brad and Milinda's attempts at plundering, Mom announced, "Everybody get dressed. We're going to church in half an hour."

In future years Robbie would postpone his early-morning excitement and stay in bed until at least 9:30 a.m. to avoid any possibility of disrupting Easter with church. "Why the hell do we have to ruin Easter with going to stupid church?" Robbie shouted as tears filled his eyes. This had started out as one of the best days ever, but the rug was being pulled out from beneath his feet. Robbie hated church. Fortunately, the Clines only made it to church on Mother's Day and an occasional Easter, but that was too often for him.

"With a mouth like that, you probably need to start going to church every weekend," Robbie's mother snapped. Mrs. Cline always tried to raise her children with good morals and Christian values while only rarely getting them to church. Mr. Cline typically led the resistance, since Sunday morning was the best time for him to sneak away and play golf. But when Mrs. Cline was determined to get her way, her husband would reluctantly submit. So with Mr. Cline on board, their biannual visit to Mile High Methodist was developing a certain inevitability.

As she slipped into her Sunday best, Mrs. Cline shouted out from her bedroom, "Make sure to brush your hair after you get dressed." Ironically there was no suggestion of brushing teeth along with brushing hair. It was later often speculated that little Robbie Cline eventually became Robert Cline, DDS, due to a mouthful of cavities that had caused him to spend a little too much time in the dentist chair, sniffing nitrous oxide. He unwillingly brushed his hair and changed into some decent clothes.

The Cline parents headed out of the house, where their six-year-old, green Ford Taurus sat in the gravel driveway. Dad strapped Milinda into a child safety seat. Robbie ran out the door after grabbing one of his helium balloons for the short car trip to church. Little Brad clumsily followed with his own balloon.

On the road Mrs. Cline fixed her lipstick using the rearview mirror while pleading with Robbie, "Please don't act up in your Sunday school class today."

Mr. Cline skillfully navigated the short trip down Wadsworth Boulevard using only the side mirrors. Robbie was getting bored, so he looked to his little sister for entertainment. He took advantage of Milinda's car seat, which resembled a straitjacket and left her defenseless to his badgering. Milinda was pretty, with cotton-fine hair that Mrs. Cline had arranged into a do fit for Sunday school.

When Mrs. Cline finished her lipstick and momentarily looked away from the rearview mirror, Robbie vigorously rubbed his balloon over Milinda's hair, introducing upon it a heavy static charge. Mini looked as though she had walked through a hurricane. Her hair stood on end, while its electric charge was strongly attracted to the polyester ceiling upholstery of the Taurus. Little Brad followed Robbie's example, with the balloon assault now coming from both sides. In her straitjacket-styled safety seat, Milinda's only defense was to let out a blood-curdling scream.

Mr. Cline slammed on the breaks, pulled the car off the road, and ripped Robbie and Brad out of the backseat to give them an execution-style, roadside spanking.

Robbie immediately started running down the sidewalk. He wouldn't easily submit to a spanking, so Little Brad was swatted first. After finishing with Brad, Mr. Cline chased and eventually overtook Robbie, who proceeded to wiggle like a cat in a bathtub. As the wiry third grader twisted and kicked, his dad managed to get enough of a grip with his left hand, to deliver a few good shots to the backside with his right hand.

Meanwhile, back at the car Mrs. Cline did her best to reassemble Milinda's hair, with little success. Robbie and little Brad had managed to generate an irrevocable static charge, and their sister's fine hairdo now looked much like a fuzzy dandelion that had gone to seed.

Both Milinda and Brad were now crying, but Robbie had managed to hold it together—that is, until Mr. Cline violently popped the Easter balloons with his car keys.

"Those were from the Easter Bunny!" Robbie screamed, with tears now streaming down *his* face.

By the time the Cline's pulled into the church parking lot, they were a pitiful sight. They had clearly been in a minor battle on their way to Sunday worship and weren't filled with the same joy as the more regular attendees.

While the Cline parents hurried to check their younger children into their Sunday school classrooms ten minutes late, Robbie walked himself to his third-grade room. His Sunday school teacher was Mrs. Stone, a decorated church member of twenty-seven years. She loved the church and hated children, which made her a perfect fit to be the third-grade Sunday school teacher. She was stern and as rigid as her heavily starched gray skirt. She kept order at all times. Lessons were carefully planned, and the children were expected to have a respectable knowledge of biblical timelines they learned from her weekly lectures and color sheets. This expectation was a problem for Robbie, since biannual attendance left him with a spotty understanding of any biblical history. Robbie was uncomfortable in this environment, as he was always one of the smarter kids in public school, but in Sunday school he was the only kid who was completely lost.

Robbie coped with being a standout champion of ignorance by acting up and causing trouble. This day he was ready to break Mrs. Stone, but little did he know that Mrs. Stone was ready to break *him*.

"Hello, Robert," Mrs. Stone snapped. "I see you're late as always." Then she murmured under her breath, "When you're parents decide to show up at all." She promptly invited him to, "Come sit in the circle with the other students," where there were no more chairs. Robbie unsuccessfully shuffled around, trying to find a spot until Mrs. Stone happily grabbed the only remaining student chair from the back of the room. It was a leftover from the preschool class, and it was a few sizes smaller than those of his classmates. She had the children widen the circle to make room for Robbie to sit in the very short chair right next to her.

The forty-five minutes of lessons that followed always seemed like they lasted for hours. As usual, Robbie couldn't make sense of the lecture, which was part of a bigger timeline that had been presented throughout all the other weeks he hadn't been in attendance. Robbie really tried to follow the sermon, but sitting next to Mrs. Stone made it even more difficult to concentrate. She smelled like mold, beef soup, and the aerosol hair spray which rigidly controlled her large brown-with-gray-accent bouffant.

Besides her love for the more insignificant details of biblical history, Mrs. Stone had special knowledge of hell and the devil. It seemed to Robbie that she knew more about hell than someone who had actually lived there. When she talked about Satan, it would always scare Robbie a little, and make it hard for him to sleep for a couple of nights.

While Mrs. Stone rambled on about the Serpent in the Garden of Eden, Robbie looked to entertain himself at the expense of the little girl sitting on his other side. He sneakily licked his finger and reached up from his small chair to stick his bony digit into Paula Papalusa's ear, successfully executing the wet-willy. He quickly retracted his hand before Mrs. Stone could witness the offense. Paula promptly and justifiably tattled on Robbie, while the rest of the children in the circle erupted in laughter. Robbie had momentarily taken control of the room, much like he controlled the events in his own home.

Mrs. Stone acted quickly, grabbing Robbie by the arm and dragging him across the room, while his tiptoes barely touched the ground to shuffle along beside her. She fired a lesson about Judas and Beelzebub to the child dissident as she quickly sat him in a corner, which was thoughtfully named "the sin bin." Then Mrs. Stone regained control of the group as she quickly twisted her neck back around to the circle while firing a seething glare.

The wrinkly, slumping stockings that reluctantly draped Mrs. Stone's ankles sagged a little lower with each stomp that she took back to the circle. She finished her lecture, and then had the children move to their workstations to color a picture of Adam and Eve so it could be inserted in their timeline workbooks.

One would have thought the Easter lesson would have had something to do with the biblical Easter story. However, Mrs. Stone had special knowledge that the traditional dates when Americans typically celebrated holidays were arbitrarily decided by the Catholic Church, and pagans. According to her independent studies, the world had begun on this day six thousand years ago, so their lesson would focus on Adam and Eve. Robbie found it disturbing that, according to Mrs. Stone, it wasn't actually Easter. But he knew she was wrong, since it was the day the Easter bunny had come.

After a period of seclusion, intended to encourage repentance, Robbie was instructed to rejoin the group and take part in the coloring project. He was a little confused about the Adam and Eve story, since his third-grade class from school had recently taken a trip to the Denver Museum of Nature and Science. Mrs. Riley, his loving third-grade teacher, had guided the children through the displays that seemed to show real monkeys that had turned into real cavemen, who had eventually turned into people. They had apparently been dug up and stuffed for display in Denver's own museum. Robbie had seen the real monkey men, just like the drawings in his science book. There was no picture of Adam and Eve in his science book. Besides, if Adam and Eve were real, the museum curators surely would have had them stuffed and placed in an exhibit.

Robbie needed to make a statement and regain control of the Sunday school class. He artfully colored Adam with a nice Denver Bronco uniform, while the smaller Eve received a ragged Oakland Raider uniform. He thoughtfully labeled the picture "GO BRONCOS." This was one of his best pieces, especially considering that he'd drawn it all while reaching upward to the table from his undersized chair.

A natural leader, Robbie managed to get some of the surrounding boys to follow his example, which would of course ruin this timeline book entry for the regularly attending children. Mrs. Stone took pride in the timeline books that each child would give to his or her parents at the end of the year. The well-thought-out project demonstrated her in-depth knowledge of biblical events.

When Mrs. Stone walked by and noticed Robbie's blasphemous desecration of the color sheet, she gnashed her teeth, and ripped the paper from beneath his orange crayon. "This looks like the work of the Devil himself," she snapped, as she crumpled up the sin-defiled worksheet and threw it into the wastebasket.

The furious Sunday school teacher grabbed Robbie once again by the arm and hurried him across to his spot in "the sin bin." The other children laughed until Mrs. Stone spun back around toward the group. She marched back to Robbie's cohorts and sternly explained that hell wasn't a place where any of them really wanted to end up. She quickly supplied new color sheets to the children, who needed to correct their unholy heresies. Robbie didn't get a new color sheet as it seemed pointless. There would be no timeline book for him. Mrs. Stone knew he would likely attend only one or two more times through the rest of the year anyway.

As Sunday school finally drew to a close, Mrs. Stone had the children line their chairs up in a row in front of the classroom. She grabbed Robbie's small chair and placed it at the end of the line. Then she signaled for him to come out of "the sin bin" and take his place with the class so they could all sing her favorite song, "Onward, Christian Soldiers," before rejoining their parents.

When the singing ended, Mrs. Stone opened two cardboard egg cartons filled with the most beautiful Easter eggs any of the children had ever seen. Robbie instantly recognized that the twenty-four perfectly decorated eggs had been created with an apparatus that was available all last month on a TV infomercial for $19.99. Robbie had begged his mother to purchase the device, which could have been a family investment, bringing joy to the Clines on Easter for years to come. But like most things wonderful, the Cline parents had said,

"It's too expensive," leaving their kids to color eggs with the standard vinegar-fizz tablets.

At least now Robbie would have one of the fabulous eggs he could have only dreamed about creating on his own. As Mrs. Stone moved down the line of children, she let each one pick an extraordinary hard-boiled piece of art. Being last in line, Robbie got a little nervous that Mrs. Stone might run out of eggs before she reached him. He silently counted the children ahead of him in line and compared the tally to the number of eggs in the cartons. Mrs. Stone approached the end of the row, and Robbie was relieved to see there were three more eggs than there were children.

For some reason, however, along with all the beautiful eggs, there was one dark-brown egg that looked like one little Brad had made at home by dipping it in all five of the vinegar tablet color solutions. Mrs. Stone's brown egg had a tiny off-center sticker of a chicken holding a carrot. Robbie quickly recounted to make sure there were enough of the beautiful eggs for him to get one. Yes, he had counted correctly; there would be two fabulous eggs in addition to the brown egg by the time Mrs. Stone reached the end of the line.

Mrs. Stone finally arrived at Robbie's position. Like all the other children, he extended his hand toward the carton, but Mrs. Stone pulled back sharply and snapped, "I made *this* one special for you." Her hand passed over the last two perfect eggs, and she grabbed what would eventually be known to Robbie as the "atheist Easter egg." She smirked as she handed the ugly, brown egg with the off-center chicken sticker to Robbie and sarcastically whispered, "Happy Easter."

Robbie slumped, took the egg, and then walked slowly through the other children, who were comparing their Easter eggs for impeccable color and quality. He kept it together while he walked out the door and down the hallway, but he burst into tears at the first glimpse of his parents. He ran into his mother's outstretched arms and explained breathlessly through sobs, "The other kids had…had…had…the good eggs and I…I…got the only br…br…brown one."

Mrs. Cline tried to spin the episode by explaining to Robbie that his egg was special because it was different from all the others. But Robbie wouldn't be consoled.

The brown egg incident ultimately led to a meeting between the Clines and the church minister. Robbie would eventually have little memory of the outcome of the meeting, other than that the minister suggested the Cline parents might try to spank their children a little more often. Robbie would, however, always remember the Easter egg that sealed the deal about God. The whole God thing had always seemed like a stretch anyway, especially when everything he studied in school and saw on TV suggested that God was make-believe just like Santa and the Easter bunny, the make-believe holiday superheroes.

THE ALLEY

June 21, a little more than ten years later

A sweltering midnight wind blew an occasional piece of garbage through a dark, rat-infested alley in Brooklyn near West Thirty-Fifth and Neptune. Dressed all in black, Rais Rasil was hidden in the shadows behind a large, sour smelling Dumpster that baked in the suffocating summer heat. He waited restlessly, alternating glances down the alley and back to his wristwatch. Rais was already on edge in the sketchy meeting place when a sudden vibration startled him.

It was only his cell phone. He retrieved it from the inside pocket of his black leather jacket and answered nervously in Arabic. The caller barked orders, also in Arabic, while Rais looked over his shoulder every few seconds to make sure he was still alone.

"Yes, sir…Yes, sir…I understand, sir…Yes, I'm sure he will be here…Yes, I will remind him. They have to be from our home land… Thank you, Mudir; you are a very fair man."

Rais grimaced when the person on the phone began hollering. He tried to speak between the caller's outbursts. "I'm sorry…Sir, I'm sorry…No, sir, please…Nobody is near me. I am alone…No one heard me say your name."

The call was abruptly disconnected. Rais was trembling as he put his cell phone back into his pocket. He looked nervously toward a flickering streetlight at the end of the long, dark alley when he was startled once more, this time by a stray cat that jumped down from the garbage bin and landed next to him. The cat looked up and hissed, scaring Rais into a frantic flurry of kicks down toward the stray. "*Xara!*" Rais swore in Arabic and spit at the cat.

Narrowly evading the boot and the spit, the cat hissed again and then darted out of sight.

A faint siren howled into the night, and Rais was getting more anxious by the second. The meeting was supposed to have taken place over ten minutes ago. If things didn't go as planned, his boss, Mudir Al-Shaitan, wouldn't be pleased. Consequences would certainly be severe.

Suddenly, a strange man appeared out of nowhere, facing away from Rais under the distant streetlight at the end of the alley. The man paused to take a long draw from the end of a cigarette and flicked the butt into the gutter before turning slowly out of the light and toward Rais into the alleyway. The siren drew closer, causing Rais's pulse to climb. The stranger, now walking toward him, didn't seem concerned about the bad neighborhood, or the approaching siren. With each step away from the streetlight, the stranger entered deeper into the backstreet and closer to Rais, while sinking farther beneath a cover of shadows. The man continued to advance slowly, while Rais's heart beat even more rapidly.

Now only ten feet away, the man could finally be identified by his smell. He reeked of dirty leather pickled in pot and cheap whiskey. This was the person Rais was supposed to meet.

Emerging from a veil of shadows and standing at six foot three inches tall was Jude Wilcox. He was a mountain of a man who wore black leather motorcycle chaps over dirty, faded jeans. Wilcox didn't have a shirt. Instead he wore a black, leather biker's vest that hung open, revealing skin that was splotchy and reddish pink from overexposure to the sun. The skin that wasn't pink was covered with tattoos; the most notable of which was a swastika on his right arm. An abused liver made Wilcox's eyes yellow. Atop his head, he had orange hair worn tight in a crew cut. His face was red with brown freckles and deeply pitted scars left over from his long childhood battle with acne. The parts of his teeth that weren't blackened from crystal meth were as yellow as his eyes.

"Jude?" Rais asked with a noticeable tremble in his voice.

"Yep," Jude replied in a raspy Mississippi accent.

"Here it is, just like we discussed." Rais pulled a medium-sized duffel bag from beneath his jacket and threw it into Jude's arms.

Wilcox didn't say a word. He immediately opened the bag and frantically rifled through its contents. He pushed through a pile of hundred-dollar bills, causing several to flutter to the ground. Wilcox didn't even notice that some of the money had fallen. Instead he focused on a small plastic baggy of cocaine resting amid the cash. He immediately pulled out the coke and took snort after snort while more hundred-dollar bills fell and blew down the alley. He stopped snorting just long enough to look up at Rais and ask, "Is this all the blow?"

"This is just a fraction of your payment, like we agreed. As soon as we verify that the job is done, I will contact you with the location of the rest of the cocaine and cash. But remember, this has to happen tomorrow."

Jude took another snort. "I know, I know. Tomorrow," he said.

Rais continued, "Remember. It has to be bloody. It has to be horrific. And, it has to be children."

Jude held the empty baggy of cocaine up to his nose, turned it inside out, and tried to sniff any residual powder that could have been stuck to the plastic. "We already went over this yesterday," he said. "I know."

Rais grabbed Jude by the shoulders and looked into his yellow eyes to make sure he was listening. "Remember, the children have to be Muslim, and everyone has to believe an American was responsible."

2

COLLEGE

June 21, one year later

Dr. Ted Ritchey was an organic chemistry professor at Fort Lewis College in Durango, Colorado. The department chair was a brilliant chemist and an excellent instructor. Ritchey could have taught at any university in the world, but he'd chosen the small mountain college because it was located in one of the most beautiful areas he'd ever seen. Plus, the La Plata Mountain range just north of Durango was the perfect location for his alpine llama ranch.

Ritchey was six foot seven inches tall with a slight curve in his back that had developed through years of bending over to look down into the eyes of all the normal-stature people. No matter what the season, the professor wore a khaki jumpsuit, a small llama-fiber stocking cap, and matching llama wool socks to work. He was a bit peculiar looking, like all the chemistry faculty at the college. Dr. Ritchey had a thick, curly beard that thoroughly covered nearly all his facial features. He had what appeared to be more beard hair covering his arms, hands, neck, and virtually all other exposed parts of his body. Rumors had circulated among Ted Ritchey's students that the professor had more than likely been covered with moles due to a chemical-induced mutation brought on by too much time spent in the lab sniffing solvents. The theory was that he'd synthesized an organic hair-replacement product to cover his moley skin, but it had obviously worked a little too well.

Enrolled in Ritchey's lab class was pre-dental student and chemistry/foreign language major Robert Cline. He had grown to be six foot two with dark hair and dark eyes. He was slender but muscular. Although Robert had an athletic build, his crowning achievement in sports had come from the ultra-nurturing Lake Middle School in Denver, where he'd once received an award for being the second-best player on the school's second-string football team. Needless to say, he wasn't attending college on an athletic scholarship. Robert was a very good student, who knew his future acceptance into dental school depended on perfect grades.

Dr. Ritchey stood in front of his students, holding a beaker that contained an unknown substance: the subject of a qualitative analysis experiment. The professor exposed two glimmering, white teeth in a sea of beard hair when he giggled from the excitement of demonstrating the proper protocol for determining the identity of the substance.

Despite his excellent focus, Robert couldn't help but turn away from the mad scientist's demonstration and look out the lab window to watch other students out on the college lawn, playing Frisbee or climbing the rock wall. Summer studies were painful to endure when the Colorado outdoors had so much to offer. But Robert kept his summer class schedule jam-packed to complete his double major in three years. Many students at Fort Lewis also took summer classes, since the college offered June trimester credits and campus housing at substantial discounts. However, most students took a light load, leaving time to enjoy the climbing, mountain biking, and rafting Durango was famous for.

Focus on chemistry now, and someday reap the benefits, Robert thought as he tried to concentrate. I'll eventually have a great job and time to travel the world, while the Frisbee players will be waiting tables at the pancake house. He turned back to Dr. Ritchey's lecture after taking one last look at a few college girls in bikini tops as they passed by the window.

Robert's lab partner was Omid from Jeddah, Saudi Arabia. Theirs was a symbiotic alliance, in which Omid, an engineering major who hated chemistry, got through the required subject with extensive aid from Robert. In return Robert used class time and study time with Omid to begin learning Arabic, a language not offered at the college.

While Robert painstakingly pursued the identity of their unknown substance, Omid would assist as best he could by gathering necessary supplies like clean beakers and test tubes.

Robert skillfully tested the unknown substance, while Dr. Ritchey circled the lab to assist the more befuddled students with their questions.

Also circulating through the lab was Carl, the college chemistry lab facilities and equipment coordinator. He wore a ten-year-old, once-white lab coat. His hair was relatively short, black, and straight with comb-mark grooves still left behind from his quick morning grooming session. Carl's black, horn-rimmed glasses had a small obstructive crack in the center of the right lens. Most of the time, his right eye peered independently from the left in search of clarity. Carl rarely spoke but was friendly and helpful. He walked through the lab, making sure students were on the right track. When not in the lab, Carl could be found in the chemistry supply closet. The standing joke among students was that he actually lived in the spacious beaker and pipette storage area, and there was little evidence to suggest otherwise. Between Dr. Ritchey and Carl, organic chemistry lab ran efficiently about 95 percent of the time.

Robert was precisely adding a chemical indicator to the beaker that contained his unknown substance when a high-pitched scream startled him. "Dr. Ted's on fire!" one of Robert's classmates shouted.

The fire had started when Dr. Ritchey was helping a female student weigh a few grams of sulfur powder on a balance. Somehow the student's Bunsen burner had ignited a patch of the professor's arm hair, setting the doctor ablaze.

Dr. Ritchey normally had a deep voice, but his scream alarmed several octaves higher than usual. "Fire blanket! Fire blanket!" Ritchey shrieked, running across the lab like a meteorite entering the earth's atmosphere. He shouted out, "Stop, drop, and roll," as if to command himself to quit running around in a panic. He dove and rolled around on the floor, screaming more fiercely, "Fire blanket! Fire blanket!"

As the roomful of students looked on with concern but without the slightest idea of how to assist, Carl leaped from his lab supply closet with a well-used fire blanket. The blanket had multiple char marks and a few holes, but it would be Dr. Ritchey's lifeline. Carl ran across the lab and leaped onto his boss with the blanket. He diligently patted out the flames, all while the professor squealed and convulsed like a witch in a pool of holy water.

Carl's quick response had saved the chemist and kept the burn damage to a minimum.

Fortunately Dr. Ritchey's condition looked a lot worse than it was. He stood up, coughing and sputtering from the bitter-smelling smoke that now filled the lab. His singed hair was still smoking when he thanked his loyal employee, Carl.

Ritchey's clothes had held up rather well, since he always treated them with one of his inventions: a fire-protectant resin spray that burned hot on the outside while forming an insulative skin below the flames. Only a few holes had burned through his khaki jumpsuit. His home-raised llama fiber cap and socks, however, hadn't fared as well. In addition Dr. Ritchey's body beard appeared to be scorched. It was replaced by black char and singed hair, which still made discerning his facial features difficult. Ritchey chuckled about the incident through what was left of his smoking beard. His distinctive two front teeth glimmered through the heavy char marks on his face.

Surrounded by his concerned students, Ritchey insisted that he was OK and that class would continue since lab time was limited during the abbreviated summer session. In spite of his protest, EMTs arrived and took him away for medical attention.

With the professor en route to the hospital, lab was officially canceled. So Robert and Omid hurried to the dorm. For the first time this semester, they would be able to hang out on the campus lawn on a weekday and enjoy a beautiful Colorado afternoon like all the other students.

Robert retrieved his baseball and a couple of mitts from his dorm room before heading outside. He attempted to play a little catch with Omid in the June sun. The task proved to be challenging, since Omid threw like a middle-school cheerleader using her off hand.

The friendly game ended after a cowboy clique from their dorm walked by. Calvin, the leader of the group, shouted, "Hey, Osama, you ain't very good at tossing them baseballs, but I sure bet you can launch the hell out of a grenade!" The group laughed and rudely imitated Omid's awkward throwing form.

Robert snapped back, "Well, if it isn't Calvin, the meat major. Why don't you wipe the horse shit off your boots and get to studying for your 'meat cuts' final? You don't want to blow it in the fifth year of your associate's degree in ag."

"This is only my fourth year, ass wipe."

Robert was relieved that the group kept moving and didn't stop to escalate the verbal exchange.

Frustrated with the clumsy game of catch, Robert motioned to his friend to head to the campus climbing wall. "Let's go find those business majors in bikinis, Omid," Robert said in his best Arabic.

Omid laughed and gently corrected Robert's grammar but passed on the request. "I need to get back to my room now, but maybe tomorrow," Omid said, again in his native tongue.

3

FIVE PASSENGERS

The next day, June 22, 4:00 p.m., Eastern Time. Fredericksburg, Virginia

Three Saudi nationals—Rais Rasil, Turhan Rauf, and Aaquib Ali— paced impatiently next to their luggage in front of a small, unmanned Fredericksburg passenger train station in ninety-five-degree heat. Next to them, Lee E. Roberts and his new wife, Betty, sat on a bench, going over plans for their honeymoon in New York City.

Rais motioned for Aaquib to watch the suitcases, while he and Turhan walked around the far side of the station house to have a discussion in private. Aaquib sat nervously next to their six large pieces of luggage while keeping an eye on the American couple next to him.

If you had looked at thirty-two-year-old Lee as he stood up and watched for the train, you wouldn't have figured that he could have ever attracted a bride. His hair, styled by his mother, could only be described as a coonskin mullet with muttonchop sideburns. It resembled the hat worn by Davy Crockett. Lee always dressed in sleeveless flannel shirts. His mother removed the sleeves and used the material to sew him a special, new birthday quilt each year. Lee was stocky with a poorly toned, double-value-meal physique that showed through his sleeveless shirts almost as much as the stream of underarm sweat from the Virginia humidity. His faded blue jeans were tight. They struggled to package his large rear end and pudgy thighs. Lee's steel-toed work boots looked good, but they had never been worn for work. He had always been unemployed, and he'd lived with his mother right up to the day before yesterday, when he married Betty.

Betty looked like she'd traded down to hitch Lee, at least when looking at her from a distance and in poor lighting. For a thirty-five-year-old, Betty could have easily passed for fifty. She didn't smile much. She tried to hide that she was missing a couple of front teeth. From time to time, she would flash her spotty grin during a heavy smoker's cough. Smoke and hot coffee helped keep Betty very thin. She wore short, cutoff jeans and her favorite faded, orange, skintight tube top. Her skin was tan and leathery like a cowboy boot. Her hair was long and a little dirty. She had the names of three ex-husbands tattooed on various parts of her body. Before they were married, Betty had told Lee that they were the names of three of her cousins. Her cover-up was partially true since one of her ex-husbands was indeed her second cousin.

Betty and Lee had matching green wedding-band tattoos that Lee had crafted with an Inkstar Diablo gun he'd purchased for twelve dollars on eBay. Lee's tattoo was a little crooked compared to Betty's, since he was left handed and had used his off hand to place his own band. Theirs was a match made in the Appalachian woods, and for all the couple lacked in charisma, they more than made up for with ignorance and friendliness.

"Where all you fellas from?" Lee shouted to Aaquib, who was now pacing alone, around his group's luggage.

At first, Aaquib didn't utter a word. He only responded with a silent look of confusion, but then tried to speak. "No Americk," he said while nervously shuffling his feet. Sweat poured from his forehead as he looked back toward his travel companions, who were now done talking. They were just starting to return to the luggage.

"Hey, do you know if you're allowed to have a ferret on the train?" Betty barked. "We're going to use some of our wedding money to get us a ferret in New York City." Betty sounded as if she may have just recovered from a long battle with bronchitis, but her vocal cords had been finely tuned by years of chain-smoking and alcohol abuse.

After walking back to the group, Rais stepped in front of Aaquib and answered Betty in a heavy Middle Eastern accent. "No, ma'am, we have not taken the train before, and I'm not sure what policies they hold for animals." Actually, Rais and his travel companions *had* taken the train before, carefully mapping the route and destination. The train was almost always a bit late but never this late. It had been due at the station thirty minutes ago.

Betty turned to Lee and spoke in a gravelly whisper that the three Saudi nationals could easily overhear. "I think those guys are Italian." She looked over at the three men and waved. European men had always been a turn-on to Betty. She hadn't actually met many Europeans, but she'd seen a lot of them on the Travel Channel.

Finally the railroad-crossing signals lit up in front of an intersection near the station. An approaching train whistle blew in the distance.

"Here it comes, baby!" Lee shouted. Betty and Lee threw themselves into one another's arms and kissed with passion—so much passion, in fact, that one of Betty's remaining teeth loosened up a bit more than it already was. She pulled back and slapped Lee. "Baby, be careful! You know what the doc said about my pyorrhea."

While Lee and Betty carried on, a large military transport truck full of soldiers from nearby Quantico Marine Base pulled to a stop behind the railroad crossing just fifty feet away. At the same time, the train engine crept past the crossing, but instead of the Amtrak, it was a long, slow moving coal train. Seeing that they'd be held up for a while, a few soldiers got out of their camouflage truck to stretch.

The three Saudis were visibly troubled by the proximity of the U.S. soldiers. Aaquib frantically ranted something in Arabic to his travel companions. Rais ordered the panicked Aaquib to stay calm and continue to stand by.

"I don't think those guys are Italian, Bett," whispered Lee. "I'm pretty sure they're speaking Spanish."

Ignoring her new husband, Betty waved and shouted toward the troop-transport truck. "God bless the USA! Go marines!"

Lee joined in, "Support the boots on the ground! Yee hew!"

All the excitement caused Betty to start coughing uncontrollably. Her coughing suddenly turned to choking. One of the soldiers started jogging toward her to see if she was OK.

"What do we do, Rais?" Aaquib whispered frantically in Arabic, not taking his eyes off the advancing soldier.

"Sit down!" Rais ordered back.

Turhan calmly reassured them, "We are OK. Allah is with us. Just sit down." Sweat poured down his neck, drenching the collar of his shirt.

Suddenly, Betty coughed up the thing she was choking on. It was her last remaining upper-right molar; the one Lee had loosened with his aggressive kiss. "You son of a bitch, Lee. Now I ain't gonna have anything to hold in my fake flipper tooth that doc's gonna make me." She slapped Lee repetitively on top of his head and across his face with her bony, leathery hand. Lee tried to comfort her and simultaneously fix his now-demolished mullet.

Just then the railroad crossing lifted. The soldier, now only fifteen feet away, shouted a concerned "Are you all right?"

Lee promptly turned from Betty, sucked in his belly, and stood at attention while saluting. "Yes, sir. Thank you, sir!"

Betty shrieked, "No, I ain't all right!" She slapped Lee across the back of his head again. "I just married a dumb ass!" Then her tone softened. "But you sure are cute. My name is Bett."

The marine sergeant waved awkwardly and chuckled through a half smile. Then he turned and jogged back to join his fellow soldiers at the railroad crossing. The coal train whistled in the distance, and the troop transport truck disappeared across the tracks and down the road toward the marine base.

Rais, Turhan, and Aaquib instantly engaged in an animated but muffled argument, while Lee picked Betty's tooth up off the ground. He put it in his mouth and swished it around from cheek to cheek to clean it off. Then he tried to convince her to let him reinsert it. "I saw this once on MD TV, Bett. If you clean it off real good before you put it back in, it'll be just like new."

Suddenly the railroad crossing lit up again. The curbside station chaos was for a moment quelled as the two groups quietly waited to see whether their train to New York was finally here. After all, this waiting was cutting into Lee and Betty's three-day honeymoon.

Rais, Turhan, and Aaquib were also running late for an appointment. They were supposed to make contact with the president of the

United States, who would be attending the NBA finals basketball game at Madison Square Garden, located directly above Penn Station. So much for making the pregame pyrotechnics. At this point they would be lucky to make it by half time. Their boss, Mudir Al-Shaitan, would not be pleased. In fact, if they were late, the consequences would undoubtedly be severe.

The train slowly pulled to a stop at the curbside of Fredericksburg Station. A lanky man in his late forties with a name badge reading "Conductor Phil" emerged from a door situated between two passenger cars. He was dressed in what looked to be a fifteen-year-old, blue-and-gray, company-issue uniform. He looked down at the group of five and shouted as if he were announcing the train's arrival to a crowd of a thousand people. "Amtrak northbound carrier to DC Union Station, Thirtieth Street Station-Philadelphia, with final stop at Penn Station, New York City! Tickets, please."

Rais, Turhan, and Aaquib pushed forward with suitcases in hand and presented their tickets. As they started to board, the gangly conductor exclaimed, "I'm sorry, gentlemen, but you will have to pull those bags up yourselves. Union says I don't handle anything over thirty-five pounds."

The explanation of no help with bags over thirty-five pounds was standard and universal among conductors. Frankly, it even seemed to apply to bags weighing as little as twenty pounds, with most employees taking full advantage of the union's worker protections. Heavy government subsidies assured that no matter how unprofitable the train was, it would continue to chug down the track. There appeared to be no urgency to keep passengers happy, because the train would operate with or without them. On previous trial runs to New York, the Saudi nationals had noticed that about 50 percent of the train employees were friendly, while only 20 percent were helpful. Also there had never been luggage security checks. It was just this apathy and lack of customer service the group was looking for.

Rais and Turhan struggled to get their suitcases around Conductor Phil, who didn't step to the side to facilitate boarding. Then the two men turned back to assist their friend, Aaquib. But just as Aaquib moved to lift his suitcases up onto the train, Lee pressed ahead and bellowed to the conductor, "Excuse me, sir, but I was wondering if we are allowed to bring a ferret on the train."

Conductor Phil promptly raised his hand into the faces of Lee and Aaquib. "No pets on board unless they are service animals!"

"What's a service animal?" Lee quizzed.

"Well, you know, a Seeing Eye dog or something of that nature," the conductor replied.

Aaquib nervously tried to slither around the discussion and board the train. Conductor Phil quickly raised his hand into Aaquib's face and said, "Please wait your turn, sir."

Standing on the train behind the conductor, Rais spoke up. "Excuse me, sir, but he is with us, and we would like to sit together."

The conductor turned sharply and held his hand up to Rais's face, shouting, "Stand down, Hussein!"

Oh. It slipped out before he could catch it. Phil had already been sent to ethnic-sensitivity training three times this year. The last time had been over an altercation with a fellow employee in the dining car, where he found himself fighting over the last maple log in the glass pastry case. An anti-Semitic comment had been made, leading up to his apparent victory in the battle of the doughnut. Phil claimed the maple log as well as a two-day training session meant to help him make better choices about racial labeling. He was warned that one more trip to sensitivity training would result in a switch to the midnight run, where there were fewer staff members and passengers to offend.

"I mean…" Phil took a deep breath. "I understand your frustration, sir. I will be with you shortly." Not bad; just like he'd practiced. Hopefully this would defuse the situation.

Then Lee interrupted, "Well, does it count if I'm disabled? I have my medical marijuana card, because my back is real bad. It would be kind of like a service ferret."

Suddenly another train employee, the lead conductor, popped out from the adjacent passenger car and shouted, "We've got to get this train moving! We're already forty-five minutes behind!"

"This guy's trying to bring a ferret on board," Phil countered.

Then Betty hollered, "We ain't got no damn ferret!" She slapped Lee across the back of his head, again throwing his coonskin mullet into disarray.

"I'll get my wand, and we'll just do a full security check," the lead conductor said. He tried to push back into the train, but the passageway was getting crowded. He struggled to get around Rais and Turhan, who nervously waited for their friend. "Please be seated, gentlemen," he barked at the two men.

Rais and Turhan began to explain that they were waiting to assist their friend.

Interrupting, the lead conductor shouted, "Please be seated!" He was growing impatient.

Rais and Turhan reluctantly grabbed their suitcases and moved into the nearby passenger car, bickering in Arabic all the way to their seat.

"Just wave Aaquib on," Rais exclaimed. "We can do this without him."

Turhan snapped back, again in Arabic, "No! No! He has my bag. He has the detonator!" They nervously looked back out the window at their friend.

After a brief disappearance, the lead conductor reemerged with a TSA-style screening wand, ready to inspect the disruptive curbside passengers. There would be no ferret or any other animal boarding his train. The lead conductor had served three tours in Vietnam. He had twenty-five years of service on the tracks, and the rules would not be broken on his watch. "Screen their bodies and bags," he ordered, handing the wand to Phil.

Conductor Phil stepped down off the train and approached Aaquib, Lee, and Betty. Like a TSA sky marshal, he gripped his wand, which in this case would be used to detect a ferret. More customarily the wand was meant to detect metal, electronics, and explosives.

Rais and Turhan looked on in horror from their window. The train was their chosen instrument because security for passengers boarding at the unmanned station was nonexistent. Rais quickly pulled out his cell phone and called Mudir Al-Shaitan. "We have a problem," he insisted to his leader. Rais was shaking as he explained the situation to Al-Shaitan in Arabic. Abruptly, the call ended. Rais slowly lowered the phone to his lap.

Turhan looked at his partner inquisitively. Rais shook his head, indicating that he didn't want to discuss their boss's reaction. Helpless, they both looked back out the window.

By this time Conductor Phil had already rummaged through Lee and Betty's luggage, and now he was moving on to wand their persons. Aaquib stood trembling next to Lee. He was drenched from the heat and humidity. Phil passed the wand down Lee's right leg toward his knee and adjacent to Aaquib's bag, causing the device to flash and beep.

"I think we've found our ferret, sir!" Phil shouted back to the lead conductor.

Aaquib gasped for air in a panic. It was his bag that was setting off the wand, and he knew he would be discovered.

The lead conductor stepped down off the train and started patting down the area of Lee's knee that seemed to have caused the wand to beep. Meanwhile, Conductor Phil moved to Betty and started to pass the wand over her, triggering a somewhat less intense alarm response. Phil immediately set down the wand and reached up to begin hand-searching Betty. She reacted quickly, punching Phil in the stomach. "That's my IUD, you son of a bitch," she shrieked. "I already told you we ain't got no freakin' ferret!"

Rushing to interrupt the physical assault, the lead conductor stepped between Phil and Betty. He promptly recited union bylaw 213, declaring, "Any physical attack of a railroad employee will result in the passenger being denied entry onto the train. Furthermore, Amtrak rules clearly state that no animals are allowed on board. Ma'am, sir, you will not be boarding this train."

With Betty and Lee belligerently protesting, Conductor Phil turned to Aaquib and said, "Sorry for the inconvenience, sir. You can go ahead and join your friends on board."

Aaquib struggled with his suitcases, so the lead conductor extended his hand and grabbed one of the bags in an attempt to lift it up onto the train. Snickering, the conductor asked, "Oh Lord, what do you have in here, a bomb? You're going to have to get this on board yourself. Union bylaw five two seven states that train employees are not allowed to handle bags heavier than thirty-five pounds."

Rais promptly got up from his seat and returned to the entryway to help Aaquib with his bags. They chirped frantically back and forth in Arabic as they headed toward their seats.

Conductor Phil murmured under his breath, "This is America, not Pakistan. Speak English." Phil had the bad habit of talking louder than he realized. After securing the entryway, the lead conductor pulled Phil aside and wrote out a pink slip, mandating another appointment to ethnic-sensitivity training.

The train pulled away, leaving Betty and Lee behind as they screamed every profanity imaginable. There are a number of obscene gestures a person can make with his or her body, and Betty and Lee knew and used them all. Just before the train finally disappeared down the track, Lee dropped his blue jeans and briefs to expose a desperation moon of disapproval.

Betty snapped her aggression away from the train and shot it straight into Lee. She beat on his chest and shouted, "You ruined my honeymoon, you piece of shit!"

As the final audible blast from the train's horn sounded in the distance, their anger turned to passion, and Lee kissed Betty as aggressively as ever.

4

THE SNIPER

The same day, 4:00 p.m., Eastern Time

J oe Stanford, the six-foot-nine forward from Southern California, was the first person to arrive at Madison Square Garden for what he hoped would unfold as a modern-day battle of David vs. Goliath. His team, the Oklahoma City Thunder, was built mostly of talented overachievers, but Stanford was the club's only true superstar. Tonight the Thunder would face the mighty New York Knicks. Over a short two-year span, the Knicks had managed to acquire six of the league's top scorers from the past two seasons. Eight players on the New York squad had won titles with their previous teams.

Oklahoma City was clearly outmatched. If they were to defeat the powerhouse Knicks, they would have to rely on exceptional teamwork. The only chink in the armor for New York was the tendency of its individual stars to slip into a selfish "me first" game. But the Knicks had overcome lapses in teamwork with raw talent, leading them to the best regular-season record in league history.

Through the entire year there had been accusations that Nicholas Riefka, New York's team owner from Russia, had cheated the league's collective-bargaining agreement and salary cap. Sports commentators kept busy debating conspiracy theories. Many suggested that in addition to salaries on the books, there were payments made to players under the table from foreign interests. Nobody could explain how the owner of the league's worst team through his first five seasons could suddenly convince such a distinguished group of athletes to sign for half of their normal earnings. With no basketball experience, Riefka had unexpectedly put together a championship shoo-in overnight. Yet despite multiple investigations, all the numbers were in order, and the league-imposed salary cap didn't appear to be violated.

As Joe Stanford started his warm-up on the lonely garden floor, his focus was superb. He shot for nearly an hour from all distances with sniper accuracy. He knew he would have to be perfect to defeat the Knicks. Stanford appeared to be up to the task, draining shot after shot.

Only after making ten straight three-pointers at the end of his workout did Stanford notice that the arena had already filled to nearly half of its capacity. Many of the New York faithful had been jeering at him for the last thirty minutes. But on this day the biggest stage in the world wouldn't affect his concentration. Twenty thousand New York fans, including countless movie stars and even presidents of the United States and Russia, would be in attendance. None of that mattered to Stanford. He had a job to do, so he kept shooting.

Suddenly, Stanford's focus and shooting streak were broken. A blinding camera flash and badgering shout blasted from advancing New York reporter Peter Azzi. "Joe!" the sportscaster called out while standing on the court just a few steps in front of the basketball star. "Why weren't you willing to accept the offer that would have made you a member of this world champion New York Knicks team?"

The sharpshooter just smiled and assured him, "They're not champions yet." He added, "Pete, I've told you before. All of the true sports legends throughout history made their own teams great. They didn't take giant sums of money to get together with other stars on a team that attempted to buy a title."

"But Joe," the reporter argued, "the Knicks didn't buy a title. The salaries are all under the cap. You met with Riefka. Do you know something the rest of us don't?"

"No comment, Pete," Stanford said as he turned away from the court and disappeared into the locker room to meet up with his teammates.

5

DORM FOOD

The same day, 4:00 p.m., Mountain Time

Robert was taking notes in his Friday afternoon organic chemistry lecture. He was surprised that Dr. Ritchey had shown up only one day after his accident. The professor's arms, hands, neck, and face were completely wrapped in bandages, and he wore a new khaki jumpsuit and llama-fiber hat. Oddly, he looked the same as ever, but instead of resembling a beard-hair mummy, he now looked like a mummy, mummy. As the professor recounted the lab accident, he giggled, exposing two small front teeth in an agglomeration of wound dressings.

Omid leaned over and whispered to Robert, who was sitting next to him, "You would think a burn victim would at least take one or two days off work."

But Dr. Ritchey loved his profession. He would rather teach than do almost anything. Besides, the abbreviated summer session didn't allow for any missed days.

With genuine excitement Dr. Ritchey danced from PowerPoint to chalkboard. His passion for teaching chemistry was palpable. This passion must have been contagious, since Robert noticed that he too was developing a true interest in the subject. Before taking Ted Ritchey's class, Robert had believed that earning a chemistry degree was simply a necessary hoop one jumped through to get into dental school.

After finishing a surprisingly stimulating lecture on the kinetics of photoisomerization reactions, Dr. Ritchey announced that a Student

Christian Fellowship meeting would be held at his mountain home at 7:00 p.m.

The professor declared, "I will be presenting the case that evolution could not explain the beginning of life, because DNA is required to synthesize polymerase proteins, yet polymerase proteins are required to synthesize DNA." Dr. Ritchey proselytized through his bandages, "I will show, at the chemical-cellular level, how God had to have created these life-essential, starting-point molecules at the same time." He handed out info sheets to interested students as they filed out of the classroom.

"Wow," Robert whispered to Omid. "How could a guy this smart be so ignorant?" If Robert hadn't been so fond of Ted Ritchey, he certainly would have turned him in to the administration for preaching in class. Robert tried to inconspicuously slide out of the classroom, while a group of students he referred to as the "Onward Christian Soldier Club" surrounded the professor. Ass-kissers, he thought.

Robert had almost made it out the door when Dr. Ritchey stopped him. "Hey, Cline," the chemist called out.

Robert grimaced and stopped in his tracks. He slowly turned and walked back into the lecture hall. As he approached the podium in front of the room, the soldier club dispersed. "What's up?" Robert asked hesitantly.

"Will I see you this evening, Robert? We'll be grilling some burgers and ribs. It should be a lot of fun." Dr. Ritchey had taken a personal interest in Robert, who maintained the highest grade in the class. The gangly professor smiled and handed Robert a sheet of paper with his address and instructions to get to his house.

"No thanks, Doc." Robert headed toward the exit again while stuffing the paper into his backpack. "I've got a genetics test to study for and a paper to write for my French class. Besides, there's an NBA finals game during your little meeting. I'm not so sure about *your* God, but I do know it's definitely time to worship the basketball gods."

The look on the professor's face showed he was clearly disappointed. He didn't have a chance to respond before Robert ducked out the door.

"Thank God it's Friday," Robert said to himself while he walked across campus to the J. F. Reed Library. He was supposed to meet Emily from his French class to help her proof her final paper. They would only have a couple of hours to study before the dorm cafeteria closed for dinner.

Ehh, dorm food, Robert thought while he skipped up the steps to the library. It was the minimum requirement to sustain the life of a poor college student. He was still feeling a minor stomach disturbance from the cafeteria chili he'd eaten for lunch just four hours earlier. Surely dinner would be an equally disappointing culinary desecration. Even while suffering a stomach ache from the previous meal, Robert was still hungry.

Robert entered the campus library and instantly became uncomfortable. This overly serious and ominously quiet cathedral was the chosen venue of his study partner, Emily. Robert preferred the comforting chaos of the dorm, where he did his best studying. After a little searching, he found Emily working on her French paper at a computer station in a quiet corner.

She's so beautiful, Robert thought as he approached his friend. Her long, blond hair was pulled up in a ponytail, revealing her flawless face. But Robert was fixed on Emily's amazing legs, scantly covered by her skimpy summer clothing. She was perfect, unlike some of the girls in the hippie college town, where all too often beautiful legs were corrupted with hair or covered by dirty, homemade tie-dyed clothing. But Emily was flawless, not succumbing to the bohemian culture that many students of the college belonged to.

"Looks like you're making good progress here," Robert said, sitting down next to his classmate.

"No thanks to you," she answered. "You're late, and I'm lost. I don't think I'd even be passing French without your help." She grinned at him, batting her eyelashes.

"Quiet down over there!" came a whispering shout. It was Calvin and his cowboy gang, sitting at a round table fifteen feet away. Robert hadn't even noticed them when he arrived. They were taking turns holding up flash cards with various cuts of beef while quizzing each other on steak names and corresponding bovine anatomy.

"What a bunch of dumb asses." Robert chuckled as he slid closer to Emily and spoke more softly. "What the hell are they going to do with an ag degree?"

Ironically, Calvin, the meat major, would eventually go on to own a large cattle ranch in Paonia, Colorado, and become a millionaire many times over.

"Here, read what I have so far," Emily said. "I think my verb conjugations are all screwed up."

In a perfect French accent, Robert responded, "Laissez-moi voir" (Let's have a look). He began reading and making necessary corrections.

Emily quickly lost interest and started searching through her large sequined purse for some ChapStick, which was swimming in a sea of feminine necessities. Her iPhone began to vibrate. "Hey, Robert, will you watch my purse? My roommate's texting me. She's in the library, but she can't find us. I'm going to go meet her at the front desk."

"Sure," Robert replied with regret as he continued to polish her paper. While Emily walked away, Robert wondered why all hot girls had unattractive and obnoxious best friends.

After Robert finished proofing Emily's work, he pulled up his own report from the college cloud and started putting the final touches on his paper.

Fifteen minutes had passed since Emily left the table. Robert completely finished his paper and started studying for Monday's genetics test. Getting bored, Robert looked over at the cowboy study group. Calvin was holding up a meat flash card. Robert called out, "Porterhouse" in a voice just loud enough for them, but not the librarian, to hear.

Calvin shouted back without restraint, unconcerned that he was in a library. "Hey, smartass, how 'bout I come over there and knock out your two front teeth? You ever seen a dentist without front teeth? And that's a shank roast anyway, jackass!" His elevated voice earned him a stiff warning from a nearby librarian.

Robert was relieved that the librarian intervened, since Calvin was nearly twice his size. Besides, even if he could hold his own in a physical confrontation, the ag posse would be standing behind Calvin for backup.

While the librarian scolded the agriculture majors, Robert noticed a bright-yellow flyer on the floor next to his foot. The heading would have gotten the attention of any starving student. EARN $1000 PER MONTH WHILE WE PAY FOR COLLEGE. He picked it up and read further:

> Imagine yourself traveling to exotic locations and living the ultimate adventure while serving your country in the CIA. The US government is looking for a few qualified students from the medical field to enroll in a new program that allows you to finish your degree from anywhere in the country while completing clandestine cadet training. Future professionals from all branches of health care are needed. Earn $1,000 spending cash each month while you're in school and let the government pay your student loans when you graduate. Simply spend college breaks receiving accelerated training at our facility in Chantilly, Virginia. In addition, we enroll you in supplemental private courses near your home throughout the school year.

> Upon graduation from med school and concurrent completion of CIA specialty agent training, you will work in your field in the private sector while earning additional pay for participation in special agency intelligence operations.

> Visit Nobel Hall on June 25 at 1:00 p.m. and speak with retired CIA officer and recruiter, Gars Toulgood, to see if you have what it takes to join this elite team.

Wow. A thousand dollars a month, Robert thought. I wonder if they need dentists. He quickly entered the recruit date into his cell phone calendar. He'd always wanted to travel the world. This could be just the ticket.

Suddenly, Robert's stomach groaned like a wounded animal. He immediately felt a massive shift of colon content. His digestive system bellowed loudly again as he was nearly bent over from pain. "Holy cow," Robert whispered to himself. "Where's Emily?" I've got to get to a bathroom right now, he thought as sweat beaded on his forehead. His stomach now made dysfunctional plumbing groans even the ag posse could hear from fifteen feet away.

"What the hell was that?" Calvin asked in a more restrained volume. "Are you shittin' your pants over there?" The ag posse erupted in laughter.

Actually, Robert thought that *was* a possible outcome if he didn't get to a bathroom quick. He looked down at Emily's purse and sighed. He had a couple of gay friends, but he certainly wasn't comfortable holding a purse and sending the signal that he himself might be homosexual. He couldn't force himself to gather her blingy handbag and carry it for a mad dash to the restroom. It's so freakin' sparkly and big, he thought while the chili from lunch twisted his intestines into knots. Thinking fast, Robert grabbed his phone and dialed Emily's cell number to get her back to the table.

"I don't know you…, and this is crazy…." Emily's personalized ring tone, "Call Me Maybe," rang out from her oversized purse.

"Oh no," Robert whispered through a cramping grimace. "She left her phone in her bag."

"Nice ringtone, sweetie!" one of the meat majors called out in a shouting whisper. The rest of the posse, thoroughly entertained, erupted in laughter again.

The hit melody played for just a moment before Robert pressed the end call button on his phone, but the damage had already been done. It was as if Carly Rae Jepsen herself had been inside Emily's tote screaming, "Look at this guy with a purse!"

Robert could not leave Emily's purse behind to be stolen, but he definitely couldn't strap it over his shoulder and carry it into the bathroom. He needed a plan. He decided to leave the purse on the table and run past several rows of bookshelves to find Emily. Then he would quickly return to check on it before venturing out in another direction.

He jogged north, looking down six or seven aisles with no luck. So he jogged back to make sure the purse was still OK. The Chili Troll inside him stabbed his intestines with mini daggers as he switched vectors. He ventured out on another brisk departure from the table, looking for his lost study partner. Robert carefully settled into a speed walk that wasn't so fast that it would loosen the tsunami that might explode at any second. Ten more aisles; still no luck. He quickly returned to the table.

Finally, Robert gave in to the waves of agonizing cramps that would let him continue the search no more. A bit of a germaphobe, he usually made it a point to reserve public restroom visits for only the gravest of emergencies, which this had turned out to be. He grabbed the sequined purse, careful to hold it in a manly way, and sprinted at full throttle to the closest men's room.

On the rare occasion that Robert did enter public restrooms, he usually stopped just outside and took a deep breath he would hold for the entire visit. But during his sprint, he decided not to bother, as he realized the ensuing session would probably take a while. He nearly collided with two other students, who reached the men's room door just as he arrived.

"Nice purse," one of the students chided. Both laughed.

At this point all pride had to be set aside so Robert could rid himself of the toxic venom that stirred within him. "Very funny," he shot back while rushing past the comedians into the undersized, light-blue stall.

He frantically constructed a toilet paper cover over the seat while trying to juggle the purse and not touch anything to contaminate himself. Cradling the purse, he sat and tried to hold back until everyone cleared out of the lavatory. This was growing more and more difficult with waves of pain shooting through his abdomen. He squeezed his eyes shut and clenched his teeth while he rocked from side to side. They've got to leave soon, he thought.

All of the sudden, Carly Rae Jepsen's voice sang out again, this time with kind of a concert hall quality, echoing another verse of "Call Me Maybe," through the plumbing of the men's room walls.

Robert's eyes popped open. It wasn't him calling this time, so he immediately rifled through the contents of the purse, trying to find the phone. "Where the hell is it," he pleaded to himself during a desperate but futile search. He relented to frantically squeezing the outside of the bag, hoping to blindly press the button that would make the girl anthem of the decade stop.

"Are you OK in there, toots?" One of the two male students called out with a chuckle from the lavatory sinks.

"I thought you were supposed to apply eyeliner in front of the mirror, not in the toilet stall," the other cracked.

Finally Robert gave in. A poosplosion of unholy magnitude was immediately followed by a putrid fetor.

The two students started to laugh but were abruptly stopped by their own choking. "What the hell!" one cried out through a gasping cough. "That dude smells like he ate a zombie for lunch." They both rushed for the exit, fighting to be the first one out.

Once Robert had exorcised the beast, he calmly departed the powder-blue stall and strolled to the sink, feeling light as a feather. He made a mental note to never again eat the school chili. Robert set down the purse, wiped the sweat from his forehead, and washed his hands thoroughly. Then he again grabbed the purse in as manly a manner possible and proceeded through the lavatory exit. Robert passed another student on *his* way to the restroom.

"Nice purse," the student jabbed smugly.

You'll be thinking "nice purse" in a second, thought Robert.

"Oh dear heavens no!" choked the student after opening the restroom door. He abruptly slammed the door shut and made an about-face. He nearly tripped as he scurried away to find an alternate men's room.

Robert returned to the study table, only to find Emily and her roommate already waiting for him.

"Nice purse," cracked the roommate, who stood at four foot nine in heels. She measured five foot one if you counted the hair bumpit. Her dark-orange, spray-tanned legs squeezed out of the taut fabric of her miniskirt.

"Yeah, thanks. I've had quite a few compliments already," relented Robert. He explained to Emily that he hadn't wanted to leave the purse behind to be stolen.

"We have to take off now, Robert," said Emily. "We're heading to my parents' house in Albuquerque for the weekend. But thanks so much for the help." She grabbed her things, and then leaned in close to give him a soft kiss on the cheek. "See you Monday in French class." She waved seductively, while her friend rolled her eyes. Then the two girls disappeared around a bookcase.

Somehow the kiss made that little nightmare worthwhile, thought Robert. He looked at his watch. Oh no, six o'clock. The cafeteria's closed. I won't be able to eat now until morning. Actually, he was having a hard time thinking about choking down more dorm food after his disagreement with the school chili.

Robert stuffed his books into his backpack. He walked out of the library while checking to see if he had enough money to bankroll a modest fast-food dinner. George Washington stared back at Robert from the lonely one-dollar bill resting in his wallet. Was he expecting a twenty? He knew he didn't have any money, but he had to look just in case.

Walking back to the dorm, Robert brainstormed to come up with a plan to feed himself. He entered his room and plopped his books on his bed. Grabbing the remote control, he turned on ESPN to preview the night's NBA finals matchup.

Just then he remembered Dr. Ritchey's party. The Onward Christian Soldier club is going to sing "Kumbaya" and fantasize about Jesus on a Friday night, he thought. This didn't interest Robert in the slightest. "But they're also going to have barbecue and I'm invited." Robert dug through his backpack, frantically searching for the wadded-up invitation with the address and map to Dr. Ritchey's house.

"Found it." Map in hand, he threw on his Oklahoma City Thunder cap and bolted out the door.

6

THE PARTY

The same day, 4:30 p.m., Eastern Time

Madison Square Garden was rapidly filling to capacity. The record crowd was getting ready to witness an event featuring a New York squad that rivaled any all-star basketball team ever assembled. Watching the arena fill was New York Knicks owner Nicholas Riefka, the forty-year-old son of a Russian mineral tycoon. Riefka's family had amassed enormous wealth by exploiting vast coal and mineral reserves in Siberia. The Riefka mineral money flowed faster than Nicholas could spend it. He lived an extraordinary life, investing the family fortune in glamorous business ventures he knew nothing about. In addition to owning the Knicks, he had also acquired a European soccer team and a major movie studio in the United States.

Riefka easily moved in and out of circles of movie stars, sports celebrities, and leaders of nations. He would often invite high-profile guests to sit with him courtside immediately behind the home team bench. But on this night Riefka wouldn't be sitting courtside. Instead he would watch from his luxury suite in order to accommodate security for the world's biggest celebrity, Jackson B. Dunham, the president of the United States of America.

President Dunham had insisted on attending the Knicks finals game despite heavy discouragement from the secret service. Riefka provided the president's security team and members of the military full access to coordinate an impenetrable safety net. An army of secret service agents stood watch in and around the arena. In addition,

29

National Guard troops patted down everyone entering and leaving Penn Subway Station below the Garden. Ten Black Hawk helicopters, which hovered over Manhattan Island, provided the finishing touch. Each Black Hawk was fully armed with grenade launchers for potential ground threats, and antiaircraft missiles for air defense.

The president arrived early and mingled, boasting to others in the luxury suite that he was the nation's biggest Knicks fan. He quickly spotted Nicholas Riefka and pushed through a crowd of celebrities to walk over and thank the team owner and reliable party contributor. "I can't tell you how grateful I am that you have bent over backwards to help me be here tonight. I haven't seen my favorite team win a championship since 1972 when I was ten years old."

In addition to President Dunham, Riefka's guest list read like a who's who of sports legends, billionaire tycoons, and Hollywood megastars. Russia's president was also a guest of Nicholas Riefka. But he was more interested in securing continued United Russia Party contributions than watching the game. He showed up just before tip-off, much to the chagrin of Jackson Dunham. Upon arrival he ordered two shots of vodka, and then approached the president. The Russian head of state dove into what appeared to be a prepared oration.

"Hello, Jackson, we have much to catch up on. I have not seen you since the Healed Earth World Summit in January. I hope you understand I just cannot submit Russia to your stringent environmental restrictions. America should know—"

President Dunham quickly interrupted, "Listen, Vladi. Tonight I'm here to be a fan and watch the game, not to discuss politics." While he was talking, the president took off his suit jacket and handed it to one of ten secret service agents in the suite. Then he placed a Knicks conference champion cap on his head. "As far as I'm concerned, Planet Earth can crumble to the ground around me during this game. This is my home team." He patted the Russian president on the shoulder. "We'll just have to save the world some other day." Unconcerned that he'd probably just set back already-strained relations with Russia, Jackson Dunham slid off to take a seat between two retired NBA Hall of Famers.

Besides the rich and famous, a number of less notable attendees circulated the luxury suite, including the team's general manager, personnel directors, and a handful of people who were thought to have helped assemble the superstar Knicks. But the unlikely mastermind who'd actually built and bankrolled the New York Knicks super team would not, and could not be in attendance. Instead of rubbing elbows with presidents of the United States and Russia, this improbable architect would watch the game from six thousand five hundred miles away.

This man was forty-eight-year-old Mudir Al-Shaitan, a secret business associate of Nicholas Riefka and the true force that had sculpted the Knicks superstar roster. Instead of taking the rightful seat of honor in the Madison Square Garden (MSG) luxury suite, Mudir Al-Shaitan would watch the event of the century unfold from his fabulous five-thousand-square-foot penthouse suite occupying the eightieth and eighty-first floors of world-famous Kingdom Centre Tower in the stunning city of Riyadh, Saudi Arabia. Al-Shaitan wouldn't be rubbing elbows with VIPs in MSG. Instead he was hosting dignitaries from all ends of the Middle East, including supreme leaders from Saudi Arabia, Iran, Jordan, Egypt, and the seventeen other Islamic nations of southwestern Asia and Northern Africa.

Such gatherings were unusual due to centuries of infighting and strife between the innumerable Middle Eastern political factions and religious sects. But a new reality was emerging with a campaign focused on eventual amalgamation of the region. Mudir Al-Shaitan was instrumental in the unification process, setting his sights on the goal of birthing a cooperative Middle Eastern nation.

Al-Shaitan's NBA finals party was peculiar; devoid of the typical fans dressed in their favorite player's jerseys. Instead most guests in the magnificent penthouse overlooking the Riyadh skyline were dressed in customary full-length Muslim thobes or bisht robes. Still others at the gathering wore modern three-piece suits with more traditional turbans or ghutra scarves. All the party guests were men, and most spoke in some dialect of Arabic or Farsi.

The apparent interest of Persian Gulf leaders in basketball could certainly be viewed as unexpected. But everyone in the high-rise penthouse ballroom was of great influence, and attendance was primarily motivated by the opportunity to gain some political advantage. Just before tip-off, Al-Shaitan's guests casually mingled and indulged in extravagant Middle Eastern cuisine, while they were waited on hand and foot. There were two servants for every invitee, and every reasonable request was granted. Mudir spared no expense to entertain the region's top dignitaries. All the men at the party were relaxed and seemed to enjoy the gathering.

Centered on one massive granite wall of the enormous, two-story penthouse grand room was a magnificent eighty-inch, flat-screen television tuned in to the NBA broadcast. The party moved forward with virtually no guests noticing that game one of the play-off finals between the mighty Knicks and the Oklahoma City Thunder had tipped off. Across from the giant television, on the opposite side of the suite, a toe-to-ceiling wall of sparkling glass exposed the picturesque, late-night Riyadh skyline, which appeared to be sleeping under careful watch of Kingdom Centre Tower. Oil money had built this Middle Eastern cityscape that rivaled any in the world.

The unnervingly handsome Mudir Al-Shaitan had jet-black hair and olive-colored skin. He dressed in a custom black Armani accented with matching power tie and turban. Normally he charmed everyone with his brilliantly nefarious and jagged smile. But this evening Mudir mostly scowled while frequently darting out of the penthouse grand room to bark orders into his cell phone. He paced about, only occasionally stopping to speak with guests.

At one point Al-Shaitan stopped pacing just long enough to angrily demand that a servant bring the guests more kabsa and tea until his phone rang. It was Rais Rasil calling from the US.

"We are on the train," Rais proclaimed. "The luggage is secure. The plan is set in motion."

Mudir quickly ducked out of the grand room and snapped back at Rais. "The plan had better be in motion. Do not forget that your families are in a warehouse in Mecca. If you fail, they will all die. Tell Turhan and Aaquib!" he raged.

"Please have mercy," pleaded Rais. "Give us time. The train was very, very late."

"If you have not carried out your obligation by half time, your son will be the first to die," growled Al-Shaitan. He abruptly disconnected.

Mudir Al-Shaitan was a very wealthy government dignitary in the Saudi kingdom. He'd grown up as the son of a construction manager, living in a modest home in Mecca. Young Mudir had been an excellent student who eventually received a Middle Eastern outreach scholarship to attend prestigious Oxford University in England, where he earned the combination philosophy, politics, and economics degree. He now acquired his wealth as a broker of sorts. Among other things he was involved in the financing of terrorist training camps and coercion of US oil companies.

It had been said that if you wanted to do business in Saudi or anywhere in the Middle East, you first dealt with Al-Shaitan, who always took a cut from every deal. Al-Shaitan had been officially named the overseer of foreign aid to Saudi Arabia five years ago. He held similar unofficial positions in Kuwait, Iran, Egypt, Jordan, and four other Middle Eastern nations. He had successfully renegotiated a deal to bring unprecedented sums of US money to Saudi Arabia, even after the US House of Representatives had banned aid to the kingdom in 2007.

While Mudir Al-Shaitan hurried in and out of the grand room of the million-dollar suite, Sheikh Hujjat Aashir from Syria pulled aside a Saudi prince named Aahil Naqvi. The sheikh whispered, "I was told that you might have information about how your country secured aid from America. Since Iran recently signed their aid package, Syria has wondered why we are being left out in the cold."

He looked around to make sure no one in the room was listening to the conversation, before he continued. "Certainly Syria's relationship with the United States has been strained in recent years, but with *Iran* even acquiring four billion annually, we feel our position could be stronger than ever. Syria's president has put me in charge of procuring an aid package of our own. Is it true that Mudir Al-Shaitan can help me?"

The massive Prince Naqvi, who weighed north of four hundred pounds, quickly engulfed the baklava pastry he was holding and wiped the sticky glaze from his fingers on his bisht robe. Then he gave a crushing hug to the sheikh while chuckling energetically. Unlike Sheikh Aashir, the prince seemed unconcerned that others might hear and boldly replied, "My friend, if Mudir was able to acquire four billion dollars per year for Iran, then surely he could pull US dollars to Syria." He continued, "Al-Shaitan began bleeding America five years ago when he consummated a deal with the president of the United States to send five billion dollars per year to Saudi Arabia."

Prince Naqvi went on to explain how the United States provided $5 billion annually to help the Saudis develop energy alternatives to the petroleum they produced. The money was pledged in exchange for a promise that Saudi Arabia would reduce oil production by 5 percent per year over the next twenty years. In theory, this would supposedly result in complete replacement of all fossil fuels with only clean energy alternatives. This was only a component of the comprehensive US-initiated global conservation plan named Healed Earth. The very idealistic plan was easily sold to foreign countries with these massive American-tax-dollar aid packages.

The same plan was sold to the American people through a $200 million advertising campaign. Healed Earth was part of President Jackson Dunham's all-inclusive blueprint to create a global community that used only 100 percent clean energy. Dramatic Healed Earth television commercials in the United States always opened with scenes of diseased citizens coughing through gas masks in treeless cities under dark, smoky skies. The commercials always ended with the earth being healed, showing birds singing in the trees of green countrysides. Revitalized actors would take deep, fresh breaths while removing their gas masks. According to President Dunham, Healed Earth would eventually save us from pollution and global-warming effects that would otherwise kill us all.

Prince Naqvi pointed out to Sheikh Aashir that the United States was generous with Healed Earth packages, even for minor oil-producing countries. "This is precisely why Syria will qualify for Healed

Earth money," exclaimed Naqvi. "The president of the United States said that all countries must join the initiative in order to truly heal the earth. This initiative seems to be independent of a country's relationship with the United States, yet dependent on the negotiating powers of Mudir Al-Shaitan. President Dunham promised that Healed Earth will enable all the world's automobiles to run exclusively on electricity or pure corn ethanol within twenty years. Dunham himself has said no countries can be left behind." He insisted, "Syria will not be left behind, especially with Al-Shaitan's help."

"But why would the Saudi kingdom agree to gradually reduce and eventually extinguish their oil production for a mere five billion dollars per year?" probed Aashir. "Oil revenues in your kingdom exceed three hundred billion dollars per year. Syria would never agree to such restrictions."

The conversation had attracted several men in the room to join and listen as the Sheikh continued to rant, "We all know how stupid the Americans are. Yes, they drive small, feminine electric cars that burn clean on the road, but most of the clean electricity comes from high-emission coal plants. And if corn ethanol is America's hope, then they are also doomed. All of our best petroleum engineers know that one and a half barrels of petroleum energy are required to produce a one-barrel equivalent of corn-ethanol fuel." Aashir, Naqvi, and the handful of men who now gathered around them all laughed together.

Everything Sheikh Aashir and Prince Naqvi had stated was true, but it was also true that under the umbrella of Healed Earth, the global emissions had continued to climb as steadily as before its implementation. However, careful manipulation of pollution data presented in the US advertising campaign pointed out that because of Healed Earth, there was a decrease in pollution. This was accomplished by comparing current emissions levels with the values of previously *projected* emissions increases. Although emissions were actually up 2 percent from the year before, they were down 3 percent from the projected increase forecasts of 6 percent. So in US government math, an increase was actually a decrease. Nightly public service ads on prime-time television featuring Hollywood stars and pop icons would overwhelmingly flood Americans with the manipulated facts.

Naqvi proclaimed, "Don't worry, my friend. Five years ago Al-Shaitan gladly accepted Healed Earth funds from the United States and promised the five percent annual oil production decrease. In reality Saudi oil exports to the United States have decreased by five percent, which has resulted in an American increase in cost of fuel at the pump to an unprecedented six dollars per gallon." The well-fed Prince let out a powerful laugh that carried above the noise from the gathering. "We send less oil and gasoline to America, yet they pay us more. We earn more profits from the US than ever before." Even more men had gathered around, listening to the conversation, and the entire group joined in laughter.

Naqvi continued, "Although Al-Shaitan made sure that US exports were reduced by five percent, he also ramped up black market oil exports to China to record levels. The Saudi kingdom has continued to produce as much oil as ever, my friend. We still extract and refine over four point five billion barrels per day. So gentlemen, the kingdom is cashing in on three things: US Healed Earth tax dollars, more profits from higher gas prices, and more revenues from China."

"Here's to the stupidity of America!" proclaimed Naqvi as he led the men to raise their glasses and toast together. The group had now grown to twenty, nearly half of the guests in the room.

All at once the party guests noticed Mudir Al-Shaitan rushing through the suite, prompting them to cheer in unison. Al-Shaitan was shouting into his cell phone but looked up and smiled briefly to acknowledge the accolades. He stormed out of the grand room as quickly as he had stormed in.

The head of the General People's Congress in Yemen grew angry while listening to the conversation. He interrupted, pumping his fist in the air and shouting, "Why would we want to take American money when we do not need it? America sends their filthy dollars to our people instead of sending shackles and chains! Taking American money means following their president's policies. Yemen will not be a slave to America!"

Still more men gathered into the conversation, which had now taken all attention away from the basketball game, that already drew little interest. Many of the men whose countries weren't receiving Healed Earth money began to chant, "We will not be slaves of America! We will not be slaves of America!"

Only the thundering laughter of Prince Naqvi rose through the disturbance that had ensued. "You fools!" Naqvi laughed as the group again became quiet. "It is Mudir Al-Shaitan who is the slave master, and America the slave! Mudir only agrees to take the money if there is no US oversight. He is making America weak by taking their tax dollars and still selling them less petroleum for more money. Just look at the news. American cities are struggling. Their economy is in ruin. The American dollar is weak. Only Mudir Al-Shaitan manages the Healed Earth aid. The United States merely writes the checks."

Prince Naqvi paused only long enough to stuff a giant baklava pastry into his mouth, engorging his massive frame. "In addition to the five billion that he had acquired for Saudi, Mudir also personally brokered similar US stimulus-backed aid packages for Kuwait, Afghanistan, Egypt, Jordan, and the United Arab Emirates, to mention a few. The more Al-Shaitan takes from Healed Earth, the more America becomes weak and the more our Muslim countries are strengthened and united."

The prince had energized the group at the party. The playoff game on the giant television had become mere background noise. Knicks fans from Madison Square Garden were chanting, "MVP! MVP!" as their leading scorer approached the free throw line. At the same time all the guests attending the party at Kingdom Centre Tower began to cheer, "Mudir Al-Shaitan...Amir of Muslim man!"

"Wait...Wait...," shouted Prince Naqvi. When the crowd quieted, he continued, "Mudir is a rising leader in the movement toward a unified Middle East. He has become very powerful and extraordinarily wealthy. As a condition of acquiring the aid packages, Al-Shaitan required personal payment of twenty percent from each of the countries he represented. This made the already-wealthy Al-Shaitan a billionaire many times over. And the money continues to flow each year.

In the five years since he began to negotiate these aid packages, he has managed to put billions into his personal bank accounts and investments." Naqvi stuffed another fistful of hors d'oeuvres into his mouth.

This revelation seemed to disturb Sheikh Aashir. He lowered his voice and quietly probed, "So Al-Shaitan is getting wealthy. Why such a large cut? And why couldn't we skip the middle man and get the Healed Earth money without Mudir?"

Prince Naqvi erupted in laughter, muffled by a mouthful of baklava. But the laughter quickly subsided as he began tipping and then staggered toward a chair. His eyes rolled back in his head, while the giant prince tipped sideways into the arms of three men, who spent all their strength trying to break his fall. One of the men shouted, "He's having a heart attack! Do something!"

At the same time Prince Naqvi collapsed, Mudir Al-Shaitan stormed through the room. He was barking into his cell phone, completely oblivious to the unfolding medical emergency. Mudir nearly collided with a woman who was rushing over to the fainting prince. While the group of dignitaries looked on in panicked paralysis, the thirty-five-year-old woman, who wore no head covering to hide her sensuous, black hair, emerald-green eyes, or flawless olive complexion, sped to assistance. Just a fourth the size of Prince Naqvi and wearing a simple black dress that fell softly over her pleasant curves, the mystery woman grabbed a syringe from her purse and quickly injected its contents into his massive arm.

"Prince!" the woman shouted in a heavy Spanish accent while slapping his cheeks. "Prince, wake up!" She pounded on his chest and scolded, "What have I told you about taking too much insulin just so you can binge? You giant child, wake up!" Naqvi slowly regained consciousness, while the woman took her finger and swept the remaining pastry out of the prince's mouth. "How can I control your blood sugar when you are so reckless? This is the second time this month that I've had to inject you with emergency glucose!"

The reprimand continued as she marched toward the exit and shouted back over her shoulder, "Don't eat another thing until I retrieve my medical bag and test your blood sugar!" The woman

stormed out of the penthouse suite, ultimately heading to the prince's limousine eighty floors below, ranting to herself in her native Spanish all the while.

Prince Naqvi was still regaining his faculties moments after the beautiful woman disappeared. The group of men surrounding Naqvi was very concerned with the prince's well-being. But they were even more concerned that a woman without proper coverings would dare talk to any man in such a manner.

"Great Prince," proclaimed Sheikh Aashir, "this disrespectful woman will be tried and sentenced to flogging."

Naqvi, now completely alert, laughed once again. He reached up from the floor and grabbed more baklava from a server passing by, while he reassured the sheikh. "No, silly sheikh. There will be no flogging. That is my personal physician. Her name is Dr. Linda Gasol. She first saved my life when I was vacationing in Almeria, Spain. I pay her three times the salary she earned in her public health clinic to travel with me." He stood up and chuckled while wiping the crumbs from his beard and ghutra. "Now she saves my life once a month! Just three weeks ago she amputated my little toe when it turned black from gangrene."

The room became silent after the Prince gave an awkwardly gruesome description of how Dr. Gasol had removed his dead toe with a butter knife in a Mediterranean resort hotel room. Naqvi grabbed three lumet il adi pastries from a servant's tray and stuffed all three into his mouth simultaneously. He roared in laughter, breaking the tension of the moment. His fellow dignitaries joined in the laughter.

"Now where was I?" asked Naqvi. "Oh, yes. Mudir has become wealthier with Healed Earth money, but he has used much of his wealth to help unify our Muslim nations. I understand that tonight he will unveil his final unification plans and show our region's position of strength to the entire world."

"I still don't understand why America will only work with Al-Shaitan. Why couldn't I get Healed Earth money for Syria without Mudir's involvement?" asked Sheikh Aashir.

Naqvi looked carefully around the grand room. Seeing that Al-Shaitan wasn't nearby, he leaned in and continued speaking in a near whisper. "Why do you think an American president would really throw away so much money?" The group of dignitaries all gathered in close so they could hear. "It was Mudir's plan to take a percentage of Healed Earth money received by our nations and funnel it through private Middle Eastern companies. The very same money is then returned back to the US through five American super PACs that campaigned to reelect the president. It is in this way that President Dunham was able to take usually untouchable tax dollars and channel them into his own reelection efforts. Super PACs were able to launder nearly one point five billion US tax dollars per year for the last five years to help put the president back in office for a second term."

Sheikh Aashir held his hands up to his ghutra scarf and shook his head. "This is all very confusing," he said.

"No, no silly Sheik it is all very simple," Prince Naqvi replied. "Mudir's entire plan was genius. It benefits President Jackson Dunham and all of our region's participating nations. President Dunham was able to use unprecedented quantities of his taxpayer's dollars to buy his reelection amid a terrible American economy. At the same time Mudir's plan channeled massive amounts of US Healed Earth dollars to the Middle East, strengthening the economy in our region. It drastically reduced Middle-Eastern exports of fuel to America, but gas prices went up, allowing us to earn more money for less petroleum. Yes the money helped to make Al-Shaitan filthy rich. But many have enjoyed great prosperity from his plan, all while it helped lay a foundation for the eventual establishment of a unified Islamic Nation. Mudir will unify the entire Middle East through shrewd diplomacy and calculated strength in a way that ISIS, Hamas, and the Muslim Brotherhood could have only dreamed about."

Aashir prodded. "But I have heard that President Dunham has threatened to pull back on Middle Eastern aid since he was reelected."

Naqvi laughed as he engulfed three more lumet il adi. "This is one of the very reasons Al-Shaitan has gathered us together this late evening. Mudir tells me he will show us how we will…"—he paused—"pressure America into not only maintaining, but expanding Healed Earth aid to the Middle East."

7

JAZAR (THE BUTCHER)

Mudir Al-Shaitan paced anxiously in his master bedroom, oblivious to the sparkling Riyadh skyline that rested below Kingdom Centre Tower. He stared impatiently at his cell phone, only glancing out his window at the night sky for a moment, before looking back down at his cell phone. He was annoyed by periodic outbursts of laughter and chanting from the grand room on the other side of the granite walls.

Mudir had spent years meticulously preparing for this one momentous evening so that everything would be perfect. If all went according to plan, this would forever be remembered as the night that a unified Arab nation was born from centuries of division and chaos. It was also supposed to be the night that would elevate Mudir Al-Shaitan to the pinnacle of power in the Middle East. But thus far, events were not unfolding according to plan.

Mudir's anxiety had gradually steamed to anger. His anger was now boiling to rage. He was too preoccupied to enjoy his own party. He feared his opportunity to give birth to a budding Persian-Arab union of states was slowly slipping away. Impatiently, he dialed his cell phone.

A man named Abdul Muntaqim answered from a warehouse in Mecca. "Tell me, great zaiem, what will you have me do?"

"Kill their families," Mudir growled.

Abdul hesitated and then stuttered into his cell phone, "All of them? All of them, my caliph?"

"Yes! 'Kill them' means kill all of them," blasted Mudir. His face was turning reddish purple, and spit flew from his mouth when he shouted. Then Al-Shaitan's phone began to vibrate and beep into his ear, interrupting the call and his tantrum. He looked down at the incoming number. It was Rais Rasil calling from the train. "Wait, Abdul. Hold the line," ordered Mudir.

Al-Shaitan transferred to the incoming call. "What is happening, you bumbling simpletons?" he snarled.

"Have mercy, great leader," pleaded Rais. "Our train just passed through East Rutherford, New Jersey. The mission will be complete in only fifteen minutes."

"This was supposed to happen nearly an hour ago," snapped Mudir. Engorged blood vessels bulged from his head and neck. "My guests are getting restless. You cannot understand the pressure you have caused me! You are making me look like a fool!"

"Forgive us, great one," begged Rais. His voice quivered as he spoke. "We will be ushering in your glory shortly." He nervously changed the subject. "Please, sir, our families…They are safe?"

"For now they are safe, you imbecile. I will deliver to them mercy if you deliver the payload. I will wait only fifteen minutes more." Al-Shaitan abruptly disconnected the call and reconnected with the other line only to hear shouting and confusion.

Back in Mecca, Abdul was barking orders to his subordinates, who were guarding the captive families of train passengers Rais, Turhan, and Aaquib. Abdul and five other men had been holding the wives and eight children of the train warriors. A minor skirmish had just broken out in the warehouse after one of the teenage children tried to escape. Abdul was very tense and was startled when the call with Mudir Al-Shaitan reconnected. "*Metherh klehelettah?*" he asked, requesting Mudir's orders.

Mudir Al-Shaitan didn't speak, but instead he took a deep breath while slowly walking over to the master bedroom window. He took a few moments and calmed himself while looking out at the night sky. His reddish-purple skin cooled back to its olive complexion, and then he answered, "Let their families share in the glory and sacrifice of the three train heroes. They are all martyrs and will receive their rewards in heaven." He closed his eyes and took another deep, calming breath, now in complete control of his emotions. He spoke softly as if with great empathy. "Kill their families." He immediately disconnected.

Mudir Al-Shaitan felt liberated, like a heavy weight had been removed from his shoulders. He calmly walked over to his bed and picked up the jacket of his Armani suit. He straightened it and put it on. As he opened the bedroom's giant cherrywood double doors and contently strolled into the grand room to join his guests, he didn't look like a man who had just ordered the execution of eleven innocent people. In fact, he was very accustomed to giving murder directives, and it always gave him a sense of exhilaration and well-being.

Exactly one year ago Al-Shaitan had arranged the deaths of two Pakistani children living with their father in the Midwood section of Brooklyn. Four-year-old Baraah and her seven-year-old sister Atikah had been playing at the Kelly Memorial Playground when they were abducted and eventually butchered by Jude Wilcox, a white male from Mississippi, who had spent much of his life in and out of prison on drug charges.

The killer was a cocaine and crystal meth addict known to have loose ties to a neo-Nazi hate group in Manhattan. At the directive of Mudir Al-Shaitan and through coordination of train passenger Rais Rasil, Wilcox had been hired to carry out the murders. Instructions were given to make sure the killings, and treatment of the bodies were horrific. It was of utmost importance to Al-Shaitan that the apparent murder motives were simply American intolerance and hatred of Muslims.

Little Baraah and Atikah's decapitated bodies were found in Wilcox's slum apartment. He'd dipped their tiny, dismembered hands in their own blood to stamp-print a giant American flag on his living room wall. He smeared in big letters, "Get Out of New York, Muslim Dogs," again in blood. Wilcox's dead body was also found in the apartment, covered in the children's blood. The cause of death was an overdose of crystal meth and cocaine. The quantity of the drugs in his system could have easily killed three men. Later, an investigation revealed that Wilcox had acted alone, and the only motives were racial bigotry and hate. The FBI never traced the large quantity of drugs used as payment for the murders to Mudir Al-Shaitan, the true orchestrator of the atrocity.

The deaths of Baraah and Atikah had dominated the world media for weeks. In a live interview, their weeping father could only repeat, over and over, that his beautiful girls were innocent and pure. He collapsed while struggling to speak to national and international reporters of their horrific fate. Only two days after the interview, the father of the murdered girls was found hanged to death in his apartment; an apparent suicide.

Rage spread like an inferno through the Muslim world. The Middle East united in protest against American hatred, brutality, and religious intolerance. Animosity toward the American killer and his nation catalyzed an unprecedented amalgamation of all countries in southwestern Asia and Northern Africa.

Through the year President Jackson Dunham had issued multiple apologies to Muslim nations. He assured them that the hatred of a few Americans was, "not indicative of the collective hearts of our citizens." But radicals in the Muslim world wouldn't be consoled in their anger toward the US. Hatred of America exploded, all while Muslims never realized that it was actually one of their own, Mudir Al-Shaitan, who was responsible for the murders. But was he really one of their own?

Al-Shaitan openly proclaimed his Islamic faith and used it frequently to build relationships with the richest and most powerful men in his region. Mudir was respected as a unifier of Arab nations through shrewd business dealings and his strong dedication to Islam, yet his most unifying acts were often inspired by deeply rooted evil. In reality Al-Shaitan was only Muslim for political convenience. He only looked to his people's god when others in the Islamic world were watching. Deep down Al-Shaitan despised any notion of a higher power. Nonetheless, he outwardly embraced the Islamic religion, masterfully using it as an instrument for manipulation.

Mudir entered the grand room with a devilish grin, walking lightly until he collided with Dr. Linda Gasol, who was just returning with her medical bag. The collision caused her to trip and break the heal of her shoe. Al-Shaitan caught her in his arms, preventing her fall. She was the most beautiful woman he'd ever seen.

"*Cerdo torpe!*" exclaimed Dr. Gasol, disgusted because Al-Shaitan had run her over yet again. Fortunately Mudir had no idea that *cerdo torpe* means "clumsy pig" in Spanish.

Al-Shaitan replied, "No need to thank me, my beautiful princess." He easily picked her up and charmingly kissed her hand. As their eyes met, Dr. Gasol was captivated by the confident, controlled charisma of Al-Shaitan. He handed the doctor to three servants, who whisked her away despite her protest.

"Keep her busy for a while," Mudir ordered in Arabic. Then he called out to reassure her, "They will find you some new shoes, my darling."

The party's head caterer spotted Mudir and rapidly approached, ranting, "Beloved leader, the party is not going well at all."

"What do you mean?" quizzed Mudir. "Everybody looks to be gathered together and eating happily."

"I just wonder if we should have planned the party around a cricket or World Cup match." The caterer continued nervously, "Nobody is even watching this game."

"Thank you, *nadil*" Mudir said condescendingly to his servant. Al-Shaitan wasn't about to allow the babbling of an idiot disturb his new calm demeanor. "I will take that under advisement. Maybe next time I will have you coordinate the entertainment." Mudir pointed to Prince Naqvi, who was waving in their direction. "Now get back to work. It looks like the good prince over there needs some more baklava."

"Yes, sir," said the caterer, respectfully miffed. He turned and stomped away prattling quietly to himself, "No he certainly does not need more baklava." He continued to complain under his breath until he finally disappeared into the kitchen. And disappear he did. After that evening, the servant was never seen again, anywhere by anybody.

Al-Shaitan was walking slowly through the grand party room when he received a text message from Rais Rasil on the train:

Only 5 minutes. Praise to Allah. Bless you for your
mercy, Great Mudir Al-Shaitan.

Mudir put his phone back into his suit pocket and calmly strolled
unnoticed past the crowd of huddled guests. He inconspicuously took
a seat in a large, comfortable chair in a shadowy corner of the grand
room.

It was of no interest to any of the party guests that the basketball
game playing on the big flat screen had just entered the fourth quarter. It had been an epic seesaw battle that had record numbers of television viewers throughout the world. Yet the indifferent assembly of
Middle Eastern leaders focused their attention on the party's extravagant cuisine and political deliberation.

With the basketball play-by-play in the background, the party
guests noisily debated until there was an instant and startling interruption. A sharp wave of thunderous bellowing blasted from massive
speakers mounted throughout the grand room walls. Kingdom Centre
Tower itself shook from the moaning roar exploding through the
penthouse suite. It was as if a mother alien ship had landed atop the
fabulous skyscraper. All the guests ducked down. Some even spilled
their drinks while dropping to the ground, and covering their heads
with their hands. The monstrous moans reverberated through the polished granite floor. Only after a few moments could the guests discern
that the giant subwoofers were blasting the *adhān*, or the Islamic call
to prayer.

While the party guests stood up and gathered themselves, many
covered their ears to muffle the deafening wailings that were so beautiful to them at lower volume. The limited attention that had been
given to the basketball game was abruptly redirected to the opposite window-covered wall. Bass thundered, announcing the entrance
of a giant, retractable, high-definition projection screen that slowly
crawled along a track and spanned from the two-story celling down
to the granite floor. Once in full display, the thirty-foot IMAX screen
overbearingly filled one side of the room, completely consuming the
wall of windows.

The volume receded to a powerfully captivating but less painful level. The *adhān* moaned through the walls, and all eyes were instantly fixed on a brilliantly crisp presentation that began to play on the newly revealed giant screen. The high-definition video looked like it had been filmed through the eyes of a hawk in flight, soaring over the most beautiful wonders and attractions of the Middle Eastern region. While the basketball game quietly played to the backs of the guests, everyone was captivated by the crystal-clear, flyby images of Egypt's pyramids, Jordan's ancient city of Petra, and the world's tallest building, Dubai's Burj Khalifa. The breathtaking, ten-minute aerial tour of the Middle East mesmerized the party guests.

While the video played on, the prerecorded voice of Mudir Al-Shaitan exploded through the walls, interrupting the *adhān*. Al-Shaitan thundered like a god, proclaiming, "This is the majesty of our land!" A pause was strategically placed for applause, and the party guests cheered on cue. The aerial tour continued with a pass over the mystic, petrified waterfalls of Pamukkale in Turkey. Mudir's voice again shouted out, "We are one people! We will no longer be slaves to the West! Instead, the time has come to build our unified Persian-Arab nation. We will build this nation on the backs of America!"

As more Middle Eastern wonders flashed across the screen, there was yet another pause in the narration. The power of the stunning presentation overwhelmed the party guests. Many of the dignitaries in the room shed tears of joy while cheering and pumping their fists.

The deafening shouts of Al-Shaitan continued. "Take my hand as I lift our new nation, the United Persian-Arab Caliphate, to the mountaintop." The video flyover picked up speed as it rapidly stormed up to the snowy peak of Iran's Mount Damavand, the highest mountain in the Middle East. The guests watched as the camera soared above the mighty peak and into the clouds above.

The flight rose up through the clouds and into the sky, picking up more speed as it jetted toward a tiny golden object glowing in the distance. As the radiant image approached, the Islamic call to prayer resumed, roaring to a deafening pitch. The party guests were mesmerized by the magnificent sights and sounds. Finally the glowing object came into focus and filled the enormous screen. It was a gold coin, slowly rotating in the sky. On one side of the coin was an embossed image of two children held in the arms of the Islamic angel, Hafaza. The two children on the coin were murder victims Baraah and Atikah.

"The name of the new currency of the United Persian-Arab Caliphate will be the Baraah in honor of the martyred sisters!" roared the voice of Mudir Al-Shaitan. The elated party guests cheered in unity.

The gargantuan image of the gold piece slowly rotated past its thick pleated edge to the coin's opposite side and the embossed image of New York City's Madison Square Garden, prompting an instant deflation of the euphoric unity that had just moments ago filled the room.

Prince Naqvi, who had been uncharacteristically silent throughout this most impressive demonstration, leaned over to his friend Sheikh Aashir and whispered jokingly, "I think I'll call heads and not tails." He looked around to make sure no one else was listening and continued, "Maybe Mudir has gone crazy. No Muslim would agree to use a coin depicting an American landmark."

Awkward silence replaced Al-Shaitan's thundering narration and the howling *adhān*. A thick haze of uneasiness smothered the grand room, while the giant coin on the IMAX screen continued to revolve slowly.

The eerie lull allowed the guests to hear barely audible boos from the crowd in the basketball game telecast, which still played quietly on the screen behind them. Joe Stanford had just stepped up to the free throw line in an attempt to tie the game, much to the chagrin of the jeering New York City faithful.

From the looks on the faces of the Kingdom Tower party guests it appeared that they also wanted to boo the insulting notion of putting an embossing of a New York City sports arena on a Middle Eastern union coin, but no one made a peep.

The brief stillness was interrupted by the NBA theme song that suddenly blared through the walls. Several men in the room had attended American universities and recognized the NBA anthem, but even to them it held little meaning. The gold Baraah vanished from the giant IMAX screen, and was instantly replaced with a New York

Knicks logo, followed by a collection of the team's season highlights. In the background an eerily sexy, robotic female voice began narration in Arabic. "Join me, fellow citizens of the Middle East, and thank Mudir Al-Shaitan for assembling *your* New York Knicks."

The puzzled party guests stood in silence with jaws dropped, while the demonstration took on a new and confusing twist. "This is the favorite team of New York native and United States President Jackson Dunham, but this is *your* team, Arab warriors." A two-story photo of President Dunham filled the giant screen before returning to the larger-than-life Knicks highlights.

Everyone in the grand room looked baffled. The presentation was so absurd that they had no choice but to keep watching the giant screen, all while the finals game still played quietly on the smaller screen behind them.

The silky, smooth narration continued. "Why did Mudir Al-Shaitan choose the New York Knicks? The American president would never miss a Knicks championship playoff game in New York." The giant screen played a short video clip from earlier that evening, showing Jackson Dunham watching the game in Madison Square Garden with Knicks owner Nicholas Riefka and Russian President Putin.

The robotic voice went on, "How the Knicks? New York has not made it to the NBA finals since 1999. The great Mudir Al-Shaitan came to Nicholas Riefka with a brilliant plan. Mudir made under-the-table payments of one hundred million dollars to each of five superstar players in the league. In exchange the players joined the Knicks while agreeing to provide rarely seen endorsements of Middle Eastern products. These endorsement contracts didn't count against the league-imposed salary cap, allowing each player to also draw his normal team salary. American greed ensured that this championship team was assembled. Mudir Al-Shaitan ensured that this championship team was assembled."

Then the female narration gradually grew in volume and morphed back to the shouting voice of Al-Shaitan, which caused all eighty stories of Kingdom Centre Tower to tremor. "Tonight in Madison Square Garden, Russian President Putin, who opposes a Persian-Arab nation sits *where I put him!*" Allah himself wouldn't have spoken with such a deep, thundering roar. "American President Jackson Dunham, who threatens to withdraw Healed Earth money and opposes our region's unification, sits tonight *where I put him!*"

The overpowering volume and splendor of the newly revealed twist sharply redirected and focused any loss of attention that had occurred during the more awkward moments of the presentation. The meaning of the revelation was still unclear to the party guests, but the entertainment value was certainly captivating.

The live NBA finals broadcast abruptly appeared on the two-story IMAX screen before them, while it also still played on the eighty-inch screen behind them. Mudir Al-Shaitan quietly got up from his chair in the shadows and walked to an elevated pedestal of rose onyx in the center of the room. The television volume withered to near silence as the game, nearing completion, played on.

"Thank you, my friends, for coming this evening," Mudir declared, speaking softly into a small microphone. "I hope you are enjoying yourselves." Then he stepped down slowly and strolled back toward his seat in the shadows. Before confused party guests had a chance to sort out the meaning of the evening's convoluted presentation, and before Mudir had made it all the way back to his seat, the game on both magnificent screens imploded to white static with a deafening, metallic reverberation blast that startled everyone in the grand room but Al-Shaitan.

Perplexed by the abrupt interruption of the broadcast and the apparent indication of the party's conclusion, the invited dignitaries spent a few moments exchanging good-byes and gathered their belongings in preparation for departure. No one in the grand room was concerned that the broadcast had stopped before the game's conclusion. It was very late, and most everyone seemed happy that the party had ended.

Then, isolated in a corner of the giant IMAX screen, a thirty-by-fifty-inch rectangle lit up with a live emergency news broadcast from Channel 5 in New York. The relatively small newscast tile looked like a tiny, rectangular island in a sea of static, which filled the remainder of the enormous screen.

Street reporter Terrell Booker looked like he'd been in a coal mining accident. His face was covered with dark powder. His clothing was torn and singed. He positioned himself in front of a camera and tried to speak into a microphone that seemed to be malfunctioning. Earlier, before the game, Booker had been conducting interviews, for the six o'clock news, with fans who were leaving Penn Station and entering Madison Square Garden. Now the whole world watched him deliver the very first newsfeed from a desperate scene of rubble, fire, and flashing emergency lights.

When Booker's microphone wasn't cutting out, sirens roared, overpowering honking car horns and screams. Behind the reporter, rescue crews rushed to help injured victims. Overwhelmed emergency workers were outnumbered by the wounded nearly three-hundred to one. While Booker frantically worked on his microphone, tears streamed down his cheeks, cutting through the dark powder that covered his skin. Finally, sound flowed freely, and Booker attempted to shout over the cacophony of a mortally wounded city crying out in agony.

"This is Terrell Booker from FOX 5 in midtown Manhattan. I'm on location in front of what's left of the post office on Ninth Avenue and west Thirty-Third." Ashes poured from the sky, while Booker looked into the camera and continued. "Something unspeakable has occurred tonight!"

Prince Naqvi, sheikh Aashir, and all the Kingdom Centre Tower party guests gathered in around the small corner of the giant screen and watched in amazement. "Is this really happening, or is this just part of the show?" whispered Aashir.

Naqvi motioned for the sheikh to be quiet, and they all continued to listen.

Booker choked and coughed through thick clouds of smoke that shrouded him while he tried to describe the indescribable scene in Manhattan. "Madison Square Garden is gone! The entire block between Eighth Avenue and Thirty-Third Street is gone! Penn Station below is a giant, fire-breathing hole in the earth."

Adding to the horror of the scene, air-raid emergency sirens joined the hellish symphony with a ghostly howl.

Suddenly in the Kingdom Tower grand room a second fifty-inch tile of video replaced a section of static in the middle of the giant IMAX screen and played simultaneously with Channel 5. The volume from Channel 5 remained strong, competing with a now equally loud CNN Special Report. Some of the Kingdom Tower party guests stayed with the broadcast in the corner of the giant screen, while others moved to the newly displayed center tile.

"This is Dolf Vizter from the CNN newsroom in Washington, reporting on what seems to be an enormous explosion that has engulfed Madison Square Garden in flames. Early reports near the explosion lead us to no conclusion other than that all twenty thousand people who were inside the Garden are feared dead. Mind you, this includes thousands of fans, all the players from the Knicks and Thunder, and yes, our beloved president, Jackson Dunham, who was in attendance and is thought to have been caught in the blast."

"You're now seeing live video from helicopters overhead, confirming that Madison Square Garden, which once towered immediately above Penn Station, has all but vaporized. Also, multiple buildings in the surrounding areas have either been destroyed or sustained heavy damage, causing expected death tolls to climb as high as thirty thousand. In addition, a white-hot fire is now threatening to tear well beyond the original blast radius."

Three more fifty-inch tiles lit up with live broadcasts from around the world. All reported on the massive explosion in New York, which appeared to have originated just below Madison Square Garden in Penn Station, the central hub of subway and Amtrak commuter trains coming in and out of New York City. The Kingdom Tower party guests stepped back in an attempt to take in bits of all the newscasts in front of them on the giant screen. The volume rose as more stations lit up to replace static.

"This is Cooper Andrews reporting from the rooftop of Time Warner Center in New York City. Even as we look down over the city, thirty blocks away from the blast, the streets are filled with horror. Traffic is completely clotted in the veins of Manhattan. Right now you can see we are focusing our cameras on subway exits below where people have been trampling each other while trying to escape. It appears that this is the case all over city subway stations, with smoke and some sort of toxic gas fuming from the underground train system. We are now getting confirmation that the origin of the blast was indeed the subterranean Penn Station."

The Giant IMAX screen was now over 70 percent filled with newscasts as a FOX News Special Report appeared, occupying a space of its own. Anchor Briant Bayer was visibly rattled while he spoke. "Breaking news just in; we are back on air after an apparent explosion rocking Penn Station and overlying Madison Square Garden momentarily cut off power to all of Manhattan. We regret to report to you that it has been confirmed that the entire New York Knicks team, the OKC Thunder, and all of the Madison Square Garden fans attending tonight's NBA finals game are dead. And barring a miracle and some hope that the president received early warning and escaped, it is feared that the beloved Jackson Dunham is also dead."

Five more tiles filled the giant screen. A BBC correspondent somberly reported in a heavy British accent, "The magnitude of the blast initially caused US officials to speculate that some sort of nuclear explosion had been detonated from Penn Station below MSG. However, we do not yet have confirmation of radiation fallout. Of course, we will be monitoring the situation closely." Though clearly disturbed, the BBC anchor reported with a much calmer demeanor, having the Atlantic Ocean to buffer her from the terror raining on the people in the streets of New York. "One can only speculate that this may be some sort of retaliation for the much-publicized murders of Baraah and Atikah exactly one year ago today."

The Kingdom Tower guests, who had just minutes earlier been planning early exits from the seemingly awkward so-called basketball party, had sudden comprehension of the sinister orchestration of the event. They were held in place by the gravity of the history unfolding before their eyes, and for their eyes. None dared to speak. They simply looked in fear and amazement from one broadcast to the next.

For some in the Middle East, hatred for America ran deep. But for others it seemed like the hate was merely something one participated in for sport out of tradition, something passed on from generation to generation. Though some Middle Eastern radicals were truly twisted with disgust of Americans, many in the room had American friends. Many of those friends were former classmates from American universities, where most Middle Eastern dignitaries are educated. Prince Naqvi could only fear the worst for one of his brothers who lived in downtown Manhattan close to Madison Square Garden. Yet a growing, deep sense of fear in the grand room ensured that not a tear was shed. Neither Naqvi nor any of the men in Kingdom Centre Tower would express even the smallest hint of protest.

It was now clear to everyone at the party that Mudir Al-Shaitan had just blown up Madison Square Garden. His power was palpable in the room. Al-Shaitan had instantly attained a new level of respect while simultaneously triggering fear, not only at his party, but all over the world.

All at once Al Jazeera TV trumpeted from the eighty-inch plasma screen behind the guests, causing everyone in the grand room to turn and watch. Cameras again focused on what was left of MSG. Reporter Haaziq Arafat proclaimed, "Twenty thousand fans, who only moments ago cheered on their teams, are now merely ghosts haunting a wrecked section of midtown Manhattan."

Al Jazeera shifted to interviews of leaders from multiple terrorist organizations. "Death to the Great Satan and praise be to Allah for avenging the murder of Baraah and Atikah," shouted a Hamas cleric. The Taliban, ISIS, and al-Qaeda shared consensus that Allah himself had inspired the attack of America's greatest city. But terrorist commanders quibbled for recognition, each claiming that his faction was in fact responsible for the blast. Many sects tried to grab the power that would certainly mushroom from carrying out the unthinkable act they hadn't actually perpetrated.

"Fools," Al-Shaitan said softly to himself while smiling. He still sat quietly in the shadows and watched the giant screens, which showed others trying to take credit for his meticulously engineered assassination and attack on American soil. But this too was part of the plan. Disorganized terror cells would raise burning American flags, diverting the United States to focus on false enemies. If there were to be any retaliatory attack, it wouldn't be launched against Mudir Al-Shaitan, the true mastermind of the gruesome assassination. Mudir chuckled while he quietly stood up from his seat in the dark corner and strolled out of the grand room, unnoticed.

Finally another panel lit up on the massive IMAX screen. A World News correspondent and personal friend of the president spoke with a trembling voice as she reported, "Tonight our greatest fears have been confirmed. The president of the United States is shown here on video just minutes before Madison Square Garden and everyone in or near the fabled arena was annihilated. Our president and tens of thousands of innocent people are dead..." She tried to gather herself while holding her hand up to her mouth in an attempt to muffle her weeping. After an extended pause she shrieked while wiping away tears from her mascara-smeared face. "This can't be happening!"

"Yes, you whore! This *is* happening!" The startling retort blasted through massive speakers after both video screens abruptly cut away from the terror and confusion of media multicasts. On the giant screen a monstrous, shadow-cloaked image of the shouting Mudir Al-Shaitan towered over the guests. He was now being filmed live from another room in the penthouse suite. On the smaller screen to the rear, the rotating golden Baraah coin returned.

"President Jackson Dunham is no longer of use to the East! I have chosen to remove him and replace him with his more timid vice president, Bo Jaden." Mudir Al-Shaitan held out his arms on the massive screen. "It is now the time to join me while I tether new American president Bo Jaden and make America our slave. The wheels are turning for us to emerge as the most powerful and respected nation in the world. Welcome, brothers, and walk tall as countrymen, in the new United Persian-Arab Caliphate!"

Then in an instant the screens went black and the thundering sound system was quelled. The motor that began retracting the giant IMAX screen purred softly as the sleeping skyline of Riyadh gradually reappeared through the wall of glass.

No one in the room said a word. Instead the guests carefully gathered their belongings and headed out into the darkness of a new unsettled world.

8

THE DEBATE

The same day, 6:30 p.m., Mountain Time

Robert hurried, nearly skipping toward the dorm parking lot. Looking for his car, he immediately noticed the beautiful, new, glossy-black Audi TT convertible with black leather interior. He quickly pulled the keys from his pocket and walked next to the driver's-side door of the sleek twin-turbo sports car. Then he turned to the passenger-side door of his 1984 Pontiac Phoenix hatchback parked in the adjacent spot. He opened the weather-faded, blue passenger door and bent down to awkwardly climb over the passenger seat and stick shift median, eventually tucking himself into the driver's seat. He reached back and grabbed the passenger-side door with his outstretched fingertips, managing to swing it shut as the gearshift dug into his hip.

The driver's-side door of his beat-up, blue Phoenix was orange and came from a more stylish 1979 model Phoenix of a completely different body style. Robert had purchased the model and color-mismatched door from a junkyard a year ago after the original rusted door simply fell off its hinges when he'd cornered a little too sharply. Unfortunately the old driver's-side door couldn't be salvaged, since an eighteen-wheel semi-truck ran it over immediately after it hit the asphalt. One of Robert's friends had simply welded the improperly fitting, orange replacement to the frame. The repair was strong but it rendered the driver's side door permanently shut.

Robert inserted the key, and the engine reluctantly turned over, bracing itself to add more mileage to an odometer that already read,

"280,000." As he backed out of the parking lot, Robert admired the counterfeit Healed Earth emissions sticker affixed to his rear window.

Healed Earth pollution requirements were stringent. If a car passed the yearly test, its driver could still take to the road only after purchasing the sticker for $400. If a vehicle's carbon-output levels were a bit elevated, a high-emissions penalty sticker could be purchased for $700. If emissions exceeded the maximum tolerance, car owners were required to pay a $2,000 fine, and the government took the car away to be recycled for scrap metal. Robert's roommate, Russ, paid his way through college by artfully crafting counterfeit stickers and selling them for just fifty dollars each. But since the roommates were lifelong friends, Russ had let Robert have his counterfeit sticker for a six-pack of beer and a medium Black Jack pizza.

Robert carefully negotiated his Pontiac through the jagged San Juan Mountains that towered over Durango, searching for Dr. Ritchey's forest home. Pavement eventually turned to gravel, testing the broken-down suspension and badly worn struts. With one eye on the road and one eye on the car stereo controls, Robert hardly noticed the herd of twenty elk he passed. He was too busy trying to tune into the signal for the NBA finals basketball game.

Dr. Ritchey's shabbily constructed map indicated that Robert was in the right area, but there was no mountain home to be found. The map had a poorly drawn picture of a llama next to a stick-figure house. The gravel road twisted through aspen- and pine tree-covered mountains, but there was no house and no llamas.

Robert was growing more and more frustrated that instead of the game, his radio blared only static. This was typical of the Phoenix radio ever since the rusted antenna had blown away in a stiff wind.

According to the map, Robert should have encountered his professor's house miles ago. He flipped the paper over, wondering if it was upside down. As he struggled with the map, Robert didn't notice that something large had wandered right in front of his car. He looked up just in time to skid to a stop only inches in front of the woolly beast that stood before him, unstartled, chewing its cud. Though deer and elk were common in the San Juan Mountain range, llamas were not.

OK, I must be close, Robert thought. "Move, you stupid camel!" he shouted.

The animal continued chewing, indifferent to the car that had almost hit it. Robert honked his horn, but the standoff continued. Finally surrendering, he ground the gears into reverse and redirected the car through an adjacent ditch around the unyielding, overgrown alpaca.

Robert took one more sharp corner on the winding mountain road before he was greeted by a rustic wooden ranch sign. It was suspended by a pine frame and was hanging over a narrow gravel drive. Lettering was burned into the sign and read, RITCHEY LLAMA RANCH.

Robert drove under the sign and passed a few more llamas before parking next to ten other student cars in front of the mountain home. Motivated by starvation and the growing smell of barbecue, he energetically crawled over the stick shift and out the passenger door. Then he hurried across the gravel driveway and skipped up the front steps. A handwritten sign taped to the house read, FORT LEWIS COLLEGE STUDENT CHRISTIAN FELLOWSHIP. THOU SHALT ENTER WITHOUT RINGING THE DOORBELL.

Wow, how corny. Robert thought. He sighed and whispered to himself, "This is going to be painful." After letting himself in, he walked across the hardwood floor and looked out through a sliding-glass door, where a group of students were mingling on a large, rear patio deck. He hesitated for a moment, and then took a deep breath before stepping out onto the deck.

"Robert, I'm so happy you decided to come." Ted Ritchey exploded into Robert's space bubble and patted his favorite student on the shoulder.

Robert's raging appetite was somewhat tamed by the sight of barbecue sauce smeared on Dr. Ritchey's bone-white bandages. The kind-hearted professor flashed his two trademark teeth through mummy wrap and a red ring of mesquite glaze.

"There are ribs, dogs, and burgers. We overdid it a little, Robert. I always forget that summer session turnouts aren't quite as strong. So anyway, eat all you want. Oh, and make sure to try my homemade sarsaparilla." Dr. Ritchey proudly held up his home-brewed soda pop in a recycled Coors longneck bottle.

Root beer? What a bunch of party animals, thought Robert. "Thanks, Doc," he said while sliding out from under the shadow of the towering chemist...or alpaca rancher...or preacher...or whatever he was. Robert loaded his plate and noticed that his hunger again strengthened when he wasn't looking directly at Ted's food-stained bandages. Like any young male college student, he ate two hamburgers and three hot dogs with ease. Then he had no trouble downing a giant piece of chocolate cake that was freshly baked by Mrs. Ritchey.

While he moved around the group and talked a little to each of his students, Dr. Ritchey downed his own piece of chocolate cake. He gradually found his way to the front railing of his large deck. A majestic evergreen-covered mountain ridge served as his backdrop. "I want to thank everyone for coming," said the professor. "Hopefully you didn't have any trouble finding the place."

Dr. Ritchey paused for a second to lick chocolate frosting off his bandage-covered fingers before continuing. "I'm going to go ahead and begin our discussion. But first, would anyone like to volunteer to open in prayer?"

Robert, a bit sunburned from his previous afternoon on the campus lawn, turned from red to grayish white as panic struck at the idea of being called on to lead a prayer. Oh, shit. Dr. Ritchey always calls on me in class, but in chemistry I usually know the answers, Robert thought while clenching his teeth. He tried to duck down behind a couple other students. If Robert had believed in God, this would have been a great time to pray that Dr. Ritchey wouldn't call on him to lead the prayer.

Then David, a student suck-up Robert knew from first-semester calculus, raised his hand to volunteer. Robert's color returned, while David bowed his large head, which supported an even larger curly hair dome. David's eyes closed beneath his big, thick glasses, and he recited a sincere prayer, to which Robert paid no attention.

So now church begins, thought Robert. He sat impatiently while trying to check the score of the basketball game on his cell phone.

Great, no bars. Who the hell would live up here in the middle of nowhere? He looked back through the sliding-glass door for the television he could hear playing inside the house. Mrs. Ritchey was using the TV in the kitchen to keep her company while she diligently baked to feed the hungry guests. Robert completely tuned out the discussion and tried to come up with a good exit strategy. He'd already gotten what he came for. My work here is done, he thought.

Suddenly his wandering attention was seized by Dr. Ritchey's probing. "Robert," said Ritchey with his two front teeth glistening through barbecue sauce and now chocolate-frosting-stained bandages. "Let's suppose you were on a boat in the Pacific and journeyed to a secluded island that was known to have never been visited by man." Ritchey paused, still smiling.

Robert sat for a moment with a befuddled look. He finally replied sarcastically, "OK?"

"As your tiny boat reaches the shore, you look up to see a beautiful bronze statue of a stallion raised up on its hind legs." Ritchey paused again, waiting for Robert to respond.

"Right," said Robert smugly.

"My question for you is simple," continued Ritchey. "Where did the statue come from?"

Robert paused for a few seconds, readying himself to match wits with the professor. "Can I ask a question, Ted?"

Dr. Ritchey's grin subsided only long enough for him to sip some homemade sarsaparilla through his bandage hole. Then he answered, "Why sure, Robert. Ask away."

"Are you sure it's a stallion, or could it actually be an alpaca?" chided Robert.

The rest of the students laughed, while Robert only smiled, knowing he was starting to gain the upper hand. One could only sense a blush through Dr. Ritchey's mummy wrap.

"Very funny," conceded Ritchey. "They're llamas, not alpacas. But the statue is of a stallion. And the question is, where did the statue come from?"

The laughter subsided, and Robert calmly answered, "If a bronze statue of a stallion is sitting on the beach, then it was made by somebody and then put on the island. If it's a real statue of a horse, it had to be man-made. Plus, bronze is a man-made alloy of copper and tin."

"Wait a minute," replied Dr. Ritchey through his now root-beer-moistened mouth hole. "No, I already said that humans have never been to the island. So who put the statue there?"

David raised his hand while bouncing in his chair.

Clearly annoyed, the professor called on his student, "Yes, David?"

David smiled and pushed up his glasses as he answered. "Moses?"

Ignoring the ridiculous answer and the quiet chuckles of the other students, Dr. Ritchey turned back to Robert and said, "You've told me that you believe in science and natural processes. So, isn't it possible that this perfect, bronze likeness of a stallion was produced by millions of years of erosion of a piece of bronze that naturally accumulated from tin and copper in the environment?"

Robert said nothing. He only made a face with one raised eyebrow, expressing his doubt.

The professor continued, "OK, so all of your experience and logic lead you to conclude that someone made the statue and put it on the island. Then let's start over. Now you come to the same island where no humans have ever been, but instead of a statue on the beach, you see a living, breathing stallion. How did it get there?"

Robert replied confidently, "Come on, Doc, the zoology class I took from the college that employs you teaches that the horse evolved from lower life forms. You're not going to deny evolution now, are you?"

Ritchey smiled and shot back, "Wait a minute. You just said that something as simple as a statue made of a whopping two-element alloy could in no way be created by nature over billions of years. Now you're telling me a complex, living stallion made from exceedingly complex chemicals like DNA and protein merely came into existence over time. You claim that my relatively simple statue was created, while the infinitesimally more complicated living being came from nothing?"

"Sure. Everyone knows that," Robert replied smugly.

Dr. Ritchey continued, "Students, remember that in chemistry we actually require *evidence* to back our theories. Also consider that Darwin came up with his theory of evolution in the 1800s before we had any knowledge of the cell or DNA, the chemical blueprint for life. Ask your zoology professors to show you biochemical mechanisms for how things evolved rather than simply proving their point with cute drawings of monkeys gradually turning into men."

Robert became energized, thinking he had the professor cornered. "What about when certain bacteria become resistant to penicillin, Doc? We see that evolution every day."

"No, Robert. That resistance comes from bacteria *losing* a gene for a characteristic that once made them susceptible to the antibiotic." Dr. Ritchey smiled and took another pull of sarsaparilla before he continued. "If we're talking about real evolution, you should be able to give me an example of meaningful DNA being *constructed* from mutations, and something being constructed from nothing. If *your* example illustrates evolution, then one could say that if a person who lived next to a house with barking dogs had a baby without ears, that baby evolved because now it doesn't have to hear the annoying barking."

Determined to win the debate, Robert pressed on. "OK, Doc. So you want biochemical proof of DNA addition? What do you have to say about the primitive light sensing cells of the tubularian worm? My zoology professor says that light sensing organs from a similar species eventually developed into the eye found in vertebrates today. So, if we don't have common ancestors with the worm, then why do we share common organs? And, how can you say that the species that inhabit earth are supposedly unrelated?"

Ritchey smiled and nodded. "Very good. So since a tricycle has tires and an airplane has tires, is that evidence that the airplane came from the tricycle? Or could it be that since they have common parts, they have a common creator?"

"You aren't really going to compare biological organisms to tricycles and airplanes...Are you?" Robert asked condescendingly.

Dr. Ritchey grinned again, exposing his two front teeth through his root-beer-moistened bandage hole. "Let me guess. Your zoology professor shows you pictures of a simple worm eye. Then they show a diagram of how a single DNA base pair gets misreplicated. Finally, they show a picture of the vertebrate eye and tell you the case is closed. But no one has ever demonstrated how millions of perfectly coordinated and useful DNA base pairs must be *added* and not just mutated or misreplicated in order to cause the simple light-sensing eye of a worm to evolve and form the video-camera-like eye of vertebrates. For that matter they don't even propose the DNA-level mechanism of how the genes coded for the worm eye were assembled from nothing in the first place. You haven't been shown chemical and DNA-level evidence because none exists. All I'm asking is that you demand real biochemical proof like you would in all other disciplines of science."

"Well, if it isn't true, then why would it be taught at your college and in all schools all over the world?" rebutted Robert.

"Unfortunately a very vocal and political faction of the scientific community has fought to maintain a hundred-and-sixty-year-old idea, all while modern biochemical evidence suggests something very different. It's funny that any scientist clearly understands how the nonfunctional eye from our horse statue, that's made of a whopping two elements, must be created. Yet the logic we apply to reach that conclusion simply evaporates when considering the biological machinery found in the eye of an actual horse. With any other scientific process, you use logic and demand proof, yet with evolution we are satisfied to have blind faith in a theory developed in the 1800s that's based on speculation backed only by more speculation."

Robert, now a bit perplexed, searched his mind for yet another rebuttal in the intensifying debate. Then suddenly Mrs. Ritchey interrupted the discussion when she burst through the open sliding-glass door onto the deck and cried out in horror, "Come into the family room and turn on the television! Something terrible has happened." She disappeared back into the house, and the group quickly followed.

The students and Mr. and Mrs. Ritchey gathered around a small television set and looked on in disbelief. They watched as a monumental tragedy unfolded in front of the world.

Emergency crews exhumed dead bodies on live television, while sirens and smoke rose from the scene around FOX correspondent Terrell Booker. He explained that the president of the United States and at least thirty thousand other innocent people had been killed in the most horrific attack on American soil ever.

"Madison Square Garden is simply gone," said Booker. The entire block between Seventh and Eighth Avenue in Manhattan is gone. As many as ten other buildings have been destroyed. What was initially feared to be a nuclear explosion, due to its sheer magnitude, has now been shown to be a monstrous blast triggered by an experimental, highly-explosive Octanitrocubane bomb. It appears that the bomb, which exploded from an Amtrak train, caused an enormous detonation of one of the city's main natural gas lines under Madison Square Garden. The NBA finals game that was unfolding in the once-fabled arena was abruptly interrupted and will never reach a conclusion. The lives of those in and around MSG have been instantly stolen by an act of pure evil."

While the FOX correspondent tried to describe the indescribable, cameras panned away to the background. There, a terrified five-year-old child with torn pajamas walked down the middle of Thirty-Fourth Street, sobbing and calling for her parents. All around her sirens screamed, and emergency air raid signals moaned like hounds rotting in hell. The little girl, with dirty face and scorched hair, had crawled from the wreckage of the now crumbled New Yorker Hotel, where her parents' dead bodies were buried in a tomb of concrete rubble. She cried out, "Mommy! Daddy!" over and over again.

Her parents didn't answer her cries. They would never again answer her cries or wipe away her tears. Instead a moment was captured on camera that would forever symbolize the tragedy. A New York City fire fighter in full gear approached the child and slowly bent down before her. The hero cautiously and tearfully extended his arms and pulled the little girl into his grasp, holding her tight. Then the rescue worker carefully stood, lifting the child as he looked down at her, and then up at the fractured city that towered above. The two slowly disappeared from view and into the fire-lit darkness.

None of the students in Dr. Ritchey's home said a word. Instead they were completely still, sobbing while staring in disbelief at the television.

Quiet tears streamed down Dr. Ritchey's face. He sputtered when he finally broke the silence and asked the group to gather together. "We need to pray right now," he said.

The students slowly formed a circle and held hands. Dr. Ritchey reached out to Robert, who pulled back and angrily erupted, "If there really was a God, how could he have let this happen? How?"

Ritchey sobbed, "I don't have an answer right now, Robert. Just please pray with us."

Robert raised his arm to wipe the tears from his face and backed toward the exit. "Thanks for the wonderful food, Mrs. Ritchey, but I've got to go." He hurried out the door and drove away.

9

PEACE

Mudir Al-Shaitan was introduced to the US Senate and the world stage just one week after the horrific bombing of Madison Square Garden. The overwhelmingly conservative majority in the US House of Representatives had spent the week rattling their sabers in a cry for war against another ill-defined terrorist group in the Middle East. But the US Senate, though almost equally divided between Republicans and Democrats, was a more moderate, predominantly peace-seeking audience. Television cameras from all major networks focused on Al-Shaitan speaking from the Senate chamber podium alongside Bo Jaden, who had just been promoted from vice president to president.

With war and peace hanging in the balance, the live telecast played to anxious households in the United States and all over the world. Al-Shaitan would offer a sinisterly sincere apology and denounce the radical terror organizations that had claimed responsibility for the MSG bombing. Like an Academy Award-winning actor, Al-Shaitan convincingly promised to personally destroy all terror groups in his region.

Just one week removed from being the vice president, silver-haired Bo Jaden stood quietly by. He had a grave expression that periodically yielded just enough to show off fifty thousand dollars' worth of dental work that he had completed in the eighties. He was being led by Al-Shaitan like a puppy on a leash, eager to make his mark on history like a yellow mark in the snow.

Mudir Al-Shaitan spoke empathetically in English, burdened only by his heavy Middle Eastern accent and periodic pauses to dry his tears. "No words will ever heal the wounds of Americans who lost friends, family, and a beloved president in the tragic and senseless bombing of your historic New York arena. The collective world cries for the late President Jackson Dunham, and every one of the thirty-three thousand and sixteen people who were killed in this most ferocious act of terror perpetrated by combined forces from ISIS, al-Qaeda, and Hamas."

Al-Shaitan's voice strengthened as he continued. "Our world has offered no remedies to terrorism, as repeated acts of violence occur generation after generation. Instead, nations recycle failed solutions that only intensify hate and escalate atrocities. Why have innocent Americans continued to die, and why have previous attempts to rid the world of terrorism failed?" asked a weeping Al-Shaitan. "Because efforts have come from America with force, and without concern for the Islamic people." While Mudir spoke, the television picture cut away to short video clips of children who had been wounded by US bombs during conflicts in Iraq, Afghanistan, and Syria.

The camera refocused on Al-Shaitan and the president just as Bo Jaden interrupted, "Mudir, on behalf of the United States of America, please also accept *my* apology for all of those senseless deaths inflicted by previous administrations. But you can rest assured that I will continue the legacy of deceased President Jackson Dunham by committing to extinguish American military operations in the Middle East." A tear trickled down his cheek. "And furthermore, we can still never apologize enough for the brutal murders of little Baraah and Atikah on our own soil."

"Thank you, Mr. President." Mudir smiled and bowed his head for a moment. He fought back more crocodile tears before looking back into the cameras to resume his speech. "My promise to America is that I will personally hunt down and bring to justice those responsible for the MSG bombing. I also promise to recruit terror organizations to fight for humanitarian causes instead of destructive causes. And those terror groups that will not convert their wicked agendas to missions of peace will be dealt with harshly from within—with Persian and

Arab authority and with the ultimate authority of Allah, the god of my people."

A standing ovation from the Senate chamber interrupted Al-Shaitan. Applause exceeded normal duration to the point of being awkward for the speaker and the entire world watching on television. Eventually there was quiet, and Al-Shaitan continued. "Finally I pledge to unify all Middle Eastern territories with a new peace, a peace we will share with America. I am pleased to announce that we have already secured the voluntary annexation of twelve of our region's countries to form our modern state, the United Persian-Arab Caliphate, over which I will preside. Former republics that once sponsored terror like Iran, Syria, Afghanistan, and Libya will now join moderates like Saudi Arabia, Egypt, Turkey, and Pakistan, accepting statehood in our bright new nation. Radical factions in the region will be forced to live in temperance and practice moderate Islam as mandated through me from Allah himself. Our people will no longer be identified by bickering ethnic subgroups or religious sects. There will be no Sunnis to battle with Shia or Turks to clash with Kurds. Whether living in Egypt or Jordan, my brothers will unite with only one national identity."

As Mudir Al-Shaitan spoke, his voice began to crack. He held up his hand and turned away to cough.

President Jaden quickly grabbed a bottle of water, unscrewed the cap, and handed the bottle to him. "Here you go, buddy" he said.

Al-Shaitan took a drink and smiled at Jaden. "Thank you, my friend." He continued, "As a newly unified country, we will forge world harmony with cooperation from our allies in the United States." Mudir turned away from the cameras and looked into the eyes of President Jaden before continuing. "Our new Persian-Arab Union will commemorate the tragedies that finally ushered peace between the Middle East and America through our new currency. While Al-Shaitan spoke, the telecast showed the image of the slowly rotating gold coin with embossings of murdered Baraah and Atikah on one side and "MSG" on the other. "Our new currency, the Baraah, will forever shine as a tribute to lives lost but also as a symbol of a new lasting peace and cooperation."

The telecast cut back to capture another lengthy ovation from the Senate floor. President Jaden, still standing, clapped with exaggerated sweeping arm movements. He smiled through a thoughtful frown, exposing a mouth full of porcelain crowns that shined bathroom sink white. He nodded and spoke softly to himself. His lips read, "Beautiful..., beautiful."

Mudir Al-Shaitan motioned for quiet, and then continued. "More important than remembering the sorrows and conflicts of the past, is looking forward to progress and cooperation in the future. Our new central government will be located in Dubai. There we have acquired the Burj Khalifa, the world's tallest skyscraper. The mighty Burj will serve as our Union capital building and as a beacon of the new era of peace and cooperation."

The telecast switched to a picture of the magnificent 163 story tower that needled through the sky, reaching a remarkable 2,722 feet. "From here I will reign in radical factions from the entire Middle East and expand a lasting bond with America."

Cameras zoomed back to Al-Shaitan, whose voice intensified. He called out in a commanding tone, "Unification and peace will not be easy. We will need financial support from the United States. The late Jackson Dunham has already helped restore our planet with Healed Earth grants in our region. Now President Jaden is making a bold proposal for healing the *citizens* of our earth by helping my new country build its own United Persian-Arab Caliphate anti-terror force."

President Bo Jaden stiffened his upper lip and took over the microphone. He stood up tall and straight, speaking with pride and authority of the first major accomplishment he would make as US president. He boasted, "I will not rush the American people into another senseless war." The Senate erupted in applause again. Its members stood in an ovation that lasted nearly thirty seconds.

Jaden quieted the audience and continued. "As a demonstration of our commitment to peace, I am proposing a cut in US military spending by fifty percent. With a fraction of this tax savings, we will be able to help the new United Caliphate build its *own* anti-terror task force." The announcement prompted many in the Senate to stand and cheer in support, while others jeered in protest. Arguments between senators erupted, and pandemonium ensued.

"Please hear me out!" Jaden shouted. Order was restored, and the new president continued. "The diversion of US dollars to Arab anti-terror forces will benefit us all. Did you know that of the nine hundred billion dollars of annual military spending, the United States currently devotes fifty percent to the war on terror? With my bold plan, we will now spend nothing to fight terrorism."

"My fellow Americans, I believe that terror is a weed that can be most effectively exterminated by attacking at two fronts. First, the United States will stop feeding the weed. 'How do we do this?' you ask. By cutting military spending and extinguishing all US military operations in the Middle East, we also cut the anger that we feed into the region.

"Second, we must destroy the terrorism weed from the root. So in addition to cutting our own military spending by four hundred fifty billion dollars per year, we will send one hundred billion dollars per year to the new United Persian-Arab Caliphate. Mudir Al-Shaitan has agreed to use this money to tear out the root of the terror weed from inside the Middle East, the only place the root can be reached. This will save the United States three hundred fifty billion dollars per year, and we will finally have an anti-terror policy that works."

Yet another standing ovation from most in the assembly interrupted the president. Cheers lasted for over a minute, while Jaden exchanged glances with Al-Shaitan and chuckled in triumph over his Faustian pledge.

Jaden waited for quiet and continued. "In addition to an incredible savings of tax dollars, no value can be placed on American lives that will be saved. I can promise you that thousands of civilian and military lives will be spared. Because in the past we chose to fight, nearly six thousand three hundred servicemen and women were lost to wars in Iraq and Afghanistan. On my watch we will lose no more. And with the indefinite suspension of US military operations in the Middle East, the much-justified hate for our country will simply disappear, as will atrocities like nine/eleven and MSG."

Applause from progressive and moderate senators rose to a frenzied level, all while a handful of stanch conservatives walked out in protest.

"Finally...Finally..." The president had to motion for silence before he could continue. "Finally, the decrease in military spending will allow us to invest in America and do some nation building right here at home, while our greatest threat turns into our greatest ally led by Mudir Al-Shaitan!"

Mudir joined in to add, "Sadly, lives will be lost in the Middle East before we reach a lasting peace, but they will no longer be American lives. Arab peace can only be bought with Arab blood. Tens of thousands of Americans have died in terrorist attacks, and while fighting terror over the last fifteen years. It's time to say, 'No more!...No more!...No more!...'"

The senators that remained in the auditorium jumped to their feet, chanting, "No more." They applauded more feverishly than ever as the new president of the United Persian-Arab Caliphate embraced the new president of the United States of America. The chanting erupted into cheers as both men turned and faced the assembly, clutching their hands together and raising them in unity.

US television commentators covering the event were quick to point out the appalling behavior of unyielding, right wing senators who "in one of America's finest hours" walked out of the assembly in protest. An MSNBC anchor summed it up as well as any, explaining, "Some right-wing Americans will forever cling to the past disgrace of anti-Islamic bigotry, hate, and love of war. But thankfully, those who embrace hate are becoming a dying minority in this new era of peace and healing."

10

DENTAL SCHOOL

October. 7:50 a.m., approximately four years later. Lincoln, Nebraska

Robert Cline sped in his Pontiac Phoenix down Cornhusker Highway, racing toward the University of Nebraska College of Dentistry. The third-year dental student had just finished an early-morning Tae Kwon Do class as a supplement to his summers of training for a new CIA Special Medical Team Service Program. The karate class had gone a little long, and now Robert was running late for his 8:00 a.m. fixed-prosthodontics lab.

Robert's instructor for the lab was retired navy dentist Dr. Glen Ivanspade, who promised in his syllabus and reminded students daily that he locked the lab door at 8:01 a.m. Any late arrivals would not be admitted and would receive an F in the class, ultimately resulting in dismissal from dental school. Though the threat seemed too unreasonable to enforce, one excellent dental student had already been lost to Dr. Ivanspade's strict protocol.

Robert sped through a yellowish-pink streetlight before slowing down to forty-five mph in observation of a twenty-five mph school zone. He carefully dodged a Fifty-Second Street cross guard who frantically waved his handheld stop sign at the multicolored, rust-laden torpedo. Robert zipped down Fortieth Street and turned into the University of Nebraska College of Dentistry's patient-only parking lot, where he skidded to a stop. He tore his lab coat on the gearshift while scrambling over the center console and out the passenger door.

Robert sprinted from the parking lot into the dental school and rushed down the stairs toward the basement. He passed his slower running classmate Gordon Chang, and just slipped into the prosthodontics lab through the closing door.

Dr. Ivanspade was pushing the door closed with his right hand while looking directly at the watch on his left wrist. Chang, managed to wedge his head into the doorway, just preventing its closing. Ivanspade seemed disappointed that he'd just missed the opportunity to fail two more students, which would have invariably resulted in their dismissal. He made a point of treating his students like the hundred members of the Republican Guard he'd single-handedly captured in Iraq and marched across the Ash Sham Desert during Operation Desert Storm.

"Looks like you just got smoked out of the jungle, Charlie!" barked Ivanspade down at Gordon Chang's trapped head.

"What a racist asshole," whispered Robert to a classmate as he took a seat at his lab station.

"Please let me in, Dr. Ivanspade. I made it on time," pleaded Chang while struggling to force the rest of his body through the door.

"It's a good thing you have a big head, Charlie," barked Ivanspade through a half grin. "Now sit down before I change my mind."

Gordon rubbed his stinging head, while he walked to his lab bench.

Sixty-five-year-old Ivanspade had silver hair his barber kept high and tight. Wearing a white, freshly pressed lab gown, he walked past his dental students, inspecting them like an army sergeant looking over his battalion. He stepped slowly toward his desk at the front of his spotless laboratory until he was confronted with unacceptable disorder.

Ivanspade grimaced while one of his polished, black combat boots stepped firmly on a green four-by-four-inch piece of paper that rested on the floor. He bent over to pick up the small sheet and commanded, "I will not have clutter in my dental lab! A cluttered lab leads to accidents." He flipped the paper over, summing it up through black, horn-rimmed glasses.

The leaflet was one of millions just like it that had been placed throughout college campuses across the country. The tiny campaign

flyer had a picture of President Bo Jaden in the corner. With one eyebrow raised above his military-issue glasses, Ivanspade read the text aloud to the class. "Come get your piece of the pie! Join your fellow students and earn sixteen dollars an hour to help reelect the president!"

"Humph," grunted Ivanspade with a frown. He quickly closed his hand around the paper, and then squeezed his fist, crumpling the small leaflet into a compact wad. He clutched his fist so tightly that had the leaflet been coal, it would have emerged as a diamond. He continued walking toward the front of the room, and then threw the tiny political advertisement into a wastebasket before stepping around his desk and facing the forty-student class.

"I can't imagine anyone shit-all stupid enough to vote for that pinko commie bastard Jaden," sneered Ivanspade. "If he's not shipping all of our tax dollars to the Arabs, he's hiding behind Healed Earth to ban the most useful substance ever known to man: dental amalgam."

The students chuckled nervously.

"What's so funny, Charlie?" shot Ivanspade to Chang, who had a red mark on his forehead from the edge of the lab door. "This country is going down the shitter, and all you can do is sit there and laugh!"

In a public dental college, tenure was sometimes more important than competence, but Ivanspade wielded both. He had twenty-five years of service at the university and was one of the nation's top prosthodontics teachers. But like many professors at dental schools, he was there due to an assortment of personality flaws that made him unfit for a more profitable career in private practice. But if a person could overlook a hint of bigotry, military rigidity, and right-wing radicalism, Ivanspade wasn't a bad guy.

"OK, now we've got a lot of work to do. We have a limited number of torches and centrifuge wells, and we need to get our gold crowns cast before clinic this afternoon. Now get to your stations!" commanded Ivanspade.

The forty dental students quickly divided up into groups of five and took their wax tooth molds to one of eight workstations that were each overseen by often more personable "part-timers" (a.k.a. local dentists who had successful private practices but helped teach at the dental school because of their love of the profession).

Robert's part-timer was Dr. McGraw, a retired dentist from the rural farm community of Firth, Nebraska. Students in Robert's class guessed that Dr. McGraw was between eighty-five and one hundred years old. Hair hadn't warmed McGraw's head for at least fifty years. Like most older dentists, he had broken-down, jagged teeth, ill-repaired dental restorations, and the bitter odor of periodontal disease—all resulting from too much time spent caring for the mouths of others while leaving no time to attend to his own oral health. McGraw was an excellent dentist, who was able to accomplish any dental procedure without remembering or worrying about the scientific minutiae that guided his more cautious students.

McGraw's student group was diverse. In addition to Robert, there was Jim Davis and Chris Engles, both from Rawlins, Wyoming. Like McGraw, the UW grads were cowboys who weren't afraid to let details stand in the way of getting things done. Then there was Qumiir Tabotabauii from Iran. Qumiir spoke broken English with a heavy accent. Whenever possible, he sought out Robert, who helped fill in the gaps of understanding by repeating lab instructions in Qumiir's native Farsi language. Finally there was thirty-seven-year-old student, Dr. Perry Wilford. Perry was twelve years older than most of his classmates. He was an MD with residency training in plastic surgery. He also had a master's degree in engineering, and now hoped to add "DDS" to his already lengthy professional title. Until they got to know him better, the more competitive dental students were threatened by Perry Wilford, MD. Initially, Robert and his classmates worried that Perry's medical degree would give him the upper hand in the competition for limited scholarships the College of Dentistry offered.

"I need one of you cherry pickers' lost wax molds," exclaimed McGraw in a gravelly voice. He lit the blistering-hot torch that was resting next to a cabinet that housed a three-foot, circular centrifuge well. "I'll demonstrate the technique for making the first crown." Qumiir quickly grabbed a pair of long-handled tongs and pulled his plaster mold out of the wax-melting oven. He handed over his mold, trusting that Dr. McGraw would cast a perfect crown to be delivered to his patient in the upcoming afternoon clinic.

"Safety glasses!" shouted Ivanspade from the front of the room, prompting action from those who had forgotten to put on their protective eyewear.

"Oh, the hell with safety glasses," grumbled Dr. McGraw under his breath as he began to melt the gold alloy in preparation for completing Qumiir's casting.

Perry Wilford, MD piped in, "Dental materials professor Beatty told us that looking at the flame without safety glasses could cause retinal damage, and gold splatters could burn the cornea."

"Stand back!" hollered McGraw as the gold pennyweights morphed into a hot, fluid orange ball. Robert, Qumiir, and Perry Wilford took three steps back, while the Wyoming boys moved closer and leaned over the molten orb.

McGraw reached down into the casting well, released the holding pin, and then quickly pulled his arm out of the way. The second the pin was released, the centrifuge spun violently, shooting liquid gold into the hollow tooth mold, while hot drops of molten metal flew through the air. McGraw was delighted, giggling as the centrifuge finally slowed to a rest. He used the long-handled tongs to grab the blistering-hot mold and submerged it into a tub of water. The water bubbled turbulently, cracking the plaster and releasing a perfect gold crown ready to be polished.

"Now who wants to try?" asked McGraw. The Wyoming boys pushed forward to be next. Robert wanted to observe another time or two to be sure he had just the right technique. And then there was Dr. Perry Wilford, who also preferred to wait. The entire class had slowly discovered that Perry's lengthy list of degrees had crowded his brain with so much information that it paralyzed him from accomplishing practical tasks.

Davis and Engles, wearing matching University of Wyoming sweat shirts, completed their castings and moved on to the polishing table.

Robert was set to go next, but Dr. McGraw turned to Perry Wilford, MD. "OK, set your mold in the centrifuge," he said in his gravelly voice. "Here's the torch."

"I was hoping to watch one more before I tried," said Perry. He didn't take the torch but instead pushed it back to Dr. McGraw.

Robert started to step forward, but Dr. McGraw pushed the torch back to Perry. "I said *you* are next." Clearly irritated, McGraw still managed to maintain a forced smile. He was starting to breathe rapidly through his opened mouth, clouding the small workstation corner with the smell of the sour cornmeal mush he'd eaten for breakfast.

Perry reluctantly placed his wax mold in the device, also known as the "broken arm centrifuge." Some wondered if the name came from the rumor that these devices had fractured the arms of one or two slow-moving dental students.

The plastic surgeon/engineer/dental-student had a subtle tremor as he approached the dangerous arm breaker with the flame he feared just a little bit more than the centrifuge. Just as he got ready to melt the gold, the frightened student stepped back with torch in hand and looked up at Dr. McGraw. "Now, it's the reducing zone of the flame that I need to touch against the gold, correct?"

McGraw's smile was instantly fractured. His normally smooth, snow-white head developed horizontal frown creases that stepped from his eyebrows all the way back to his neck, interrupted only by two or three very suspicious-looking moles. "What the hell are you talking about, Perry?"

"Dental materials professor Beatty says that we need to hold only the reducing part of the flame on the gold and not the oxidizing part. Otherwise we will introduce impurities." He continued nervously, "And I like to be called *Dr.* Wilford or *Dr.* Perry, not just Perry. I *am* a doctor."

McGraw stood silently bewildered, with his mouth hanging open in amazement, staring at his highly educated pupil. "Doctor?" McGraw shouted. He started laughing. Vertical smile lines collided with the horizontal frown lines that hadn't completely disappeared. "It doesn't look like you're doing any plastic surgery here. Now melt the damn gold, Perry!" growled McGraw.

"I just need to make sure I am using the electron-rich, reducing portion of the flame to ensure the best possible casting like we were taught in dental materials," snapped Perry.

McGraw's irritation quickly turned to anger. His pasty-white skin changed three shades of red, and with an open-mouthed grimace he went from looking like a snowman character in a Claymation Christmas special to a jack-o'-lantern from a Halloween horror flick. "I don't know what in the hell you're talking about, you moron. Now touch the blue part of the flame against the gold."

Dr. Perry was becoming more confused. "So the blue part is the electron-rich zone?"

Robert was getting restless, as he still needed to finish his crown before his patient arrived in clinic. He understood the question and tried to clear up the confusion. "Yes, Perry, the blue zone is the reducing zone, and the yellow zone is the oxidizing zone. Now finish and get out of the way."

Perry Wilford, MD licked his lips. He took a swallow and a deep breath, and with torch in hand he slowly approached the centrifuge. He cautiously brought the flame to within six inches of the gold, paused for a moment, and abruptly pulled back. "How can I keep from touching the gold with the oxidizing zone of the flame when the electron-rich reducing zone is *inside* the oxidizing zone?"

McGraw had reached his limit. "Give me that, you prim little sissy!" He lunged forward and, with corn-country strength, ripped the torch out of Perry Wilford, MD's limp grasp. He swung around to the well and liquefied the gold pennyweights to a hot globule.

Robert could actually see Dr. McGraw's angry reflection in the small, swirling, orange mirror surface of the molten gold.

"It's the blue part of the flame!" shouted McGraw. He released the holding pin and watched as the centrifuge violently spun the liquid gold into the lost wax mold. With tongs in hand he plunged the mold into the nearby tub of water. He giggled like he always did when the water bubbled and the plaster fractured, leaving behind yet another perfect casting.

"You're next, Robert," said McGraw, as his pasty-white complexion returned and the horizontal folds in his head became vertical lines of delight.

Robert quickly completed his casting. Then he hurried back to his lab bench and polished the molar crown much like a jeweler would polish a fine pendant.

Dr. Ivanspade walked by, looking over Robert's shoulder. "You're the last one here, Cline. Lab closes in two minutes."

"Almost done, Doc," replied Robert as he finished and presented his creation to the instructor.

Ivanspade traded his horn-rimmed glasses for the telescopic loupes that hung from his neck. "Good triangular ridges...Nice line angles...Your cusp of Carabelli is a little weak though. You know the cusp of Carabelli is my favorite nonfunctional cusp, Cline." He paused, rubbed his chin with his hand, and groaned while he contemplated. Then he abruptly called out, "A minus!"

Ivanspade hated to praise his students. He shrewdly used the minus, which had no deleterious effect on grade point average, to break down the confidence of any student he reluctantly awarded an A.

"I'll try harder next time, Dr. Ivanspade, Sir." Since the CIA demanded the highest grades from its medical team cadets, Robert gladly took the A and ignored the unwarranted disparagement implied by the minus. He gathered his things and rushed out the door to grab lunch before clinic.

Recognizing that his student was unfazed by the minus, Ivanspade followed Robert to the doorway and shouted down the hall behind him, "If that cusp of Carabelli doesn't jump off the tooth next time, that A minus will be an F minus!"

At times, the mental abuse and torment at the College of Dentistry was much more intense than the POW resistance training Robert had received over the summer as a CIA cadet. If the dental school couldn't break him, he would certainly be able to withstand eventual capture and torture by the Red Chinese or the Taliban.

Robert entered the York Memorial Student Lounge and sat next to his classmate Qumiir, who was watching the news on television while finishing his lunch.

"*Merhaba*," said Robert.

"Oh yes, hello, Robert," Qumiir replied, grinning. Studying so far from home, he loved that there was a student he could talk to in Farsi.

"*Uakahteh elu hudeah?*" Robert asked.

"Yes. Yes, lunchtime," answered Qumiir.

"No, you're supposed to answer in Farsi, not English," said Robert, wanting to practice the language whenever possible. The CIA had arranged for him to log on to nightly web courses provided by the Defense Language Institute, but he thrived on refining his accents through personal conversations.

Qumiir laughed. "Well, then you shouldn't have asked the question in Arabic,"

Even with his extensive studies, Robert struggled trying to sort out the major languages in the Middle East where well over twenty separate tongues and even more dialects are spoken.

"Hey, there's your buddy Mudir Al-Shaitan," Robert said, pointing to the television.

Qumiir looked up, and both students watched the world news anchor's report highlighting the major accomplishments of the president of the United Persian-Arab Caliphate. In the past four years, Al-Shaitan had personally overseen public executions of nearly two hundred terrorists convicted for their involvement in the murders of President Jackson Dunham and the other thirty-some thousand victims of the Madison Square Garden bombing. Mudir Al-Shaitan's more notable execution targets included former heads of state of Syria, Iran, and Yemen. The report clearly showed that in the four years since the bombing and subsequent establishment of Al-Shaitan's United Caliphate, there hadn't been one documented act of terror perpetrated against American citizens.

While the news anchor celebrated the United Persian-Arab Caliphate president, Qumiir turned to Robert and proclaimed, "Mudir Al-Shaitan is not *my* buddy. He has taken possession of every Islamic country in the Middle East, while America stands idly by. Al-Shaitan calls himself a caliph, savior of Muslims, and a prophet. But I am not so sure. How many Islamic holy men have spilled so much Muslim blood? The very fact that he named Dubai the capital city of the Persian-Arab Caliphate is, in itself, suspicious. It is a western-influenced metropolis, not a holy city. How can he be a prophet?"

The newscast shifted to coverage of a Middle Eastern summit, where President Bo Jaden was signing a monumental nuclear disarmament treaty with Al-Shaitan. In this time of unprecedented peace, the agreement called for reduction of US nuclear warheads by 50 percent. Both men had crusaded for the treaty that, according to Al-Shaitan, was "needed to bring the world's nuclear arsenal into balance." Jaden reassured the American people that they were now safe from former rogue, terror-sponsoring nations that were now annexed and bridled by the charismatic president of the United Caliphate.

Chris Engles walked over, wiping a mustard spill from his lunch off his Wyoming sweat shirt. He pointed to the television screen and asked, "Who's the chick standing next to Bo Jaden's wife?"

"That's Dr. Linda Gasol-Al-Shaitan, the Caliphate president's wife," answered Qumiir.

"That guy looks kind of like 'the most interesting man in the world' from the beer commercials," added Engles. "His wife's got to be twenty years younger than him. She's way hot."

Then Jim Davis, the other Wyoming cowboy, walked up to the group and interrupted. He held up a "Get Your Piece of the Pie" leaflet like the one that had upset Dr. Ivanspade. "Hey, do you guys want to come downtown with me tonight to work at the election headquarters?"

"I don't think so," Robert replied. "I've got a pool certification scuba diving class at six." Robert had missed out on the CIA's intensive scuba training that regular cadets took at Camp Perry, the agency's training facility near Williamsburg, Virginia. Time at Camp Perry, a.k.a. "The Farm," was extremely valuable, and dental school summer breaks were only three weeks long. So during their limited time at Camp Perry, the Special Medical Team cadets were engrossed in types of training that couldn't be completed at home. He desperately wanted to tell his friends that his upcoming evening scuba class, offered to the public by the Professional Association of Diving Instructors (PADI), was part of his supplemental CIA preparation, but of course nobody was allowed to know that he was a cadet in training.

"Come on, it's easy money," Jim said. "My friend did it last night. It's a one-time-only thing where they pay you sixteen dollars per hour. For the first two hours you just cut out more of these little 'Vote for Jaden' leaflets. While you work, they give you all of the pizza, pop, and doughnuts you can eat. Then you spend the third hour just spreading the papers around campus. You just put them anywhere. Finally, you get on a bus with everybody else, and they take you down to the early-voting center to vote. That's it. They bring you back downtown and give you sixty-four bucks cash."

"What the hell?" blasted Engles. "It's like they're paying you to vote for Bo Jaden. That's illegal. He can't do that."

"No, no," replied Davis. "It's paid for by one of the independent companies that contributes to a Bo Jaden super PAC. The president has nothing to do with it. Plus, you don't have to vote for Jaden. You can vote for whoever you want."

Free food and cash would have normally appealed to Robert, but with dental school paid for by the CIA and his $1,000 monthly stipend, time was now more valuable than money. "You guys have fun with that tonight. I'm out of here," said Robert. "I've got to get a good clinic instructor today because I need to seat my crown and try to get a filling done." He was being optimistic, as most students accomplished only a single restoration in the typical grueling four-hour dental college appointment. He started out the door.

"Watch out!" Engles shouted after him. "I think Dr. Crow is on the floor today!"

Robert hurried up the stairs and through the sophomore clinic, where underclassmen were practicing taking impressions on each other for study models. Giggling second-year students Melanie and Carmen cornered Robert while holding something repulsive. It was an impression that Melanie had taken of Carmen's upper teeth. But the impression also extended five inches downward past the soft palate to include about one-third of Carmen's esophagus. Robert felt a dry heave well up in his throat at the sight of it.

Everybody in dental school knew the story of how Robert, a gagger, had erupted like a vomit volcano during the same exercise just last year. His buddy and excellent dental student Derek Harbour had executed a much less intrusive impression, but chunks had flown nonetheless.

"Carmen didn't even flinch." Melanie laughed.

Carmen smiled and nodded boastfully while wiping some of the overflow, white rubbery impression material from her chin.

"Oh, that's horrible." Robert chuckled. "I'd love to stay and gag with you, but I've got a patient in ten minutes." He waved and thanked the underclasswomen for being thoughtful enough to show him their handiwork while he hustled away to the junior and senior clinic cubicles.

Robert meticulously set up his workstation, readying himself for what he hoped would be a very productive session. At precisely 1:00 p.m., he headed out to find his patient, Mrs. Bertrand, who was sitting in the dental college's large, crowded waiting room, reading a cooking magazine.

Mrs. Bertrand dressed neat and conservatively. She wore her graying brown hair up in a tight bun. She was always cold, so as usual, she wore a white knitted sweater over her flower-pattern, long-sleeve blouse. As soon as she saw Robert approaching, she immediately pretended not to notice him. She looked down at her wristwatch impatiently.

"Hello, Mrs. Bertrand. I'm ready for you."

"Oh, you're here. I was just about to leave. I've been waiting for over thirty-five minutes," accused the fifty-eight-year-old widow as she peered over her readers up to Robert.

"I'm sorry, Mrs. Bertrand, but the appointment is scheduled for one, and they don't allow us to start until then." University of Nebraska students were well trained to absorb whatever abuse their patients could dish out with the understanding that most bad behavior was simply a manifestation of their fear of dentistry. One of the school's missions was to help reverse the misconceptions and phobias people had about dental visits, and dissipating castigation was a requirement for winning over the distrustful patient.

"Well, next time don't schedule my appointment for twelve thirty if the clinic doesn't open until one."

Psycho, thought Robert, as no appointments, including hers, were ever scheduled at 12:30 p.m. "I'm sorry, Mrs. Bertrand. I will try harder next time."

Robert offered his hand and took his patient by the arm, walking her up to the payment counter. All work at the dental college had to be paid for prior to treatment.

"Well, the university certainly makes sure to get their money, don't they?" whined Mrs. Bertrand as they approached the payment counter.

Robert handed his paper work to the clerk, who pecked her computer keys and arrived at the total. "OK, Mrs. Bertrand, it looks like three hundred dollars for the crown, and Robert has planned one of your fillings today as well. So that will be another fifty-seven dollars. Oh, and fifty more dollars to purchase your Healed Earth certificate, since it looks like they will have to remove old dental amalgam to get to your cavity."

Mrs. Bertrand flashed an angry smile and scolded, "That's ridiculous. I don't know if I'm going to be able to do this today." She started to cry, and rifled through her purse. "I'm a widow on a fixed income. Maybe I should just get all of my teeth pulled and get dentures."

The clerk consoled her. "I'm sorry, Mrs. Bertrand, but in private practice that same crown would cost over one thousand dollars, and the same filling is close to three hundred."

"Well, maybe in private practice my appointment would start on time. I'm just going to have to give you a check and get a loan to pay my heating bill." Mrs. Bertrand angrily wrote a check from the bank that her deceased husband had directed as president and where she was still a majority shareholder. She ripped the check out of her checkbook and handed it to the clerk, while chastising "This ought to pay for the dean's vacation in Hawaii this year. Have him send me a postcard."

Robert and the clerk exchanged dumbfounded glances as Mrs. Bertrand's two-carat diamond ring got snagged on the lining of her purse, while she tucked away her checkbook.

"OK, let's head on into the clinic now, Mrs. Bertrand," said Robert. He quickly escorted his patient back to the dental chair in one of eighty identical work cubicles. "Just sit here and relax for a minute while I go get signed off with an instructor," he said.

"How could I possibly relax when they keep it so cold in here?" she pecked. "You're going to need to have somebody turn up the heat because I am just freezing."

"Of course. I'll see what I can do, Mrs. Bertrand," Robert said over his shoulder as he quickly walked past several other students to the clinical instructor station. He opened his patient's chart and entered the instructor cubicle, hoping to draw either Dr. Haisch, Custer, Chafee, or Koka. Anybody with a pulse will be great as long as it isn't Dr. Crow, he thought.

Robert waited behind another student for Dr. Haisch, the head of the Adult Restorative Dentistry Department, while Dr. Crow sat alone, working a crossword from the *Lincoln Journal Star*.

Just as Haisch signed off his student and started turning toward Robert, Dr. Crow looked up from his chair and asked, "What do you have today, Cline?"

"Oh, nothing. I was just waiting for Dr. Haisch."

"It appears that he's busy," Crow pointed out. "Let's take a look."

Dr. Crow was balding and sort of resembled The Grinch minus the green complexion but including the creepy, long fingers. After an unsuccessful attempt at private practice, Dr. Crow had spent twenty years working for the Department of Health and Human Services treating low-income and underserved populations. His Health Department patients never really had a choice to switch to another dentist. This arrangement worked great for Crow, who had the bedside manner of corn on the cob. He was now the faculty dentist most avoided by students at the college.

"Uhhm…" Robert paused while brainstorming to come up with a plan to maneuver away from the advancing Crow.

Dr. Crow slowly removed the chart from Robert's hands. He glanced over the proposed treatment critically, reading aloud, "A crown seat on the upper-left first molar and a filling on tooth number nineteen." He looked up at Robert and smirked. "Do you really think you have enough time to get all that done before five? He had a special talent for derailing plans and finding flaws in the flawless. His favorite saying, which he often uttered right before making a student start a project over, was the dreaded, "Don't fall in love with a failure."

Dr. Crow slowly wrote his signature on Robert's paper work, which signified that they would be regrettably yoked for the afternoon. Even with Mrs. Bertrand being his most difficult patient, Robert most often worked through her idiosyncrasies and accomplished his tasks. But with Dr. Crow on board, Robert feared this session wouldn't be as productive as he had hoped. The willing student took a deep breath, adjusted his attitude, and guided Dr. Crow back to his cubicle to meet Mrs. Bertrand.

"Looks like your dental student has planned to seat your crown and complete a filling today."

"That's why I'm here," replied Mrs. Bertrand with a scowl.

"Well, a whole lot of things are going to have to go right to get all that done in one four-hour appointment," cautioned Dr. Crow. "This is a learning clinic, and we have to check each step to make sure our students are practicing University of Nebraska dentistry and not iatrogenic dentistry," he said with a smirk.

The faculty dentist turned to Robert and breathed heavily into his face with his typical smoker's breath accented with the enchiladas he'd just eaten for lunch. "I'll leave you two alone now. Come get me when you're ready to cement your crown," Crow mumbled through a sarcastic grin.

An ever growing number of high-speed handpiece drills screeched, paused, and screeched in a random ensemble played to a nervous audience by the junior and senior dental student orchestra. Over half of his classmates were already going to work on their patients, while Robert washed his hands. He put on his gloves and mask, sat down, and started to recline his patient in the dental chair.

With a resisting squirm Mrs. Bertrand snapped, "Now remember my vertigo. I can't go back this far, Robert."

"Of course, Mrs. Bertrand," Robert replied apologetically. He tilted her chair back up to a near-sitting position before she reluctantly approved. Robert tried to see inside her mouth while he sat, with limited success. Eventually he relented to standing while leaning over the patient, who seemed focused on making her appointments as difficult as possible.

Robert often wondered why on earth somebody would want to make things so hard on the person who was trying to provide optimal care. Wouldn't it enter her head that she might not get the best result if she intentionally presented too many obstacles? Still, Robert took the University of Nebraska College of Dentistry mission statement very seriously. It read, "Only settle for excellence no matter how difficult the task."

"OK, now turn your head to the right just a bit, and I'll remove your temporary crown."

Mrs. Bertrand gave only a minimal hint of a neck twist.

"OK, turn just a little more my way," Robert politely requested.

"My head doesn't turn that way!" shot back Mrs. Bertrand.

What a freak, thought Robert in exasperation. "That's OK. We'll just see what we can do," he responded with waning compassion. Robert figured the best approach would be to climb up on the old spinster's lap, manually turn her head, and duct-tape it to the chair before going to work. "I'm putting a little balm on your lips now to keep them moist," he said speaking softly.

Somehow, despite all the resistance, Robert managed to try on the crown and check his work. "Looks like a great fit," he said. "Now I'm going to give you a little numby stuff on the lower left so we can work on your cavity. Then I'll go get Dr. Crow to check before we fill the tooth and cement the crown."

Robert applied topical anesthetic to his anticipated injection site with a cotton swab. Mrs. Bertrand began to pucker and spit. "That tastes terrible. I need suction."

Robert calmly suctioned the excess gel from his patient. "Is that better?" he asked.

She shot him a glare that assured him he could do nothing to please her.

"OK, let's get this all nice and numb," said Robert. He did his best to hide the 27 gauge, one-and-a-half-inch-long needle attached to the surgical steel syringe from his patient. Stiff old Mrs. Bertrand, who just moments ago couldn't turn two degrees to the right, now looked like a possessed kid from an exorcism movie, almost spinning her head 360 degrees to see what he was doing.

"That's the needle, isn't it, Robert? You know how I hate needles."

"Just a little mosquito, Mrs. Bertrand. I'll be very gentle," he assured her.

Robert craftily shielded her eyes with his left hand as he positioned the syringe with his right. The mulish patient opened only enough to allow the student's thumb and the 27 gauge long shaft needle into her mouth. She flexed her tongue and cheeks, covering the anatomical landmarks of the ensuing mandibular block with stubborn musly soft tissue.

"OK, now try to open just a bit more and turn to the left," said Robert in a gentle voice. He couldn't see inside his patient's mouth at all. His frustration level rose sharply, as did his pulse which climbed to well over one hundred beats per minute.

With a mouth full of thumbs and needles, Mrs. Bertrand managed to shoot back, "That's as far as I can open, and my head doesn't turn that way!"

Robert took a deep breath, looking down at the nickel-size opening Mrs. Bertrand was making with her puckered lips. Feeling the tongue and cheeks squeezing his thumb and trying not to stab her in the wrong spot with the needle, he remembered the college mission statement: "Only settle for excellence no matter how difficult the task." He injected her as he had learned:

1. Penetrate one inch until you feel the resistance of mandibular ramus bone meet the point of the needle.

2. Pull back slightly and aspirate for blood to make sure there would be no epinephrine-containing anesthetic injected into an artery or vein. Injection into a vein would cause a dangerous delivery of epinephrine directly to the heart.

3. Finally, inject the contents of the syringe slowly, over sixty seconds, to avoid rapid tissue tearing and undue pain.

"Hurry!" murmured Mrs. Bertrand, pushing on the syringe with her thick, meaty tongue as she spoke. She jerked, moving her mouth out of the operatory light's focus. Robert couldn't see anyway, so her move out of the light didn't even faze him. He was, however, irritated when she began to squint in pain from the misdirected light beam, which now hit her sensitive eyes square in the pupils.

Still injecting, Robert explained, "It hurts worse when we go fast. The numbing medicine will make it better as we go, if we go slowly."

"I need to swallow," she muttered in a panicked gurgle while grabbing the student's hand and trying to pull it out of her mouth.

Robert's pulse pounded to 120 beats per minute. "Just a few seconds more. You're doing great," he said softly while smiling. You crazy bitch. Let go of my hand, the voice in his head screamed.

"OK, now that wasn't so bad, was it?" said Robert after finishing the injection. He tried to make conversation while waiting for the anesthetic to kick in.

After ten awkward minutes, he said, "OK, let's test your numbness. I'm going to squeeze your lip and tongue to see if we're ready."

"It's numb!" snapped Bertrand as she looked at her watch impatiently. "Can we just get started? I feel like I've been here all day."

"Sure," conceded Robert. He tried to negotiate a somewhat more reclined chair position, with no success. The frustrated dental student stood awkwardly and hung over Mrs. Bertrand, trying to complete his work while jumping through endless hoops.

Robert carefully removed decay and prepared the tooth for its filling. Mrs. Bertrand's annoyed face suddenly winced as she sharply pulled away from the moving drill. "Ouch! I can feel that." She frowned as her eyes welled up with tears.

Completely exasperated, Robert knew he would have to ask Dr. Crow for another carpule of lidocaine before he could proceed.

Robert stepped back and turned around, almost running face-first into Dr. Crow, who'd been entertained while watching the student struggle.

"Having some trouble?" sneered Crow through a half-mouth grin.

"Oh. Yes, I guess I need some more anesthetic, Doc," the defeated student replied.

Dr. Crow said, "Move aside." Nasty was about to meet nasty as the no-nonsense doctor pulled a carpule of lidocaine from his white lab coat and loaded it into the syringe right in front of Mrs. Bertrand's face. He lowered her into a completely reclined position. She didn't protest. She knew it would be no use.

"Open," demanded Crow. Robert marveled as Mrs. Bertrand's nickel-sized mouth suddenly stretched to the diameter of a large apple.

Dr. Crow inserted his thumb and grabbed hold of the patient's jaw, clutching it firmly in his grasp. He abruptly wrenched her head and neck ninety degrees to the left, held up the syringe, and injected its contents in less than three seconds. The vinyl of the dental chair battled the leather of Mrs. Bertrand's shoes, squeaking while she squirmed. She punctured her purse with her fingernails as she squeezed it, while Dr. Crow squeezed the syringe plunger.

Crow pulled up the light to see what was left to do. "I can't see when you keep moving around!" scolded the instructor. Mrs. Bertrand fearfully stopped moving away from the light.

With no delay the high-speed drill was unholstered, and Dr. Crow advanced.

"Aren't you going to wait for the anesthetic to work?" snapped Mrs. Bertrand.

Dr. Crow didn't respond; instead he started to drill, putting all his weight behind his tool. After five minutes and a few squeals and tears from Mrs. Bertrand, Crow stood up and said, "Fill it."

As the professor walked away, Robert called out, "Do you want to check my crown before I cement it?"

Crow didn't stop walking and didn't look back. "Cement it!" he hollered just before he sat down and went back to work on his crossword puzzle.

"You lucky son of a gun," said fellow student Darrin Moore from the adjacent cubicle. "Last week Dr. Crow was checking my crown and said that the floss contact was too tight. Then he ground off the contact with my high speed and said the contact was too light and that I would have to remake the crown. I told him I could solder it, but he said—"

"'Don't fall in love with a failure,'" Robert finished his friend's sentence. "I know. He loves to shut down a project."

Robert returned to his patient, quickly completing her filling and cementing her crown before Dr. Crow changed his mind. Mrs. Bertrand seemed much more appreciative of his gentle approach after just one round in the ring with the ever-rigid Dr. Crow.

Finally, after Robert released his patient, he cleaned up his cubicle and gathered his things. He walked out to his car and chuckled as he removed what he thought was another Bo Jaden leaflet from beneath his windshield wiper. "Oh my God, it's a hundred-dollar parking ticket."

He *had* parked in the patient parking lot after all. In the future Robert would always remember to throw away alumni donation requests from both his dental school and undergrad college, feeling that each had made out very well with aggressive parking-ticket policies. He reluctantly put the ticket in his pocket, climbed in the passenger side of his Pontiac Phoenix, crawled over the stick-shift, and reached back to close the passenger door before speeding off to scuba class.

Robert so looked forward to the day when he'd be practicing dentistry and working for the CIA. The first thing he planned to do after graduation was to junk the Phoenix and move into a more James Bond/DDS worthy model, perhaps a Jaguar or BMW.

11

THE PUPPET MASTER

Approximately one and a half years later

Bo Jaden sat at his desk in the Oval Office with a small group of friends and cabinet members. He was gloating over the recent confirmation of his newest appointee to the Supreme Court. This had been the president's second Supreme Court Justice confirmation since his landslide election victory a little over a year ago when he carried all fifty states and watched his party take back the house majority. The new justice gave the party a two-judge edge and strengthened the president's death grip on politics in the United States.

Jaden's personal secretary, Susan Quinn, walked into the room and stood quietly. She waited for a break in the conversation before raising a finger to get the attention of the commander in chief.

Jaden noticed his secretary but continued talking; ignoring her even though she was obviously anxious to cut in.

She finally interrupted politely. "Excuse me, Mr. President."

"Can't this wait, Suz? I'm in a meeting." He immediately redirected his attention back to his pals. "Now where was I?"

"I'm sorry, Mr. President, but Mudir Al-Shaitan is on the phone for you."

"Oh for God sakes, Susan. Tell him I'm in a very important meeting. I've got a country to run here."

Jaden returned to his conversation. "Did you see the look on the Senate majority leader's face once he figured out he couldn't get enough votes from his own party to block our new appointee? Classic!" Jaden and his friends laughed boisterously.

"Please, Mr. President," Susan said. "Persian-Arab Caliphate President Al-Shaitan says it's urgent."

"All right, all right. I'll take the call. Now go get us a few cups of joe, would ya, Suz?" The president flipped up his hand and waved on his secretary.

Jaden put his feet up on his desk and boasted to his friends, "Sit back and enjoy while the puppet master pulls the strings of our Arab pawn."

He picked up the phone. "How the hell are you, Moody?" Jaden asked obnoxiously while smiling and giving a wink to one of his advisers.

After a brief pause, the president of the United Persian-Arab Caliphate replied in a slow, composed voice, laden only by his Middle Eastern accent. "This is Caliph Al-Shaitan."

"Yes, sir. How's my brother from another mother?" Jaden chuckled.

"I was calling to congratulate you on your confirmation of yet another Supreme Court justice, Bo Jaden."

"Well, thanks so much, Moody. And I just want to tell you that I appreciate the hell out of ya." Looking at his advisers, Jaden held the phone up to his ear with his shoulder and motioned with his hands, pretending to control marionette strings while struggling to hold back laughter.

Then Al-Shaitan said something that abruptly turned Jaden's smile into a concerned frown. His complexion changed from healthy pink to white. The president pulled his feet off his desk, sat up straight, and replied, "I understand. We appreciate everything you're doing. You know that the United States of America has been your number one advocate but..." Jaden waved his friends to go on and waited until the room cleared.

President Jaden switched to speakerphone and nervously paced the Oval Office, not wandering far from his desk. "Mudir, I just have to beg you to consider waiting until the midterm elections. I could be a lot more helpful after we win back the Senate. We're one election away from getting a stranglehold on this country. A move right now on Israel would undermine everything my party has promised the American people about its relationship with the Arabs and peace in the Middle East. The one thing we don't need for the upcoming election is to get the entire Bible-thumping base on the right energized about their Holy Land."

Al-Shaitan spoke with poignant authority. "I need to annex the Palestinian territories and honor them with an overdue statehood in the United Caliphate. The Israeli prime minister continues to threaten an attack on my country if we absorb Gaza and the West Bank, but the Palestinian people overwhelmingly support their annexation. We both know Israel won't make a move without backing from the United States. So I need you to assure me that you will support the Persian-Arab Union and not Israel in this matter."

"Well, Moody, I just can't let you do that right now," Jaden replied arrogantly.

"You don't understand," Mudir replied as he laughed. "Super PAC kickbacks from Healed Earth money are covered with your fingerprints. The US taxpayer dollars that I pumped back into your campaign could be revealed with one phone call to the *Washington Post.* How do you think your countrymen will respond when they find out that it was *you* who was responsible for paying cash for votes with Healed Earth dollars; with *taxpayer* dollars? How will they respond when they find out that nearly five billion Healed Earth dollars trickled back into your campaign?"

"That would be a public relations disaster for you as well," returned Jaden angrily. "How about I pull back *all* of the Healed Earth aid, and Arab unification aid? Then what?"

Initially, Mudir didn't say a word. Instead he calmly looked out his office window from the one-hundred-sixtieth floor of the Burj Khalifa in Dubai. He slowly pulled a tin of English Dunhill tobacco from his jacket pocket. Then he opened the tin and placed a wad of the tobacco into his favorite pipe. He lit it, took a big draw, and exhaled while growling, "Luckily we have used your country's unification aid wisely to subsidize our nuclear arsenal. As you know, Pakistani nuclear warheads are now in my control. We have also cultivated our Iranian plutonium-enrichment program to double our weaponry, all of course financed exclusively with US money."

Mudir shouted, "So go ahead and stop aid, you fool!" Spit flew from his blistering, red face. "Israel could be annihilated with only a fraction of our nuclear missiles!" He paused and regained his composure again before lowering his voice. "And we can use the rest of our arsenal to temper your infidelity, if need be."

"Don't bullshit me, Al-Shaitan," Jaden barked back. "You know that even after our scale-down, the United States of America could wipe out the Persian-Arab Caliphate four times over with our nuclear capabilities."

Mudir took another puff from his pipe and replied calmly, "Well, that's the difference between you and me. If you take us out, we are martyrs. My people believe that I am a prophet. If my *brothers* are murdered by Americans, I say they will be together with Allah. This is what they desire. So either way I win."

Mudir lowered his voice and spoke more sharply. "How about you, Bo Jaden? How about your people? How is their faith in their president or their Christian God? Millions in the Persian-Arab Union will step forward to die for me, their caliph, because they believe that when I speak, it is as if Allah himself has spoken. Will millions in the United States step forward to die for Bo Jaden and his Healed Earth tax scandal that I can turn into headline news as soon as tomorrow? Do your people believe that you speak on behalf of their God, Bo Jaden? You attend mass once a month and nervously throw a five-dollar bill in the collection plate while cameras roll. Nobody in America thinks that your words are divinely inspired."

Mudir paused again and took another long draw from his pipe before he continued. "Let me help you understand, Bo Jaden. When you control the voice of the people's god, you control the people. When you control the money, you control the people. In the United Persian-Arab Caliphate, I control both." Al-Shaitan started shouting. "I may not speak for your God, but in your country, I control the money!

I control you, Bo Jaden! I put you in office, and I will take you out of office if necessary!"

Jaden was silent.

Mudir laughed in a slow, sinister cackle and continued again calmly. "That's what I thought. Healed Earth money will continue to flow, but I will need a five-percent increase that will signify to me your continued cooperation and gratitude for my help with your campaigns. Defense aid will also continue, but again I will need an increase due to Israel's aggressive resistance to our acquisition of the Palestinian territories. You will pressure Israel to turn over Gaza and the West Bank this month. Do you understand?"

Jaden paused for a moment, then responded, "Please, Mudir—"

"I said, 'Do you understand!'"

Jaden took a deep breath and searched his thoughts for an answer. "I guess my hands are tied. I'll do what I can."

"Excellent, Bo Jaden. I am sure you can convince the American people that Gaza and the West Bank belong to the Palestinian people, and the Palestinian people rightfully belong in the United Caliphate. You may not be a great president, but you certainly are an excellent salesman, Bo Jaden. After all, you have sold the American people everything I have ever led you to sell them."

Al-Shaitan took another long draw from his pipe. "I look forward to speaking with you again, Bo Jaden."

An abrupt dial tone rang from the speakerphone after Mudir Al-Shaitan hung up.

The president was in a state of panic. He'd cut defense spending at home and given billions to Al-Shaitan for Middle Eastern unification and anti-terrorism efforts. Only Jaden, the party committee chair, and the late President Jackson Dunham knew about the super PAC Healed Earth scandal orchestrated by Mudir Al-Shaitan. He knew with certainty that he'd be impeached and tried for treason if discovered.

Quickly, Jaden called a secret meeting of his top advisers. Within an hour he sat at the long oval table of the situation room, presenting his case to senior members of the military, US intelligence, and his cabinet. He struggled to convince them that, for reasons he could not disclose, Mudir Al-Shaitan was becoming a threat to the safety and security of the United States of America.

President Jaden's advisers explained that Al-Shaitan was the wealthiest, most powerful man in the world. His security was impenetrable. "There isn't anybody in the world that could touch this guy," said the director of the CIA. "And even if we could, killing him would be a suicide mission."

"What about an air strike?" probed Jaden.

The intelligence director replied, "We have very few agents on the ground in the Persian-Arab Union, and they never even get close to him. His security team keeps him moving. If we thought we knew where he was one minute, he'd be gone the next. We understand that he doesn't even sleep in the same place two nights in a row." He paused, and then asked, "What's going on? We'd never heard this guy was a threat until today. We really haven't even tried to gather much intel on Al-Shaitan because he was supposed to be some kind of hero for cleaning up Middle Eastern terrorism and ushering peace into the entire region."

Jaden jumped up out of his chair and slammed his fist on the table. "We've got to take this guy out! I'm giving you ninety days, so you'd better come up with something. Do whatever it takes!" He stormed out of the room and slammed the door, leaving his advisers staring at each other in silence.

12

DALLAS

One month later

Robert Cline, DDS, had one more patient to see on an August afternoon in the Dallas Public Health Dental Clinic. He was mandated to work in the treatment center for a two-year assignment in addition to being the only dentist commissioned to the Special Medical Clandestine branch of the CIA. Even though Robert still spent a few evenings a week completing minor supplemental training for the agency, he was already cleared and on deck to participate in special intelligence-gathering assignments.

For a twenty-five-year-old, Robert was paid well enough: $80,000 per year from the public dental clinic, plus officer's pay for each hour of supplemental agency training. As soon as he got the call, he would also earn individual clandestine missions pay. But for now Robert was frustrated working in the bureaucracy-saddled government health care system. He'd been trained to provide a high standard of treatment at the University of Nebraska, where he'd mastered all general dentistry procedures, including placement of beautiful white fillings, ceramic crowns, and dental implants. He was also highly skilled at performing orthodontics and multiple surgical procedures. But much to his dislike, Robert now spent most of his day performing the limited services the newly added dentistry benefits of the Affordable Health Care Act provided. He spent most of his days extracting teeth that could have been saved with root canals, and making dentures to replace the extracted teeth. Instead of providing strengthening crowns for badly broken-down teeth, public health dentists were forced to patch things together with giant fillings. More costly state-of-the-art procedures were excluded for the patients who qualified for care.

Robert's CIA contract required him to spend his first two years at the state clinic before he'd be allowed to enter private practice. The agency informed him that initially it would be easier to periodically break away from a government health care facility on short notice when he was needed for a mission.

What mission? Robert thought. He was even more frustrated that he'd been in Dallas for three months since graduating from dental school and CIA clandestine officer training, yet he hadn't been assigned to one intelligence operation. For now the private pilot program he took two evenings a week for the agency was the one thing he really looked forward to. He also counted down the days until he'd be able to start his own private dental practice and provide the kind of optimal care he was trained for.

Despite his frustrations Robert gave every patient his undivided, undistracted attention. He would often stay late without pay to make sure his end of the day patient's needs were met. But with this day's overloaded afternoon schedule, he was concerned that running late would cause him to miss his 5:30 p.m. flight lesson. He needed to be off right at five, as the Addison airport was a good thirty minutes away from the clinic.

At 4:15 p.m., Robert finished up with five surgical extractions on a Texas ranch hand. The patient's boots must have dragged in about a pound of mud when he'd first arrived an hour ago. The foot of the dental chair was now caked with dirt, as the mud had hardened during the procedure.

"You were a great patient, Ed. Your extractions went really well today," said Robert to his patient, whose mouth was stuffed with enough cotton gauze to muffle any attempt at a response.

"I'm going to have Nicole go over some post-op instructions with you before we set you free." Dental assistant Nicole Salcedo blinked her big, brown eyes and nodded politely, while Robert walked out of the operatory.

As he departed into the hallway, Robert ran into a twenty-foot trail of now-dried mud his patient had dragged in. In the last hour, the twenty-some clinical support staff workers must have walked around and, in some cases, through the clumps of mud without so much as the slightest effort to clean up the mess.

Over the intercom system, a page called out, "Dr. Cline, you have a patient in operatory fifteen. Dr. Cline, operatory fifteen."

Before heading to his next patient, Robert tiptoed through the mounds of dirt in the hallway and ducked his head out the back door of the clinic. There, twelve staff members sat outside, smoking cigarettes around a picnic table while taking one of three state-mandated, fifteen-minute work breaks.

"Did anybody notice that there's been mud caked in the hallway for the last hour?" he asked. "Somebody will probably want to go ahead and get it cleaned up, don't you think?"

Martha, who helped process Medicaid claims, spoke up. "The cleaning lady gets here in an hour, Dr. Cline."

"Yes, Martha, I know that the cleaning lady comes at the end of the day, but we need to keep this place looking respectable in the meantime."

All the staff members simply stared at Robert for a few seconds before he gave up and closed the door. Robert was one of three dentists who worked in the clinic. The dentists were supported by a small troop of twenty staff members. Only about five of the support crew did the majority of the work. The rest would shift from room to room, trying to avoid the doctors. In government clinics a state committee awarded raises yearly but never visited the offices or had any communication with the dentists. All pay increases were based strictly on number of years of service, with no performance consideration at all. With no incentive to perform, only a handful of employees were driven, mainly by their own work ethic.

Clearly disgusted, Robert walked down the hall toward a janitorial closet, where he found a broom and dustpan.

"All the new dentists are the same," said Martha to the others at the table outside. "I can't wait until he's been here awhile so we can get him trained to chill out." They all laughed together and continued to pass the time until five o'clock checkout.

Back inside, Robert carried the broom and dustpan toward the mess, but Nicole had just released their last patient and intercepted him. "I got that," she said, quickly grabbing the cleaning supplies out of Robert's hands. Of the five support staff that did any work in the clinic, Nicole Salcedo was by far the best. She was the glue that held the office together.

"You got a page to op fifteen," she said while she scurried down the hall and started sweeping the mounds of dirt into a single pile.

Nicole didn't usually say much. She was pleasant, but there was never any small talk—only the minimal communication needed to perform her work tasks.

"Thanks, Salcedo," said Robert, calling back to her. "You remind me of that little dog on the Inspector Gadget cartoons that never says anything but runs around making everything work." It was supposed to be a compliment, but Robert knew it probably wouldn't be taken that way as soon as he said it.

Nicole ignored him and quickly cleaned up the mess.

"Dr. Cline, you have a patient in operatory fifteen. Dr. Cline, operatory fifteen," the intercom called for the second time.

Robert walked up to room fifteen and looked at the chart that was hanging on the door. He'd be seeing Mrs. Lois Jones, a seventy-five-year-old patient who he had made new dentures for just two weeks ago. The Sticky-note on the outside of her chart read, "Lower denture causing severe pain."

Robert entered the operatory and greeted his patient. "Hello, Mrs. Jones. I hear that you're having some problems with your new dentures."

Mrs. Jones pulled her hand up to her jaw and squinted in pain. "Oh, I'm so grateful that you could see me today, Doctor. I just don't think these dentures are working out."

This news surprised Robert, since he'd seen his patient two times since he delivered her dentures, and both times she'd reported that everything was going well. "Hmm, I'm sorry to hear that you're having problems. Why don't we take a look and see what's going on."

"The top teeth are really doing fine," she said, "but about halfway through my lunch today, my lower denture started stabbing my gums, and I've had excruciating pain ever since."

Robert pressed the intercom button and requested a dental assistant to room fifteen. He figured that someone in the back would surely be done smoking and able to help him by now. Just then Nicole walked into the room to assist.

"Hey, could you grab a denture-adjusting kit for…?" But before he could finish his sentence, his trusty assistant spread the kit across the countertop, behind the patient chair.

Robert gloved up and shined his Pelton & Crane operating light into Mrs. Jones's mouth. "Go ahead and take your lower denture out for me, Mrs. Jones," he said.

With one final grimace, Mrs. Jones removed her lower denture and handed it to Robert. He stepped behind the patient chair to his workstation, flipped the denture over, and set it down on the countertop. Robert and Nicole both did a double take. Nicole frowned in disbelief, put her hand on her stomach, and looked away.

With Robert and his assistant standing behind her, Mrs. Jones didn't let the fact that she wasn't wearing the lower denture slow down reports of what her grandchildren had been up to in recent years. "Little Rudy is on a camping trip with the scouts, and Hannah, his sister, just plays the French horn beautifully…" Mrs. Jones spoke continuously, almost without inhaling, it seemed.

Robert pulled what appeared to be an entire Frito from the underside of Mrs. Jones's denture. Somehow the corn chip had worked itself beneath the denture and wedged itself under the pink, acrylic base. It looked as though it might have still been a little crunchy.

Nicole gagged and accidentally let out a small giggle at the same time.

"I've done a little work on this, so let's try it in and see if what I did helped," said Robert, while Nicole made a peculiar snort sound as she tried to hold back her laughter.

Robert stepped back around to the front of his patient and gently placed the denture back in Mrs. Jones mouth without managing to slow her talking.

"Cloe just made the honor roll, and her brother, Sam, is the state champion in track…"

"Try to bite down on that for me, Mrs. Jones, and tell me how it feels," said Robert, interrupting.

"Oh, Doctor! Bless you. They are perfect. Thank you. Thank you. The stabbing pain is gone." She grabbed Robert's hand and went back to telling him about her grandchildren.

This was usually the time when Robert told the patient that he would have Nicole finish up, allowing him to make a clean exit. But just as he was about to turn things over to his assistant, Vicky, one of the clinic's hygienists, rushed into the room in a panic and pleaded, "Nicole, Nicole, can you sterilize my instruments for me please? I'm forty-five minutes behind for my last patient, and when I asked the other assistants for help, they all said they were too busy."

"Sure," said Nicole. She promptly exited.

Mrs. Jones's seventy-five-year-old hand clutched Robert's like a vice in a woodshop. She continued, "Now Vance is going to be going to medical school in the fall. You probably already know this, but medical school is a lot harder than dental school."

People always irritated Robert when they said this. *He* knew dental school was at *least* as demanding as med school.

"Vance has a scholarship to attend whatever university he…"

Robert's mind was racing to arrive at an escape strategy while the voice in his head screamed; does this lady ever take a breath? There was no natural break to interrupt. I'm going to be late for my flying lesson, he thought as he looked at the clock and watched the time slip away. Surely Nicole will come back and save me.

While Mrs. Jones clenched his hand, Robert subtly stretched his other arm over to the wall and hit the red emergency button on the intercom pager panel, which was supposed to be the call for any available assistant to drop what she was doing and come. But no one came, and Mrs. Jones didn't even notice Robert hitting the button. She continued to clench his hand and pat his forearm with her free hand.

"Little Holly is the number one cheerleader on her middle-school cheer squad but she..."

A few minutes passed. Then 4:45 p.m. turned to 5:00, and 5:00 turned to 5:15. Nicole finally rushed in after Robert's third attempt at the emergency page. "Sorry," she said. "Dr. Erickson grabbed me to help him finish a filling."

But the rescue didn't come soon enough. Robert's flying lesson would definitely be canceled since he would be at least a half hour late. Limited runway time at Addison airport dictated that any lessons that started even ten minutes late would be rescheduled.

"Little Johnny looks just like my husband. He's the scarecrow in the school production of—"

"OK, sweetheart. I'm going to finish you up now," said Nicole as she took Mrs. Jones's free hand. It was just enough of a diversion for Robert to escape his patient's grip.

"Timmy won the essay contest at school, and he—" Mrs. Jones didn't even notice as Robert slipped out of the room, but she seemed equally happy to have Nicole to talk to anyway.

Dejected, Robert walked slowly to the mostly empty clinic parking lot and climbed into the passenger-side door of his Pontiac Phoenix. He contorted across the gearshift and into the driver's seat.

He was too worn out to make dinner, so he stopped in at the Taco Bell across the street from the clinic to pick up a large Nacho Bell Grande and a Doritos Loco Taco. He decided to go inside instead of using the drive-through, because not only did his driver's-side door not open, but the window didn't roll down either. At times he would just pass money and food through the rear driver-side passenger's window behind him, but he always hated to have to lean his neck back and explain why he didn't just use his own window.

Robert drove down Tom Landry Highway 30 toward his apartment, while his crispy taco softened in its to-go bag. He was half dazed, and completely disgusted that he'd missed his flight time. After today's class, he would have needed only two more sessions before his first solo flight.

13

BLACK OP

Robert walked into his apartment with all the energy and enthusiasm of a sea cucumber. He plopped down on his couch, grabbed the remote control, and tried to find a good baseball game on TV. He ate his Nachos Bell Grande with one hand and petted his cat, Kitty Witty, with the other. His frustration was building, and he couldn't help but wonder if he would ever get in on an actual CIA operation. His holding pattern seemed to be dragging on for an eternity.

The exhausted dentist nodded off to sleep in front of the television, which opened the door for Kitty Witty to lick the black, plastic nacho platter clean. Then, suddenly, the phone rang causing Robert to wake up with a jerk. This startled his cat who abruptly ended his snack and leapt off the couch.

When Robert answered, he was surprised to hear the voice of senior CIA Case Officer George Harpole. The agency veteran was calling to let Robert know he needed to pack a bag and be ready to fly out the next morning. Robert was even more surprised to learn the serious scope of the assignment. This would be a "black op"— a dark and dangerous covert mission that would often veer from standard protocol. Due to the unpredictable nature of this type of duty, the participation by new agents was uncommon.

"We're going to ask you to do some things that would be frowned upon by the world community, and if you're discovered, the agency and the US government will claim that you were a rogue agent operating without approval," said Harpole. "There's been an executive order to reinstate enhanced interrogation, of which you will assist."

"You mean, like waterboarding?" asked Robert

George lowered his voice and laughed with a slow and somewhat sinister cadence. "After we do what's currently on the table, the subject will be *begging* for waterboarding."

"I'm not complaining, George, but why such a serious assignment for my first mission?"

"We've suddenly got a situation in the Middle East that could bring us to the brink of war. The Oval Office has given us much more leeway than usual to deal with the issue. I can't go into details right now, but we need a dentist in the field who can work on real patients, and who will plant a device into a person's tooth without their knowledge—you know, while they think they're just getting a filling. We will then be able to use the implanted device to track the subject via global-positioning satellites."

"So I'm going to the Middle East?" asked Robert.

"Not now," replied Agent Harpole. "First, we need to see how you hold up in a high-pressure field situation. We're sending you in with two other agents to capture and interrogate a lower-level security threat. After you assist in interrogation, you will place a test tracking device in one of the subject's molars. This will be a quick op—in and out in a matter of days. If the device works and the mission's a success, you can expect to ship out to your main assignment in the United Persian-Arab Caliphate within two weeks."

"Who's the target of the test mission?" asked Robert.

"I've told you all I can right now Cline. You'll be briefed on the ground by agents 3293, and 2094. You'll know them as Kevin Smith, and Troy Mercer."

"Cool," replied Robert eagerly. "What will they call *me*?"

"What do you mean?" asked George.

"You know, my professional name. What's my mission name?"

"Uh..., you will be Robert Cline, DDS. That's your whole deal, Robert. We want people who question your identity to be able to Google you and see that you're really a dentist. You know, they can look you up and verify that you went to dental school, that you're licensed, and that you work at a Health and Human Services dental clinic in Texas."

"Wow. That's messed up. What if I get discovered?"

"You don't need an alias until you've done something, Robert. Believe me, if you're able to accomplish what we have planned for you, then you'll be able to call yourself James flipping Bond if you want to." George laughed again with a characteristic easygoing tempo.

"Whatever," Robert replied. "I'm just glad to get out of the government dental clinic for a while. That is *not* what I signed up for. So where's the test mission?"

"I can't tell you exactly. Your team will brief you and give you travel documents on location at the airport. Further details will be given by secure video conference when you arrive at your destination. What I *can* tell you is that you will be somewhere in Mexico. Part of your mission will be underwater, so you need to bring your scuba BCD and regulator—and Cline…, pack for hot and tropical."

"Perfect!" replied Robert, unable to disguise his excitement.

"Yeah, perfect," grunted George. "For my first real mission, I spent two years in Bratsk, Siberia. What a hellhole. Anyway, meet agents Smith and Mercer at Dallas Fort Worth International Airport at O' six hundred tomorrow and…, good luck, Cline." George hung up the phone.

Robert immediately sprang through his apartment, threw a couple suitcases on his bed, and stuffed them with anything he could imagine needing. He readied his scuba equipment, and skimmed through his "PADI" dive training book. This was what he'd been waiting for: world travel and adventure. Plus, this would be Robert's first trip out of the country—and Mexico! Even though he spoke seven foreign languages, Spanish was his first and favorite, having studied it since ninth grade.

As he packed his last few things and started to zip up his luggage, Kitty Witty strutted between Robert's legs, jumped up on the bed, and stepped into the open suitcase. The fifteen-pound, gray-and-white American long hair looked up at his owner as if to say, No, this just won't work, Cline. You haven't made arrangements for me.

"Oh…, K-Dub, what am I going to do with you? Looks like you're just going to have to spend a couple days with Nicole." He moved Kitty Witty aside and rechecked his bags again just to make sure he hadn't left anything out.

———

At 5:00 a.m. the next day, Robert hoisted his fully loaded suitcases into the hatchback of his Pontiac Phoenix and gently placed Kitty Witty and his cat carrier into the backseat.

Even though Robert now earned good wages from the dental clinic and the CIA, which stood to pay him up to $5,000 for his first three-day mission, he still drove the beat-up Pontiac Phoenix. A bad childhood experience with debt involving his paper route had made him very cautious about taking loans. Robert continued to drive his worn-out car and would do so until he could save enough cash to pay for a new one in full. Since the car he wanted stickered at $80,000, he would likely be driving the Phoenix for a few more years unless the wheels simply rusted off the axle.

Robert climbed through the passenger door and across the gearshift. He leaned back over the passenger seat and swung the door shut.

As Robert sped down the freeway, Kitty Witty let out a long, loud "Meow!" as if to say, It's embarrassing to ride in this piece-of-shit car. Why don't you get some respectable wheels, you cheap ass?

"Hey now, K-Dub. I found you at the pound, and I can take you right back to the pound if I have to. I'm dropping you off to spend a few days with Nicole. You two will get along great, but don't count on any deep, meaningful conversations. You're a little more talkative than her."

Robert made the twenty-minute car trip in just under twelve minutes. "There's her house, K-Dub." He quickly grabbed the cat carrier and balanced a litter box and sack of food on top before he blindly negotiated the sidewalk and stepped up to Nicole's door.

Just as Robert strained to reach for the bell, his competent dental assistant abruptly swung open her front door. "Efficient as always,

Salcedo." Robert was amazed that Nicole was always ready and one step ahead of him. "Thank you so much for taking Kitty Witty for me on such short notice. You really are the best."

Nicole quickly grabbed the carrier and stack of supplies, while Kitty Witty protested. "Meow."

"Have a nice trip," Nicole said professionally as she closed the door in Robert's face.

Wow, she's pretty chatty today, thought Robert. "Thank you!" he shouted appreciatively through the closed door. He skipped down the steps, flew into his car, and sped off for the airport.

Just as Robert pulled into the airport parking complex, the odometer on his Phoenix painfully rolled to three hundred thousand miles. He parked quickly, liking the fact that he could squeeze into the tightest of spots with no concern over impending door dings.

The sun was just starting to rise. Robert grabbed his two large suitcases and entered the airport, struggling as he tried to outrun the uncooperative rollers on the overloaded bags. He hurried to the designated meeting place, a terminal-E Home Team Sports Bar that was known for its hot wings and the Dallas Cowboys sports paraphernalia that adorned the walls.

The rookie agent looked around for his contacts. He had never met Troy Mercer, but Agent Kevin Smith had helped train Robert and the other medical team cadets in emergency parachute flight evacuation. Smith seemed like a good guy, though he jabbed regularly that the med team training was more like a short-course country club version of the rigors regular field agents endured.

Robert sat down and ordered coffee and a bagel, while he reviewed verb conjugations from one of his college Spanish books. The surrounding twenty flat-screen televisions that replayed old Dallas Cowboy Super Bowl highlights only presented a mildly irritating distraction to the lifelong Denver Bronco fan.

A familiar voice interrupted Robert's concentration. "What's up, Doc?"

Robert looked up to see agent Kevin Smith standing over his table. Smith was in his early forties, with salt-and-pepper hair covering all but a baseball-sized empty patch on the crown of his head. He was tall and *had* been athletic, but 150 extra pounds were now hitching a ride on his muscular frame. All that spare weight had landed above Smith's waist. One could only feel empathy for his comparatively skinny legs and knobby knees, which reluctantly supported his massive upper body.

"Are you spending a month touring Europe, Cline?" razzed the decorated, twenty-year tenured agent, while looking down at Robert's large suitcases.

Before Robert had a chance to defend himself, Agent Troy Mercer appeared out of nowhere. Mercer dropped an envelope labeled "Operation C58" on the table next to Robert's bagel.

"How's it going, Kevin?" Mercer asked. The veteran colleagues shook hands. Then, turning to Robert, Mercer said, "And this must be the good Dr. Cline?" He extended his hand to Robert, who stood up and reached out to shake it.

Agent Troy Mercer, an ex-Navy Seal and former all-American tight end for the Syracuse Orange Men was in his mid-thirties. He had dark black hair sculpted by no shortage of barber-grade hair grease. He was an accomplished field agent, just starting his tenth year with the CIA. Although Robert was strong and in good physical condition, he felt a little small and weak compared to Mercer who boasted a chiseled granite physique.

With an unmistakable New York accent, Agent Mercer picked up where Agent Smith had left off. "So Cline, is this all *your* luggage? Who are you traveling with—Paris Hilton or something?" Mercer and Smith exchanged looks and enjoyed a few chuckles at Robert's expense.

Robert tried to be cool, but his expression failed to mask the irritation he felt from being the butt of the joke. "Yeah...well...you know... I've gotta make sure my shoes will match my belt and that I'm ready for any occasion," he countered.

"Take it easy, Cline. We're just messing with you," said Mercer. "Come on. I've got a secure room provided by the Fort Worth Naval Air Station. Once we get there, we can go over phase one of the mission.

Oh, and you'll need your credentials." Agent Mercer handed US Navy security badges to his two colleagues.

Inspecting Robert's badge, Mercer continued to prod. "Looks like you will go by your real name then, huh, Cline? George told me you wanted a mission name. Maybe if you grade out OK on this assignment, they can change your name to Paris." The senior agents laughed and patted each other on the back, while they grabbed their single carry-on bags and led the way to the meeting room.

Robert pulled out his wallet and dropped enough cash on the table to cover his breakfast and a tip. He picked up the "Operation C58" envelope that contained his travel documents and stuffed it into one of the pockets of his cargo shorts. He struggled to keep up while following behind with his enormous suitcases. The bags seemed even bigger than they really were, and they were making him a bit self-conscious now that they were the subject of such amusement for his colleagues.

Mercer and Smith reached a naval-security checkpoint and waited for Robert to catch up with his luggage. Then the three agents flashed their badges and walked into a private room, where they sat around a small, round table. Agent Smith began the briefing. "OK, boys, if you open up your 'Operation C58' envelopes, we'll go over phase one of our mission: travel and security of temporary residence."

Robert felt like a kid at Christmas as he ripped open his envelope and sorted through his paper work. Documents included customs forms, a passport, and a ground transportation voucher from the airport in Cancún, Mexico, to Puerto Juarez. There were also ferry tickets and a key to a beach house on the Isla de Mujeres, plus $500 of per diem cash and a credit card. "Nice," exclaimed Robert. I wonder if the agency would let me stay a couple extra days, he thought.

Robert came to the bottom document, a coach ticket for Frontier Airlines. "What the hell is this?" asked Robert. This was not the type of air transportation he expected, thinking that the group might fly on a private charter jet. "I can't believe we're flying coach on a commercial carrier."

Agent Mercer's expression showed grave concern. "Oh..., well, actually the agency had arranged for a Cessna Citation X private jet, but once they found out how much luggage you were bringing, they decided we needed to take a *big* plane." An eruption of laughter interrupted Mercer's concerned look. He and Smith were thoroughly enjoying Robert's first mission, which hadn't even gotten off the ground yet.

"Here's the deal, Robert," instructed Agent Smith through diminishing laughter. "Most of the time an agent wants to kind of blend in with everybody else. You aren't flying around in private jets and walking around in tuxedos."

Robert made a mental note to make sure not to let either of his partners see the tuxedo he'd neatly packed in one of his suitcases.

"OK, let's get down to business," said Smith as he put on a pair of reading glasses and sorted through his paper work. "You can see from your travel documents that we board in forty-five minutes and touch down in Cancún International Airport at approximately ten a.m. We will get on a chartered van and take a half-hour drive to Puerto Juarez. From there we'll board the ferry and take a short boat ride to the small island, Isla de Mujeres. Once on the island, Robert will secure ground transportation from a local rental company with the credit card you should have found in your packet." Smith looked above the rim of his readers at Robert and warned, "Don't spend two hundred dollars a day on a rental car, please."

Smith continued, "Troy, you will make contact with Juan Chavez, our agency asset and dive master on site. His dive shop, Isla Aquatics, is right across the street and around the corner from the Isla Mujeres port. You'll confirm tomorrow's day trip, which will include a morning snorkel of some sort and an afternoon shipwreck dive. Looks like Juan has already established this, but please confirm that we will be in the group with Pablo Alva, the subject of our mission. Any questions?"

"So I just get the car and pick you guys up in front of the ferry?" asked Robert.

"Yep. Then we drive to the windy side of the island and find our rental house. I guess it looks like a giant seashell."

"That's a little odd," said Mercer.

"Well, Troy, I think it's Case Officer Harpole's idea of a joke. George thinks that three guys staying together in a giant seashell would make us look like we were three male lovers on a vacation ménage à trois or something. You know, like we're going to have a threesome weekend fling of some sort. At least that's the rumor at the agency."

"Well, I guess we will just have to prove that theory to be false," Mercer said in his heavy Brooklyn accent as he winked at the two other agents.

"Now, Troy, remember that you are not supposed to impregnate the natives. Please plan on being on your best behavior. After we're settled in the shell house, we should have four or five hours to chill out. We can hit the beach, snorkel a bit, and even look for some bikini models. Just stay out of trouble." The agent in charge looked at his two partners and said, "OK, let's go. We've got a plane to catch."

"Wait. So what's our actual mission, Agent Smith?" asked Robert eagerly.

"We'll go over details this evening on a video conference call with Case Officer Harpole at eight thirty p.m. But real quick—no more 'agent this' or 'last name that.' I *can* tell you that we're supposed to be two college professors and their dentist friend, all on a dive trip together. So I'm no longer Agent Smith, just Kevin. Agent Mercer is Troy, and Cline is Robert or Doc." Kevin looked up and nodded, waiting for a response.

Robert and Troy nodded and responded sarcastically in unison, "Yes, Agent Smith."

Kevin, Troy, and Robert got up and headed toward their gate. They arrived just as the plane started boarding.

Robert had hoped to sit next to his fellow agents on the plane but regretted that his wishes came to fruition as Agent Smith, or Kevin, spilled well over into Robert's coach seat from the left, while Agent Mercer, or Troy, instantly fell asleep and blew heavy garlic breath into Robert's face from the right.

As uncomfortable as he was, Robert somehow fell asleep.

The flight passed as if it lasted for only a moment. The landing gear hitting the hot runway at Cancún International startled Robert awake. He was disappointed that he had slept through the approach into the airport, having wanted to look out at the Caribbean Sea during descent.

Troy, whose head was now resting on Robert's shoulder, had slept through the landing. The garlic breath now competed with an odor Dr. Cline diagnosed as early periodontal disease. Robert moved away into the Kevin-filled zone of his own seat, causing Troy's head to drop, instantly waking him.

Oh, freaking sick, Robert thought as he noticed a cantaloupe-sized hair grease stain on his shirt, where Troy had been peacefully slumbering. He hoped the six-inch streak below the large stain was simply a dripping from hair grease, but he feared the worst. Drool! the voice in his head screamed as a gross-out wiggle-shiver shot up his spine.

"All right, bedfellows, we've got ground transportation waiting," jabbed Kevin as he stood up and grabbed his only bag from the overhead compartment.

The three agents worked their way through the airplane cabin and into the airport. They passed Mexico's customs without a glitch and picked up Robert's suitcases. They walked through sliding glass doors, leaving behind the well-chilled interior of Cancún International Airport, abruptly transitioning into a damp, penetrating jungle heat. Ground transportation was on standby, ready to whisk the men away to Puerto Juarez, where they hoped to catch the 11:30 a.m. ferry.

Robert, though eager to be on his first mission, was impressed with the plentiful palm trees, but so far he wasn't as excited about the rest of the Yucatán scenery. He couldn't wait to see the ocean, but so far there was nothing but highway and vegetation. The van traveled at excessive speed along the sun-scorched asphalt road, passing an occasional Coke stand nestled in a dense jungle canopy.

Finally they passed by a body of water known as Cancún's Nichupte Lagoon, which Robert mistook for the Caribbean Sea. He had expected something a little more picturesque. Robert mumbled to himself, "Wow, it looks kind of murky." He'd been looking forward to scuba diving but figured he wouldn't be able to see anything unless it was right in front of his face under this muddy-looking swamp. He decided the location wouldn't be as nice as he'd expected, but he was still pumped about being on his first real mission.

For the remainder of the van ride, the three men made small talk with the driver, Hector. When speaking Spanish or any language, Robert always thought it was important to try to use the proper native accent. He was annoyed with Troy, who was the first person he'd ever heard butcher the language with an irrepressible Brooklyn gringo accent.

The closer they got to the Puerto Juarez ferry, the more run down the surroundings became. They could see Miami-style hotels far across the murky Nichupte, but their trajectory was in the opposite direction. Soon the hotels and lagoon were out of sight. It appeared that the van was heading farther away from anything resembling paradise and deeper into a ghetto. With each passing block, the roadway became more perforated with potholes. The somewhat-respectable-looking houses they had passed near the lagoon were growing scarce, replaced by shacks with particleboard roofs and glassless windows. Garbage was piled up all around the primitive, living structures. Still more garbage floated down gutters in what looked like either mud or raw sewage.

Hector finally pulled into the parking lot in front of a concrete block building with a Puerto Juarez sign. The three agents climbed out of the van and into the hot, humid tropics. The air was stagnant and clammy. This can't be right, thought Robert. Where's the ocean? All there is around here is jungle, garbage, and asphalt.

Troy and Kevin discussed what would be an appropriate tip, while the four-foot-eleven Mayan driver labored to remove Robert's suitcases from the rear compartment. Robert handed him ten dollars while asking which way to the sea. "*Donde esta el mar?*"

Hector pointed toward an archway in the building to their right and said, "*A traves de la puerta.*" Then he switched to broken English. "The boat is leaving only in five minutes."

"Let's go!" shouted Kevin over his shoulder while he rushed through the passageway toward the ferry. "Next boat doesn't pick up for two more hours!"

Robert hurried along after Kevin, while Troy stopped to purchase a giant hot dog and fried banana from a street vendor.

"Hold on. I'm freakin' starving over here!" shouted Troy, who was stuck trying to calculate the 12.8 peso for one-dollar exchange rate.

Weighed down by the overpowering heat and his heavy luggage, Robert dragged his bags through the archway at the front of the concrete-block building and passed through a short, dimly lit hallway. When he emerged on the other side of the building, he was instantly kissed by a cool Caribbean breeze and mesmerized by the fire-aqua-blue sea before him. In awe of the beauty of the crystal-clear ocean, he stopped in his tracks with his jaw dropped open.

"Hurry up, you idiots! We're going to miss the ferry!" Kevin shouted back, startling Robert out of his hypnotic trance. The tranquil moment was then thoroughly extinguished by the smell that rose up from Troy's street vendor hot dog as he ran past.

"Yeah, hurry up, rookie," shouted Troy through a full mouth of hot dog meat.

Robert refocused and pulled his wobbling luggage over wide joints in the long, rickety wooden dock leading to the ferry. The spaces between each wooden plank jarred the suitcases, at times flipping them off their wheels altogether and causing them to sluggishly drag on their side. As soon as Robert got one suitcase flipped over onto its wheels, the other flopped onto its belly. The dock attendant was just raising the plank when Robert picked up both fifty-pound bags and sprinted, just boarding before the ferry pulled away.

Robert tipped an attendant on board, who took his suitcases to the deck below. Bouncing up the steps to the open deck above, Robert joined his partners and marveled at the pristine water.

As the powerful boat headed out to sea, Kevin badgered Troy about the stupidity of ordering a hot dog from a street vendor in Mexico. "You're going to get worms, man. That hot dog looks greenish gray."

"I already got worms when I was in Afghanistan," Troy argued. "I have immunity."

Robert was sitting right next to Troy but barely heard a word. He was overwhelmed by the picturesque seascape. The water seemed to grow more clear and blue the farther the boat traveled from shore. A magnificent pelican with a five-foot wingspan glided overhead under an occasional fluffy, white cloud before diving sharply to snatch a bright yellow tropical fish for lunch. The clean, blue Caribbean Sea stretched to the horizon, only interrupted by the white-foam wake of the ferry and an occasional windsurfer riding a wave in the distance.

"Sail away, sail away, sail away," played faintly on the radio in Robert's mind, as the scene was so fairy-tale perfect that he nearly wondered if he was dreaming.

"Belch!"

Robert didn't know what ripped him out of his trance first. Was it the vulgar, bellowing sound of Troy's release of stomach gas? Or maybe it was the odor of stomach acid, street vendor hot dog meat, periodontal disease, and fried bananas. No, no, it was definitely the quarter-inch chunk of chewed-up hot dog meat that Troy's burp had propelled onto the back of Robert's hand.

"Oh my God!" Robert jumped up like he'd been abruptly stabbed in his back with a spear. He thrashed his hand violently, trying to shake off the meat chunk. "That's the nastiest damn thing that's ever happened to me! It's only rivaled by you drooling all over me on the freakin' airplane! Shit!"

Robert usually thought of himself as unflappable, but in this case he was clearly flapped. Troy and Kevin tried to hold back their laughter, but for seasoned agents, nothing was more entertaining than watching their less experienced colleagues struggle to fit in.

"Sorry, Cline," Troy offered through poorly veiled amusement. "I think that frankfurter upset my stomach a little."

"No kidding?" Robert shot back angrily. "A hot dog from a street vendor in Mexico upset your stomach?" The thought of it *was* actually a little funny.

Robert walked across the deck of the ferry and took a seat as far away from the other two agents as possible. He gazed back into the crystal-blue Caribbean and tried to get back into his "Orinoco Flow." He looked off into the horizon, trying not to think about the large stain on his shirt or the germs on his hand from the meaty belch. Robert was really wishing he had some hand sanitizer. He was starting to think that maybe he and Troy wouldn't end up being the best of friends. He tried to adjust his attitude so he could enjoy the remaining ten minutes of the boat ride.

After the ferry docked at Isla de Mujeres, the three men disembarked together. They strolled over to the street named Calle Medina next to the pier.

Kevin got the agents organized, "OK, Troy, you make contact with our dive master. Case Officer Harpole says we're going to need a small motor boat and a catamaran sail raft for tomorrow evening, so I'll see what I can find. Robert, you secure some ground transportation—and remember, keep it under a hundred bucks a day please. Let's meet right back here in thirty minutes."

The three agents split up. Kevin turned back toward the beach to look for boat rentals. Troy crossed the street and purchased a tamale and churro from a street vendor en route to confirm plans for tomorrow's dive.

Robert paid a female ferry worker behind the ticketing counter to watch his suitcases. The rookie agent quickly weaved through traffic, crossing Calle Medina to search for a rental vehicle. He hurried up and down the narrow tourist-filled streets, politely turning down demands from local shop owners to purchase a Mexican poncho here or a sombrero there. "*No, gracias,*" repeated Robert continually.

He encountered several rental centers, all providing either scooters or four-man golf carts. This sucks, he thought. Robert was really hoping to get ahold of a European sports car worthy of agents on an important mission. He certainly looked forward to driving around in something a little more exotic than his Pontiac Phoenix.

As he quickly weaved up and down the handful of streets of the very small pueblo, an especially persistent shop owner ran through the doors of his tiny store and badgered, "Whach you need, I got it. Bracelet, T-shirt, Cuban cigars?"

"*No, gracias.*" Robert smiled and continued walking past the pushy store owner.

"Mexican blanket, tequila, sunglasses? I got Rolex watch. Berry cheap price for you, amigo."

"*No, gracias.*" Robert had now put about ten yards of space between himself and the salesman. He figured he'd finally shaken the guy but braced himself to ditch another.

"How about sunscreen? Really works! No Healed Earth!" The shop-keeper shouted out, as it appeared his customer was slipping away.

Robert stopped walking. He paused for a moment, and then turned back to the store owner who had finally caught his attention.

"Come on. I show you." The four-foot-ten Mayan descendant took three steps for every one of Robert's. He eagerly guided the American down the sidewalk past several locals, who also stood just under five foot tall. Robert felt like a giant as he followed the shop owner and ducked his head to enter the small doorway of the tiny store.

Together he and the salesman passed the regular display items and slipped into a small, windowless back room. The dark room had walls lined with shelves of contraband, including a few small handguns, several strains of marijuana, and sure enough, sunscreen that was now the subject of a strict Healed Earth crackdown. In January the United States and the United Nations had signed international laws banning traditional sunscreens due to their oils and other chemicals that, after applied, could eventually wash away to contaminate groundwater. The US government treated the pollutants in traditional sunscreens with as much care as they would uranium. Swimming in lakes, rivers, or oceans while wearing sunscreen that didn't display the Healed Earth seal of approval warranted a stiff international fine of $1,500.

Although international law governed the pollutants in sunscreen, enforcement was strictest in the United States. Far less attention was paid to the ban in foreign countries.

"*Por favor, puedo tener dos bolletos de la Banana Boat SPF cincuenta?*" Robert practiced his Spanish as he asked for two bottles of the Banana

Boat Sport SPF 50. "But can you pour the stuff into a Healed Earth-approved bottle?"

Many people sought after the now-illegal sunscreen produced prior to Healed Earth restrictions. Newly approved sunscreens claimed SPF protection of over 200, but they just didn't seem to work. People would burn easily with even the strongest available protection. In addition, skin cancer rates had nearly tripled in the years after the Healed Earth ban. The sunscreen and skin cancer controversy had prompted a US government study that concluded Healed Earth-approved sunscreen was "more effective" than the banned sun protectants of old. The study explained that the increased incidents of sunburn and skin cancer were attributed to "higher-intensity solar rays penetrating to the earth's surface due to pollution damage in the atmosphere." Even though independent studies that followed demonstrated the ineffectiveness of Healed Earth-approved sunscreen, the US government, environmentalist groups, and the national media ridiculed those results.

Oddly enough, the country's leading catsup mogul and wife of a Massachusetts senator had won the exclusive contract to produce government-subsidized, Healed Earth-approved sunscreen. Robert thought it was no coincidence that Healed Earth-approved sunscreen smelled quite a bit like mayonnaise. In fact, commercials promoting the approved sunscreen boasted that the product was so safe, it could be eaten.

Robert took one of the bootleg bottles and held it up to his nose, sniffing to make sure there was no mayonnaise smell. "Nope. Toxic coconut-pineapple perfume just like the good old days."

As the eager store owner transferred the black market lotion into empty Healed Earth sunscreen bottles for an additional twenty pesos, he worked hard to try to make another sale. "You need Thirty-Eight Special or smoke a little Mexican red, amigo?" he asked, pointing to a shelf with jars of marijuana and a few handguns.

"*No, gracias.* I think I've purchased enough illegal stuff for today." Robert paid for his under-the-counter merchandise and ducked out of the store. Back to the hunt for some respectable spy wheels, he thought.

Robert walked up and down each of the seven narrow streets that made up the tiny village, searching with no success. Every block had a scooter and golf cart rental shop owned by the same company. He finally decided to go inside one of them and ask a shop attendant if there was any place on the island that rented real cars.

"*Hola, amigo.* You need scooter?" asked the four-foot-eleven-inch man behind the counter, whose left-central incisor was dark gray and distinctively longer than its neighbor.

"Well, actually I was hoping to rent a car. Are there any car-rental agencies on the island?"

"No, I'm sorry, amigo, but Isla de Mujeres is a very small island. It is better for golf cart or scooter."

"So there's nowhere on the island where a person could rent a real car?" probed Robert.

"Well, yes, probably someone could rent a car, but it would be very expensive," replied the man apologetically in a heavy Spanish accent.

"OK, now we're getting somewhere. I don't care if it's expensive. I want to rent a car, something exotic." Robert had regrettably given up speaking Spanish as it seemed to him that everyone in Mexico preferred to speak English anyway.

"Hold on, amigo. I need to contact my cousin Raul." While Robert waited for the attendant to make a phone call, he chuckled, thinking, On an island this small, you probably couldn't find any two people who *weren't* cousins.

"OK, amigo, Raul is coming. He owns all of the rental shops. Only give me five minutes."

Robert looked at his watch impatiently. He was supposed to meet the other two agents back in front of the dock in ten minutes. Besides, the beach just next to the ferry station looked pretty nice: white sand, clear-blue water, and no shortage of girls in bikinis. He wanted to have a little time to check it out. As he looked out at the beach across the street, the roaring engine of a 2010 Mustang startled him. It skidded to a stop in front of the rental shop.

The windows of the muscle car were blackened entirely with tint. A red, white, and green decal of Mexico's flag completely obstructed the rear window. Base-blasting subwoofers in the trunk boomed mariachi music, while the custom-chrome side pipes thundered and smoked a bit. The Mistichrome paint changed continually from deep purple to emerald green depending on the angle of the observer. Beneath the car, bright-purple neon under glow pulsated to the rhythm of the bass and shined brighter than the competing light of the island sun.

A four-foot-eleven-inch native islander, wearing snake skin cowboy boots with the snake head still attached, stepped out of the muscle car. He wore spotless white jeans held up by a snakeskin belt that matched his boots. He looked a lot like his employee behind the counter but with a more presentable set of teeth.

"Raul!" the shop attendant shouted as he ran out to the curb to greet his cousin. "My friend here wants to rent a special car for his time on the island."

Raul reached out to Robert, and the two shook hands. "*Hola, amigo.* What do you think about this one? It is my own personal vehicle. I will rent it to you for just three hundred dollars a day."

"Uh…, well, it is very nice, but do you have any European sports cars?"

"Don't worry, my friend," assured Raul. "This one has European leather seats."

"What other types of cars do you have?"

Raul looked insulted by Robert's lack of enthusiasm. He answered with disgust in his heavy Spanish accent. "You can rent this, or the scooter, or the golf cart."

Robert didn't reply right away, prompting Raul to begin bargaining.

"OK, I tell you what. For you only two hundred fifty and no pay gas. *Escucha!* Big speakers, amigo!" Raul reached into the car and turned up the mariachi music to a deafening clangor.

Robert was really hoping for something like a Jaguar or Bugatti. But the Mustang, while a bit gaudy, was still several steps up from his Phoenix and even a few more notches better than a four-man golf cart. He figured he'd have to throw in some of his own cash, but he had plenty. Besides buying a sack of cat food here and there, he saved almost every dime he earned from the Dallas dental clinic.

"OK, I'll just do two days for now," said Robert enthusiastically. Papers were signed, money was exchanged, and keys were secured. Robert tried to enter through the driver's-side door but nearly got stuck between the steering wheel and seat, which had been adjusted for the much shorter Raul.

"Let me help you, amigo." Raul moved Robert out of the way and adjusted the automatic seats. "Look. You move it with *buttons*. Very nice, eh?"

"*Gracias*, Raul." Robert stepped into the rumbling rod and adjusted the mirrors. He hit the seek button on the stereo to find something a little more Spanish contemporary. But the seek rolled full cycle and landed back on the island's only channel. Well then, he thought, mariachi it is.

As Robert pulled away, he noticed, for the first time, signs posted every thirty feet, warning in Spanish and English that the maximum speed on the island was twenty-five kilometers per hour. That's only fifteen miles per hour, thought Robert after calculating the metric conversion in his head. "What the hell!" He hit the steering wheel with an open hand.

Robert drove three blocks away from the ferry along the beachside road, then pulled through a small roundabout, turning back toward the pier. He observed the speed limit but enjoyed testing the acceleration of the vehicle in short thrusts from five to fifteen miles per hour, and then back to five. He could see his partners on the sidewalk just a block ahead. He pulled up to the curb in front of the two agents. It was great to have a driver's-side door that opened, and Robert jumped out of it, revealing himself from the veil of the black-tinted windows.

Kevin and Troy stood with dropped jaws. "What the f…!" blasted Kevin. "What are you doing, Cline?"

"What?" asked Robert. "Am I late?"

"No, but where the hell did you find this monster?" snapped Kevin angrily.

"Chill out. I spent my own money—"

"Get back in the car, Cline. Now!" ordered Kevin as he swung open the passenger side door and dropped down into the seat. Robert got back in and took the wheel.

Kevin lowered his window and motioned to Troy. "Hold tight." Then turning to Robert, he demanded, "Drive!"

Robert drove slowly for a few blocks toward the edge of the village, while his senior agent vented some steam. "Robert, I know that it takes time to learn what the agency expects of you, but never in all my years at the CIA have I ever seen anyone pull such a boneheaded stunt. We're supposed to blend in to our surroundings, not wave flags to draw attention to ourselves. This car looks like it's been shipped in by the Tijuana Mafia."

Trying to defend himself, Robert argued, "They didn't have anything else. I was looking for a European sports—"

"Don't say another word. How many European sports cars do you see on this speck of an island? We are drawing the attention of every local and tourist as we speak. As I understand it, the agency has big plans for you if you can pass this test, but you're going to have to grow up in a hurry, Cline. This is not a James freakin' Bond movie. Our mission here is important. But for whatever reason, the director says your special training as an agent and a dentist will soon put you in the middle of the most consequential operation in decades. So quit defending yourself. Talk less, learn more, and trade in the Batmobile for a damn golf cart!"

"Yes, sir. You're right." Robert took a U-turn just south of the village and headed back to the pier. He dropped off Kevin, and then continued a few blocks more, stopping in front of Raul's shop.

"What's the matter, my friend?" asked Raul, running out of his rental center as Robert got out of the vehicle in defeat and approached with the car keys.

"I guess it's just more than I need right now. What do you say we trade straight across for one of the four-seater golf carts?"

Raul eagerly took the keys and had his long-toothed cousin pull the finest golf cart out of the garage. After all, he'd just made an extra

$400 for nothing. "New tires, amigo," said Raul while proudly handing over the key to the deluxe cart of his fleet.

Robert pulled away in the golf cart, while Raul and his cousin stood in front of the shop and waved. He again circled the roundabout and puttered up in front of the pier for a second attempt at picking up his partners. He got out and approached the lady who was watching his suitcases. He tipped her for taking good care of them. Then the three men got in the cart, and followed a map that guided them from the calm side around to the windy side of the four-mile-long, half-mile-wide island.

They reached the windy-side beach house, which was shaped like a giant seashell. Robert cautiously pulled into the cobblestone driveway.

How is it blending in if we stay in a house shaped like a shell? Robert thought but dared not say.

Troy and Kevin went inside, leaving Robert behind to clumsily drag his suitcases over the large cobbles and washed-out joints in the driveway.

Robert finally managed to muscle his luggage through the front door of the shell house. It was overwhelmingly apparent that the interior decorator had been shooting for a flamboyant Caribbean island/Mayan fusion decor. The walls were adorned with pastel art. A full-sized, pink rowing oar with a topless mermaid painted on the blade hung mounted over the doorway. A large mural on one of the walls depicted three Mayan women canoeing into the white-capped waves of the Caribbean. The living room couch was a white stone carving of the reclining Chac-Mool Mayan god holding aqua-blue cushions. The bright sun shined through large windows, splashing the walls with ample light by day. At night the room would be just as bright with light glowing from multiple conch-shaped wall sconces and bursting from a chandelier made of at least twenty blown-glass puffer fish hanging from the tall living room ceiling.

"Let's get on some swim trunks, head back to town, and grab a bite to eat," said Kevin. "Then we should still have a few hours to hit the beach." The agents headed upstairs, where each found a bedroom.

They hurried to change so they could take advantage of some free time before their operation started.

Robert heaved his suitcases up onto the bed, which was shaped like a giant clam draped with a pink, pastel duvet. He opened his bags and carefully pulled his surfboarder shorts and flip-flops from beneath his tuxedo. After changing, he covered himself from head to toe with his newly purchased sunscreen. Then Robert shot downstairs into the main level and waited impatiently for the other agents. It was almost one in the afternoon, and the half bagel from breakfast wasn't holding him over anymore.

Kevin appeared from his room next. He wore faded-green swim trunks that hung to mid-thigh and looked as though they'd been with him for all his years of service to the agency. The elastic waistband around his trunks strained to keep from snapping. It had been meant to secure the swimsuit of the much smaller man that Kevin had been when he purchased it twenty years ago. Kevin rested his left arm on his massive belly, while his right hand glided down the handrail of the staircase.

"I'm getting too old for this, Cline. It'll only be another five years, and then they'll stick me behind a desk back at the agency in Langley." He walked past Robert and looked through the window at the waves crashing into the rocky shore just below. "You know, Robert, Troy is a pretty-good guy and a damn-good agent. I can tell the two of you aren't hitting it off, but you need to give him a chance."

"I know," Robert replied. "I didn't get much sleep last night because I was excited to get going on my first assignment. I think stuff's just getting on my nerves more that it normally would. I'm pretty sure we're going to be fine."

Just then the muscle-chiseled Troy blasted through the door of his room and stood at the top of the stairs. "Ladies await," he announced in his heavy Brooklyn accent. He had combed a new glob of barber's grease through his hair and traded in civilian clothes for a silky, black Speedo. He strutted down the stairs, obviously proud of his grotesquely oversized bulge. As he walked, the small, silk piece of material struggled to hold back the mass of manliness.

Nasty, thought Robert. He was beginning to notice that he thought better of Troy when he wasn't in the room.

Kevin shook his head in disbelief and pointed out, "Being dressed like that will surely prompt the locals to think exactly what Harpole intended, that we're a threesome on a holiday of hot monkey love."

"Well, at least everyone will know who the bull monkey is," Troy boasted.

Robert felt a bit of a gag welling up in his throat but managed to hold it back. "All right, off to the Bentley now," Robert said in an English accent as he held up the keys to the golf cart.

The three agents headed for their not-so-exotic transportation at about 1:15 p.m. They blazed back to town, nearly reaching speeds of seventeen miles per hour on the road that ran next to the ocean on the windy side of the island. The sun was hot, but the sea breeze kept them comfortable. They circled around to Calle Medina on the calm side of the island, where the water was still. They parked on the street back near the ferry dock.

Earlier Robert had noticed a bar and grill called Jax next to the village's only roundabout and across the street from a pristine beach. The place looked clean, and the sign in front indicated that it was operated by an American. Since Robert was a very picky eater on his first trip out of the country, he was most comfortable trying an American-owned restaurant.

Troy was putting in a plug for a sketchy-looking food joint named The Soggy Nacho, which operated from a tent on the beach across the street from Jax. Ultimately, though, Troy was won over by the sign at Jax, which read, "If it's not on the menu, we will make it anyway."

"I'm dying for some good Alfredo," said Troy. The waiter assured him that shrimp fettuccini Alfredo was one of Jax's off-the-menu specialties.

Robert, starved from not eating for seven hours, gorged himself with a giant fajita platter. Kevin had the famous Jax Burger, and Troy enjoyed a special order of shrimp fettuccini Alfredo with extra garlic.

And I thought the garlic smell was just starting to wear off a little, thought Robert.

Kevin and Troy each downed a few mugs of whatever Mexican beer was on tap, while Robert, the designated golf cart driver, had an Orange Fanta.

After the agents paid their bill and got ready to head to the beach for a couple hours of sea and sun, their waiter stopped them at the door. "Hey, you guys might want to spray yourself with some of this insect repellant. When the sun falls in a few hours, the mosquitos will go on a fifteen-minute feeding frenzy."

"Won't it wear off by then?" asked Kevin.

"No, don't worry. This is the good stuff. None of that Healed Earth crap you get back in the States. It lasts for hours and won't wash off."

The three men sprayed away, while Robert made a mental note that before returning home, he would buy some illegal bug spray to go with his illegal sunscreen.

The agents thanked the waiter and crossed Calle Medina, evading a few scooters and golf carts to get to the beach on the other side. Troy, in his black, silky Speedo, led the way. He strutted to an open-air, beachside bar, ordered a drink, and plopped himself down on a beach chair in the sand next to a group of college girls, who were playing sand volleyball in their bikinis. Kevin and Robert followed, parking themselves on chairs nearby.

"There," Troy said. "If I get tired of watching these ladies playing volleyball, I can look at the ocean."

It was 2:30 p.m., and the sun was hot. The seawater was calm, and the air was still and humid.

"So, if you guys are going to hang out here for a while, I might walk around the coast to the northeast beach and do a little bodysurfing. The map says it's only about three-quarters of a mile back to some bigger waves on the windy side," said Robert.

"We'll be right here, soaking up some rays," said Kevin, who made no attempt to look at Robert to his right. Instead he stared directly at the girls playing volleyball to his left.

"I don't think any of those gals are even old enough to be your daughters, Kevin," said Robert.

"Well, I don't have to *worry* about that because I don't have any daughters, Cline. Those ladies are fair game."

"Good luck," Robert said, chuckling. "Oh, and I'm going to leave this sunscreen that I bought. It's the old kind they banned because of the whole Healed Earth-pollution thing. You guys should use some, or you'll get fried."

Troy took the bottle. "Thanks, Cline. I take back all the nasty things I've been saying about you when you're not around." He applied the lotion to all parts not covered by his offensive, black mankini.

"Come on, Robert. You don't buy into that sunscreen conspiracy theory bullshit, do you?" asked Kevin. "That's just a bunch of anti-government rhetoric. I've got my own Healed Earth stuff right here, and it works just fine. You guys go ahead and pollute the water. Maybe you can kill a few turtles with that stuff."

Kevin began to lather himself with his own sunscreen and asked, "Hey, Mercer, can you put some on my back?"

The growing smell of banned, artificial pineapple/coconut lotion, Healed Earth mayonnaise lotion, and of course garlic from Troy's shrimp Alfredo filled the air like a peculiar tropical island macaroni salad. The sight of the rubdown and the ill-assorted medley of smells caused Robert's stomach to turn a bit.

"I'll be back in a few hours." Robert waved over his shoulder as he headed toward the north point of the beach.

Troy posed in his beach chair with one knee up and legs spread toward the volleyball coeds, while he and Kevin drank several beers and exchanged stories from past missions.

Before the volleyball game dispersed, agents Mercer and Smith drifted off to sleep. The unforgiving afternoon rays pushed down on them, as the sun inched slowly across the sky before finally dipping behind some clouds far off on the horizon.

As the sun set, Robert reappeared from his three-hour journey. He walked up next to his two colleagues, who seemed to be entrenched in a snoring contest.

"Oh my," Robert said to himself as he approached the other two agents. Kevin had a nasty sunburn. This looked like it would be painful. It could have been a lot worse, but luckily, during the second hour of his two-hour nap, the sun had ducked behind the shielding of a nearby thatched umbrella. The Healed Earth stuff works just fine, huh? thought Robert.

It appeared that Troy had fared much better after using the black market sunscreen. He hadn't been shaded at all from the thatched umbrella, but initially he seemed to have evaded even the slightest sunburn.

Robert stepped between the two agents and decided to wake them. He leaned over to nudge Troy but stepped back after noticing something horrible. "What the hell is that?" Robert whispered to himself. Somehow some shifting had taken place while Troy was sleeping. A breach in containment had occurred, and something had managed to escape from the not-so-secure packaging of the black, silk Speedo. Robert turned away in disgust as he realized that the blood-red, sunscorched object hanging out of the little, black bikini bottom was Troy's left testicle.

Still looking in the opposite direction, Robert pushed on Kevin's shoulder to wake him and pointed toward Troy. Kevin sat up on his chair and looked over at Troy. "Oh, that's not good at all," he said. Kevin wanted to look away but couldn't help but to stare in disbelief. "Put something over it."

"I'm not getting near that thing," replied Robert.

Troy continued to snore when suddenly, just as the waiter at Jax had warned, legions of mosquitos swarmed the beach, sending people not wearing insect repellent scrambling for cover. Luckily, the three agents had thoroughly covered themselves with the extra potent bug spray, which seemed to be protecting them. But just as Troy's unexpected escapee hadn't been covered with sunscreen, it also didn't benefit from as much as a squirt of insect repellant.

Within seconds, around a half-dozen mosquitos landed, attracted to the blood-red, inflamed skin that had slid past the security of the black mankini borders. Troy woke up with a sudden jerk and hollered, "Shit! What's going on?" Still half dazed from sleep, he looked down and frantically swatted at the mosquitos. "Oooh!" he screamed and jumped up out of his beach chair.

Troy immediately ran toward the ocean with a peculiar limping stride. "It freaking stings! It freaking stings!" he yelled over and over. Running into the water, he abruptly turned and ran back out as quickly as he had entered. "Shit! Shit!" The salt water seemed to cause the burning to intensify.

Robert and Kevin wanted to laugh, but they knew the pain was severe. These parts were no laughing matter among men.

Kevin looked down, assessing his less severe but still somewhat-painful sunburn that covered most of his body. The sun had spared only a few areas that had been sealed tightly and protected by an assortment of fat rolls, leaving a few oddly placed stripes of virgin white skin. He looked up at Robert and said, "Maybe there's something to that sunscreen after all, Cline."

Robert and Kevin walked out to the shore to help their colleague, who by this time had wrapped a towel around his waist and left the mankini to be taken out to sea by the slow persistent waves. "I can't let anything touch it," Troy said, nearly crying. He put one arm over the shoulder of each of the other agents, and they helped him limp back to the golf cart.

"Well, at least you won't be impregnating the natives this time," Kevin said, chuckling as they got into the golf cart. They putted away from the setting sun, back toward the shell house on the other side of the island. They made a brief stop at a small grocery store to purchase supplies to cook for dinner. Troy used a little of his per diem cash to buy an iced grouper. He slipped the fish under his towel and held it next to his burn.

The three agents made their way back around to the shell house and pulled into the cobblestone driveway. While they had been at the beach, the two small boats Kevin arranged for had been delivered and were thrashing in the waves next to the rocky shore below. One was a fourteen-foot fiberglass panga fishing boat and the other, a tiny catamaran sailboat. Both were poorly tethered to a large, wooden beam that was wedged into a crevice in the rocks.

While Troy held onto his thawing grouper and carefully limped inside, Kevin and Robert attempted to better secure the boats to shore amid the wind and crashing surf. Kevin found an assortment of ropes in the panga boat. He and Robert struggled in the waves but managed to tie the boat, named the *Hay Caramba*, rigidly to the shore, protecting the large outboard motor from crashing against the rocks.

Once the *Hay Caramba* was secure, Robert grabbed a single rope and balanced in the waves next to the smaller sailboat. He wound the rope around the single wooden mast until he noticed that the one-person hobby craft was extremely light. So he pulled the catamaran completely out of the water and rested it on the cragged sea bank.

A bit concerned, Robert asked, "We're not going diving tomorrow from these rickety things, are we?"

"No. This Alva guy is a big shot drug lord," replied Kevin. "He has a very extravagant lifestyle, does everything first-class. Our boats and equipment are going to be top notch."

"So what's up with *these* rattletrap boats then?"

"Not sure, Cline. George will tell us in our video conference in about an hour. We better go in and grab a bite to eat before our briefing."

Robert and Kevin headed back up to the shell house just as the last glow of twilight disappeared. They walked in and joined Troy for a quick dinner. Then a little before 8:00 p.m., the three men descended in a row down the stairway into the beach house basement.

Kevin was the first one down the stairs. Catching a glimpse of what the agency prep team had assembled, he turned back to Robert. "Well, what do we have here, Doc? Looks like somebody knew you were coming."

In the center of the dimly lit one-room basement was a portable, military field dental chair complete with a delivery unit that holstered an air-water syringe, high- and slow-speed drills, and suction tubing. A portable, pole-mounted operator's light had been left on, shining on an assortment of dental instruments wrapped in sterile packs atop a small medical cabinet that rested behind the patient chair.

Troy, who seemed to be feeling better, plopped himself down in the patient chair and demanded, "Hey, Cline, come take a look in my mouth. I think they messed me up in the navy. One of the dentists was using a bunch of these metal tools, and they broke big chunks of enamel off my teeth. I haven't gone back to a dentist since." He opened his mouth, waiting.

Robert didn't move but stood with arms crossed and replied, "They were breaking chunks of tarter off your teeth, Troy. You have periodontal disease, and not going to the dentist again for several years has certainly made it worse."

"What do you mean, paradoxil disease?" Troy looked very concerned. He remembered acquiring an STD on a mission in North Korea once but he'd been cured with a few rounds of antibiotics. "You think I've got a disease?"

Kevin interrupted, "Get away from that stuff, Troy. We're not supposed to mess with it until we get our orders from George."

Right on cue, a blinking red light and series of high-pitched beeps signaled that Case Officer George Harpole was trying to make contact. The three agents quickly gathered around a satellite video phone resting on a small table in the corner of the basement. Harpole's face appeared on the ten-by-twelve screen.

Harpole was in his mid-seventies. Over the years his thick, black hair had gradually been replaced mostly by baldness and a little, well-kept gray around his ears. His ever-present, short, gray moustache didn't hide his mischievous smile. George's teeth were mostly straight, with just enough irregularity to give him rugged character.

At a time when the agency encouraged most of its employees to retire at sixty-five, the brass kept begging George to stay. Before joining the CIA, he'd worked his way through college by fighting forest fires as a smoke jumper. After joining the agency, Harpole worked on the front lines of world-changing missions. Most noteworthy were the years he spent providing key intelligence that led to the decline of the Soviet Union. It was often said that Harpole's covert activity was an instrumental catalyst to the tearing down of the Berlin wall. George had eventually moved away from fieldwork to become one of the best-connected operations directors in the agency. Intelligence insiders knew that if you had the ear of George Harpole, you also had the ear of the president of the United States. That was, of course, until the past two administrations tried to temper the influence and activity of the CIA.

"Hello," said Harpole, trying to hold back a smile. "From here it looks like the three of you are enjoying your three-day escapade in the little shell beach house."

"Yeah, George, I'm sure all the locals are talking," conceded Kevin.

George was thoroughly pleased with himself and laughed for a few moments, but then he changed his tone. "All right, let's get on with the briefing. You already know that you'll be meeting our embedded agent Juan Chavez with Isla Aquatics tomorrow at 7:30 a.m. You have a reservation to go out with drug cartel leader Pablo Alva on a morning dive in an area known for its high concentration of whale sharks, followed by an afternoon scuba at the *General Anaya* or C58 shipwreck site."

"What do you mean, dive with sharks?" asked Kevin in a troubled voice. He'd completed all the scuba certifications required for agents and hated every mission that required diving. Kevin loved boating on the ocean and was an expert navigator. He would gladly deep-sea fish for hours, but he preferred to catch fish, not swim with them.

"Juan will fill you in on the dives tomorrow, Smith," replied George, ignoring and enjoying Kevin's exhibition of anxiety. "We know from five years of tracking that Alva leaves his estate in Colombia and books a dive trip with the same dive shop every year at this time. It's the only time that he travels alone. No wife, no friends, no security guards."

"Come on. No security? You've got to be kidding," challenged Troy.

"No security," George assured. "Juan Chavez has been our asset on the ground, working in this dive shop for three years now. Based on the intelligence we've gathered, we believe Pablo Alva leaves everyone behind so they don't report back to his wife, who's insanely jealous and quite possibly as ruthless as Pablo. The cartel leader dives every day and drinks and womanizes every night for a week. He must figure that if nobody comes with him, then nobody slips up and tells mamma." George laughed.

"The scuba trip has been set up so it will only be the three of you going out with the dive master; and Alva." George continued, "You'll be at sea for the better part of the day, so you should have plenty of time to get friendly with the guy. While you're on the boat, invite Alva to the beach house for some tequila. Maybe tell him there will be some interesting senoritas there."

"What if he doesn't want to come?" asked Kevin. "Can the dive master help us out?"

"No way. We can't blow Juan's cover. We have him in and out of dive shops all over Mexico and the Caribbean, helping agents gather intel on a variety of subjects. To Alva, Juan is dive master and a familiar face but nothing more. Besides, all our info says that booze and women will be all the bait you need."

"OK, so what do we do when we get him back to the shell?" asked Kevin.

"Let me give you a little background first. Pablo Alva is currently the kingpin drug lord of Colombia. He is in charge of, or is involved with, everyone who traffics cocaine, opium, and marijuana from Colombia and Mexico. He used to deal more heavily in marijuana until it was legalized two years ago in all fifty states. Funny that most backers of marijuana legalization insisted that decriminalization of hemp use would put drug lords out of business." George chuckled. "Did they really think these guys would drop their pot pushing and get legitimate jobs as CPAs or investment bankers? It was really only after marijuana became legal that Alva added opium to his list of drugs smuggled into the US."

"But you mentioned that Alva still does traffic some marijuana into the United States. What's the point of that now that it's legal?" asked Robert.

"Turns out you can get the Mexican pot cheaper because it's under the table. No taxes. Currently our government pulls in an estimated five billion dollars per year in taxes on legal pot sales. That has nearly eclipsed tax revenues for liquor sales. So when you think about it, Alva's illegal drugs are taking away from government tax on legal drugs. Bottom line is that the heavy taxation means the US government is now in the recreational marijuana business, and Alva is our main competition for drug money."

George continued, "You really only have two objectives, guys. The first: extract as many names and locations of high-status players in the trafficking ring as possible. The war on drugs is in full throttle to ensure that Uncle Sam keeps the annual five billion dollars of tax revenue flowing. I have deniable orders from the president that enhanced interrogation is on the table. And that's where you come in, Dr. Cline."

"What do I do, George?" Robert asked.

"Well, you can see that our prep crew has set you up with a fully functioning mobile dental office. You'll just sit back and let your two partner gorillas there rough Alva up a bit. They will get him all comfy in the dental chair behind you, possibly tying him down in case he's a dental phobic. Then just do what dentists do best, Robert. Scare the hell out of him and hurt him." Amusing himself, George had to pause for a chuckle before continuing. "You'll notice that we gave you an array of instruments, including anesthetic syringes. Be advised, however, that most of the cartridges don't actually contain anesthetic."

"What do you mean?" asked Robert.

"They contain a caustic solution known as the 'devil's fire.' It's a nontoxic venom that burns like hell when injected. Everyone who goes to the dentist hates the shot, but yours will hurt a lot more than usual. Then, of course, since your syringes contain no anesthetic, the guy won't be numb when you really go to work."

"Uh...I'm kind of surprised that they didn't tell me about any of this stuff in training, George," said Robert skeptically.

George let out a slow, friendly chuckle. "I'm telling you, Robert, this kind of thing has been frowned upon as of late, but the United States is stepping it up to subdue its competition in the recreational drug market. Of course the real objective is much more serious." His tone became very grave. "There's a much greater national security threat that you're going to be facing head-on in a matter of weeks. The executive office is unshackling the agency temporarily so we can help get world power back in our court. Operation C58 will really serve as a test for you, Robert. It's a high-stress mission, and we need to see how you hold up."

"So I just give the guy a shot or two and drill on a few teeth until he talks?" asked Robert.

"Yeah, and maybe do one or two extractions as well. Just have fun with it. Be creative." George laughed, prompting Kevin and Troy to join in with slightly more nervous laughter.

"Now, go over to the second drawer of your mobile dental cabinet, Robert," ordered George. "When you open it up, you'll find two small vials that contain tiny electronic devices."

Robert walked over and found the vials. He walked back to the video satellite phone and asked, "So what are these?"

"In your hand you have a pair of GPS tracking and guidance devices, one of which you will implant into one of Alva's molars. You will have to drill out the equivalent of a moderately deep cavity preparation, set the device in his tooth, and then cover it with a permanent composite filling."

"So when we're all done with that, do we just let him go?" asked Robert. Troy and Kevin exchanged a quick glance, knowing the answer might not sit well with the rookie.

"Oh my, no," replied George. "You will wait until at least midnight so the island Coast Guard will be off patrol and then inject the patient with a sedative. Next, the three of you will load Alva into the panga boat and tie the catamaran sailboat to be towed behind. Then you'll head out to sea about five miles or so, tie Alva to the catamaran, and turn back toward the shell house."

"What then? Do we just leave him there?" asked Robert.

"Well, sort of. You need to stop about a hundred yards away from the sail raft and wait. Then Kevin will call by portable satellite phone, signaling a stealth bomber five hundred miles away, off the coast of Florida. The bomber will launch a prototype, long-range, supersonic missile that will be guided by the device you implanted in Alva's tooth."

"We're launching a missile into the guy's face?" asked Robert in disbelief.

George laughed in a slow, unapologetic tone. "Well, I guess so." He continued laughing.

After the laughter subsided, he said, "There will be nothing left of the catamaran or Alva. But you three need to stick around to verify that. Now, there has been some testing of this device but never on a live person, so confirmation of the strike is of utmost importance."

"So what do we do with the second device?" asked Robert.

"That's only a backup... in case you drop the first one down Alva's throat. We've already tried to test an ingested device, and it just doesn't seem to work."

"What kind of dentist do you think I am? I'm not going to drop anything down his throat."

"Actually, it would be kind of a nice touch if you would drop a few things down his throat..., you know, to get him nervous about his airway. It seems to really help with interrogation." Harpole chuckled again. "But, if we accidently lose one device, we will definitely need a backup. And it's not that we don't trust your clinical skills. We know you were one of the top graduating dentists in the country, but your patient will likely be a little wigglier than most, so one slipup would be understood."

George continued. "Once the mission is complete, get back to the shell house, get a few hours of sleep, and be ready to catch the six a.m. ferry so you can make your flight out of Cancún at O' ten hundred. Once you leave, our ground prep crew will clean up any mess you make and get rid of the portable dental unit. It will be like you were never there. Any questions?"

"What if someone hears Alva screaming?" asked Robert.

"Oh, no worries. The prep team has made sure to come in and sound-proof the basement. Just make sure to keep the door closed when the doctor is at work."

Robert was blown away. Nothing in his training had prepared him for this—and on his first mission. Troy and Kevin were also taken aback, as the agency simply hadn't engaged in this type of operation for years. All three stood silent.

"OK then, men. You need to get some rest so you're on your game in the morning. We'll make contact again just before you take Alva out to sea, but otherwise I'll see you back in Washington for debriefing in a couple days. Any questions?"

After no response, George changed the subject. "Oh, and before I disconnect, could one of you guys pick me up some of the old, banned sunscreen down there? The VA hospital just burned another damn basal cell carcinoma off the top of my head." He twisted his neck and pointed to a bandage covering a recent surgical wound. He turned back. "If I have to keep using that Healed Earth crap, I'm going to need to get a toupee to block the sun," he said, laughing.

The screen went black.

14

THE *GENERAL ANAYA*

7:20 a.m., the next day

Robert, Kevin, and Troy pulled into town and parked their golf cart in front of Isla Aquatics. Kevin wore his same old, worn out swim trunks from the day before, and the year before, and the past two decades. Troy went conservative, choosing more traditional surfer shorts in favor of a second Speedo. Dive master Juan Chavez stood in front of the dive shop, awaiting their arrival.

"*Hola, amigos,*" Juan said, welcoming them.

Juan was tall for a Mayan descendant, five foot three inches, with darkened skin from the relentless Caribbean sun. He was completely bald but good looking. Even though he was short and round, he was rock strong. Juan had lived on nearby Cozumel Island for two decades, working as a scuba instructor before the agency recruited him. Now he instructed agents for specialty dive certifications and coordinated liaisons like the one that was about to take place with Pablo Alva.

Robert brought all his own scuba gear that he'd purchased immediately after his open-water certification at the hot springs crater near Heber City, Utah. He hauled his equipment into the small dive shop, while Juan sized Troy and Kevin for rental wet suits and buoyancy control vests, or BCDs.

No wonder these guys travel so light. They're using shop gear, thought Robert.

"Any word from Pablo Alva yet, Juan?" asked Kevin.

"He called last night from his hotel on the island and said he would be here. Hopefully he didn't get arrested."

Apparently Pablo would spend as many as a third of his nights on the island in *la cárcel*, or Mexican jail. The island police were generally forgiving to tourists, but Pablo regularly and intentionally broke the law with drunk and disorderly conduct. He frequently slept off a tequila intoxication in a jail cell and paid a heavy fine just to do it all again the next evening.

"I hope this thing is a go," said Kevin.

"Don't worry, my friend," Juan reassured him. "Pablo is always late, but he will be here."

Once Kevin and Troy had been outfitted with scuba equipment, Juan's assistant, Felipe, made several trips across Calle Medina to the dive boat, transferring gear with a wheelbarrow. He hauled tanks, wet suits, and fins, crossing the street and the sandy beach to a boat parked in a very small marina.

After transporting Troy and Kevin's gear, Felipe approached Robert and asked, "*¿Puedo ayudarte con su equipo senor?*"

Wow, somebody on the island actually speaks Spanish, thought Robert. He'd been looking forward to practicing the language but was disappointed that everyone spoke mostly English to visiting Americans. But Felipe was asking to haul away Robert's equipment…, and it was all brand new. What if something got stolen or misplaced? Robert politely declined, making up the excuse that since the gear was new, he would familiarize himself with it a little more while he waited for Pablo Alva.

Thirty minutes passed, and Kevin was getting impatient. He paced from the shop, across Calle Medina to the beach, and back several times. He looked down at his watch at least two or three times a minute.

While Kevin paced, Robert kept busy practicing his Spanish by making small talk with Felipe in the dive shop. Troy purchased a breakfast burrito and a giant chorizo sausage from a street vendor just outside. He ducked back into the shop, eating from both fists.

"We just ate breakfast forty-five minutes ago, Troy," said Robert, shaking his head with raised eyebrows. "There's something horribly wrong with you."

"This is freaking-amazing chorizo, Cline. You should try some." Troy held up the two-inch-thick spicy sausage, offering Robert a bite.

"Nope, I'm good," said Robert, turning his head away while trying not to smell the beastly chorizo.

Just then Kevin walked back into the shop, demanding, "Where the hell is this guy? We were supposed to get on the boat forty-five minutes ago."

"I don't know, amigo," Juan replied. "He's usually a little late but—"

A roaring engine, screeching tires, and muffled mariachi interrupted Juan. The squeak of a car door preceded a sudden boost in music volume and the smell of heavy engine exhaust. The assortment of snorkels and masks on the shop's shelves began to vibrate as massive bass pounded from subwoofers just outside. Juan and the three agents walked out to the street to see what was going on.

Just below them, parked halfway up on the sidewalk of Calle Medina, sat the 2010 Mustang with purple and green Mistichrome paint. Black, tinted windows were interrupted only by a Mexican flag decal filling the rear window. The bright-purple, underglow lighting system pulsated to the mariachi music that blared from the backseat subwoofer.

Stepping out from the driver's-side door emerged Pablo Alva. "Hola, Juan. ¿Como esta amigo? How you like my wheels?" Alva shook hands with Juan and patted him on the back.

Robert raised one eyebrow and shook his head in disgust at Kevin, who somewhat apologetically shrugged back at him. Looks like we would have blended in with this guy just fine, thought Robert. He watched as Alva showed off the very car that had earned him a stiff reprimand.

Colombian drug lord Pablo Alva was nearly six feet tall. He had dark hair, dark eyes, and a Hollywood smile.

Drug cartel leaders must have a good dental plan, thought Robert.

Juan introduced Pablo to the three agents using their cover: two college professors and their dentist friend. "These guys will be going on our trip with us today," the dive master explained.

Then Juan, Pablo, and the three agents walked across the street to the marina. Robert was loaded down with gear, since he hadn't let Felipe transport his equipment. But his excitement over diving with whale sharks fueled his pace as he continually had to make a conscious effort to slow down and wait for the group. They met Felipe at the dive boat named *Raya Isla*. Once loaded, they sped off north through the beautiful Caribbean waters. They navigated toward the Gulf of Mexico to an area rich with the largest species of shark in the world.

It was a clear, hot day, but the canopy of the *Raya Isla* protected the group from the sun's unforgiving rays. For the first half hour the water was pristine, aqua-blue, and glass calm. Robert was thoroughly enjoying being at sea. He plugged his MP3 player into the boat's stereo axillary, and they glided along the water to the tropical island beat and "Hip, Hip" of "Island in the Sun," by Weezer.

As the picturesque morning faded into a memory, the midsize dive boat transitioned from the tranquil Caribbean into deep dark Gulf of Mexico waters. Eight-foot swells pounded the hull of the *Raya Isla* while Troy and Kevin tried to break through and make conversation with Alva. As the rising and falling sea tossed the boat side to side, Robert gradually slid away to isolate himself from the others.

Pablo Alva didn't seem interested in Troy or Kevin's friendship. Instead the drug cartel leader focused on Juan and Felipe, telling stories of his extravagant life while being careful not to reveal that he was Latin America's top drug kingpin. Dive master Juan made multiple attempts to spark Alva's interest in Troy and Kevin with no success.

Realizing they weren't making any progress, Kevin looked to utilize all his available resources. He carefully timed the waves as he stumbled over to Robert, who was sitting alone toward the back of the boat. "Come help us out, Cline," Kevin whispered. "We've got to make friends with this guy if we're going to get him back to the shell tonight. He doesn't want anything to do with Troy or me. I actually think Troy's butchered Spanish is pissing him off. Maybe you can get Alva talking about his teeth or something."

Robert had his eyes fixed firmly on the horizon as the unrelenting waves beat against the hull of the *Raya Isla*. He didn't answer Kevin.

"Cline, what the hell is wrong with you? You're not on vacation. We're going to need your help," Kevin demanded in his quietest whisper shout.

"I think if I talk, I'm going to puke," said Robert, still looking straight into the horizon. "If I move right now, I'm *definitely* going to blow." This was already the third spot that Robert had tried sitting in, while attempting to escape the motor's exhaust. But the fumes found him wherever he went; provoking his motion sickness the same way rotten meat provokes the arrival of maggots.

"You're not seasick, are you?" asked Kevin in disgust. "We need you to help us break the ice with this guy."

"Oh yeah. I'm seasick. Besides, nobody wants to talk about their teeth on vacation." With each pounding wave, Robert's complexion became a little greener. "I've been boating on lakes a thousand times and never had a problem. I was great on the ferry yesterday, but this is blowing me away."

Kevin wobbled back to his dive pack and carefully returned holding a small yellow pill and a water bottle. "Take this, Cline."

Robert finally looked away from the horizon. He looked down at the pill, and then up at Kevin with one raised eyebrow. "What is it?"

"Zofran. I got it from one of the agency docs. I took one before we left. It works great."

Robert knew Zofran was a revolutionary drug that worked wonders fighting nausea in chemotherapy patients. He'd never heard of its use for motion sickness, but with the prospect of several more hours at sea, he was willing to try anything. He popped the pill and took a few swallows of water.

"I'll leave you alone here, Cline, but I need you to get back in the game." Kevin patted Robert on the shoulder and teetered back to the front of the boat with the others.

Robert could only wait and hope that as the Gulf waves advanced, his nausea waves would retreat. He wanted to feel better but seemed to be getting worse until his misery was abruptly interrupted.

Felipe let go of the wheel and rang a bell just above the helm. "*Tiburones, tiburones!*" he shouted.

Robert looked up past the bow side of the boat and saw a large, black-spotted dorsal fin skimming the surface of the water. The cry of *tiburones*, the Spanish word for sharks, would ordinarily strike fear in the hearts of most, but this seemed to be just the thing to take Robert's mind off the unrelenting sea swells. Exhilaration instantly replaced queasiness as Robert jumped up and joined the rest of the group.

Juan gathered the men in a circle and went over the dive plan. "As I have already told you, amigos, we will be skin diving with the whale sharks. No tanks. They come close to the top of the water and skim for plankton. You will see them perfectly just beneath the surface without diving deep."

While Juan explained the procedures, Felipe worked diligently, laying out masks, fins, and snorkels for each of the men at the boat's port side. With years of experience at sea, Felipe moved easily, as if on dry land. His balance was not even slightly affected by the heavy motion and steady waves.

Juan continued, "Felipe will drive the boat into the path of one of the whale sharks, and two of you will dive with me into the water. Then we swim alongside the shark until we can't keep up. After we lose sight of the whale shark, we get back on the boat so we can track down another mighty fish for the next two divers. There are hundreds of these magnificent creatures in the area. Remember, this is a private trip, so we will go out as many times as you would like. We just need to leave enough daylight for our afternoon shipwreck scuba dive."

Kevin interrupted, "So you're saying that we jump in the water *directly in the path* of these sharks?" He was clearly concerned. "Is that really a good idea?"

Juan laughed. "Don't worry, amigo. They will slowly turn and swim right around you. They are beautiful and graceful but not aggressive. They are, however, very powerful, sometimes reaching forty feet in length and weighing up to twenty tons. One whip of the tail from an agitated whale shark would generate plenty enough force to take out any one of us. So please do not touch the shark. They will leave you alone if you leave them alone. Besides, there is a mandatory ten-thou-sand-dollar fine and a minimum ten-day immediate incarceration for anybody caught touching even so much as a fin of one of these gentle giants."

Juan looked into the eyes of each of the men to make sure they understood. "Any questions, amigos?"

Everyone but Kevin was already putting on their gear. "I don't seem to find my snorkel here," said Kevin, looking bewildered while shuffling through his equipment. He had intentionally misplaced it, hoping to at least miss out on the shark dive.

"No problem, amigo. I have an extra for you," said Felipe, smiling as he bailed out the agent who didn't want to be bailed out.

"Oh, yeah, thanks, Felipe. I really appreciate that."

Felipe quickly grabbed Kevin's mask and attached the backup snorkel for him.

"Felipe, let's get in front of one of these giants," ordered Juan, prompting his assistant to again man the helm. "Pair up and decide who's going first."

Robert was standing ready, decked out with his mask, snorkel, and fins. The Zofran and excitement had completely cured his seasickness. Pablo, who'd been on several whale shark dives through the years, was also ready. Troy was busy helping Kevin figure out the tightness of his mask adjustment. It was clear that Kevin was stalling. He was hoping he could waste enough time to allow for some storm clouds to roll in and interrupt the shark dive. But the sky stayed clear.

Felipe steered in front of a relatively small whale shark. "It's a little one; only about twenty-five feet!"

"Shit...Only about twenty-five feet," said Kevin under his breath as he tried to accidentally drop one of his fins overboard.

"I got that for you, buddy," said Troy, catching the fin before it hit the water.

"OK, *Roberto y Pablo, vamanos!*" shouted Juan enthusiastically.

Robert and Pablo followed Juan, jumping fins first into the green, plankton-rich Gulf. After the bubbles in front of his mask cleared, Robert looked right into the eyes of a nine-ton beast swimming slowly toward him with mouth wide open. He instinctively thrashed his arms and kicked his fins to get out of the way of the approaching behemoth.

The giant shark seemed to pay no attention to the three divers, only subtly turning to swim past them. Dive master Juan lifted his head above water and shouted, "Swim, amigos! *Vamanos!*"

Pablo was already swimming ahead as fast as he could alongside the young whale shark. Robert got over his initial shock, and began kicking with all his strength to keep up. The powerful tail of the shark slowly and gracefully glided from side to side, but the propulsion generated was far more than a man with fins could produce. Even though they were swimming at full speed, the divers were quickly losing ground.

All of the sudden, Pablo reached out and grabbed the wide, flat pectoral fin on the side of the great whale shark. The fin was almost as big as Alva. Juan motioned frantically for Pablo to stop. The drug lord managed to hitch a ride for just a few moments before the shark whipped its tail violently and flung him loose.

This guy's kind of a wild ass, thought Robert.

The three men followed the giant fish for a few minutes more until the creature, with no known predators other than man, finally dove down and disappeared into the deep.

The divers surfaced, spitting out their snorkels and pulling down their masks. "That was incredible!" hollered Robert while treading water.

Pablo had gone on whale shark dives each of the last five years, but he was equally excited. "Did you see her take me?" he shouted.

Juan pleaded with Pablo about grabbing the shark's fin. He had to disguise his anger so as not to compromise the mission. "Amigo, this can be very dangerous. We are in their environment." Even though he was an agency asset, Juan was a diver first, and he was passionate about treating the wonderful creatures with respect.

"I'm sorry, amigo. I won't do it again," said Pablo through a poorly suppressed grin. Alva was carefree and reckless. He had no intention of honoring Juan's request. As long as no sea-patrol boats were nearby, he would do just what he pleased.

"OK, amigos, let's get back in the boat and let the others try. After we rest, I'll take you out a few more times."

Felipe sped the *Raya Isla* around to the three men.

Troy looked down from the deck, eager for his turn. He shouted over the noise of the motor, while the boat rocked next to the three divers. "How was it, Cline?"

"Just completely breathtaking," Robert replied, laughing in delight.

Kevin looked out into the water, wearing his mask and fins. His giant belly hung over his worn-out swim trunks. Despite his bad sunburn from just the day before, his color was stark white. Agent Kevin Smith, who'd fearlessly jumped out of airplanes into enemy territory, played Texas Hold'em at gunpoint with Fidel Castro, and even slept with one of Saddam Hussein's wives while Saddam was in the next room, was scared shitless.

Robert and Pablo climbed up a small ladder onto the boat, energized from the amazing experience. Juan, still angry about the fin grab, followed with fake enthusiasm.

The dive master and his assistant traded places, and Felipe quickly readied himself to get into the water. They trolled a few hundred feet until they crossed the path of another whale shark, which was even more massive than the one before.

"Jump in!" shouted Juan from the helm.

Felipe quickly jumped, but Troy waited, having picked up on the fact that Kevin was not OK with this. "Come on, Kevin, let's go."

Kevin's legs could not bend or step, and they certainly would not jump. Fear shackled him to the platform on the edge of the dive boat. His fist was riveted around the frame of the boat's Bimini top.

Felipe shouted up at the agents, "*Vamanos*, amigos. The fish is coming!"

Kevin's eyes focused like lasers on a giant dorsal fin that broke the surface of the water and moved straight toward the boat. His toes curled and gripped the edge of the platform like a vice. He would not be able to force himself to enter the water right in front of a thirty-foot shark. But before he knew what was happening, Kevin was the catalyst to a sudden splash. He was upside down in the deep-green gulf, with a mouth full of salt water so concentrated that it bludgeoned his taste buds and burned his throat.

Kevin, spitting and choking, popped his head up and looked at the boat above him just in time to see Troy jump over his head into the ocean. "You freaking pushed me, you son of a bitch!" shouted Kevin as he continued coughing up seawater while violently swinging his arms to splash Troy in the face.

"The fish was coming!" shouted Troy as he laughed and spit back the water from Kevin's angry splashing.

"Yes, the fish is coming. Come on, amigos!" Felipe motioned for the two agents to follow and dove to chase the whale shark.

Troy adjusted his dive mask and began swimming with Felipe. Kevin took a quick peak beneath the water through his mask. Oh shit, he thought, while watching the beast move toward them. A wave clapped over his snorkel from above, causing him to choke on yet more seawater. His head immediately popped up for air.

Robert shouted down from the boat at his senior agent. "Are you OK?"

"There's something wrong with this freaking snorkel," Kevin barked back as he lifted his mask and spit out the mouthpiece, trying to clear it.

By the time Kevin got his gear resituated and looked back underwater, he could only barely see the shark's giant tail swaying side to side fifty feet ahead. He was feeling much more comfortable at this distance and began swimming, trying to intentionally not catch up to Troy, Felipe, or the shark.

After the mighty fish dove out of sight, dive master Juan sped ahead in the *Raya Isla* and picked up Troy and Felipe. Kevin, now worried that the shark might reappear, picked up his swim pace. He had fallen at least seventy feet behind the other divers who were already drying off on deck by the time he swam up to the boat.

Like Robert and Pablo before him, Troy was completely amazed with the encounter and couldn't wait for his next turn. "What did you think?" Troy shouted down to Kevin while offering his hand to help his senior agent onto the ladder. "Wasn't that sweet?"

Trying to appear enthusiastic, Kevin replied, "Yeah. That's a once-in-a-lifetime deal. But I don't know if I'm going to be able to go out again. There's something seriously wrong with this snorkel."

Robert wanted to point out that Kevin's snorkel was one of very basic design: a single-piece breathing tube with no valves or moving parts. There couldn't be a whole heck of a lot that could go wrong with this type of snorkel. But this was obviously Kevin's tactic to get out of another dive, and Robert decided to let it rest.

As the sun slowly rolled across the clear-blue sky, Robert, Troy, and Pablo each had a chance to skin dive with at least five more giant whale sharks. Meanwhile, Kevin observed comfortably from the boat's deck. Frequent wildlife-protection patrol boats managed to deter Pablo from grabbing any more fins. He had more money than discernment, and he wouldn't have minded paying the $10,000 fine. Alva didn't, however, embrace the thought of spending the remainder of his vacation days in jail.

"All right, amigos!" shouted Juan over the motor. "Now that we are all back on the boat, let's get moving. It's getting late, so if we still want to do our shipwreck dive, we need to get going. On the way back we will be traveling with the current, but it is still over an hour's trip to the *General Anaya* site between Isla Mujeres and Cancún."

Alva pulled a large Cuban cigar from his equipment pack. He held the Cuban tightly between his teeth and talked around it while digging through his bag for a lighter. "Come on, Juan, I have never seen so many whale sharks in one spot. Let's chase a few more." He found a lighter and struggled to ignite the flame with his wet hands. "If it's dark when we get back, we can dive the *General* at night. I know you keep underwater lights on the boat," Alva said, just as he lit the cigar. He blew a few puffs of smoke in Robert's face and slapped Kevin on the back, accusing, "Unless, of course, our gringo friends here are afraid of diving in the dark."

"Well, that would be great, Pablo, but the Mexican Coast Guard recently placed a ban on shipwreck diving at night due to problems with people lifting artifacts from wreckage for souvenirs." Juan skillfully got Alva refocused. "If we leave now, amigo, we will have just enough time for a one-tank dive."

With Pablo in agreement, the dive boat started back toward Isla de Mujeres, riding along the waves instead of bouncing over them. The trip was considerably smoother and quicker than it had been in the morning. Robert, Troy, and Kevin continued to try to make a connection with Pablo Alva, but he still showed little interest. Troy suggested that they all get together in the evening for a few beers, but Alva didn't even acknowledge the request. Kevin was growing more and more concerned that they wouldn't be able to lure him back to the shell house at all. He was starting to consider an alternate plan, such as kidnapping, but that would be risky, and chances of being discovered were high in such operations.

After a short hour-and-a-half boat ride, the *Raya Isla* reached waters over the *General Anaya*, a US World War I minesweeper that had been decommissioned and sold to the Mexican navy. It was intentionally sunk in the 1980s with the sole purpose of artificial reef formation for recreational scuba. The C58 dive site was very popular and crowded at times. But with sunset approaching, only a few dive boats remained over the sight, and they were all loading up to head back to shore. Shortly after arriving, Juan's group became the only boat that remained in the area.

While Felipe prepared to set anchor, Juan laid out the dive plan. "We will go down together and circle the *General*. We can enter portions of the vessel since it was split open by Hurricane Wilma in 2005. The ship has a few internal passages we will not be entering. These passages are very constricted, and it is just too dangerous to attempt penetration. You will see many tropical fish and possibly some turtles or rays. We spent a little too much time with the whale sharks, so we only have a little over half an hour until sunset, which means we will need to cut the dive a bit short. I will signal when it is time to surface."

"Are there a lot more sharks in this area?" asked Kevin. "I just think I'm going to have a much better time seeing them with my scuba gear tonight. That snorkel ruined my entire dive earlier." He was trying to save face from his cowardly morning but really was hoping for the assurance that there would be no sharks.

"So sorry, amigo, but there just aren't many sharks around here. Maybe only a few small nurse sharks, but as you know they have no *dientes*, or teeth, and they are harmless."

"Hmm...Well that's too bad," said Kevin, looking gravely disappointed while actually feeling quite relieved. Robert saw right through his display of machismo, noticing that while Juan spoke, Kevin frequently raised his eyebrows and took worried glances over the boat railing into the water below. The horizontal lines of his furrowed brow read like a book, exposing the fact that he was actually more than a little concerned about the idea of even running into a toothless nurse shark.

Juan continued, "We will use the PADI dive buddy system, so I need you to pair up. You will look out for each other. Stick with your partner. You should all have three thousand PSI in your tanks. Once your air gets down to five hundred PSI, let me know and then head to the top. If one of you goes up, your buddy needs to go up with you. But when I surface, we all need to surface. So decide who your dive partner will be. Oh, and be careful. The current is very strong today. If you start to get swept away, just go with your partner to the surface and Felipe will pick you up in the boat."

Alva had already decided that he didn't care much for Troy, and he didn't want to be held back by Kevin, who was already struggling to put on his scuba gear. He looked up at Robert and said, "*Mira que es yo y tu*," indicating that he'd chosen the "vacationing dentist" to be his dive buddy.

Robert was more than a little concerned with this arrangement, since Pablo had proven to be completely reckless. Putting his safety in the hands of a drug lord was a bit more than Robert had hoped for on his first scuba dive in the ocean.

While Pablo finished checking his dive gear, he spoke brashly to Robert in his heavy Spanish accent. "You better keep up, *partner*."

Juan and the four other divers jumped into the water and started to descend slowly toward the wreckage of the *General Anaya* sixty feet below. Kevin got stuck at a depth of twenty-five feet. He was having trouble regulating the pressure in his ears. While waiting for Kevin, Juan noticed that there was a small but steady stream of air bubbles leaking from his regulator hose. The dive master knew Pablo was temperamental, and aborting the dive before it began could cause him to storm away once they reached shore. That would, of course, compromise Kevin, Troy, and Robert's chances of getting him back to the shell house. He also knew the leak would cause him to run out of air much faster than usual, but he was an experienced diver and was good at conserving air, so he decided to continue.

Juan signaled for the others to wait for Kevin's ear pressure to regulate, but Pablo continued to dive deeper, ignoring the request. Juan waved Robert on, indicating that he should follow his dive partner.

As Pablo and Robert descended toward the wreckage, a deep-creaking and metallic-pounding sound filled the water around them. The eerily haunting noise came from what must have been a thousand pound, rust- and coral-covered door swinging slowly back and forth in the current. A heavy chain fixed to the door to hold it open periodically clanked against the hull of the sunken *General Anaya*. A sign on the door displayed skull and crossbones and read, PELIGROSO. MIRA DENTRO, PERO NO ENTRE! (DANGER. LOOK INSIDE, BUT DO NOT ENTER!). The door led to the only area of the ship where diver access wasn't permitted.

Hundreds of bright-blue and yellow tropical fish passed in and out of the great ship, but the remaining sunlight that filtered through the water was rapidly fleeing, and shadows began to cloak the *General Anaya*. Just below Robert, a giant orange-and-green parrot fish used its powerful beak to crush coral on the sea bottom. The loud cracking sound of the crunching coral joined the melody of the creaking door, clanking chain, and ever-rushing scuba regulator bubbles. The two divers watched the parrot fish for only a minute before Pablo was back on the move.

This guy needs to pop a little Ritalin, Robert thought. He has the attention span of a middle-school kid with ADHD. Robert stayed close, making sure not to lose sight of him.

As Pablo and Robert worked their way around the shipwreck, Juan, Kevin, and Troy finally approached their planned depth. A majestic eagle ray with a twelve-foot wingspan glided just below the three late-comers and just above Robert and Pablo. The peaceful ray clearly startled Kevin, who was already breathing heavily.

Juan signaled for the group to stay together. He planned to guide the divers through the coral-crusted ship's open rooms. Before entering the wreckage, Juan noticed a turtle feeding on some sea grass on the ocean floor. The five men stopped to watch, but when the turtle became annoyed with their presence and swam away, Pablo took chase.

Juan pounded on his air tank to get Pablo's attention, but it was clear that the cartel leader was not to be contained. Alva chased the turtle for nearly fifty yards, with the group reluctantly following. Eventually, Pablo gave up and turned around. The divers struggled against the heavy current for a hard swim back to the *General Anaya*.

The scene slowly faded to a dark, bluish gray as the shadows of sunset chased away the usually brilliant colors of the fish and coral. Dive master Juan had stayed down as long as possible, but he saw that his air had already dipped to four hundred PSI, and the stream of bubbles leaking from his regulator was intensifying. He pointed to his air gauge and gave the signal that it was time for the group to ascend. Kevin had anxiously breathed his tank down to five hundred PSI without the assistance of a leak, and Troy didn't have much more air. Robert still had close to eight hundred PSI left in the tank. He doubted Pablo concerned himself with such petty details as how much air he had remaining.

The last few rays of the setting sun managed to penetrate the water, shimmering a reflection off the silver scales of a six-foot barracuda just twenty feet away. The ominous fish flaunted razor-sharp teeth and appeared to be frozen still, suspended in the stiff current. It stared at the divers with one eye.

Ignoring Juan's signal to ascend, Pablo swam aggressively toward the long barracuda, which continued to remain completely stationary in the water. Only Robert followed, thinking that the dive buddy system in this case seemed to be more of a hazard than a safety measure.

Troy motioned to Kevin, suggesting they should also swim over for a closer look before their ascent, but the senior agent fearfully held back and hovered at a safe distance. Kevin breathed heavily with anxiety, hoping Pablo wouldn't scare the barracuda his way.

The stream of bubbles leaking from Juan's regulator strengthened, taking his air down to only 250 PSI. He aggressively pounded on his tank to get the divers to follow him to the top. Pablo ignored the request, but Robert looked back to acknowledge and gave a hand signal, indicating that he was still good on air and would try to stay with Alva. Juan nodded in agreement and gave the OK sign just before he rose to the top with Troy and Kevin.

Now it was just Pablo and Robert alone beneath the darkening sea. Robert took a deep breath from his regulator. This guy's probably going to get me killed, he thought. He watched as Pablo finally reached the barracuda, eventually causing it to break stillness and retreat slowly backward toward the shipwreck. Alva fearlessly advanced even while the ghoulish fish opened its jaw fully as if to warn that he was getting too close. While the cartel leader backed the barracuda into a corner against the rusted helm of the *General Anaya*, Robert began to fear that this could only end badly. Surely the spooked monster fish would feel trapped. Won't it inevitably lash out and use its razor-sharp teeth to cut right through Pablo? Robert thought. What is this guy doing?

Just when it appeared that the barracuda might be threatened enough to attack, a shocking metal crash resonated through the water. The startled fish darted past Pablo like a torpedo into the darkness and was instantly out of sight. Again a loud metal crash blasted through the water. It was the door that had been chained open only a while ago. The chain had pulled away from its anchor, leaving the weighty metal door free to swing open and then slam shut with the current.

Pablo looked at Robert for a moment, and then turned back toward the door. He swam to the door and strained with all his strength to pull it open. Ignoring the DANGER. DO NOT ENTER! sign, he signaled for Robert to follow and disappeared into the hull of the ship.

Shit! thought Robert. What in the world is wrong with this idiot? There's no way in hell I am going through that door. This has got to be the most reckless imbecile I've ever seen. Robert held on to a coral-crusted railing on the ship and stood by, figuring that Pablo's short attention span wouldn't permit him to spend much time in his most recent, ill-advised adventure.

Robert waited for nearly five minutes, while visibility continued to fade. He checked his air gauge and was startled to see that it had dropped to just below five hundred PSI. Still, there was no sign of Pablo Alva. Each time the door swung open, Robert tried to look inside, but he could see nothing but darkness. He pulled his underwater flashlight out of a pocket in his buoyancy vest and aimed it into the *General*, but only saw an occasional fish. Finally, Robert contemplated returning to the dive boat, thinking Pablo may have swum out through another passage and ascended unnoticed.

All of the sudden, Robert heard a faint pounding between crashes from the metal door. Could that be Alva? he thought. Against his better judgment, he waited for the current to help open the door, and then followed his flashlight beam inside the *General Anaya*. The entrance led to the World War I minesweeper's control room. The flashlight cut through the pitch-black interior of the ship, revealing four walls covered with oxidized switches and levers. A single interior doorway led to a long, narrow hallway and what appeared to be another even darker room.

Robert had received extensive CIA operative training, but like other special medical team agents, his training was primarily geared toward missions that utilized his specialty: dentistry. Agents Smith and Mercer were probably right; training for special medical team cadets was more of a country club version of the preparation *real* agents received. His dive instruction hadn't even been in the ocean. This was turning into something quite a bit more extreme than anything he'd prepared for. He breathed heavily, looking at his glow in the dark air gauge, which dipped down to four hundred PSI.

Although Robert hadn't been a big fan of Agent Mercer up to this point, he was thinking that this situation would have been a little more appropriate for the ex-Navy Seal. Why did *I* get stuck being Alva's dive partner anyway? He tried to think of one good reason for entering deeper into the ship's hull instead of simply retreating and heading to the top. This wasn't the part of the mission a CIA specialist dentist should be executing. With that in mind, he made the prudent decision to exit the ship.

Then, there was more pounding. While underwater, there is no sense of sound direction, but it had to be Alva, and he had to still be inside. Robert tried to swallow around the mouthpiece of his regulator, but his throat was as dry as desert sand. There wasn't enough air left in his tank for such indecision. Overwhelmed by fear, he decided it would still be best to exit the ship and go to the surface, but only after a quick swim through the hallway and a look into the dark room.

Robert cautiously swam through the long, black passage, aiming his flashlight down the hall, hoping to see no sign of Pablo Alva, so he could get out of the ship and swim to the top. He cautiously passed through the opening at the other side, entering into a confined instrument room.

Wonderful, thought Robert. He immediately saw his careless dive partner trapped in an entanglement of barbed wire and netting, which had originally been put in place to protect an entire wall of navigation instruments. Pablo had attempted to weave through the barricade in hopes of breaking away an artifact. His tank, regulator tubing, legs, and arms were completely intertwined with the wire and netting, leaving Pablo thrashing and twisting himself farther into a braid of ensnarement. Alva frantically motioned for Robert to help and gave the diver's hand signal for low air.

Low air? No shit, thought Robert, looking at his own pressure gauge, which now read only 350 PSI. He approached in an attempt to untangle his dive partner, but Pablo thrashed his arms in a panic, knocking Robert's air-regulator hose out of his mouth and his mask completely off his face.

An unforgiving rush of salt water flooded into Robert's nose, mouth, and eyes. He was instantly blinded without his mask. Robert's lungs burned for air as he fought with all his strength to pull away from Pablo, who now had him locked in a death grip. Once he broke free, the rookie agent quickly reached through the darkness and located his regulator air hose. He reinserted the mouthpiece, purged the pungent salt water from his mouth, and then gasped for a much needed breath.

Still blinded, he bent down and felt his way to relocating his mask. After repositioning the water-filled mask, he took a deep breath from his regulator and exhaled air through his nose to expel all the liquid just like he'd learned in his PADI scuba training. At first he lifted his eyelids slowly, but then he blinked rapidly to get rid of the sting from the salt.

Even though Robert's eyes were burning, at least he could see. His stomach was turning from the concentrated salt water he'd swallowed, but at least he was now breathing. His adrenal glands were pumping epinephrine into his bloodstream like a fire hose pumps water on a fire. Robert tried to remain calm, but panic was overtaking him. Why the hell should I bother to try to save this freak, just so I can help kill him in a few hours? What are the chances that trying to rescue him won't get me killed? Questions flashed through his mind almost as quickly as his air was vanishing.

Robert looked at his air gauge, which now read three hundred PSI. He took a deep breath, knowing he only had one last attempt to free Alva. He pulled a knife from one of the pockets in his buoyancy-control vest and signaled for Pablo to calm down as he approached him for a second time.

The drug lord violently swiped his hand in front of his neck, giving the signal for no air. He repeatedly pointed to his pressure gauge, which now read zero.

Robert's nerves were shot, but he tried to stay cool. As the rookie agent came closer, Pablo thrashed again in a panic. He frantically pulled at Robert, who finally dropped the knife and flashlight, further dimming the already-shadowy underwater instrument room. He grabbed hold of Pablo's arms, tightly clamping them to stillness. Looking eye to eye, Robert slowly shook his head "no" in an attempt to calm the panicked drug lord. At the same time he unhooked his emergency second-stage breathing regulator from his dive vest and put it in Alva's mouth. Robert used all his strength to keep Alva still with one hand, while he again signaled to stay calm.

After Pablo took a few breaths, he settled down, allowing Robert to release his restraining grip. The rookie agent bent down and extended his arm, while Pablo's emergency air hose stretched down to Robert's tank. He reached out with his fingertips and managed to grasp his flashlight and knife without dislodging Alva's airline. Once the items were secured, Robert stood back up and handed the flashlight to Pablo. He showed Alva his own pressure gauge, which read only 250 PSI and was now being depleted twice as fast with both men breathing from Robert's tank. Pablo slowly raised both arms above his head, signaling submission.

Robert quickly went to work, using his knife to cut through the netting, while Pablo held the flashlight. The rookie agent raced against the clock, trying to outrun death itself. He sawed desperately at the heavy netting, now committing to free Pablo or die trying. How did this idiot get so twisted in this mess? thought Robert.

He was able to cut away all the netting, but somehow the barbed wire kept Alva secured firmly in his underwater tomb. Air pressure was down to 150 PSI, and his knife was no match for the wire, leaving Robert frantically trying to solve the convoluted puzzle. He pulled and ripped by hand in hopes of untwisting his dive partner. The water in the beam of the flashlight quickly took on a rose-colored tint as blood oozed from barb-torn wounds on Robert's hands and arms.

The efforts to untwist the barbed wire from Pablo were completely unsuccessful. In a final attempt to free the drug lord, Robert went back to his knife and aggressively sawed at his partner's dive vest and part of his wet suit. He hacked and tore through the heavy material, reaching the point of complete exhaustion. Finally, using his last ounce of energy, while clamping his teeth around his rubber mouthpiece and letting out a desperation shriek that bubbled through his air regulator, he was able to rip through enough material to pull apart Pablo's buoyancy vest, leaving the empty air tank behind and freeing the cartel leader.

Pablo lunged for the door, but Robert immediately restrained him and reestablished his controlling grip. The rookie agent signaled that they would go together slowly. Pablo nodded in agreement, knowing that he had no other choice as they both pulled air from the same tank.

Breathing was now met with noticeable resistance as the tank air dropped to fifty PSI. With arms locked the two men swam through the long, dark hallway into the larger area of the ship's hull. Only faint rays of ocean-filtered moonlight leaked through the ship's heavy exterior door when it periodically swung open. The men timed the opening and swam through. They ascended the now-dark Caribbean Sea as slowly as possible in an attempt to avoid being afflicted with the bends. Nitrogen gas, saturated in their blood, threatened to bubble out of solution as a speedier-than-usual ascent would be necessary with dwindling air.

As the men strained to draw even a shallow breath from the now empty tank, Robert dropped his weight belt to help ease their climb for the last fifteen feet. The fight for survival was so strong that neither man even noticed the half-dozen circling reef sharks that were attracted to the steady stream of Robert's blood.

Pablo gasped for oxygen as his head finally broke through the water to the plentiful air above. Exhausted, Robert also took a deep, life-giving breath at the surface. Then he held his flashlight up so they'd be noticed by the crew of the *Raya Isla*, that was searching for them in the distance.

"*Me salvaste la vida*. You saved my life. *Me salvaste la vida*," said Pablo as he treaded water and grabbed both of Robert's shoulders, holding him at arms' distance. "I did not even bother to listen to your full name. What is your name, my friend?"

"Cline...Robert Cline," said the agent, emotionally and physically drained and breathing heavily.

"Robert Cline, you are my brother!" shouted Alva. "You have saved me. I owe you my life." Pablo hugged him with all his strength, laughing through tears of gratitude. "You will always be my brother, Robert Cline. *Mi hermano para siempre.*"

Though completely disgusted with the drug lord's reckless behavior, Robert was also overcome with emotion and felt a strange connection to Pablo, born of their mutual dance with death. "We made it, Pablo." Robert laughed, shaking his head in disbelief. "We made it."

The dive boat sped toward Robert's flashlight beam. During their ascent the strong current had caused Robert and Pablo to drift nearly three hundred yards away from the anchored *Raya Isla.*

"What happened?" shouted Juan from the boat.

"Robert Cline saved me!" Pablo grabbed Robert's bloodied hand and held it up out of the water triumphantly. "I owe him every minute of my life until I die!"

Felipe threw the ladder over the side of the dive boat and extended his hand to help the two men climb on board.

Kevin and Troy looked down at the divers. "What went on down there?" asked Troy in his New York accent.

Now on deck, Pablo threw his arm around Robert's shoulder and held tight. "This man is a hero. He is my brother. You are a great man, Robert Cline."

Robert tried to withhold his emotion with limited success. Luckily the darkness of night and the water dripping from his hair disguised the tears that were streaming down his face. A combination of the grueling rescue, Pablo's expression of gratitude, and Robert's knowledge of the gruesome events that would follow later that evening were simply overwhelming.

"We've got to get out of here!" warned Juan. "If the island Coast Guard finds us, we will all spend some time in prison."

As the *Raya Isla* sped back to Isla de Mujeres, Pablo described the adventure in animated fashion to the other divers. While Pablo recounted his predicament and rescue, Kevin leaned over to Troy and whispered, "I think we've got a breakthrough. Alva wouldn't even talk to us earlier, but it looks like he's suddenly in love with Cline. Now he'll come back to the shell with us for sure."

15

THE DENTAL VISIT

After reaching the marina, Felipe unloaded the *Raya Isla* while the rest of the divers walked back to the dive shop. There they took a few shots of tequila to celebrate Pablo's rescue. Kevin seized the opportunity to invite Pablo to continue the celebration. "We've got lots of beer in the fridge and fresh grouper to grill back at our beach rental," he said. "I'm sure Robert would want you to come."

Standing next to Robert, Pablo flung his arm around his rescuer's shoulder. "I will do anything for this man. He is my brother," the drug lord exclaimed. "Of course I will come."

Kevin convinced Pablo to leave the Mustang back at the dive shop, promising to drive him to his hotel if he drank too much. Kevin, Troy, Robert, and Pablo jumped into the golf cart and putted around the island until they eventually pulled into the cobblestone driveway of the beach house.

Pablo stuck to Robert like they were long-lost twins newly reunited after being separated at birth. He put his arm around his rescuer's neck and pulled him in close as they walked up the driveway. It was becoming clear to Robert that the drug lord would continue to violate his very small space bubble as long as they were anywhere near each other. But they were *brothers* now, after all, and Pablo constantly reminded him of this.

Light from the full moon unveiled the peculiar shell shape of the beach house. Pablo quickly pulled his arm from around Robert's neck and stopped in his tracks. His expression turned from carefree to

suspicious apprehension. "Hey," he said in a most serious tone. "You guys aren't gay, are you?"

"What?" asked Kevin. "No, no, absolutely not. Why…? Oh, this shell thing? It's just that we got a smoking deal on this rental…A week for seven hundred bucks. We didn't even know it was going to look like a shell until we got here."

"Yeah, we've all got girlfriends." added Troy.

They awkwardly paused for a few seconds, which seemed more like an eternity. "Ah ha ha ha," Pablo laughed, looking as relieved as he had when Robert made the final cut that set him free from the *General Anaya*. "I knew you guys weren't gay. Whoa, that would have been bad: three gay guys in a girly house. Ha ha ha." He slapped Robert on the back and gratefully flung his arm back around his rescuer's shoulder.

They all walked into the big shell, and Troy closed the door behind them.

"Nice place," joked Alva, looking at Kevin and Troy. "Looks like the perfect house for you two girls. But you better keep your hands off my brother." He briskly rubbed Robert's head, messing his hair. "Hey, where are the *baños*?" he asked. "I think I already had too much tequila at the dive shop."

"Just down the hall." Kevin pointed the way.

The second Pablo let go of Robert, Troy grabbed the large rowing oar that was mounted over the front door and took a home-run swing straight into Alva's face. The broad paddle cracked against the drug lord's skull, tearing away his left eyelid and sending blood and splintered wood flying through the air.

Pablo instantly dropped to the floor, where he laid motionless.

"What the hell is wrong with you, Troy? Are you trying to kill the guy?" accused Kevin, shaking his head in disgust. "We're supposed to keep him alive so Dr. Cline here can torture him while we interrogate him."

"He'll be fine," argued Troy. "I took a little off my swing."

Troy and Kevin quickly grabbed the limp Alva and dragged him down the stairs to the soundproof basement.

"Make sure the front and back doors are locked, Cline!" Kevin shouted from the stairwell. "Then hustle down here and check this guy out for us to make sure he's not dead."

Robert, clearly irritated, hurried through the house, checking the doors while mumbling to himself. "So now if he's dying, I suppose you're going to want me to try to save him again so we can kill him. I'm a freaking dentist, not a neurosurgeon. Maybe if you wanted him alive, you should have considered a submission tactic other than a blunt blow to the head."

"What was that, Cline?" Kevin shouted from downstairs.

"Oh, nothing, I'm just locking the back door now," hollered Robert. These guys are about as smart as a couple of turnips, he thought as he hurried down the stairs.

As soon as Robert entered the basement, Kevin shut the door, securing the soundproof seal. Troy had already gone to work muscling Pablo into the dental chair. He used heavy-duty cam straps and four rolls of duct tape to bind the drug lord's arms, legs, and chest to the chair.

"I bet a few of the pediatric dentists I know would like to have a guy like you in their noncompliant children's room," joked Robert. Before dental school, he'd assumed that pediatric dental offices had theme park atmospheres with balloons, puppets, and sugar-free cotton candy. Instead, many resembled asylums with papoose boards, strait-jackets, and soundproof rooms. While most general dentists enjoyed working on well-behaved children in their warm and inviting family offices, they reluctantly sent the "screamers" to the pediatric specialist, where they were firmly managed with restraint and discipline.

"Go see if he's OK, Doc," said Kevin, while Troy continued to fetter Alva.

"Uh, yeah, he's definitely not OK," responded Robert, while he checked Pablo's pulse and lifted the closed eyelid that hadn't been hit by the oar, "but he should live. He might even regain consciousness. Looks like a concussion and a fractured left eye socket." Robert looked up at Troy. "Good work, Agent Mercer."

"Well, I *did* bat four hundred in high school back in Brooklyn," boasted Troy.

"OK, make sure you have everything you need to work on this guy, Doc," ordered Kevin. "And Troy, please save a little duct tape for later. We're going to need some of that to tie him to the catamaran."

Standing behind the dental chair, Robert put on his gloves and mask. He organized his instruments, arranging extraction forceps and diamond bits for his high-speed drill. Then he arranged the supplies he would need to place filling material over the missile-guidance transmitter.

Alva continued to lay strapped to the dental chair unconscious, until Robert hit the compressed-air control-pedal, with his foot. The high-speed handpiece instantly screamed out in a bone-chilling, high-pitched squeal. Startled to consciousness, Pablo asked, "What's going on?" He turned his head to look around just as he came to.

Troy quickly ripped off another long piece of duct tape and wound it around Alva's forehead and the chair's headrest like a rodeo cowboy hog-tying the hooves of a steer. "Don't move your freaking head!" shouted Troy. He punched Pablo in the stomach.

"Yeah...Doesn't look like we're going to have to worry about that anymore," said Robert sarcastically. "Does the agency offer anger-management classes, Troy?"

"Well, actually I did take a few sessions with—"

"All right, take it easy there, Rocky. Now let's get busy." Kevin tried to gain order. "You two need to focus. We've got a lot to do here."

Unable to move his head, Pablo looked up with his good right eye at Troy and Kevin standing in front of him. Blinking was no longer an option for his left eye. It was now fixed open since the eyelid was completely torn away. The naked pupil drooped off to the side, peering into an empty corner of the room, firmly aimed, and motionless from muscle damage. His good eye began frantically darting all around independently from its still partner. "Where is Robert Cline? You haven't hurt him, have you? I will kill you if you have done anything to harm even a hair of his head."

Robert still stood behind the dental chair, just out of Alva's sight. He took a big swallow, instantly feeling a little sick.

"You're buddy, *Dr.* Cline, is standing right behind you," answered Troy, laughing.

Pablo looked back with his one good eye, while Robert leaned forward over the dental chair, giving a nervous wave. "Hey, Pablo, you're not going to believe this—"

"What is happening? You saved my life. We are brothers!"

Troy interrupted him with another brutal blow to the abdomen.

"He's with us, Pablo," Kevin said. "We're all US intelligence agents, and we know about you and your drug cartel. You've been retained for crimes against the people of the United States of America. You're going to have to cooperate and give us some information so nobody gets hurt." Kevin pulled a micro sound recorder from his shirt pocket and held it over Pablo. "We need the names of your growers, transporters, and distributers in the US."

Alva tried to spit in Kevin's face, but the senior agent stood just out of range. "I will never give you names. Those people are family. Family never betrays family." His good eye looked back at Robert and formed a tear that rolled down his cheek. Only blood dripped from his misaimed wounded eye, since the tear duct had been completely crushed by the oar. "I know *you* will not betray me. You saved me because you are a good man, Robert Cline. You are my brother."

Robert took a deep breath. At this point he realized it would be harder to help kill Pablo Alva than it had been to save him.

Troy ripped another piece of duct tape off the roll and pressed it tightly over Pablo's mouth, driving the back of the cartel leader's head into the dental chair. "Shut up!" he screamed.

"So how are we going to get him to talk with duct tape over his mouth?" chided Robert.

Troy shot back, "You just get your drill going, Cline. I'll pull off the duct tape when we're ready to make him talk."

Kevin took charge of his younger colleagues as he calmly walked to the foot of the dental chair. "All right, Cline, I've got a list of questions from the agency here. I'll ask Alva a question, and if he answers, we move on to the next item. If not, you give him a shot, or do a little drilling, or pull a tooth. If you think it will be helpful, you can cut off a piece of his tongue, but don't cut off so much that I can't understand him if he answers a question."

It was suddenly becoming clear to Robert why Kevin had been assigned to this mission. It obviously hadn't been because of his expertise in scuba diving. No, it was definitely due to his experience at orchestrating enhanced interrogation. Agent Kevin Smith understood that talking about planned torture in front of the subject was often more effective than the torture itself. In fact, Robert would later learn that Kevin was frequently able to get the information he needed without leaving so much as a scratch on his subjects.

Kevin turned to Troy and said, "OK, Mercer, get the tape off his mouth and play dental assistant. Do whatever Doc needs."

"What the hell ever," responded Troy, not appreciating the female insinuation that went along with being a dental assistant. He abruptly ripped the tape off.

"I knew you were gay…, *dental assistant Mercer*," growled Alva up to Troy.

"No! I'm your worst-freaking nightmare, you son of a bitch!" Troy pulled back his fist to deliver another blow.

"Stop! Sit your ass down in the dental assistant chair and wait for my instruction!" barked Kevin.

Troy lowered his fist and followed Agent Smith's command.

"All right," said Kevin. "Let's start with something easy. I need the name and location of your top distributor in the US."

"*No hablo Ingles*," replied Alva defiantly.

"Don't bullshit me, Pablo," said Kevin calmly. "You know we all speak Spanish here."

"Yeah, *yo hablo Espanol* asshole!" shouted Troy in his heavy, Brooklyn-accent Spanish.

"You sound just like the New York streetwalker I met last year in Cuba," sneered Alva. "Maybe she was your sister. *Puta!*" he shouted in Spanish, meaning "whore."

"You'll think *puta!*" Troy quickly rammed his fist into Pablo's face two times before Kevin ran over and grabbed his arm on the third swing.

Kevin clutched Troy's shirt with both hands and flung him across the small room, where he hit the wall and fell to the floor. Then, after storming over and pressing his forehead against Troy's forehead, Kevin began shouting, "Control yourself, Agent Mercer! Do what I tell you and only what I tell you!"

Kevin was strong, but Troy was stronger and could have easily overtaken him. Instead, Mercer submitted to his superior. "Yes, sir."

Robert looked on in astonishment, while Pablo spoke up to him softly. "Hey, Doc, do you think you can fix this?" Pablo used his bloodied tongue to push the tooth that Troy had just knocked out, from the inside of his cheek, up to his puckered lips. He gently spit out the tooth. The bloodied upper-central incisor rolled down the side of his face past his destroyed, drooping eye. It fell to the concrete floor, where it made a clicking noise as it bounced to a rest.

"Just cooperate and answer their questions," warned Robert, hoping to see the intensity of the scene drop several notches.

"I will not answer any questions, and you will do what you have to do, my brother, but I forgive you. I know you are only doing your job. You are a good man, Robert Cline." He flashed a wrecked, bloody smile up at his newest and greatest friend.

Robert was not feeling good about the mission at this point. It would have been a whole lot easier if Alva wasn't acting so indebted to him. Robert had been trained that captured subjects would pretend to be overly friendly to gain sympathy and then stab you in the back once you let your guard down. But Pablo seemed so sincere.

Troy reassumed his position as dental assistant, and Kevin stood back at the foot of the dental chair. "Please don't talk to Cline, Alva," ordered Kevin. "Now, who's your main distributer in the US?"

"OK. I give up, *jefe*," Pablo replied. He paused for a second, and then began laughing with his bloodied smile and missing front tooth. "It is Mercer's whore sister."

Kevin immediately shot a piercing look at Troy, indicating that he would stay under control. Then Kevin looked down at Alva with a smile and said, "Dr. Cline knows how to make you talk." He waived his hand at Robert and barked out an unapologetic order. "Give him a shot, Doc!"

Robert was nervous but maintained a cool outward appearance. It wasn't really the CIA training that kept him calm as much as his dental school training. At the University of Nebraska College of Dentistry, he had to perform countless procedures on patients for the very first time while acting like he was a seasoned expert. Just like in dental school, he sat behind the patient, turned to his supply cart, and carefully attached a 27 gauge long shaft, inch-and-a-half needle to a cold, surgical steel syringe. But instead of lidocaine, he inserted a carpule of the "devil's fire," the distinctly orange fluid that was specially designed by the agency to burn like a welder's flame when injected.

"Show him the needle, Cline," instructed Kevin.

Out of habit, Robert hid the syringe from Pablo's sight. He never let his regular patients, young or old, see the needle.

"Oh yeah, sorry," Robert apologized. Since enhanced interrogation had been omitted from CIA protocol, Robert had no real training in the area. His anxiety rose, but his hand was steady as he pivoted his chair until he was hovering over Alva. He unsheathed the 27 gauge long shaft needle directly over Pablo's face. The drug lord's broken eye aimed motionless off to the side, while his good eye focused sharply on the light passing through the drop of orange liquid forming at the tip of the needle.

"Who's your distributer, Pablo?" demanded Kevin, raising his voice.

"Do what you must, but I will not tell you anything."

Kevin gave a nod. Robert acknowledged the signal and got in position to give the injection. Pablo did his best to pull back, flexing every muscle in his body and trying to twist away. Troy ripped off a three-foot strap of duct tape and wound it tightly around Alva's neck and the dental chair, causing Pablo to grimace and labor for air.

"I bet this is how you treat...your whore sister!" Alva strained to speak in much more than a whisper, while the duct tape squeezed his throat and vocal cords.

Robert tried to inject Pablo, who no longer wiggled but sealed his lips tightly. The rookie agent looked back at the table of supplies, where he found a device known as the Jennings Gag. The gag is a stainless steel ratcheting apparatus that, once inserted, can be used to stretch and hold a person's mouth as wide open as necessary. Robert had seen one of these in his dental school's museum of Civil War dentistry, but he'd never actually used such a device. He reluctantly grabbed the gag and turned back to his patient, only to see Troy holding Pablo's lips in each hand while pulling apart his mouth. Alva tried to scream but only made a wheezing noise through his duct-tape-compressed throat.

"Get in there, Cline!" shouted Troy just before Pablo managed to pull his lips out of the agent's grip. "Son of a bitch!" Agent Mercer let out a loud yelp and jumped back as pain shot through his little finger. Alva had bit the agent, managing to draw a little blood. Troy shot a look back at Kevin, wanting the OK to pound Pablo into submission.

Calmly ignoring Troy, Kevin turned to Robert. "If he won't open his mouth, just stick the needle through the outside of his face, Doc."

As Robert advanced to inject through Pablo's cheek, the drug lord quickly decided to submit and opened his mouth. Robert quickly placed the Jennings Gag and squeezed it several times, ratcheting it to a secure position. "That's not too tight, is it?" he asked, clearly concerned.

"What in the hell do you care if it's too tight, Cline?" screamed Troy, who was on the brink of losing control. He quickly reached over and pushed Robert out of the way. Then he rapidly squeezed the powerful gag ratchet handles four more times, causing a gruesome pop sound to radiate from Pablo's temporomandibular joint. Alva's good eye rolled back in his head, while his damaged eye remained fixed and aimed off to the side. Pablo had passed out just before he'd had a chance to scream.

"Shit, you dislocated his jaw!" shouted Robert.

Troy screamed into Robert's face while spit flew from the corners of his mouth. "This isn't dental school, Cline! We are dealing with matters of national security, so if you don't have the guts for this, maybe you should go back to your clinic in Texas and wiggle out loose baby teeth for the tooth fairy!"

"Well, we're not getting much interrogation done now that the guy's passed out, are we, smartass?" shot back Robert.

Agent Smith quickly inserted himself between Troy and Robert and pushed Troy back. "Cline is right. You need to get yourself under control. A little garden-variety dental work will probably be all we need to get the information the agency wants. Plus we have strict orders to keep Pablo alive so we can test the guidance device on a living person. A little controlled pain and a lot of talking are what we're looking for."

Kevin pressed his index finger into Troy's sternum and continued, "This whole interrogation is turning into chaos, and we just don't need that. Alva hasn't had a chance to talk between you smashing him in the face with an oar, knocking out his tooth, choking him with duct tape, and dislocating his jaw. Hell, he couldn't give us any information even if he wanted to. If you do one more thing that is not a response to a direct order from me, you will face disciplinary measures back at Langley."

While Agent Smith got Agent Mercer back under control, Robert quietly backed off the ratchet and removed the mouth gag. He firmly grabbed the unconscious Alva's dislocated jaw with both hands, placing each of his thumbs over the drug lord's lower molars. A double thump resonated through the room as the young dentist maneuvered Pablo's mandible back into its normal position.

Alva slowly regained consciousness prompting Robert to quickly reinsert the Jennings Gag. He ratcheted it, opening the drug lord's mouth for firm restraint but at a reasonably comfortable position. He also used a scalpel from his instrument packet to loosen the duct tape around Alva's neck.

Kevin returned to his spot at the foot of the dental chair, and Troy reluctantly resumed his role as dental assistant.

"Are you ready to talk, Pablo?" asked Kevin. After a pause and no response, the senior agent signaled for Robert to resume.

Dr. Cline injected the 27 gauge long shaft needle through oral mucosal tissue to a depth of one inch, until he could feel the bony resistance of the mandibular ramus. Pablo was shaking, and clearly bothered by the thick needle's penetration; but even without topical anesthetic, Robert had a good technique and caused more anxiety than pain up to this point. Then the dentist/agent pushed the thumb handle of the syringe, introducing the devil's fire around Pablo's inferior alveolar nerve. Instead of the customary numbness of the tongue, lower lip, and jaw, the injection site burned hot, as if being poked with a scorching iron probe. Pablo's neck restraint had been loosened just enough to permit him a blood-curdling scream, but not enough to permit even the slightest wiggle.

Robert removed the needle and looked on as the pounding burn traveled to areas normally anesthetized. The drug lord frantically and unsuccessfully tried to cool his burning lip with the saliva on his tongue. Then the devil's fire spread through soft tissue to his lingual nerve, giving his tongue the same blistering torment. Pablo let out another scream so loud that the three agents worried the soundproofing of the basement would be inadequate. Tears streamed from Alva's good eye and blood trickled from his wrecked eye as he screamed over and over again. Only periodic and frantic gasps for air interrupted the pain-induced shrieks.

As the screams continued, Robert wondered how Pablo could have survived if the caustic liquid lasted as long as regular anesthetic. But just then, the screaming subsided. Luckily, devil's fire had been specially reformulated to last for only five minutes. Original preparations of the substance lasted for up to an hour, making subjects so irrational and overcome with pain that it interfered with interrogation dialogue. Two subjects had even gone into cardiac arrest as a result of the unrelenting agony from the longer-acting formula.

"Robert Cline, I forgive you…You are still my brother, but you are a terrible dentist," panted Alva, trying to regain his breath and straining to be understood while talking around the mouth gag.

"It's burning medicine. I'm actually good at giving shots," replied Robert in defense of his dentistry skills.

"Are you ready to talk?" asked Kevin.

"Never."

"OK, another shot, Doc," ordered Kevin.

Robert reluctantly reloaded his syringe, while Pablo's good eye looked up and backward fearfully.

"No, no, no, no!" hollered Pablo just before Robert injected. He quickly listed the names and addresses of three drug distributers, while Kevin took notes.

"You aren't bullshitting me, are you, Pablo?" quizzed Kevin.

"No, I'm giving you good information. I promise."

Kevin paused, looking on with a skeptically raised eyebrow. Then he pulled out his satellite cell phone and rapidly entered several digits. "Hey, Harpole, it's Agent Smith. How's it going?... Yeah, we've got Alva strapped to Dr. Cline's dental chair here.... No, he wasn't wanting to talk, but after a little dental work, he's got some info for us. I just thought I'd verify that these are real names and addresses."

Kevin read off the information he'd taken from Pablo. He waited while George entered the data into his computer back at the George Bush Center for Intelligence in Virginia.

Kevin continued, "Yeah, I understand." He laughed. "Isn't that the way it always goes?" He folded up the phone and put it back in his pocket.

"All right, George says none of the addresses you gave me even exist, so I assume the names are also bogus. Go ahead and take out a molar for me, Cline."

Beads of perspiration formed on Robert's forehead. At the same time sweat streamed down Pablo's face. Robert was breathing heavily, while Pablo was gasping for air. "Come on, man, just give them what they want," Robert lobbied as he turned to his instruments and reached for the number-twenty-three forceps, also known to dentists as the "cow horns." The twenty-three, shaped with two sharp claws, was designed to clamp beneath the gum line and wedge under the bone between the double roots of mandibular molars. Robert was hoping the mere sight of the most horrific looking of all extraction forceps might cause Pablo to simply give in.

"Do what you have to, my brother, but I cannot betray my family." Pablo closed his one good eye and braced himself.

Robert reluctantly squeezed the jaws of the cow horns around Alva's lower left first molar. As the instrument wedged into the bone between the tooth's roots, he used the forceps' leverage to apply heavy force to one side, then to the other. Pablo screamed and tried to push the instrument away with his tongue... to no avail.

"Don't you have it out yet, Cline?" asked Troy.

Irritated, Robert replied, "These teeth usually have really long roots. Most of the time I use my high-speed handpiece to cut them in half and remove each side individually, but I don't have the right drill tips for that." With every tug Pablo squinted and squealed.

"Just pull harder, Cline. You're holding that thing like a girl," criticized Troy.

"Well, I'll have you know that there are lots of woman dentists who pull teeth. This thing creates so much leverage that a child could use it. The trick is not breaking the tooth off at the gum line."

Alva winced and cried as Robert kept working and arguing with Agent Mercer.

"Who the hell cares if you break it off at the gum line, Cline? Just break it off!"

Only Robert, who was used to deciphering the words of his patients while he worked, understood Pablo who pleaded, "No, please, no."

"Yeah, just go ahead and break it, Doc. It will work all the same for what we're doing," added Agent Smith.

Shit, thought Robert. He'd never broken a tooth away from the root. He was trained not to. He wondered if he should simply submit his resignation right now and walk away. But quitting in the middle of a US intelligence mission was considered treason. He continued to push and pull, while the tooth showed only subtle movement as the surrounding bone expanded slowly.

"Maybe we should have gotten one of those woman dentists you're talking about. Just break it off, Cline!" Troy demanded.

"I thought you were supposed to shut the hell up!" barked Robert while he continued to push and twist. He didn't enjoy inflicting pain, and he wondered if he could have been hating this as much as Alva. The operator and patient were both now drenched in sweat. A stream of blood rolled from Pablo's mouth and down his cheek just before there was a noticeable cracking sound. Pablo screamed in agony, and then coughed, splattering blood in Robert's face. The tooth was out. Robert had managed to extract it in one piece, but a large chunk of bone had also broken away from the jaw and was sticking to the roots of the molar.

Pablo's good eye rolled back in his head again as he passed out. Robert was also feeling a little faint.

"Atta boy, Doc. You strapped on your man pants. Wow, look at that hunk of bone you broke out with the tooth. I wouldn't want you for my dentist," jabbed Troy. Kevin also chuckled a bit, trying not to let Robert notice.

Assholes, thought Robert. He wadded up some cotton gauze and applied pressure to the socket to slow down the bleeding just as Pablo came to.

Alva mumbled through a mouth of hands, gauze, and the Jennings Gag. "You are keeping me from bleeding to death, aren't you? Thank you, Robert Cline."

"What did he say?" asked Kevin.

"I don't know. Why don't you just get on with this," snapped Robert. How the hell can this freak still be grateful to me? he thought.

"What do you have for us now, Pablo? I need some real names and locations," demanded Kevin.

"Nothing. I will tell you nothing."

"This obviously isn't working, Smith. I'm not going to sit here and extract all of this guy's teeth while he spits blood in my face and refuses to talk," Robert protested. "We might as well just let Troy keep punching his teeth out."

"Sounds like a good plan," added Troy.

Kevin interrupted, "No, it's not a good plan! If you don't want to keep pulling teeth, maybe you could do a root canal. I hear those are painful even with anesthetic. Besides Cline, as a specialist agent you get paid twice as much as a regular agent with your same experience.

If you don't want to do dental work, then I'm not sure what use you are to the agency.

"Root canals do *not* hurt when we use anesthetic," Robert said, standing up for his profession.

"What do you *mean* he gets paid twice as much as a regular rookie agent? That's bullshit." It appeared that smoke might start to pour from Troy's ears as the gears inside his head began to turn. He laboriously did the math that brought him to the conclusion that Robert probably already earned as much as he did after ten years of service.

"Never mind that," said Kevin. "We need to get this guy to talk. We also have to get his device planted soon. It's already eleven thirty, and there's a stealth bomber circling on standby off the coast of Florida, waiting for orders to fire. So get a little more aggressive, Doc, and get us some information."

Troy continued to be distracted by his infuriating salary calculations. "I only make a little under twice what I earned ten years ago. Cline probably makes *more* than me!"

"Can you just focus for more than five minutes, you idiot?" Kevin was losing patience with Troy.

"I have an idea," said Robert, interrupting.

"It's above your pay grade to have an idea!" shouted Troy.

"Well, apparently it's *not* above my pay grade Mercer, and this might just work." Robert hadn't realized that his specialty status earned him double pay compared to other agents, but the new information energized him a bit.

Troy turned red with anger, but Kevin wanted to hear more. "What do you got, Cline?"

"In my kit back here I have a handful of disposable syringes of Midazolam that we're supposed to use to sedate Pablo before we take him out to the boat. I use stuff like this to relax patients when I extract wisdom teeth all the time. People get real compliant when they're on it. They even start talking about things I usually don't want to hear. It's like truth serum. If you don't use too much, it won't put people to sleep. It just relaxes them and makes them ultra-cooperative. Let me inject a small dose right now. Then I'll trade in this devil's fire crap for some real anesthetic. I'll get him numb so I can get the missile-guidance device implanted without his tongue thrashing around. When that's out of the way, we can see if he'll start talking. We couldn't get any less information than we've gotten so far."

"That's a stupid idea," Agent Mercer protested.

"Let's try it," said Agent Smith.

Robert walked back to his operator position behind Pablo. He put on clean gloves and a mask. He grabbed one of the four syringes containing a solution with 1.0 mg of Midazolam and injected half of the sedative hypnotic into a superficial vein on Alva's forearm.

Within seconds Pablo's good eye drooped. He looked up at Robert, struggling to see past a heavy eyelid, while his bad eye was still fixed open and aimed off to the side.

"This should help things go a little better for you, buddy." For Robert, it was hard not to like a person who liked him so much. He was relieved to be able to de-escalate the intensity of the situation several hundred notches.

Robert mounted a new sharp 27 gauge long shaft needle onto his dental syringe and inserted a carpule of lidocaine 2 percent with 1:50,000 epinephrine. "Who in the agency orders these supplies?" he whispered critically under his breath. The anesthetic blend had a higher concentration of adrenaline than usual. "This stuff could give his ticker a big challenge if I'm not careful."

Robert used the needle to pierce the oral soft tissue. He carefully pulled back on the thumb loop, checking for negative aspiration to make sure he wasn't in a blood vessel. He knew that injecting anesthetic with such a high concentration of epinephrine into a vein could send a patient into an unstable tachycardia heart rhythm, leading to cardiac arrest. After a negative aspiration for blood, Robert slowly deposited the anesthetic. Pablo didn't flinch. He was awake but very relaxed.

Robert pulled the operator light down so it wasn't shining in Pablo's bloodied face and sat back in his chair to wait for the anesthetic to take effect.

"What are you doing Cline?" asked Troy.

"What do you mean?" Robert replied.

"What are you waiting for?" demanded Troy.

"I'm waiting for him to get numb."

Agent Mercer was incensed. "Oh, you're kidding. What is this? Some kind of dental spa now, Cline?" He turned to their senior agent. "What in the hell are we doing here, Kevin? Are we letting a rookie run the show now? This is complete bullshit!"

"Shut up and stand there with your freaking suction tube like a good dental assistant," ordered Agent Smith. "Oh, and don't give me that angry look. Your face is almost as red as your damn nut sack."

Agent Mercer's face immediately went from red with anger to red with embarrassment.

Robert interrupted, "According to the instructions they left me for placing the global positioner, I need to have a perfect four-by-four-by-four-millimeter, box-shaped tooth prep. It says if I drill too deep, the device may not transmit accurately through the filling. I'm also supposed to keep everything clean and dry when I cover it, or the electronic components could get damaged. I'm pretty sure that Pablo will need to be comfortable and still in order for me to properly place this thing and fill over it. Therefore, I will be waiting until he's numb."

Troy calmed down, and Robert gently removed the duct tape from around Pablo's head. He waited another five minutes for his patient to be fully anesthetized.

"All right, let's try this out," said Robert. "Can you turn your head my way buddy?" Pablo, almost asleep, compliantly turned toward Robert. "I spotted a cavity in there that I'm going to try to fix up for you."

"OK, amigo," the disoriented Alva responded through the Jennings Gag.

"This guy really is out of it." Kevin chuckled.

"Now, Troy, just flip the lever and hold the high-volume suction tube in the corner of his mouth there for me while I drill," instructed Robert.

Troy flipped the hand lever, producing a powerful vacuum airflow. *Whshhhhhhhh.* Pleased with himself, he smiled and boasted, "This dentistry stuff isn't that hard."

Robert began to painlessly shape a four-millimeter, cube-shaped preparation. Troy happily pulled large volumes of water, saliva, and residual blood, clearing the way for Alva to breathe comfortably.

"Squaaaaa!" A startling screech wailed from Pablo's mouth causing everyone in the soundproof room to jump except the patient, who was drifting in and out of a dream.

"What's going on, Cline?" Troy asked in a panic.

Robert quickly grabbed the obstructed suction tube out of Agent Mercer's hand, while the agent gratefully let him. Cline flipped the lever to the "off" position and removed the suction from Pablo's mouth, causing a faint popping sound.

"What was that?" asked Kevin, looking concerned.

"That was Pablo's uvula," replied Robert, chuckling. He looked up at Troy. "You don't need to get the suction back so far."

"That thing's powerful," said Agent Mercer.

"Just position it here in the corner of the cheek. It's strong enough to draw water from the back of his throat without actually *putting* it in the back of his throat." Robert placed the tip of the suction tube in the proper location, and then allowed Troy to retake control of the handle.

Robert resumed his work, while Pablo lay comfortably at rest. The drug lord periodically opened his good eye, while his bad eye remained fixed open and aimed off to the side. Troy was starting to feel quite proud of his suctioning skills, while Robert refined his tooth preparation to perfect specifications.

Turning back to his instrument setup, Robert opened one of the vials that contained the global-positioning missile guidance device and got it ready to try it into his tooth prep. He paused, thinking for a moment, and then removed the Jennings Gag. The other two agents wondered what Robert was doing until he asked, "Hey, Pablo, who are your distributors back in the United States?"

Pablo's good eye was heavy, but he managed to force it open. Then he slowly listed the names of seven of his top distributors, while Kevin grinned and took notes from the foot of the chair. "Please don't tell those other two jerks though, amigo," Pablo whispered up to Robert.

"This guy's on Mars, isn't he?" Troy said, laughing.

"Shhh." Kevin held his finger to his lips, and then pointed to Robert, signaling for him to continue.

"Where do the distributors operate from?" asked Robert. Pablo gave specific locations, including, states, cities, and exact addresses.

"Maybe I should place the device before I ask him any more questions," said Robert.

"No, no, we're on a roll here, Cline. Continue." Kevin waved his hand forward, signaling him to resume questioning.

Suddenly, Troy shouted, demanding, "Where are your growers located, Alva!"

Pablo's good eye looked slowly away from Robert, and then up at Troy. With speech impeded from numbness and sedation, he grumbled, "I will tell you nothing, you whore." He tried to spit at Agent Mercer, but at this point he lacked the necessary coordination and managed only to spray a little saliva and blood into his own good eye.

Kevin dropped his notepad to the floor, raised his hands to his head, and pushed his hair back slowly, looking up at the ceiling. "Shut the hell up, Mercer! What in the world is wrong with you?"

Pablo slowly added, "Yes…You can just shut the hell up…I will not talk to you…I will only talk to Robert Cline, *mi hermano*."

Kevin frowned at Mercer, and then nodded for Cline to continue.

"Where are your growers, Pablo?" asked Robert. "I promise I won't tell these guys."

"Yes, amigo…I will only tell you." Pablo gave locations of several drug plantations and refining laboratories across Colombia and Mexico.

Kevin and Troy tried to muffle their laughter. "Wow, it's like he knows we're standing right here, but he doesn't know we're standing right here," whispered Kevin.

Robert continued asking questions, and Pablo continued to answer. The drug lord revealed more distributers, drug trafficking transport routes, and even the name of a US senator who owned several warehouses where cocaine and pot were stored prior to distribution.

Kevin cross-checked the intelligence with Agent Harpole via his satellite phone. "Harpole says we already have some of this data, but it all checks out so far," Kevin said.

Only a few minutes after Alva had given up all the information he had, he started to become a little more alert.

"That wore off pretty fast," Robert said. He injected another cc of 0.5 mg/ml Midazolam, causing Pablo to drift off to sleep.

"OK, but don't use it all up," said Kevin. "We're probably going to need more of that later to keep him quiet on the boat. You did good, Cline. I think we got about all we're going to get out of him, so go ahead and finish placing the device."

Robert reinserted the Jennings Gag and squeezed the ratchet handles, opening Alva's mouth to a comfortable, but secure position. "All right, Troy. Get ready with the suction." Robert rinsed and dried the tooth, while Troy collected the water from the corner of Pablo's cheek. "Good job. You're better than some of my assistants back at the public health dental clinic."

His agent/assistant nodded and gave a cocky glance up to Kevin, who rolled his eyes.

"OK, Troy, now turn off the suction and just use the tube to reflect the cheek back for me a bit." Dental assistant Mercer followed Doctor Cline's instructions, flipping the lever to stop the vacuum airflow. Robert isolated the tooth with cotton rolls to keep the area clear of saliva. He brushed a thin coat of Optibond XTR dental adhesive in the tooth prep and hardened it with a curing light. He pressed the tiny activation button on the missile-guidance device, then meticulously placed it with cotton pliers into the prepared tooth at the specified orientation. He turned and reached back to his instrument table, picking up some composite resin filling material to pack around the device.

Wshhhhhhhhh.

Robert turned back abruptly and looked into the tooth. The device was gone. "What in the world are you doing, Troy?"

"What?" his dental assistant asked defensively.

"You sucked up the device! Why on earth would you turn on the suction?"

"He was getting some spit back in the corner of his mouth," said Troy.

"Where does the suction go?" asked Kevin.

"With most setups it would get trapped in a filter, but these tubes look like they go straight to sewer pipes." Exasperated, Robert exclaimed, "The thing is gone!"

"Don't worry, Doc, we've got another one," said Kevin.

"But I activated it. What if a missile gets launched into the island sewer plant?"

"No, no. I'll call Harpole back with the serial number on the vial of the backup device. They'll program the missile to follow the signal from the second transmitter. Besides, these things become inactive if they get wet, remember?" Kevin looked at Troy. "Please don't suck up the second device, Mercer."

"It's not as easy as it looks to control this thing, you know!" complained Troy.

Robert activated and placed the backup device into Alva's tooth. He gently packed composite filling material around it, being careful not to disturb the orientation of the transmitter. He light hardened the first layer of material; then he placed a second layer, sculpting the tooth back to its original anatomy. After he was finished hardening the filling, no one could have known from looking that any work had been done at all. The tooth looked perfect, as if it had never been touched.

"Nice work, Cline," said Troy. "Maybe I'd let you be my dentist after all."

Exhausted, Robert removed his gloves and mask. "Now what?" he asked.

"Well, that whole little fiasco only took a couple of hours," replied Kevin. "Island Coast Guard should be off patrol by now, so I guess we get this guy on our boat and try the guidance system out."

Kevin walked behind the dental chair and picked up the vial that had held the backup missile-guidance device. Then he connected to Agent Harpole on the video conference monitor. Harpole instructed Kevin to simply use his pocket satellite phone to text the serial number on the vial back to the agency thirty minutes before they were ready for impact.

"Make sure you guys will be at least one hundred yards away from Alva when the strike occurs," George said from the satellite video screen. "The long-range missile will launch when you key in the serial number, and it will strike exactly thirty minutes later. Please memorize the serial number in case you lose the vial. Also, please be sure to watch the impact. The agency needs visual confirmation that this thing works."

Kevin read the serial number aloud. "Five four three two one. Boy, that's a tough one. I bet it took the encryption team a while to put that together. I might need you guys to help me remember that," he said sarcastically to Robert and Troy, who were now also hovering over the video monitor.

"Five four three two one? What happened to the first device: one two three four five?" asked George. "Did you drop it down his throat after all, Cline?" He laughed in his trademark slow, rhythmic chuckle.

Disgusted, Robert replied, "Yeah..., something like that."

"All three of you need to remember the number, so we made it simple," said George. "You never know, Smith. You could fall overboard and get eaten by a shark or something. Then one of these guys would have to enter the code."

Kevin smirked, clearly annoyed that everyone at the agency had always made a joke of his rumored fear of sharks. "Don't worry, George. I'll be staying in the boat tonight."

"Well, let's hope so." His tone became more serious. "You're going to be operating in the dark the rest of the night. You will only use moonlight—no lights, and no night-vision goggles giving off heat. Nothing. We can't afford for you to get spotted. You will place four small radar-scattering devices on the panga boat and the catamaran. This will make you completely invisible to radar. Of course, once the missile strikes, island navy and Coast Guard boats will rush out to the explosion. But while they're moving in to investigate, you will slip straight back to shore, unnoticed. Any questions?"

The three agents looked at each other and back at the video monitor. "I guess not," replied Kevin.

"Good. You'll find three pairs of black, night-camo coveralls lying in the corner of the basement for you to slip over your clothes. Report back when you return to the shell," ordered Harpole. The screen went dark.

16

THE MAST

Kevin slapped Troy on the back and said, "Let's do this, big fella." The agents quickly grabbed the three black coveralls that were neatly folded in the corner. They slipped the garments over their clothes and smeared black face paint on their exposed skin to help them disappear into the night.

Then Agent Mercer went to work. He unfolded a large, black cloth sack lying next to the coveralls. He quickly unstrapped Alva from the dental chair while leaving his arms and legs tightly bound together. Troy ripped off another piece of duct tape and pressed it firmly across the drug lord's mouth, while Pablo slept comfortably with his bad eye opened and aimed off to the side. The agent single-handedly lifted Alva and dumped him into the bag. He wound the opening shut with more duct tape.

"You need a hand there, Mercer?" asked Kevin.

"I got this," said Troy. This was what he did, and this was the reason he'd been chosen for the mission. He was gorilla strong and more than capable of muscling around sedated compliant, or alert resistant subjects. Robert hated to admit it, but it probably would have been difficult to subdue and control Pablo without Agent Mercer.

Troy jogged up the stairs, looking like a young Mafia Santa Clause, all dressed in black, with his jet-black hair matching the jet-black Pablo sack he had hanging over his shoulder.

Kevin picked up his pocket satellite phone and turned it off before putting it in his pocket. "Make sure to bring more of that sleepy juice in case Alva wakes up, Cline. We definitely don't want to have him fighting us."

Robert quickly grabbed the last three hypodermics of Midazolam sedative, the true hero of the operation. He slipped the syringes into his black army fatigue chest pocket. Then he and Kevin hurried up the stairs and out the front door, locking it behind them.

Agent Smith stuck an adhesive-backed, red LED light to the outside of the door and turned it on. "The lighthouse on the southern point of the island will keep us from getting lost at sea, but this little guy will guide our boat right back to the shell house when we get closer to shore," Kevin told Robert. The two agents caught up with Troy, who had already hauled Alva across the street and down to the rocky beach.

Troy dumped the sack containing Pablo into the *Hay Caramba* panga boat, while the wind swirled and gusted. Light from the full moon illuminated white-capped waves, which continually slapped against the rocks. The three men connected the catamaran sailboat to the panga motorboat with canvas tow straps so they could pull the hobby craft behind them. Kevin and Troy quickly removed tabs, exposing adhesive on the radar-scattering devices and stuck four onto each of the boats. Then they launched the pair into the turbulent sea. Kevin manned the motor at the rear of the *Hay Caramba*, while Robert and Troy grabbed onto their seats. The powerful, little fishing boat pulled away from the shore, cutting through the choppy water while it violently tossed them about.

"Better take your Zofran, Cline!" shouted Kevin over the wind and roaring motor. He pulled two tablets from his pocket and handed one to Robert. They each swallowed a pill before seasickness had a chance to take hold.

The boat sped deep into the shadowy, moonlit night, skipping and swaying all the way. The feather-light catamaran they towed rarely kissed the blackened sea below. It mostly flew like a kite three to six feet off the water. In this area the waves were smaller but much choppier than the large sea swells where the whale sharks fed. Robert watched the lights from Isla de Mujeres fade in the distance as they sped out to sea for nearly twenty minutes. He hoped Kevin knew what he was doing, while it seemed they were about to lose sight of the island completely.

"Harpole told me to travel straight east off the coast for twenty-five minutes," Kevin shouted over the roaring motor. "That should make it difficult for the island Coast Guard to pinpoint the location of the explosion, but we're getting *way* the hell out here!" They could barely see the fading glow pulsing from the Punta Sur Lighthouse.

Kevin abruptly killed the motor. Now the only sound came from the swirling wind and steadily clapping waves. "That's as far as I go," he said. "Another quarter mile, and we are going to lose the lighthouse altogether. I don't care what George says. I'm not getting us lost out here."

Good, thought Robert.

Kevin took out his satellite phone and turned it on. He pulled up the agency and texted the launch code: 54321. "We've got thirty minutes to get Pablo tied to the catamaran and get our distance," he said. "We'd better get moving, or we'll all go up in smoke with him."

"Why did you enter the sequence already?" questioned Troy. "Couldn't you have at least let us get him onto the other boat first?"

"We have to be quick about this," Kevin said. "The island Coast Guard supposedly doesn't patrol this late, but we can't take any chances. If we screw around out here too long, we just might get noticed."

Troy plopped down on one of the seats and threw his hands up in despair. "Well, what if something goes wrong?"

"Nothing is going to go wrong," reassured Kevin.

Just then the black sack containing Pablo started to move. Indiscernible and heavily muffled shouting immediately followed. "Give him another shot of the sleepy juice, Doc," said Kevin.

Robert reached into his black coverall chest pocket and found nothing. He frantically checked his other pockets, but he knew he'd specifically put the sedative-loaded syringes in his shirt pocket. Pablo moaned and let out more muffled shouts.

"What are you doing, Cline? Shoot him up," demanded Troy.

Somehow the syringes had fallen out when Robert was helping launch the boats. Looking all around, he admitted, "I don't think I have them…They must have dropped into the water or something. I'm so sorry. I should have secured them better."

"Nothing's going to go wrong, huh?" said Troy, looking up at Kevin and shaking his head in disgust. Troy looked back downward and punched Alva twice through the bag. "If you don't shut up in there, I'm going to keep punching you!" He turned back to the other two agents. "Who needs a little shot when we've got the big cannons?" Troy flexed his massive biceps, and then quickly unraveled the duct tape to open the sack. "Why does the agency need a dentist special-ist agent anyway? The Doc busted a tooth; I busted a tooth. The Doc knocked the patient out; I knocked the patient out…twice."

In spite of his crude methods, Troy was clearly taking charge of this phase of the mission. "Let's get this done," he said. "I'm sure that missile is already a third of the way here from Florida."

Robert and Kevin balanced themselves in the bouncing *Hay Caramba,* while they pulled in the small catamaran sail craft from the tow straps. They fastened the two boats more tightly together so they could easily step from one to the other.

"You two get over onto the sailboat, and I'll hand him over to you," said Troy. He pulled the bloodied drug lord out of the black bag and flung him over his shoulder, where Pablo hung limp. Kevin and Robert carefully stepped out of the panga boat and down onto the platform of the catamaran. They both held onto the single wooden mast, fighting to keep their balance amid the turbulent, churning tide.

The men worked in the cover of the night, but their eyes were becoming well-adjusted in the moonlight.

Troy single-handedly lifted Pablo with ease across to Kevin and Robert, who struggled as a team to hold up his listless body. Each choppy wave was followed by another, and the platform of the lighter sail craft didn't provide a stable surface for standing. "Just hold on to him, and I'll trade places with you, Kevin," said Troy as he loaded himself with rope and duct tape.

Robert held tightly onto Pablo with one hand and the wooden mast with the other, while Kevin and Troy met where the boats were joined to slide past one another. Troy stepped down onto the catamaran and steadied himself by holding onto the mast with Robert.

Kevin cleanly stepped up onto the edge of the panga boat with his right foot, and completely missed the boat with his left. A horribly familiar rush of salt water filled Agent Smith's nose and throat. Extreme panic set in as his violently swinging arms and desperately kicking legs didn't seem to help the fact that he was sinking into the cool, black sea. The agent opened his eyes, hoping to see the surface, but through the sting of salt water, he could see only darkness.

Kevin tried to swim for the top, but he was so disoriented that he feared he might be swimming down deeper instead of up for air. He struggled to hold his breath for as long as possible but knew an involuntary gasp was coming in seconds. If he didn't make contact with the surface soon, he'd draw in a full breath of water and die at sea. In a moment of dark serenity, calmness set in just before death. He gave up and stopped kicking. His lungs burned for oxygen, but he mentally prepared for seawater instead. He held his breath for five seconds longer than he thought he would be able to, but the life urge for air overcame his struggle to resist breathing.

An involuntary gasp sucked in seawater initially, but only a bit. Then there was air. Kevin's large belly had acted like a buoy and floated him right up to the surface. He immediately choked up the small amount of water he'd aspirated.

"Agent Smith! Are you OK?" shouted Robert. He and Troy were bent over the edge of the catamaran where they'd been frantically searching for their senior agent.

Kevin continued to cough and choke. He was initially relieved that he hadn't drowned, but he quickly remembered his worst fear. "Get me the hell out of here before I get torn to pieces by sharks!" he screamed as he resumed thrashing on the surface of the water.

"You heard Juan earlier, Kevin. I really don't think there are that many sharks this close to the island," said Troy.

"That's easy for you to say. You're not in the damn water. Now get me out of here!"

Troy moved over to the more stable fishing boat. He lowered his hand and pulled his friend back on board. Robert stayed on the catamaran, still holding onto Alva.

"If I get dumped in the son-of-a-bitching water one more time on this mission, I'm going to resign!" Kevin was dripping wet, furious about his second involuntary spill of the day.

"Well, the next time you go in the water, you'll probably already be dead after getting hit with the missile, since you already entered the launch code," complained Troy. "According to my watch, your little swim only leaves about ten minutes to get the hell away from Alva before the rocket hits him in the face and wipes us all out."

Troy quickly climbed back to the catamaran. "OK, Cline, we need to hurry." The two agents lifted Pablo to a standing position and leaned him on the mast. "You just hold him up while I tie him onto this thing. We should be able to see him hanging here from a distance."

Robert held on, while Troy used rope and duct tape to secure the drug lord to the wooden beam anchored to the platform of the catamaran. They fettered his chest, arms, and legs securely.

Alva wasn't going anywhere. He was bound more tightly to the mast than he'd been to the *General Anaya* or the dental chair. Troy pulled the final two feet of duct tape off the roll and started to twist it around Pablo's neck before Robert stopped him. "Is that really necessary? There's no way he's going to escape, and you're going to kill him if you cut off his airway. He's supposed to be alive."

"He's probably *already* dead," argued Troy.

"No, he's not dead, but he will be soon enough," said Robert. "Why don't you show a little humanity and have some respect for the guy before he dies. We've already tortured him, and we're about to kill him. I'm pretty sure he's not going to escape with or without pressing his neck into the beam. Let's just get out of here."

"Respect and humanity?" Agent Mercer ripped the duct tape off Pablo's neck, then, turning to Robert, he chided, "This is the most notorious drug cartel leader in the world, Cline. He's responsible for ruining the lives of thousands of Americans. He doesn't need respect!" He angrily wadded the tape into a ball and threw it into the water.

Just then Pablo regained consciousness and arduously lifted his drooping head. Clearly in pain, the drug lord looked at Robert with despair.

Troy brutally ripped the duct tape off Pablo's mouth. "You have any last words, Alva?" he demanded.

Pablo gathered his last ounce of strength to straighten his neck. He spit in Troy's face and shouted, "Whore!"

Furious, Troy punched Pablo repeatedly in the ribs, and then kneed him in the groin. "I'm not going to put the tape back on your mouth because I want to hear you scream just before the missile hits you in the face!"

He punched Pablo again, causing blood to shoot from his mouth. Pablo barely clung to consciousness. His neck went limp in exhaustion, and his head drooped back down to his chest.

"Let's go!" ordered Kevin from the panga boat. "Five minutes until impact!"

Troy and Robert quickly jumped from the catamaran into the *Hay Caramba*, joining Kevin. They frantically worked to separate the two seacrafts.

While the agents unraveled the tow straps, Pablo lifted his head. "You will always be my brother, Robert Cline." Robert heard the voice but tried not to listen. "All of this changes nothing. I am still grateful that you saved my life, amigo."

Robert looked up at the drug lord for only a moment and was instantly grief struck as he saw the sincerity in Pablo's good eye. Horrified, the rookie agent immediately looked away.

Kevin started up the rumbling outboard motor just as Troy cut the final tow strap. "Go ahead and keep running your mouth, Pablo!" shouted Troy. "It'll be stuffed full of a USA warhead any minute now!"

Troy and Robert held onto their seats as Kevin carefully backed the panga away from the catamaran.

Pablo cried out to Robert. "I have done many bad things, and I am getting what I deserve, but I know you were only doing your job, my brother! You are a good man, Robert Cline!"

Robert continued looking away.

With a powerful thrust of the propeller, the three agents sped off from the drug lord, who stood bound to the catamaran.

"You are a good man, Robert Cline! I forgive you! You are a good man!" Pablo shouted, spending his last measure of strength. Then his neck went limp again, and he hung, weeping and listless on the mast of the small sail craft.

The panga boat raced to a safe distance a hundred yards away before Agent Smith killed the motor. The sea had calmed, becoming eerily still. The surface of the water reflected the moon's cool-white light and a mirrored image of the drug lord hanging on the mast.

The three agents were silent as they looked on and waited for a long two minutes, which seemed like an eternity. The sea was placid and quiet, and the sky was clear.

Suddenly, from the dark of night a starry light appeared in the sky. It expanded exponentially and began to overtake the moonlight with each passing second. The bright-orange fire in the sky grew a tail and developed a howling roar as it moved ever closer. It shined brightly on Alva as it swelled. A heavy feeling of despair overcame Robert, while he looked on through tear-filled eyes.

The drug lord momentarily raised his drooping head and helplessly gazed up at the powerful advancing light from the mast where he hung. There was a great flash with a thunderous explosion, and then there was nothing. Alva had been simply wiped clean from the earth.

The hot glow had momentarily burned the image of Pablo's execution onto Robert's retinas so he could see the shadow of Alva in his eyes even when they were closed. The retinal burn slowly faded, but the image of the drug lord hanging on the mast just before his death was permanently scorched onto Robert's soul.

Turbulent rings of waves from the explosion broke the stillness of the sea, rocking the panga boat from side to side.

"Let's get out of here before the island Coast Guard comes to figure out what the hell that was," said Kevin. He started up the outboard motor, and the agents sped back toward the distant beam from the island lighthouse.

None of the three men said a word for the entire duration of the boat ride. Gradually a few island lights became visible, while more and more joined with every passing moment. They continued to cut through the water of the calm sea, eventually spotting the red LED light that Kevin had placed on the front door of their beach rental. It guided them straight back to the rocky beach just in front of the shell house.

17

CLEANUP

The next morning agents Smith, Mercer, and Cline boarded the 6:00 a.m. ferry, leaving Isla de Mujeres for Puerto Juarez near Cancún. While they sat for the short ferry ride, the CIA prep crew was already at work cleaning the shell house.

The cleanup staff routinely traveled behind field agents and wiped away visible and invisible evidence of even the messiest missions. The crew removed large splatters of Pablo's blood, chunks of teeth and bone; even Pablo's shriveled-up eyelid. After they were finished, *no* investigator would be able to find as much as a hair from the drug lord's head. The crew removed the soundproofing insulation that they'd installed just days before. They even replaced the splintered oar that was used to fracture Alva's eye socket. They cleaned and returned the Panga boat, paying the rental fee, in addition to paying for replacement of the catamaran all together.

Robert, Kevin, and Troy sat next to each other in the cabin of the ferry's lower deck. Dark morning clouds had moved in, spilling rain and graying the Caribbean water. Robert gazed aimlessly through the window. He hadn't slept all night, replaying the entire mission over and over in his mind. He was exhausted. He was also annoyed by Troy and Kevin, who already seemed to have put the successful mission behind them.

"I can't believe I lost the damned satellite phone when I was in the water," complained Kevin.

"Yeah, but it turns out that it was a good thing you entered the launch code before you fell in. Otherwise the mission would have been dead in the water." Troy laughed obnoxiously and elbowed Robert. "Did you hear that, Cline? I said the mission would have been dead in the water. Maybe I should put in my notice and work on my stand-up routine."

"Yeah, that's hilarious," mumbled Robert, not looking away from the window.

Also not amused, Kevin continued, "Those portable satellite phones are specially made for the agency and supposedly cost four thousand dollars."

"Are you shitting me? You can't even surf the web on those things," joked Troy. "I wouldn't trade one straight across for my iPhone."

"Yeah, tell me about it," Kevin said. "What's worse is they always take this kind of stuff into consideration when it's time to hand out year-end bonuses. Three years ago I broke a forty-thousand-dollar, antiaircraft, shoulder-mounted missile launcher in Yemen and only received a turkey for my annual bonus."

Troy and Kevin continued to ramble on in the background, while Robert looked out to the gray sky. The events of the day before started to blur as the rain and waves lethargically rolled under the ferry. With each passing wave, Robert slowly blinked until he drifted off to sleep.

18

RESIGNATION

Eight hours later

Robert drank lukewarm coffee from a white Styrofoam cup while sitting in an uncomfortable, metal-framed chair with a time-faded, powder-blue cushion. He tried not to be irritated that Christmas music was playing in the middle of August in the small waiting area on the second floor of the George Bush Center for Intelligence in Langley, Virginia.

He attempted to ignore the Healed Earth-approved fluorescent tubes flickering overhead and the stains on the once-powder-blue carpet below. Robert was already stiff due to a long day of travel from the Yucatán, and his fifteen-year-old chair wasn't helping any. He tried to read a magazine to get his mind off the torture and execution of Pablo Alva, but he had difficulty getting interested in the seven-year-old fishing publication.

Robert, who didn't like to fish, was periodically torn away from a comparative analysis of trout baits by intermittent outbursts of laughter coming from behind the closed office door of Case Officer George Harpole. Robert waited nearly an hour for his very first debriefing, while agents Smith and Mercer seemed to thoroughly enjoy recounting all the mission's details to Agent Harpole.

In between eruptions of laughter, Robert found himself annoyed by the vigorous and heavy-handed typing of Harpole's secretary, who sat at her government-issue desk directly across from him. Phyllis Joyfield had been George's personal assistant the entire fifteen years since he'd moved out of the field and into the agency headquarters. Robert estimated that she might have been typing upward of two hundred words per minute.

Phyllis had a kind face, wore big glasses, and had big hair. She maintained a constant smile but seemed to have sad eyes that strained to hide a personal life filled with challenges. She wore a plus-size home-made dress that was as faded as the carpet and chair cushions in the waiting area. While typing, Mrs. Joyfield quietly sang along with her twenty-year-old Christmas CD into the microphone that hung from her headset telephone.

Why the hell do those guys get interviewed together while I have to sit out here and wait? thought Robert.

"Hey, can I ask you something?" Phyllis asked in a loud voice while she continued to pound her keyboard.

Robert looked up from his magazine, breaking away from a paragraph dedicated to night crawlers. "Sure. What would you like to know?" he asked.

"Could you pick up some milk for me on your way home?" Phyllis asked while looking right at Robert with a lonely smile.

Robert looked behind himself and all around. Surely she can't be talking to me, he thought, turning back to the secretary. "Excuse me?" he said.

"Thanks, cutie. Love you." She smiled while her eyes seemed to be full of tears that never fell. She quickly pushed a button on her phone-control panel sitting next to her keyboard and immediately resumed typing.

Oh, gosh, she was talking to someone on her headset phone, thought Robert, embarrassed. He shook his head and cringed before relocating his place in the night-crawler dissertation.

"Hi-low," said Phyllis cheerfully while typing and staring at Robert. Robert continued reading.

"Hi-low!" she said again, this time with kind of an aggressive cheerfulness.

Robert slowly pulled the magazine, which had lost its cover page three years ago, down below his eyes and looked up at the smiling secretary. "Excuse me?" he said.

"Oh, I just said hi-low. That's all," Phyllis replied, laughing energetically and smiling as big as ever.

"Are you talking to me?" asked Robert, again looking all around.

"Uh-huh," she replied, nodding and typing feverishly.

"What do you mean, high...low?" asked Robert.

"Oh, it's just what I say. It's hi...low, like a combination of *hi* and *hello* put together. Get it? Hi-low." Phyllis laughed loudly.

"OK. Sure I get it. That's great...Um, yeah, hi," Robert replied, wondering why they were exchanging greetings again after already having done so when he first arrived.

"Would you like some more coffee, hon?" Phyllis asked, still smiling and looking at Robert.

Robert looked down at his half-finished cup of joe, which hadn't even started off hot and was now very cold. "Well, maybe just—"

"OK. For all three?" she asked.

"Huh?" said Robert, bewildered. He quickly realized that she had switched from talking with him, to talking with Agent Harpole on the headset phone.

Phyllis promptly got up, prepared three Styrofoam cups of coffee, and took them into George's office.

"Coffee!" she shouted through teary-eyed laughter as she entered the office.

The dedicated secretary left the coffee behind and quickly returned to take her seat, where she resumed typing and singing with her Christmas CD.

"Would you like some more coffee, cutie?" Phyllis asked, still smiling and looking at Robert.

Am I just having a bad, freaking dream or what? thought Robert as he continued to read about trout bait.

"Did you hear me?" asked Phyllis.

Robert jerked the magazine down to his lap and looked up, irritated. "Are you talking to me?" he asked.

"Of course I'm talking to you. Who else would I be talking to?" Phyllis pushed out another aggressive, cheerful laugh.

"I'm good. Thanks." Robert wondered how much longer he would have to put up with this. They should use this lady and her freaky *headset* for enhanced interrogation, he thought. They wouldn't need to pull teeth or bring in Troy to punch people. Ten minutes in this waiting room with George's secretary would break down anyone. "No, but you don't happen to have any newer magazines, do you?" Robert asked politely.

"Nope. Budget cuts," replied Phyllis. "We used to get new ones every month until Jackson Dunham was elected president, Lord rest his soul. His party never really was a fan of the agency. We haven't had any new carpet, paint, furniture—and certainly no magazines—since they took control of the White House."

"Oh, right," replied Robert, looking back into his magazine.

"Hey, is it true that you are a real dentist?" asked Phyllis.

For the first time Robert knew for sure that George's secretary was talking to him. He feared what would follow was the same thing that would follow him for the rest of his life. Anytime a dentist was discovered in a social setting, they were asked to diagnose some kind of dental problem on the spot. Robert would eventually learn to deny the DDS when he wasn't working, but that would come years later.

"Yeah," replied Robert reluctantly.

Phyllis got up from the seat behind her government-issue, metal-frame, simulated-wood-top desk and walked over to him. "Can you tell if my dentist messed up my filling? Since I saw him last month, my back tooth has hurt me every time I eat candy." She sat in the faded-powder-blue seat next to Robert and opened her mouth widely, pulling back her cheek with her finger.

People didn't understand that flickering fluorescent light was no match for magnifying loops, operatory light, and an x-ray. "I really can't see back there," said Robert. "Your finger is pretty much covering all of your teeth on that side."

"Look closer," she said. "It seems like there's a piece out of it or something."

Why the hell are you eating so much candy that your tooth hurts anyway? he thought. "Yeah, you should probably get back in and see your own dentist if your tooth doesn't feel right."

"Oh...*Well.*" For the first time since they met, Phyllis's smile faded. She stood up and placed her hand on her chest just below her neck as if she'd been horribly offended. "No wonder he's working for the agency and not as a real dentist," she murmured quietly to herself as she walked back to her desk. "He must not be very good if he can't even figure out what's wrong with my tooth."

Before Robert had a chance to return to his magazine, his cell phone vibrated, signaling a text message from his dental assistant Nicole:

OMG. When are you going to come pick up your cat?

It's wreaking havoc with my dogs.

Suddenly, Case Officer Harpole's door was flung open, and agents Smith and Mercer emerged. "Have a great day, and send in Cline, will ya?" George hollered out from his office.

Thank God, thought Robert. This secretary lady is wearing me down.

"Jingle bells. Jingle bells. Jingle all the way," Phyllis sang while pounding on her keyboard.

"All right, Cline, you're up," Troy said in his heavy Brooklyn accent while he passed Robert and slapped him on the back. "It was a pleasure working with you, Doc. I'm on a plane out of here in two hours, so I probably won't see you again until the agency Christmas party in December."

"Yeah, Cline, it was a blast. No pun intended," said Kevin, prompting Troy to join him in resounding laughter.

Phyllis also joined the laughter.

Shit! I don't even think she knows what the hell they're laughing about. Robert was irritated, thinking that George's secretary would probably just laugh at anything.

Kevin and Troy headed into the elevator across the waiting room.

Looking straight at Kevin and Troy, Phyllis called out, "I'll see you tonight," prompting the two agents to stop, look back, and wave awkwardly. "Yeah, it looks like I might get off early today, hon, so you won't have to pick up the milk after all. Love you!" She continued gazing forward while talking to her husband through her headset phone as the elevator door closed, rescuing Kevin and Troy from the confusing conversation.

"Come on in, Robert," George hollered from inside his office.

Phyllis smiled and sang along with her Christmas CD while pounding her keyboard and staring at Robert. He disappeared into George's office and closed the door behind himself.

"Hey, here's the big hero," said George as he stood up and shook Robert's hand from behind his government-issue, metal-frame, simulated-wood-top desk. "It's great to finally meet you in person."

Case Officer Harpole looked the same in person as he did on the satellite video monitor, but he was a bit taller than Robert had imagined. George stood six feet tall and looked nearly eye to eye with Robert. Although the senior agent was in good physical condition, age and a life of hard work had bent his back slightly. Robert figured he had probably been at least six foot two when he was younger.

"Wow, I just got the breakdown on all your amazing heroics in your first mission," George said, followed by a slow, sincere chuckle. "You saved Pablo in a diving accident and used the sedative to get him talking; fantastic. You held up under extraordinary pressure, Robert. Because of you, we can file away Operation C58 as a resounding success." George was smiling, truly delighted with what he'd heard from agents Smith and Mercer. "I just think we've hit the jackpot with you, Cline. The agency only runs across people of your quality once in a great while."

For the first time since the mission's completion, Robert felt a little encouraged. "Well, I appreciate the kind words, Agent Harpole, but—"

"Oh no, no. Please call me George."

"Thanks, George. It's just that—"

"You want any coffee in there, cutie?" Phyllis's aggressive, cheerful voice interrupted over the speakerphone.

George looked up at Robert and extended his hand as if waiting for a response.

"No, I'm good," replied Robert.

"Thanks, Phyllis. Why don't you head on home early," George said just before he disconnected. "Now, let's talk about your next mission."

"Well, the thing is, George, I'm just not sure this is the right job for me. Every time I close my eyes, I still see Alva hanging on the mast just before the missile struck." Robert sighed, and then continued, "I just don't think I'm cut out for this kind of work."

George raised a concerned eyebrow. "Oh. I'm sorry you feel that way, but you know, Cline, the first kill is always a little tough." He paused to let out a slow chuckle. "Hell, I had to kill my first double agent about five minutes after I got done rolling around in the sack with her. She was a pretty little thing too. But the good news is, after the *third* kill, you stop thinking about it so much, and then they all start to run together."

"That's just it, George. I don't *want* to make torture and killing a routine. I was under the impression when I signed up that the new CIA was a kinder, gentler spy agency. Supposedly presidents Dunham and Jaden frowned on the kind of stuff that happened in Mexico."

"Oh, yeah, well that kind of goes in phases from administration to administration." George chuckled. "Bo Jaden was as bad as any when it came to putting the shackles on us; that is, until recently. Then, all of the sudden, he gave us more leeway and funding than ever."

George paused, and then turned to open a file cabinet behind his desk. He pulled out a folder labeled with Robert's name and opened it up before shuffling through the small stack of papers inside. He put on a pair of high-power reading glasses and wrinkled his forehead, straining to read the documents through aging eyes. "Looks like you owe the CIA about one hundred thousand dollars in exchange for us paying your way through dental school. This says you signed up for a minimum commitment of four years with the agency to repay that debt. It also looks like we pay you full specialist agent wages and you get to work as a dentist when you're not on missions. That's a pretty sweet deal, Robert."

George threw his reading glasses onto the middle of his desk. He leaned back in his chair, folding his hands together and slowly raising them up behind his head. "If you have a hundred grand to pay back the agency and a good lawyer, you might just be able to wiggle out of this job without doing any prison time, Cline."

Somehow Robert had forgotten that he'd signed an agreement with the agency. He hadn't ever really read the fine print that detailed penalties for default. One thing he knew for certain was that he didn't have $100,000.

"Doc, the CIA needs men with your skills and education. I just can't begin to tell you how impressed I am to hear about all you did in the Yucatán. You've already done this country a great service by helping gather priceless information about the biggest drug cartel in the Western Hemisphere, not to mention taking down the most wanted drug lord in the world." George paused, shaking his head in disappointment, but then looked back into Robert's eyes. "If you decide you need out, I guess I'll do everything in my power to help you."

Robert breathed a sigh of relief. He may have had to spend the next twenty years repaying his debt to the government, but at this point it seemed that getting out of the agency would be worth it.

George continued, "All that being said, here's why I'm going to beg you to stay. You've successfully planted the global-positioning missile tracking device, and we all saw that it worked." George reached over and hit a switch to dim the lights. Then he pushed a button on the side of his desk to activate a flat screen video monitor that filled the entire office wall behind him. With a single click of the mouse, his presentation began. "This is Mudir Al-Shaitan, president of the United Persian-Arab Caliphate."

"Yeah, everybody knows about him. The Persian-Arab Union annexes a new Muslim territory a couple times per year. He's built an empire as large as the United States. So what gives?" asked Robert. "I thought he was supposed to be some kind of hero that stabilized the Middle East and wiped out terrorism across the globe."

George frowned as his look grew very serious. "We have new information that Al-Shaitan masterminded the 2014 bombing of Madison

Square Garden and the murders of President Jackson Dunham, the president of Russia, and thirty-three thousand and sixteen American citizens. He has become the most powerful person in the entire world, and he now rules over territories in the Middle East that boast an impressive nuclear arsenal. Mudir Al-Shaitan has only recently made threats to use this arsenal to wipe the United States off the face of the earth."

"All I've ever heard from the agency is that Al-Shaitan is our greatest ally," Robert said in a concerned voice. "I haven't heard anything about him being responsible for MSG or threatening to use his weapons against us."

"This is all classified information, Cline, but it's very reliable. The problem is that the guy is untouchable. As you know, the United Caliphate capital is in Dubai in the former United Arab Emirates just north of the state of Saudi Arabia. Al-Shaitan operates his government and lives in Dubai, but he has mansions and palaces all over the Middle East. Our limited intelligence on the ground says he never sleeps in the same location two nights in a row. Al-Shaitan's security is second to none. We speculate that he usually uses body doubles when giving public speeches. He has many supporters across the world, including the United States, until recently. Now the Persian-Arab Caliphate president is our number one terrorist threat and the number one threat to national security."

George clicked his mouse, and a photograph of a magnificent skyscraper replaced the image of Mudir Al-Shaitan. The brilliant, twisting tower of glass and titanium stretched above the clouds and into the heavens. Surrounding the architectural masterpiece were otherwise-magnificent skyscrapers, which seemingly bowed down to the foundation of the majestic wonder. "This is the Burj Khalifa," George pointed out.

"I've seen pictures of the place," Robert said. "It's the tallest building in the world, located in Dubai. Didn't Mudir Al-Shaitan purchase it and turn it into the capitol building of the United Caliphate?"

"You're right on Robert."

"So what does all this have to do with me George?"

Agent Harpole clicked the mouse again, switching to a photo of a different skyscraper made of gorgeous reflective black glass contrasted against brushed steel. Atop the sixty-story tower, a stunning artistic spire pierced the Dubai skyline. "This is Millennium Tower. It's situated just blocks away from the magnificent Burj Khalifa. We've been working for weeks to set up a state-of-the-art dental office under your name on Millennium Tower's fiftieth floor. We also have a fully furnished, three-thousand-square-foot residential apartment leased for you on the forty-second floor of the same building."

The slide show switched from the building's fabulous exterior, to the modernly equipped dental office, and then to the luxury apartment.

"They want me to live and work there?" asked Robert. "But why such a nice place?"

"Our plan is that we place you near Mudir Al-Shaitan and get the word out that you're the best new American dentist in Dubai. American medical and dental training is the best in the world, and the upper crust of the Middle East demands the best. They love American doctors and dentists over there. Your office is so nice because it has to be. The state of the art facility is all part of the bait to get Mudir Al-Shaitan and his family to come to you for their dental work." George chuckled. "The president of the United Persian-Arab Caliphate wouldn't go to a dental office in a strip mall."

Robert was amazed by Agent Harpole's presentation. "So why is my apartment so nice?" he asked.

"Again, everything about you needs to demonstrate that you're a success. You should see the car they have sitting in the parking garage of Millennium Tower for you." George clicked the mouse again. "I think I have a picture right here."

The monitor switched to a picture of the Mustang with tinted windows and Mistichrome paint—the same car Robert had tried to rent in Mexico. "What do you think about that?" George paused, smiling. Then he erupted in laughter while reaching over his desk to pat Robert on the shoulder.

"Yeah, that's great." Robert turned bright red and tried to fake a smile, with little success. "So I guess the guys not only told you about it, but they even took a picture."

George continued to enjoy the moment. "Actually we always have 'PEEPs' on the ground taking photos of our agents during their missions. They usually look like tourists, and boy are they good. Nobody ever notices them, but they get us some great photos." George continued laughing. "It makes for a fun slide show at our agency Christmas party. I suspect that photo will probably show up at this year's gala."

"I'm sure," grunted Robert.

George hit the mouse again, and the Mustang photo was replaced by a picture of a Sarthe Silver Aston Martin DB9 Coup. "Actually, I understand they have *this* sitting in the parking garage for you. Everything about you has to affirm that you're first class if we're to attract Al-Shaitan."

Robert gazed in amazement at the clean, elegant contours of the esteemed luxury sports car. "That's the most beautiful car I've ever seen." Robert looked up at George and questioned, "I thought the agency was all about blending in. A hundred-thousand-dollar, twelve-cylinder Aston Martin isn't really a blend-in type of car. This thing would just scream for people to look every time it hits the road."

"Well, you aren't blending into a small fishing village in the Yucatán anymore, Robert. Dubai is one of the richest cities in the world. Every downtown building is an architectural masterpiece. The most affluent people in the Middle East live and vacation there, and they drive only the finest cars. We need you to fit in with the best of the best in Dubai."

"Wow," said Robert, astonished. "This is all simply incredible."

"You may still decide to turn your nose up at this mission and go home to live a normal life," George said sternly, "but if Mudir Al-Shaitan has his way, you may be living that normal life in a nuclear-aftermath wasteland. Robert Cline, this country needs a hero right now. Hell, the *world* needs a hero right now, and *you* are that hero. A secret resolution has been signed by the president to reinstate 'Executive Actions', or the deliberate assassination of a foreign leader. We need you to plant a device just like the one you already planted in Alva's molar. But this time you'll plant the device in the tooth of Mudir Al-Shaitan. The long-range missile will do the rest."

"What If I fail?" asked Robert, suddenly feeling like the weight of the world had been stacked on his shoulders.

"You won't fail," replied George with confidence. "We've seen you in action. You are just cool enough to get it done. You saved Pablo Alva from the shipwreck under extreme pressure. You turned around an interrogation that was going nowhere. But most importantly, you treated Pablo gently and with compassion, which you will need to do to attract Al-Shaitan and his family to your Dubai dental office. With your gentle touch and bedside manner, they will trust you."

"What if Mudir doesn't come to my dental office?"

George laughed in his characteristically slow, rhythmic tempo. "Well, the thing of it is, we've been working to put this together for a while. The office is already fully staffed with two dental assistants, two dental hygienists, and a receptionist. As we speak, they are getting things ready and waiting for your arrival. You already have a full book of appointments starting just four days from now. And Robert, six days from now you have Shahzad and Malikah Al-Shaitan, the son and daughter of Mudir Al-Shaitan, scheduled for cleanings and exams in your office."

"How did you get them to come to me?" Robert asked in amazement.

"Well, again, wealthy people in the Middle East want America's best medical professionals. We've advertised your credentials heavily and used a few assets on the ground in Dubai to spread the word about your office. We even put out word that you speak fluent Arabic, Farsi, and Spanish."

Robert looked confused. "I get the Arabic and Farsi, but what's with the Spanish?"

"Dr. Linda Gasol-Al-Shaitan, the wife of the United Caliphate president, is from Spain. We made sure to make your Spanish fluency known, and I hear that was just the bait that got her hooked."

"I don't know George." Robert raised his hands to his head and ran his fingers slowly through his hair. "The whole thing is completely blowing me away."

"Robert, this is undoubtedly the CIA's most important mission of the century. We're working in unison with the Pentagon, and even the Sluzhba Vneshney Razvedki, or SVR.... They did teach you about the SVR in your country club version of field agent training, right?"

Robert rolled his eyes and sighed. "The SVR is Russia's modern successor to the Soviet KGB. You can continue if you think I can keep up, George."

George laughed longer than was necessary, and then continued with a satisfied grin. "OK, OK, Cline. So, this unprecedented cooperation will allow us to provide the operation with maximum resources and support. We have too much invested in the mission and too much invested in you to have you back out now. The opportunity is amazing. The location is stunning. Dubai is one of the most incredible cities in the world, and outside of four days of dental work a week, you'll be free to enjoy your luxury skyscraper apartment and your luxury sports car. You'll be equipped and pampered on this mission like no other agent I can remember."

"Yeah, the location is pretty spectacular, but so was Mexico, and I still end up planting another missile-guidance device and killing another person. Plus, none of this changes the fact that I see Pablo Alva every time I close my eyes."

"Well, I have something that just might change that." George clicked the computer mouse and switched to a screen most people wouldn't have understood. It was a price list for a handful of the most commonly performed dental procedures.

"Yeah, so you have a price list for dental work. So what?" asked Robert.

"Did you take a look at the prices for these procedures, Doc?" asked George.

"Three thousand dollars for a crown, nine hundred dollars for a filling, three hundred dollars for an exam. Nobody would pay that kind of money for dental work, George."

"Oh, but they do. These are standard fees charged by the best dentists in the Persian-Arab Union capital city. These are your fees in Dubai," George said, smiling.

"So doesn't that go to the agency?" Robert asked.

"Nope. After a forty percent cut for overhead expenses, all of the profits yielded from the dental office go to you. And of course, you still get your standard CIA-operation pay. You could be working there for months before you get Mudir Al-Shaitan himself in your chair. George rolled off a few waves of his characteristically slow, rhythmic laughter. "Now, Doc..., close your eyes, and tell me what you see *this* time."

Robert closed his eyes and paused a few seconds. A grin slowly spread across his face. "I see money, George. I see a lot of money. I also see myself driving in downtown Dubai in my Aston Martin. I see the view of the Burj Khalifa capitol building from my penthouse suite in Millennium Tower." His grin turned to a full smile but then faded as he thought, Oh crap. I see Kitty Witty.

Robert opened his eyes and looked at Agent Harpole, who knew he'd just gotten his man. "Do you think it would be OK if I bring my cat?"

"Really, Cline? That's highly irregular," George said while chuckling.

"I'm still feeling a little rattled over the Alva thing. I just think it would calm my nerves if you let me bring my cat along."

"I won't promise anything, Robert, but I'll see what I can do. I suspect the agency would give you about anything you want at this point. You could be the country's only hope."

"I guess I'm in," Robert said as he reached across the desk to shake George's hand.

"Perfect," said George. "I'll be sending you briefings over the next two days."

"Am I working by myself, or are there other agents in the dental office?"

"Oh yeah, we thought we would send Agent Mercer to be one of your dental assistants." George tried to act serious but immediately started laughing.

"Yeah, no thanks," said Robert.

"Actually, all but one of the people working in your office have been hired from civilian population and know nothing of what's going on in this mission. The exception is Special Agent Olen, a twenty-eight-year-old Russian spy who will be one of your dental assistants. Olen will assist when you place the missile-guidance device."

"Olen?" Robert said cynically. "Sounds like a big, hairy Ukrainian gal."

"Actually, she's very attractive. She worked as an assistant in a Moscow dental office before being recruited by the SVR. We're getting a lot of cooperation from the Russians of course, with them losing *their* president in the Madison Square Garden bombing."

George continued, "All of the other employees believe that you contracted a regular staffing service to put them in place. But the agency actually set up our own storefront staffing service and brought in qualified people from all over the world, including a receptionist, and dental assistant who both speak Spanish and Arabic. Gotta keep mamma Al-Shaitan happy."

George handed a file folder across the desk to Robert. "Here's some mission information, including a list of the names and profiles of the people working in your office in addition to some other particulars you can study on the plane. Any questions?"

"I guess not," Robert replied.

"Perfect," said George. "You'll fly back to Texas tonight. Then get ready to be back at Dallas/Fort Worth International Airport in two days for a zero-seven-hundred, nonstop flight to New York."

Robert opened the folder labeled "Dubai" and pulled out a coach ticket from DC to Dallas and then from Dallas to New York City. "Coach? I knew this was too good to be true."

George laughed in a slow, sinister rhythm. "Of course, but then you'll fly on a private Cessna Citation M2 jet from New York to Dubai. We can be cheap when you're in the US, but you have to arrive in the caliphate capital like you're the king of dentists."

Robert continued to skim through the folder and found a wallet copy of a dental license with the name Robert Cline, DDS. "I still use my real name?" he asked.

"Well, nobody even knows you were in the Yucatán. Our cleanup crew does such a great job of erasing events. It's like you were never there. Your name is still clean. The agency doesn't start using aliases until you get into some messy situations and your name gets out," replied George.

Robert continued to read the license. "This says I went to dental school in Boston, not the University of Nebraska. What gives?"

"We just thought it sounded a little more...prestigious," said George, chuckling.

"I'll have you know that the University of Nebraska College of Dentistry is one of the finest in the nation." Robert was clearly insulted. "I'd go to a dentist from Nebraska over Boston any day."

"Well, it's just that we weren't sure that anybody in the Middle East had even heard of Nebraska, Cline," said George, who was digging his hole even deeper.

"I thought the whole deal was that people were supposed to be able to find records that I graduated from the University of Nebraska if they wanted to," accused Robert.

"Yeah, well, that used to be the case. But now, if anyone Googles Robert Cline, DDS, they will see that you went to dental school all right...but in Boston. They can also verify that if they call the university."

"OK, OK, I guess it doesn't really matter anyway," conceded Robert, who was trying not to be unreasonably difficult.

"Good," replied George. "This really is a special mission with global consequences. But you are a special agent, Cline. You're going to save our country and the world from the most notorious terrorist and dictator of our time. So just get over there and do some dental work but also have a great time. You have a quick office staff meeting scheduled the day after you arrive so you can get the group organized. Then you start on patients the next day."

"Sounds good," said Robert as he stood up, getting ready to depart.

"Oh, and one last thing before you go," said George. "This mission isn't like the Yucatán. Here you only place the missile-guidance device and alert us when that has been completed. That's it. You don't have any intelligence-gathering responsibilities."

"You mean, no torture?" asked Robert sarcastically.

"Right. Furthermore, I have been told to inform you that it would be best for you to be a dentist, have some fun, plant the device, and otherwise try to learn as little as possible about Mudir Al-Shaitan and his political activities or dealings with the United States."

Robert became a bit concerned. "What do you mean?"

George stood up slowly and walked over to his office door. He opened it, looking out to make sure Phyllis was gone and nobody else was nearby. He promptly closed it and returned to his seat. Harpole opened his desk drawer and pulled out a small, black, rectangular device about the size of a cigarette lighter; he flipped a switch on the gadget, causing a tiny blue light to flash. Robert recognized the device from his agent training. It was an ultrasonic signal scrambler that would cause enormous sound distortion in wiretapping surveillance. George was making sure that no one was listening.

"Well, let's just say we're getting intelligence that a monstrous scandal associated with Al-Shaitan penetrates deep into the US government. Countless elected officials and private US companies are twisted up in a mess of misconduct that reaches all the way to the top. It could be dangerous for you if you learn too much. We just need you to establish a professional relationship with the Al-Shaitan family, plant the missile-guidance device in Mudir's tooth, and get to your private jet, which will be waiting with a pilot on standby twenty-four hours to get you out of Dubai."

Robert frowned and slowly sat back down. His complexion turned whitish grey.

"Close your eyes again, Cline," ordered George.

Robert closed his eyes and sat still for a few seconds. He quietly whispered, "Money, Millennium Tower, Aston Martin." His color and smile returned.

"Good. Now you'd better get going, Robert. Your flight leaves out of Ronald Reagan International in just four hours. We have a driver waiting downstairs to take you to the airport."

Robert stood up, reenergized. "Thanks, George." He turned toward the exit, and then paused before turning back. He pulled a full bottle of non–Healed Earth–approved sunscreen out of his backpack and threw it over the desk to Agent Harpole, who made a perfect catch. "You wouldn't believe what I went through to get this past security. It was like smuggling plutonium." Robert turned back to the door and ducked out of Agent Harpole's office.

George, now alone, chuckled slowly and opened the bottle to take a sniff. "Artificial pineapple and coconut, just like the good old days." He squirted a little of the lotion onto his hand and rubbed it into the skin on his bald head.

19

AIR MILES

Once back in Dallas, Robert informed his staff at the Public Health Department dental clinic that he was being temporarily relocated out of state for a few weeks to help with a sudden overload of patients in another treatment center. This information was confirmed by The Department of Health and Human Services under orders from the CIA.

Robert only had a couple days to unpack from his Yucatán mission and repack for Dubai. Good thing Kevin and Troy won't be around to see this, he thought as he pulled out a third suitcase to accommodate an assortment of dress pants, dress shirts, and neck ties to be worn at work.

Robert spent some time researching the capital of the United Persian-Arab Caliphate and learned that the average high temperature for the month usually topped 99 degrees Fahrenheit. Pictures online revealed beautiful, private beaches where Western dress was permitted, so Robert made room for his swim trunks. He left his tuxedo behind but added winter clothing that he planned to use at the indoor snow ski complex, located at world-famous Mall of the Emirates.

Robert was about to embark on what promised to be an incredible adventure. He checked and rechecked his luggage the night before his journey, making sure to leave nothing behind. When he finally went to bed, he lay awake most of the night, thinking about George's pictures of the state-of-the-art dental office, his skyscraper apartment, and his Aston Martin DB9 Coup.

Robert finally closed his eyes and drifted off to sleep at 3:30 a.m. Twenty-five minutes later he was sitting in the *Hay Caramba*, watching Pablo Alva hang on the mast of the catamaran sailboat while a fire glowed in the sky. Even though he was far away, Robert could see Alva up close and heard him whisper, "You will always be my brother, Robert Cline."

The fiery light grew and the missile thundered, growing to a deafening pitch. Robert covered his ears but he could read Pablo's lips as he said, "I forgive you, my friend." There was a stillness before impact. Then Robert was startled to attention by the scream of his alarm clock. He lunged up off his pillow and sat in his bed breathing heavily, drenched in sweat. It was 4:00 a.m. and time to get up. His short sleep had been more exhausting than a night of no sleep at all.

Robert got up slowly and brewed a pot of coffee. He downed three cups quickly, burning his mouth several times in the process. Robert's eyes were tired, but caffeine lifted the pace of his heart and fueled his body with uncomfortable energy.

In just fifteen minutes he was ready to leave for the airport. Almost everything he was going to bring to Dubai had been organized the night before and neatly stacked just inside the apartment's front door. Only one thing was missing.

"C'mon, Kitty Witty. It's time to get into your cat carrier." He looked all around the apartment for the fifteen-pound fur ball before he found his pet hiding under the couch.

"K-Dub, let's go! I've got to be at the airport in thirty minutes." Robert reached to grab his sleeping cat and dragged him out from under the couch.

As always, Robert read the thoughts in Kitty Witty's eyes and figured he was thinking, *What the hell? I was sleeping. What time is it anyway?* "Meow!"

Robert loaded up the Pontiac Phoenix and raced to the airport. With plenty of time before departure, he made his way to the ticket counter, where he checked his bags and his cat.

Where are these freaks taking me, Cline? Help! Help! Kitty Witty moaned relentlessly and let out a series of blood-curdling meows. His futile cries faded away as his cat carrier disappeared down a conveyer belt for his ride in the luggage compartment.

Just before takeoff, Robert took his coach seat on the fully booked 7:00 a.m. flight to New York City. He wadded his long legs into the confined space and caught up on his sleep through the relatively short flight.

Robert and his cat were reunited for a quick ground transportation drive to Teterboro Airport, where most private charter jet traffic in the New York and New Jersey area is serviced. The uprooted K-Dub howled for the entire drive to the small airport.

The driver pulled right up to a hangar used exclusively by the CIA.

The small ground crew helped Robert get his bags loaded into the luggage compartment of a beautiful Cessna Citation M2, parked just outside the hangar. The seven-passenger Ferrari of charter jets was sleek, powerful, and piloted by Captain John Saunders. "I guess we're flying to Dubai together," said the former air force F-16 fighter pilot as he stepped out of the plane and shook Robert's hand. "I also understand you're working on a recreational rating for your own aviation license."

"Yes, sir, but this is a *machine*. The planes I've been flying in Dallas look like toys compared to this one."

Captain Saunders continued, "My boss says I'm supposed to give you as much instruction as you want up there today. There are two seats in the cockpit, and we'll be in the air for over fourteen hours. So if you want, you can sit up in the front, and I'll show you how to fly this little speed demon."

"Are you kidding?" Robert was ecstatic. "Absolutely."

The two men boarded the immaculate jet. Robert strapped Kitty Witty to one of the five fully reclining leather seats in the compact-but-roomy rear cabin. Then he climbed alongside Captain Saunders and marveled at the high-tech Garmin instrument panel in the cockpit.

"If you get tired at any point, feel free to step back into the cabin for a rest," Saunders said. "There's plenty of food back there in the mini fridge, and the seats are great—way comfortable. I've been on the radio to the tower for the last hour. It sounds like there could be a little delay, but once we get off the ground, we'll be flying right over the Statue of Liberty in the Upper New York Bay."

Saunders put on his aviation headset and handed a pair to Robert. The frustration in his voice was clear as the captain spoke back and forth to the control tower.

"Well, Robert, there was some kind of movie tribute ceremony in the city last night. Lots of pampered Hollywood stars waiting to take off, so it sounds like there are still ten planes in line ahead of us. I guess we just wait."

Traffic at the small private airport hadn't been this heavy for years. It had been down nearly 90 percent since the federal government instituted a policy requiring all private jet passengers and each of their pilots to purchase special Healed Earth certificates, costing fifty cents for every mile in the air. With the distance from New York to Dubai approaching 6,900 miles, two one-way Healed Earth certificates for Agent Cline and Captain Saunders would have cost the CIA $6,900. Fortunately, US government agencies were allowed to apply for Healed Earth exemption certificates. As a result, only government officials and the super-rich flew by private charter jet.

"Were bumping you up for departure, Saunders." The voice came in loud and clear over the cockpit radio.

"Wow," said Captain Saunders, looking at his passenger. "I'm not supposed to ask who you are, Robert Cline, but you must be important. They just pushed us up in front of a rock star, a major motion picture director, and Al Gore."

The Cessna jet taxied a short distance, passing six other private jets ranging in size. Saunders awaited the signal.

"Clear for departure," announced the voice from the control tower.

"Buckle up, Robert. This little bird might as well be a rocket," said the captain.

Robert had already fastened his seat belt. The pilot lowered the thruster, and the aerodynamic seven-seater screamed smoothly down the runway and took off, shooting through the air like an arrow. "Now this is how to fly," Robert said quietly as he sank back into his soft, leather copilot chair.

Robert watched Captain Saunders's every move. He would take in all he could, not sleeping the entire flight to Dubai. He only left the cockpit a time or two to retrieve food for himself and the captain. Even though Robert had barely slept the night before, he was driven by an unrelenting stream of adrenaline. Saunders went over the finer points of flying the Cessna Citation M2 as the ultra-sleek jet cut through the clouds like a hot knife through butter. The captain even let Robert take the controls and guided him through landing and takeoff in Paris, where they stopped briefly to refuel.

It's going to be tough to fly coach again, Robert thought.

20

HEAVEN

Architect Abdul Basit was very content. He lay slightly reclined, staring at the beautiful palace that twisted through the heavens in front of him. The fabulous tower seemed to be dancing above a garden of skyscrapers in an architect's playground. Abdul was not only content; he was overcome with joy. "How are you feeling?" asked Evie Garcia in a beautiful Spanish accent. Her dark-brown eyes caringly peered through thick, long eyelashes at Abdul.

Lying next to Evie, Abdul looked up and replied, "I think…I think I am feeling very happy." He stared at her lovely eyes. Her jet-black hair was pulled back slick, and tied neatly in a bun, leaving nothing to cover her pleasing, lovely face. Abdul was a gentleman, so he tried not to notice Evie's long, slender legs that were only partially covered by her simple black dress.

"Hello," a soft Russian voice sounded from Abdul's other side. He looked away from Evie and turned to Dzhoanna, whom he also lay next to. Her ice-blue eyes and well-defined jaw were exquisite enough to momentarily distract him from the beautiful Evie, who still waited for him on the other side. Dzhoanna's eyes were so captivating; Abdul didn't even notice she was wearing the same black dress and sleek hairstyle as Evie. "We are so glad you are here with us," she said with a flirtatious giggle.

"I too am very glad. This is the most joyful day of my life," Abdul proclaimed, now looking back and forth at the beautiful women he lay next to. A small tear ran down his left cheek. Evie caught the teardrop in a tiny two-by-two-inch cotton tissue for him.

A gentle touch on Abdul's forearm startled him. Zasu Deinas had suddenly appeared and was leaning over him. "Are they taking good care of you, Abdul?" Zasu asked in a seductive French accent. Her thick, red lips maintained a constant pucker. She was striking, with inviting curves that were draped by a simple black dress like the ones worn by Evie and Dzhoanna.

Abdul grinned a bit. His eyes were heavy. He felt sleep drawing him in, but he didn't want to look away from the beautiful ladies he was lying next to. Was this a dream, or was he in heaven? One hundred virgins was the promise of Allah. The first three were mesmerizing. He couldn't wait to see the next ninety-seven. Another tear trickled down Abdul's cheek.

A fourth dressed in black with dark eyes and dark hair entered the room. "How are you doing, Abdul?" The voice was caring and compassionate, but it seemed a little deep.

"Oh, Evie, you have the nitrous oxide up way too high." Robert Cline, DDS, peered in around the three women. "Poor guy's eyes are watering. Let's get that down about fifteen percent for you, Mr. Basit." Robert gently motioned for Evie to turn the laughing gas down.

Abdul was definitely not in heaven. If he'd spent any time in the United States watching MTV in the late eighties, he probably would have thought he was in the middle of a Robert Palmer video. Instead, he was in Robert Cline's downtown-Dubai dental office on the fiftieth floor of Millennium Tower.

The telephone rang from the next room. "Ooh, I had better go get that," Zasu declared. She let out a flirtatious giggle and waved good-bye to Abdul before returning to the front desk.

The agency subcontracted by the CIA to hire and train the dental office staff chose people based on their skill level, and willingness to pamper their patients. A high-end office would serve clientele who were used to being waited on hand and foot. It was already clear to Robert that the agency had done a fine job of selecting the ladies in his office.

"Let's get your filling started, Mr. Basit," said Robert. Evie and Dzhoanna were both standing by to assist. "I guess I'll have Evie help me with this one, Miss Olen."

Evie smiled and sat up straight in her assisting chair, while Dzhoanna, clearly disappointed, promised, "I will go sterilize Evie's instruments. Please call if you need anything, Doctor."

Wow, we're already two days in, and they're still helping each other. They're even jockeying over who gets to assist me. It would be nice to have a little of this attitude back at the Health Department dental clinic in Texas, thought Robert. "Thank you, Dzhoanna," he said.

Robert and Evie worked in perfect unison to complete the small composite filling on Abdul Basit, while the patient gazed out the floor-to-ceiling window at the Burj Khalifa and the clear Dubai sky. Dr. Cline practiced his Arabic and gave Abdul a few tips on cavity prevention before they released him.

Evie escorted Abdul to Zasu who sat behind a black glass counter at the front of the office. Robert followed, but was intercepted by one of his dental hygienists, who looked very concerned. "Dr. Cline, I'm ready for you," she said as she pulled him aside to a private office. She began to whisper frantically, "I have little Shahzad Al-Shaitan ready for his exam, but I have to warn you. He is very nervous. He's five, and it's his first dental visit. It's a zoo in there. His mother and four bodyguards are in the room with us."

"It should be fine," interrupted Robert confidently.

"You don't understand, Doctor. The guards have machine guns. I was informed by one of the guards that I would not be hurting the child. Oh, and his mother keeps scaring him, talking about needles and drills."

Robert always believed the most frightening things for children visiting a dental office were the poorly thought-out reassurances from their own mothers. "Well, let's go have a look." Robert followed his hygienist into room five, which was designated for cleanings and exams.

Each of the five operatories faced the same direction, with a stunning view of the Burj Khalifa and the city of Dubai. All were immaculate, fully equipped, and state of the art. The rooms were also very spacious, compared to any dental workspace Robert had seen. But with four security guards, Robert, his hygienist, and the patient's mother in the operatory, the polished black granite floor offered little standing room.

Robert tried to ignore the very large bodyguards standing in the doorway, wearing long, red bisht cloaks. The guards' heads were completely covered with black ghutra scarves that exposed only a small slit for their watchful eyes. Their distinctive uniforms were worn only by members of Mudir Al-Shaitan's elite secret service known as the Caliphate Guard.

The dentist squeezed past four magazine-fed assault machine guns and walked straight to Mrs. Al-Shaitan, who was sitting in a chair next to her son. "Hola. ¿*Cómo está*, Dr. Gasol-Al-Shaitan?" Robert said as he charmingly took her hand and tipped his head in respect.

"I haven't been called 'doctor' since I married Mudir," said the First Lady of the United Persian-Arab Caliphate while blushing. "Es *verdad* que habla Español." She was pleased that Robert spoke to her in her native Spanish.

"*Es un honor para cuidar de su familia*," replied Robert, stating that it was an honor to care for her family.

"Move out of the way please," said the United Caliphate First Lady, shooing two of the guards away from her side. Her Spanish accent suddenly became more pronounced. "I said go on. It is too crowded in here." Mrs. Al-Shaitan's two personal bodyguards reluctantly left the operatory, while the two other Caliphate Guard officers commissioned to protect the life of little Shahzad Al-Shaitan moved to the foot of the dental chair with weapons drawn.

Looking back to Robert, the beautiful Mrs. Al-Shaitan continued, "Where did you learn to speak Spanish, Doctor?"

"I spent some time in the Yucatán," Robert replied. Then he turned his attention from the First Lady and bent down on one knee to greet his patient, who sat nervously in the black, leather dental chair. "Who do we have here?" Robert asked, speaking in Arabic and offering his hand to his tiny patient.

Shahzad Al-Shaitan was small for being nearly six years old. He was dressed to perfection, and his dark hair was neat as a pin. He had a dark complexion, and had inherited his mother's distinctive emerald-green eyes. Little Shahzad didn't speak. Instead his lower lip curled, and he began to whimper.

"I am sorry. He is very frightened," explained his mother.

"It's OK, Shahzad. Look what I have for you." Robert showed he had nothing in his hands, and then like a magician he pulled a small toy from his nervous patient's ear. "This is for you, my brave, little prince," said Robert, handing the toy to Shahzad.

The little boy did not want to be there, but his frown turned to a reluctant smile. He clapped and took the toy, holding it up for his mother to see. Robert stood up and washed his hands in a polished copper bowl sink resting on the black, glass work counter behind the dental chair. "Let's see how your teeth look, buddy," said Dr. Cline as he put on his gloves and mask.

Shahzad opened wide, and Robert began to examine his patient. "Hmm, looks like we've got a little crowding issue in the lower front." Robert explained to Mrs. Al-Shaitan that her son's lower front adult tooth hadn't dissolved the root of the baby tooth above, causing the new tooth to come in directly behind the arch of baby teeth. "Shahzad's baby tooth didn't get loose, so we will have to set up an appointment to remove it for him."

"No, no, my poor baby!" Mrs. Al-Shaitan gasped, squeezing Shahzad's little hand. She looked up at Robert and said, "This cannot be. I would have noticed this." She held her hand up to her mouth in distress. Then she promptly stood up from her chair and looked over Robert's shoulder to see a new adult tooth forming a second row just behind the baby teeth. "Oh, dear no. How could this have happened, Dr?"

"Don't worry. It's a very common problem. When the permanent tooth is wider than the baby tooth above, it will erupt by simply sliding to the inside, forming a second row. All we have to do is remove the baby central incisor that should have been lost, and the adjacent baby lateral incisor to create a little extra space. After the two baby teeth are removed, the permanent central incisor shifts forward into perfect alignment within weeks."

"Are you sure this is the best thing?" asked the First Lady.

Chill out, lady. It's not brain surgery, thought Robert. "Absolutely; it's very routine," he said.

"I trust you, Dr. Cline. I see you went to the finest dental school in Boston," she said, referring to his diploma that hung neatly in the reception area.

Puke! The voice in Robert's head shouted, "Yeah…well, you know, Boston is one of the finest dental schools in the United States, probably rivaled only by the University of Nebraska."

"Nebraska?" she quizzed looking puzzled. "I have only ever heard of corn coming from Nebraska." Regaining her composure, the First Lady asked, "When should we pull the teeth, Doctor?"

"Let me look over the rest of his teeth, while we ask Zasu what appointments we have available." Robert finished the exam, while his hygienist went out to the reception area to check for the next-available appointment.

Zasu quickly entered the operatory with the office schedule pulled up on an iPad. She introduced herself to Linda Gasol-Al-Shaitan, speaking Spanish in a beautiful French accent. Then she looked for an appointment that would work with the First Lady's busy schedule. "I hear our little man needs just an hour with the doctor."

"Yes, I'm afraid so," replied Gasol-Al-Shaitan who was clearly stressed.

"Oh, my darling, do not worry. Dr. Cline is simply wonderful with children," Zasu reassured her.

"Yes. Yes, I know. We have heard all over Dubai what a great dentist he is," she replied, looking comforted.

Wow, Agent Harpole's crew really must have done a good job getting the word out about my office, thought Robert. "I'll stay late or even come in on the weekend if we need to," he said.

Zasu continued, "Well, it *is* Friday, but we have a slot available right now. We also have a spot available next Tuesday. Otherwise it looks like we're pretty full next week. But like the doctor says, we will work with your schedule, even if we need to stay after regular business hours."

"Oh no. My little Shahzad's birthday is next Tuesday. I don't want the biggest memory of his sixth birthday to be oral surgery. Besides, we have a huge party in his honor to get ready for. Everyone who is anyone in the Persian-Arab Union will be there with their children."

"You know, we still have your daughter scheduled for her cleaning and exam in a half hour, so if you're going to be here anyway…, maybe right now would work?"

"I have to go and pick Malikah up from ballet class now, but I suppose I could leave little Shahzad here with his bodyguards until I return with her."

"Perfect," said Zasu. "I'll tell the girls to get room one ready."

With tear-filled eyes, Linda Gasol-Al-Shaitan knelt down next to her son. She gently touched his little cheek and explained, "My baby, I'm going to leave you here with Hami and Nasir." Shahzad's body-guards both nodded in agreement while holding their machine gun's tightly. "They will protect you, my love." She fixed her son's already perfect hair as she continued, "I need you to be brave while the doctor gives you a shot and pulls your teeth. You will bleed, but you need to be strong."

What in the hell are you telling him *that* for? thought Robert, listening in disbelief. I thought she was a doctor. This is not how you work with children. "Please, Dr. Gasol-Al-Shaitan. We really try to downplay the details of our procedures with children. We're often able to place anesthetic and remove baby teeth without any awareness from the patient whatsoever." He was trying to speak over the child's head and get the concerned mother to stop offering information that would frighten the little boy.

"Excuse me, Dr. Cline, but I believe in being honest with my children. If there will be a shot and bleeding, it is best that he knows of this."

Oh, wonderful. This ought to really help us keep little Shahzad calm while we start off with him being scared to death, thought Robert. "Of course, Mrs. Gasol-Al-Shaitan," he said. Thank God she's leaving. I'll have a better chance of getting this done with these guys and their guns than with mommy Al-Shaitan.

"Good-bye, *mi-hijo*, joy of my life," said the distraught mother, with tears streaming down her face. She hugged little Shahzad like it would be their last good-bye, sending her child all the signals that something bad was about to happen. Then she turned to Robert. "Please do not hurt my baby, Dr. Cline." She grabbed her purse with one hand and wiped her tears away with the other while she briskly walked out of the office.

What a drama queen, thought Robert. "Don't worry. We'll take good care of him!" he called out behind her.

Just then Dzhoanna Olen walked into the room and bent down over Shahzad's chair. She placed a token coin in his tiny hand and said, "Hello, little mister. I want you to hold onto this coin until after your appointment. You can use it to get a prize from our gum ball machine."

Shahzad took the coin and put it into his pants pocket. He looked up at the beautiful, smiling face of Dzhoanna. Her caring blue eyes comforted him immediately. The Russian spy gently offered her hand, and Shahzad took hold.

"I'll come get you when we're ready, Doctor," said Dzhoanna. The patient and dental assistant walked hand in hand out of the room, and down the spotless, black, granite floor in the hallway. Hami and Nasir followed closely behind with their assault machine guns into operatory two, which was specially designed for children.

Miss Olen seated Shahzad in a child-sized, black, leather dental chair. The room was very clean and sterile in appearance, and at first glance, other than the small chair, it looked just like all the others. Then the dental assistant flipped a switch, causing an automatic blind to lower, blocking the sun and the view of the Burj Khalifa. At the same time, a sixty-inch television screen mounted on the ceiling above the dental chair came to life. Dzhoanna let her little patient pick from an assortment of fantasy DVDs that Robert had chosen to help him immerse his child patients into a dental-appointment adventure. "We have jungle safari, dinosaur land, cowboys and Indians, or outer space. Which adventure would you like today?" Dzhoanna asked.

"Whoa. Outer space!" exclaimed Shahzad. He smiled up at his two bodyguards, whose expressionless faces were hidden behind their black ghutra scarves. In seconds a computer animation showing a rocket ready for launch played larger than life from the ceiling above his chair. For the first time that afternoon, Hami and Nasir periodically took their eyes off Shahzad, looking up with him to watch the screen.

"I'm going to go get Dr. Cline now, sweetie," said Miss Olen just before she left the room. Almost as quickly as she left, Dzhoanna returned with Robert.

Hami and Nasir were standing behind the dental chair where the dentist would normally sit. Speaking in Arabic, Robert requested, "All right, guys, I'm going to need to get in behind him. Can you maybe stand at the foot of his chair for me please?"

The two Caliphate Guard agents pulled up their assault machine guns and glared at Robert before reluctantly yielding to his request.

"*Shukran,*" said Robert, thanking them in Arabic, while he sat down in his operating chair. "OK, little buddy, let's give you a ride in the magic space ship chair." He lowered Shahzad into a reclined position.

The little patient seemed at ease as he watched the large screen on the ceiling.

"Let's try this little astronaut nose on while you sit in your rocket ship," said Robert, gently placing the nitrous oxide mask over Shahzad's nose. "Wow, look at our little space captain." Robert worked in sync with the video to spin the appointment into a real adventure for his patient.

Shahzad smiled and used his little hands to pretend he was steering the spaceship, while the video screen showed a real spaceship cockpit. He made a cute rumbling sound, pretending to start the engine of the rocket he imagined he was in.

This is going to be a piece of cake, thought Robert, who had already notched a point in the victory column. "OK, captain, let's get ready for takeoff. But first we will have you open your mouth so I can paint on some space jelly to make your tongue sleep. That way you won't get hungry on your long flight. Now I have to warn you—this stuff tastes pretty sweet, but it's a little bit strange. Little boy astronauts usually like it, but little girls don't put up with it as well."

Robert tried to prepare his patient for the somewhat bad-tasting topical anesthetic in advance. He usually found that challenging his little boy patients to tolerate bad tastes better than little girls was very effective. He used similar tactics, encouraging his little girl patients to behave better than little boys.

Robert applied the topical anesthetic, causing Shahzad to pucker and frown a bit. The patient whined just a little, expressing disapproval with the taste.

"Wow, you're a tough astronaut," said Robert quickly. "You do much better than the girls with that stuff."

"What's wrong?" asked Hami as he and Nasir abruptly stepped forward.

"It tastes yucky," replied Shahzad with a bit of a whimper.

"Rinse it out of his mouth," demanded Nasir.

"This is just numbing jelly to help with the next step," explained Robert. "He's actually doing really well with it, and we'll be able to rinse as soon as we get him numb."

"He doesn't like the taste. Rinse his mouth now!" Nasir shouted this time, lunging closer to Robert.

Robert pulled down his mask and looked up at the bodyguards. "I need to get his mouth a little numb before we place the anesthetic, or this will not work."

He turned back to his patient, who was now becoming restless. "Can you just leave the space gel for thirty more seconds, buddy? I promise I will rinse you very soon."

Before Shahzad had a chance to answer, Robert redirected his patient's attention. "Oh, look up at the screen! We're flying up to an alien spacecraft. We need to get our laser guns ready in case they're unfriendly."

Shahzad held up his tiny hand and pointed it like a gun at the spaceships flying across the giant screen above him. He made a laser noise as he pretended to shoot at the alien ships. "Pshew, pshew!"

Agitated, Robert glanced up at the guards with a raised eyebrow, and they stepped back a bit, seeing that Shahzad was tolerating the topical anesthetic.

"I can't see the spaceships," said Shahzad, who pulled the nitrous oxide mask down off his face and continued shooting at the screen. "Pshew, pshew!"

"Oh no, captain, there is no oxygen in the ship. You have to wear the mask." Robert slowly placed the nitrous oxide back over his patient's nose, and Shahzad complied.

"Do you want that off of your face?" Nasir ranted in Arabic.

Little Shahzad looked away from the spaceships that flew across the screen and thought about the question for a second. "It is very heavy on my nose. It kind of hurts my cheeks a little."

"Get it off," commanded Nasir.

Robert's face turned red hot. His heart was pounding, causing a vein in his forehead to pulsate. He ignored the order and explained to his patient, "We'll just leave it on until we enter the atmosphere, captain."

Nasir abruptly aimed his machine gun at Robert's head, while Hami pointed his rifle at Dzhoanna. "Get it off his face! Get it off his face! It is hurting him! Get it off his face!" The bodyguards, seemingly ready to discharge their weapons, shouted frantically in Arabic at the dentist and his assistant.

Dzhoanna breathed heavily beneath her dental mask and looked to Robert for the next move as the situation escalated.

"Pshew, pshew." Shahzad aimed his pretend laser guns at his own bodyguards. "I shot the aliens, Doctor," said the little patient as he looked up at Robert.

Thank God. This kid thinks it's part of the game, Robert thought. "Yeah, I think you got them," he replied. Dr. Cline looked up at the bodyguards in disbelief, while they continued to aim their weapons.

"Take the mask off his face," Nasir growled. He put his finger on the trigger of his assault machine gun, which was still aimed directly at Robert's head. Then Hami quickly redirected his aim from Dzhoanna to Robert, placed his finger on the trigger, and shot Robert...a blistering glare that indicated he was ready to fire.

Exasperated, Robert held up his hands and rolled back in his chair. He ripped off his gloves and mask and threw them on the spotless, black granite floor. "You wait here on the ship, captain. I'm going to have to board the enemy vessel and talk to the alien commander," he said, keeping his composure and the fantasy scene intact for his astonishingly cooperative patient.

Robert stood up, walked right past of the barrel of Nasir's gun, and snapped, "We need to talk now." He stormed out of the room, motioning for the bodyguard to come along. Nasir ordered Hami to stay behind with Shahzad, and then followed the aggravated dentist.

Robert marched past Zasu at the reception area and into his private office, holding the door open for Nasir, who was right behind him.

The frustrated dentist slammed the door shut and barked at the Caliphate Guard agent. "How in the hell do you expect me to take care of my patient while you continually undermine everything I'm trying to do to help him? How do you expect me to keep him calm and prevent him from being scared when you're threatening to shoot me and my dental assistant?"

"He was uncomfortable, and it is my job to protect him and keep him from harm," Nasir argued. His angry frown barely showed through the small slit in his black ghutra scarf.

"The very next thing I need to do for that poor little guy is give him a shot, and then pull two teeth. If I can't give him topical anesthetic, the shot will hurt worse. If he doesn't use the laughing gas, I won't be able to keep him as happy. Everything we do is designed to provide the most comfortable and predictable outcome. Of course, there will be some discomfort, but if you just let me do what I've been trained to do, that can all be kept to a minimum. I use specific language that is geared toward communicating but not upsetting. There are certain things you just never say in front of children. Don't say 'needle'! Don't say 'hurt'! Don't say 'blood'! Don't say anything! Trust me, and this will go just fine. I went to dental school in *Boston*, for God sake." It made him sick to hear the words coming from his own mouth.

Nasir lowered his voice to a near whisper but shot back defensively, "The child's father holds me personally responsible if anything happens to his son. He is very ruthless. My own life is at stake." He looked over his shoulder multiple times as he spoke, obviously concerned about the possibility of one of the other guards hearing him.

"You alone will be responsible if we can't complete the procedure," Robert said, "so stand the hell back at the foot of my dental chair and keep your mouth shut! I will take excellent care of Shahzad so he will be better off when he leaves than when he came, and overseeing his well-being is your job, so do it!"

Robert's heart was pounding as he stormed by Nasir, opened his office door, and marched past Zasu. He continued down the hallway, while Nasir followed. Robert's legs trembled as he walked, considering that there was an excellent possibility that he would be gunned down from behind, but no shots were fired. Instead both men reentered operatory two.

"Hello, captain," said Robert while kneeling down next to his patient. "I boarded the alien ship, and we have the OK to continue our voyage." Robert gave a reassuring wink and stood up behind Shahzad, turning up the nitrous oxide slightly. He put on a new dental mask and washed his hands.

Robert sat down as he put on new gloves. "I'm afraid we will have to use a bit more space jelly, captain, but you are very good with it, much better than our girl captains." Shahzad looked disappointed but nodded in approval. The dentist reapplied the topical anesthetic while glaring up at Nasir as if to warn him not to speak.

Robert turned around to the spotless, black glass work counter behind him and sneakily assembled a dental syringe, screwing the 27 gauge long shaft needle into place, and then loading a single carpule of anesthetic.

Nasir and Hami each took a step forward when they caught sight of the needle, but Robert gave a controlling glare, indicating that they would keep their distance. Robert turned back to Shahzad, carefully holding the anesthetic syringe out of his patient's sight.

"Let's make sure we got your tongue and cheek sleepy enough for the rest of the mission, captain," he said. "I am going to pinch your cheek and chin a bit with my finger, fingernail, and dental tool. If I touch a bad spot, I need you to raise your left hand to let me know."

Dzhoanna helped Shahzad raise his left hand as the doctor spoke, just like he'd instructed his assistants to do in their day-one staff meeting.

Robert continued to explain, "Now you are like my puppet master, captain. If you raise your hand from a bad spot, I will squirt a stronger numbing medicine right on the area."

"He means raise your hand if it hurts," explained Nasir in Arabic.

Robert felt his anger level rising again. "No. I mean raise your hand if I make a *bad spot*," he calmly replied. The University of Nebraska Department of Pediatric Dentistry had always taught that it was best not to allow parents in the room with their children because they would send signals and use language that prompted fear. Dental professionals never used words like *pain*, *blood*, and *shot*, but nervous parents frequently blurted them out. Apparently bodyguards with machine guns would fall under the same category as parents in the room, he thought.

Robert recaptured control of the situation. "After you raise your hand, it will take exactly five seconds for the medicine to make everything better. Now let's practice on the outside." Robert pushed along his patient's cheek, chin, and neck with his finger. "Most of the time there are no bad spots, and some spots even tickle."

Robert tickled Shahzad's neck, causing the patient to giggle and pull back a bit. "OK, now be ready because I'm going to make a little bad spot." Robert used his fingers to give his patient a little pinch on the outside cheek.

Shahzad's smile instantly turned to a troubled frown.

"Oh no, bad spot! What are you supposed to do?" Robert asked quickly while continuing to pinch his patient's cheek.

Dzhoanna gently tapped Shahzad's hand as a reminder, and he immediately raised it while squirming from the mild sting that the doctor was causing from his pinch.

With wide eyes and concerned urgency in his voice, Robert began counting slowly, "One...two...three..." Robert's voice lowered in tone and decreased in desperation with each number he counted. "Four... five...ahhhhhh." Robert gave a deliberate relief sigh, signaling that his patient had done just right; making the discomfort go away with his calmly raised hand.

"I think you've got it, captain. Now let's do it for real on the inside," said Robert.

"Make sure to raise your hand if the shot hurts," warned Nasir.

Unbelievable! thought Robert as he angrily glared at the bodyguard.

With a very worried look, Shahzad asked Robert, "Are you going to give me a shot, Doctor Cline?"

Robert usually accomplished injections on small children reasonably comfortably and without them being aware of what was going on, but there was too much information flying around the room at this point. The dentist stood by his protocol. "No, my little space captain. You watch for alien ships, while I check for bad spots, just like we practiced."

Shahzad opened his mouth wide. Then, like a magician, Robert used sleight of hand to shield the eyes of his patient and slid the 27 gauge long shaft needle into his mouth.

Nasir and Hami looked on nervously. Beads of sweat formed on the foreheads of both bodyguards.

Robert was able to make initial needle penetration without a reaction from his patient, who was focused intently on the television screen above. The dentist began injecting anesthetic slowly to numb the area.

"Is he hurting you?" asked Nasir.

You flipping idiot, thought Robert while continuing to painlessly inject lidocaine to block his patient's mandible.

Little Shahzad momentarily took his attention away from the spaceships flying across the television screen and tried to answer. When he realized he couldn't speak with Dr. Cline's hands in his mouth, he abruptly shook his head to motion no, which caused movement of the needle and a tiny pinch. He let out a small squeal, prompting Nasir and Hami to aim their weapons at Robert.

"Get that needle out of his mouth!" shouted Nasir.

"Oh no, we've got a bad spot!" said Robert in a dramatically concerned voice, ignoring the Caliphate Guard agents.

"Get that shot out of his mouth!" This time Nasir was louder, and both guards advanced.

"Raise your left hand," Robert quickly reminded Shahzad as he continued to inject. Dzhoanna tapped the patient's tiny hand as a reminder. In a high-pitched voice, Robert counted out, "One...two... three..." His voice lowered and slowed, assuring the patient that the situation was improving. "Four...five...ahhhhh." He finished counting, just like they had practiced.

Robert's counting was so animated and silly that Shahzad giggled as the pain subsided. The little patient lowered his hand down to his side. But he was so entertained by Robert's goofy method that he raised his hand again. This time it wasn't due to pain, but rather to see his dentist count again with the silly voice.

"You are hurting him! Stop!" shouted Nasir.

Robert could see what was happening, so, ignoring the bodyguards, he began counting again in an even sillier voice. Little Shahzad giggled again and raised his hand three more times during the injection just to prompt his doctor's amusing reaction.

Nasir and Hami finally realized what the child was doing and lowered their weapons before stepping back.

Zasu's beautiful French accent came over the intercom speaker behind Robert. "Your hygienist is ready for an exam in operatory five, Doctor."

"OK, buddy. You stay here and guard the spaceship, while I go check for aliens."

Shahzad smiled and nodded.

Robert patted him on the shoulder. "You're a great little patient," he said before leaving the room.

Robert usually didn't like getting interrupted, but it was nice to get out of the war zone for a bit. He walked past Zasu's desk, and she whispered, "I'm sorry, Doctor."

He smiled and shrugged as he continued walking to the hygiene room.

After completing his examination on the former prince of the Arab Emirates, Robert headed back down the hall, returning to his little patient in operatory two. Evie and Zasu scurried behind him, sweeping and polishing away the dust prints from his shoes, keeping the black granite floor spotless.

"Let's see if your teeth and lip are sleepy yet," announced Robert as he reentered the room.

"They are *very* sleepy," Shahzad said while touching his cheek in amazement.

Robert sat down and explained the next step. "I'm going to push all around your two teeth to make sure there are no more bad spots. I doubt there will be any. But if there are, raise your hand, and this time I will stop immediately. Got it?"

Shahzad nodded looking up at his dentist with great confidence.

"Got it?" Robert asked Nasir and Hami.

Both men nodded.

Dzhoanna handed Robert his instruments before he had a chance to ask for them. For a Russian spy, she's a pretty good dental assistant, he thought.

Robert carefully tested the areas around the two teeth he planned to extract. "Any bad spots?" he asked.

"No, Doctor," his patient said, smiling.

Robert skillfully extracted both problem baby teeth with no awareness from Shahzad. "Wow, these teeth are way too strong for me to get out. I don't know if I can do it," he said while sneakily wiping all blood from the extracted teeth just behind his patient's field of vision.

Nasir and Hami looked confused and stepped forward, holding their assault machine rifles tightly. Shahzad lost confidence in his dentist for the first time during the appointment. "What will we do, Doctor?" he asked innocently with a concerned look on his face.

"Well…, there *is* a magic trick I could try," Robert replied. He held the sparkling, white extracted teeth in each hand behind his patient's head and then used the pointy root of one of the teeth to scrape the skin on Shahzad's right ear. Then he revealed the shiny, white tooth, rotating it in front of Shahzad's eyes. "Look what I just got out of your ear," Robert said.

"Wow! Hami, Nasir, look! Dr. Cline pulled it out of my ear!"

Relieved, the body guards chirped some indiscernible Arabic to one another before nodding at Shahzad and then at Robert.

"Do it again, Doctor!" exclaimed Shahzad, clapping and laughing.

"Let's see what we can do." Robert pulled his other hand up to the patient's left ear and gently scraped the skin before he exposed the second tooth.

"Thank you, Doctor, thank you. Did you really pull the teeth from my ears?"

Just then Mrs. Gasol-Al-Shaitan burst into the room. "My poor precious baby, is everything OK?"

"Dr. Cline pulled the teeth from my ears!"

"Did he hurt you?"

"No, no, he wasn't strong enough to get them out through my mouth, so he had to do a magic trick."

"Didn't it hurt when he gave you the shot?" she asked.

"No, he didn't give me a shot. He just rubbed some space jelly on my cheek and then checked for bad spots with his fingernail."

"Fingernail, Dr. Cline? Hmm?" Gasol-Al-Shaitan raised an eyebrow and smiled while looking at Robert.

Robert shrugged, grinning triumphantly.

Suddenly the First Lady remembered. "I need to get back to your hygiene room. I left my little girl there, and she is probably scared without her mother." She rushed out and hurried down the hallway.

"Go ahead and get Shahzad's teeth boxed up for the tooth fairy, Dzhoanna, and I'll see how his sister looks." Robert turned to walk away when a voice stopped him.

"Doctor, please wait." It was Nasir approaching with his machine gun. "I apologize for the way we behaved." Hami nodded in agreement.

"It's OK," Robert replied. "You were only trying to do your job. Don't worry about it."

"Please listen, Doctor. You were so caring with little Shahzad. Will you consider being the dentist for my own children?" pleaded Nasir.

"I'll tell you what. Leave the machine guns at home, and you have a deal." He winked and walked out of the room.

Robert strolled down the hallway and grabbed a tiny, plush toy from behind the receptionist's counter.

"How are you holding up?" Zasu asked.

"It's Friday, and we're almost done," he said.

"I've never worked in a dental office where there were so many machine guns," she whispered, laughing.

Robert smiled, held the toy behind his back, and then disappeared into operatory one.

"Are you guys ready for me?" Robert asked as he poked his face between the heads of Linda Gasol-Al-Shaitan's bodyguards, who were standing shoulder to shoulder, shielding the entrance.

"Please, go to the waiting room." The First Lady waved on her security agents, while her daughter's two guards remained at the foot of the dental chair.

Robert knelt down next to three-and-a-half-year-old Malikah Al-Shaitan. She looked up at him with her mother's green eyes while sucking her thumb like it was coated with honey. The enthusiastic, young dentist pulled the toy from behind his back and presented it to the adorable little girl, who was still wearing white tights and a tutu from dance class. "How about we trade this prize for the thumb, my little princess?" requested Robert.

Uncertain, Malikah looked up at her mother, who gave an assuring nod. Then the little girl removed her thumb, smiled cautiously, and took the toy from her dentist.

Robert looked over at Malikah's radiographs that filled the computer monitor mounted on a brushed-aluminum wall. He instantly got a sick feeling as he spotted multiple areas of decay. He hated to see so many problems on such young patients.

"Hmm. We can talk about how to cut back on the thumb sucking a little later, but for now it looks like we have a more pressing issue. Little Malikah has several cavities."

"I don't understand Dr. Cline. She brushes every day. How can this be?" Mrs. Al-Shaitan stood up and leaned over the dental chair to look at the x-rays.

Robert pulled down his mask and looked up. "We like young children to brush their own teeth at least twice a day to build the habit, but I recommend that parents help brush as well. Little ones just don't seem to be as effective as necessary. That said, I think there's more to this than a lack of brushing. Does she by chance take a bottle at night?" he asked.

"Poor little Malikah comes into the bedroom with Mudir and me every night because she is frightened. She is daddy's little girl. Mudir has a sippy cup with milk ready for her. She climbs up in bed between us and drinks only a little before she falls asleep for the night."

"I see," Robert replied with a frown. "This is a very common problem called 'baby bottle carries.' Extensive tooth decay results from drinking milk in bed. Luckily her cavities are still only moderate in depth so they can all be fixed with composite fillings, but we're going to need to come up with a plan to get rid of the milk at night."

"You don't understand, Dr. Cline. For security reasons, we don't sleep in the same place even two nights in a row. Every evening it is a different palace or mansion. She is only a child. She is scared, Doctor."

"I do understand, but dental decay can lead to serious infection, and infections can spread to other parts of the body with severe consequences. It's not just a tooth issue but a health issue. I recommend switching her from milk to water."

Linda stood up in a defensive posture. "She does not like water, Dr. Cline. It is the milk that helps her sleep."

Robert tried not to come off as insulting but he insisted, "We all want our children to be happy, Dr. Gasol, but sometimes what they want is *not* in their best interest. I'll give you some literature from the American Dental Association on this problem, and you can look it over. Please know that I only want what's best for you and little Malikah."

Awkward silence followed, while the shocked mother held her hand up to her mouth and sobbed. She was embarrassed that someone of her education and social standing had let this happen to her own daughter.

Dzhoanna broke the silence and said, "Come on, Dr. Gasol. I'll take you to see Zasu so we can set up some appointments and get

Malikah all fixed up. I'm sure this little princess will do as good a job as her brother."

Right on cue, little Shahzad walked into the room and tugged up at his mother's arm. Still crying, she ignored her son.

"It's OK, Dr. Gasol-Al-Shaitan," Robert said, patting her on the shoulder.

"Malikah is going to be fine,"

Shahzad continued to pull on his mother's robe. He motioned again and again for her to bend down.

Mrs. Al-Shaitan finally knelt down, allowing her tiny son to whisper something in her ear.

She quickly held her hand up to her neck. Her crying turned to a smile and then to laughter.

Everyone in the room looked on, wondering what Shahzad had said.

"Dr. Cline, little Shahzad just asked me if you would be our guest at his birthday party next Tuesday evening."

Shahzad looked up at Robert with puffy, gauze-packed cheeks. He smiled and nodded.

"Wow," Robert said, laughing. "That's the coolest request I've ever had." He was clearly touched by the offer. "But I don't know if your other little friends would like hanging out with me, though," he said to Shahzad.

"I insist that you come," said Dr. Gasol-Al-Shaitan. "Of course, there is a party for his friends, but there will also be a huge celebration for adults. Every important person in the United Persian-Arab Caliphate will be there." She raised her eyebrow, looking at Robert, and smiled. "And apparently, you are now the *most* important person in the caliphate. Besides, with the affluent crowd in attendance, you will have the opportunity to mingle and meet prospective new patients."

"I don't know what to say. It's such a kind offer."

"Say yes," insisted the First Lady.

"Yes."

Shahzad reached up and hugged Robert's leg. "Thank you for pulling my teeth and not giving me a shot, Dr. Cline," he mumbled through a mouth full of cotton.

"That's quite all right. You were very brave today."

The First Lady continued. "Please bring one of the lovely ladies from the office with you. The event is very formal: evening gowns and tuxedos or traditional Muslim dress."

Great! I *knew* I should have brought my tuxedo, he thought.

"I will leave directions to the party with your receptionist. We expect to see you there." Then the First Lady looked down at Malikah and Shahzad and said, "Come on, children." She gathered them together and headed out of the operatory.

At the front desk, Mrs. Al-Shaitan bumped into Nasir and Hami, who were making appointments with Zasu for their own children. Evie and Dzhoanna quickly grabbed two iPads and helped with the scheduling so no one had to wait.

Robert quietly ducked down the hall and headed into his laboratory to finish some odds and ends before the weekend. There were a couple models to pour up and cases to prep for shipping out to a crown-and-bridge laboratory back in the United States.

The office lab was unlike any he'd ever seen. Most were confined to dark, cluttered spaces that resembled large closets, but the Millennium Tower dental office laboratory boasted a large window with the same stunning view of the Burj Khalifa found in each of the five operatories.

While Robert was concentrating on pouring up a dental cast without incorporating air bubbles, a voice startled him. "Doctor." He turned to see his assistant, Evie Garcia.

"What's up, Evie?"

"I just wanted to tell you that I really love the way you cared for the children today."

Robert looked back down at his work and replied, "Thanks. You were a lot of help today."

"Dr. Cline, I didn't get a chance to tell you that I volunteer in an orphanage on the weekends. The children have many needs."

"That's great," said Robert. As Evie continued to speak, his mind wandered toward his weekend plans: touring the city of Dubai in his Aston Martin.

"It's just that I was wondering if you would consider visiting the orphanage with me Saturday. We have a small nursing station that could be used as a dental operatory. Some of the children have serious dental problems, and there is no one to care for them."

Robert was a bit irritated. He worked hard during the week, and by Friday he was physically and mentally worn out. People just didn't understand that being a dentist was stressful—not to mention there was the added stress of doing dental work with machine guns pointed at your head and having the CIA mission to complete at the same time. He had to think quickly to wiggle out of her appeal for help. "Well, that sounds worthwhile, Evie, but I still have a lot to get situated in my new condo. I probably just won't have time."

"I understand, Doctor," she said graciously. "You are a very busy man."

Feeling a little guilty and a lot cornered, Robert put down the lab work, stood up, and headed for the door. "I better get going. I'll probably just come in and finish this stuff up before work on Monday. You have a great weekend," he said.

"Same to you. And you really were great today," his assistant said, smiling. "God bless you."

Robert was halfway out the door before Evie's words stopped him in his tracks. God bless you? You've got to be kidding, he thought. He turned back and said, "I don't wait around for God to bless me. I make my own blessings."

"Well, I have hope that he will bless you nonetheless," she replied.

Robert didn't believe in God anyway, but it was growing apparent that if God did exist, a CIA agent would not be one of his favorite children. "About the best thing I could hope for is that God isn't really out there," he said. "If he was, then I'd be in big trouble." Robert winked and walked out of the room. He headed down the hallway toward the exit before another voice from behind stopped him.

"Doctor, I wanted to catch you before you left." It was Dzhoanna, the other dental assistant/Russian agent.

"What's up, Miss Olen?" he asked.

"I just wanted to let you know how great you were today," she said.

Robert was noticing a common theme. OK, butter me up and then ask me to do something, he thought. I suppose she wants me to help work at a soup kitchen or something. "Just doing my job," he said.

"Maybe we should get together this weekend and have a little fun. This is an amazing city after all, Dr. Cline."

Dzhoanna was striking and seemed to be interested. Robert figured it would be fun to enjoy all Dubai had to offer with such a beautiful, exotic woman by his side. Plus, it wouldn't hurt to talk a little about the mission away from the office, since she would eventually be assisting him when it came time to implant the missile-guidance device. Surely they would need a well-thought-out routine, as they would likely have to plant the device in Mudir Al-Shaitan's tooth at gunpoint while being watched closely by multiple agents of the Caliphate Guard.

"Cool," said Robert. "I have monumental plans for the whole day tomorrow, and I'd *love* to have you along. I'll call you later and let you know what we'll be doing. Make sure to get a lot of sleep tonight so we can turn the city upside down."

"I am so looking forward to it." she said flirtatiously.

Robert skipped past each of his five operatories. All through the day, the entire staff had worked together to keep the office immaculate. It was already prepared for seeing patients next week. He said good-bye to Zasu, who was polishing the black glass counter at the front desk. She called out to him in her lovely French accent as he rushed out to the fiftieth-floor commons area of Millennium Tower. "Good-bye, Doctor. You were amazing today."

21

THE DATE

It was Saturday morning, and Robert was flying across the desert. Only the Cessna Citation M2 had given him the same kind of power rush that the Aston Martin DB9 now delivered. With every push of the accelerator, the luxury sports coupe responded with unrestrained fury. The all-alloy, quad overhead-cam, forty-eight-valve, 5,935-cc V-12 was a beast built for the racetrack or the autobahn. But on the Sheikh Zayed Highway in Dubai, Robert struggled to keep within reasonable vicinity of the sixty-five-mile-per-hour speed limit.

Led Zeppelin's "Kashmir" played through the seven-hundred-watt Aston Martin premium-Dolby audio system, while the hot Rub' al Khali desert sun reflected off the cool Sarthe Silver paint of the supremely engineered roadster. Robert wasn't driving his rusty Pontiac Phoenix past fields of corn on the Cornhusker Highway anymore. No, instead he was commandeering one of the world's finest driving machines past a world famous architectural masterpiece; the Burj Al Arab hotel. He couldn't help but think that the Burj Al Arab looked like an art deco crescent moon that had fallen from the sky and landed gently in the Persian Gulf.

Robert had started the morning feeling tired. Last night and every night since Mexico, he'd woken up multiple times after dreaming of hanging Pablo on the catamaran mast and watching the night sky grow bright just before impact of the long-range missile. Every time he closed his eyes, he saw Pablo's image, but now Robert was awake with eyes wide open. The exhilarating drive in the luxury road rocket had him pleasantly distracted from his memories of the Yucatán.

As he approached his destination, Robert powered past a fleet of eighteen-wheel, oil-transport trucks. He swerved sharply onto a highway exit, which led him to a modest residential neighborhood inhabited primarily by Russian oil company workers. Robert looked for a suitable parking spot in front of a small-but-nice apartment complex where Dzhoanna Olen was staying. There was certainly no valet like back at Millennium Tower. Nobody better scratch this beauty, he thought, parking at a careful distance from any other cars in the lot.

Robert locked the Aston Martin and walked about a hundred feet, through the blistering desert heat, up to Dzhoanna's duplex apartment. He took one large skip over the three concrete steps leading to her front landing and rang the doorbell. He patiently waited..., but there was no answer.

He rang again; still nothing. Pulling out his cell phone, Robert rechecked the address. This has got to be it, he thought. How can she not be here? We just set this up last night. He tried knocking on the door this time, but there was still no response. He looked back around the cluster of apartments, while the sun pressed down on him. One small palm tree was planted in front of each duplex, serving as the only landscaping and providing almost no shade.

Robert and Dzhoanna had the day well planned; starting with the 10:00 a.m. morning session at Ski Dubai, followed by lunch at one of the city's many fine restaurants. They had agreed to then return to Robert's Millennium Tower condo for a swim in the skyscraper's rooftop pool. But it was already 9:00 a.m., and their morning ski reservation was fast approaching.

Robert walked back down the front steps and dialed Dzhoanna's number on his cell phone. It rang twice and abruptly switched to voice mail. "Great," he murmured. "I wonder if I have the wrong apartment."

Before giving up and heading to the Aston Martin, he took one last look back up at the front door.

Suddenly there was subtle movement in the curtain that hung in the apartment window. What the heck, he thought as the sun's rays sizzled hot on the back of his neck.

Robert walked back up to the door and knocked loudly. There was still no answer, but again the curtain fluttered in the window while a curtain of paranoia fell over him. Why isn't Dzhoanna here? Why isn't she answering her phone? What if the Caliphate Guard discovered that she was a Russian agent sent to Dubai to assist in the assassination of Mudir Al-Shaitan? What if someone attempted to kill her and she's signaling me with her curtain that she hears me but she's wounded?

During his summers of CIA training at "The Farm," Robert had learned that if something seemed wrong, then it probably was wrong. Sweat rolled down his forehead as he contemplated his next move. I'm in the big league now, he thought. Anything could happen on this mission. He considered breaking the door down, worrying that he might see Miss Olen wounded and bleeding on the floor.

But what if this is a trap? he thought.

In addition to teaching agents to be prepared for the worst, the CIA had also emphasized the importance of remaining calm. There was no room for irrational behavior that would undoubtedly draw attention to yourself.

The curtains rustled again. Robert looked around, trying to decide whether or not he could kick the door in without being noticed. There were certainly more than a handful of people moving about in the Russian community. Being careful that no one was watching, he pulled an agency-issue Ruger LCP 380 ultra-compact, semiautomatic pistol out of his pocket and held it down by his side. He took a step back so he could generate some power with his leg, but then decided to ring the bell one more time.

Yet another fluttering of the curtain was immediately followed by a subtle squeaking of the doorknob. It was slowly but noticeably turning from the inside. It turned a quarter inch to the right, and then half an inch to the left. Robert drew his pistol into a ready position and turned on the laser sight.

Who could be waiting inside the apartment? he thought. This is without a doubt an ambush.

Then suddenly, the doorknob made a full quarter turn, and the door was slowly pulled from within, rotating open only an inch or two on its hinge before coming to a rest.

"Hello...? Dzhoanna?" Robert called quietly through the cracked opening.

Finally, the portal to a certain firefight swung wide open. Robert's heart pounded as he looked through the doorway, waiting to see a mob of Caliphate Guard agents with magazine-fed machine guns aimed and ready to overpower his small Ruger. He looked straight ahead and saw nothing but an empty apartment.

"*Ukhodit*," a small voice sounded from below.

Robert looked down and saw a little girl, who couldn't have been more than two or three years old, looking up at him.

"*YA skazal, ukhodit.*" The chubby child with thin, blond hair and short, straight bangs was pointing her well-fed index finger up at Robert, telling him to "go away" in Russian.

"*Privet.*" Robert said hello back in Russian. This is obviously not the right place, he thought while looking around and wondering if he'd been noticed. "Sorry, wrong apartment," he said while gently nudging the little girl back inside the doorway and attempting to shut the door in front of her.

Before he completely closed the door, he heard another Russian voice calling from inside. "Hello, Doctor." It was Dzhoanna Olen. "Come in."

Robert, more than a bit surprised, reopened the door and poked his head in. Dzhoanna entered from a bedroom and stood before him with her hair wrapped like a turban in a small, white bath towel. Her athletic body was blessed with sensual curves barely covered by another small, white towel that was loosely draped around her. "I am running a little behind, Doctor. I could not find a sitter for little Padub."

"Padub?" quizzed Robert with a perplexed gaze.

The rookie agent looked back down at the meaty little girl, who was dressed only in some type of training diaper. Her cheeks were so chubby that he wondered if they were actually stuffed full of food. She was still staring up at him with a frown, and her index finger pointed directly at his face. "*My* mommy!" she exclaimed to him in Russian. "Go away," she grunted.

"I will be ready in just a few minutes," said Dzhoanna. "I still need to dry my hair." She disappeared back into the apartment, leaving Robert and little Padub to stand at the doorway, staring at one another.

"Guess I won't be needing this," he mumbled, putting away his Ruger 380.

Robert walked in and sat down on a small couch. The overfed little girl ran out of the room.

How can she bring a kid on an assignment like this? thought Robert, shaking his head. Does the Russian government know she has a child with her?

The CIA never sent agents on missions with their children. It was considered a serious distraction, detrimental to the safety of the child and everyone involved. Apparently Russian intelligence operates a little differently than US intelligence, Robert thought.

Robert looked impatiently at his watch. The apartment was fifteen miles away from the indoor ski complex. It was already 9:15 a.m., and Dzhoanna wasn't even dressed.

Dzhoanna walked frantically back and forth between her bedroom and the bathroom. Each time she passed from one room to the next, she looked a little bit more put together. Padub followed her, looking just as she had when Robert first arrived.

9:15 turned to 9:30, and 9:30 turned to 9:45. Robert dialed the number for the Dubai Ski Center to move back his 10:00 a.m. reservation.

"We can change your ski session time, sir, but you will have to forfeit your deposit," the customer service agent told him, speaking Farsi.

Finally at 10:15 a.m. the beautiful Dzhoanna Olen entered the front room of her small apartment, holding the hand of…"So is this your daughter?" Robert asked in a puzzled tone, looking down at the plump little girl, now dressed all in pink. Dzhoanna had pulled most of the child's thin, blond hair up into a pair of curled pigtails, with the remaining bangs hanging laser straight across the middle of her forehead.

"Yes. Her father was killed in a Chechen uprising soon after she was born," replied Dzhoanna.

"And they don't mind you bringing her along on this mission?" quizzed Robert.

"Well, the SVR doesn't exactly know she is here. Actually they do not even know that little Padub exists." Her tone became troubled. "If they did, I would be forced to resign. Please do not tell anyone from the CIA."

"I don't suppose it really matters," Robert reassured her. Then he quickly changed the subject and asked, "So, what's the backup plan for the babysitter?"

"There is no backup plan," Dzhoanna said with an alluring smile. "She is coming with us."

Wow, you're kidding, he thought. "Yeah, sure, that will be great," he said, trying to generate some fake enthusiasm.

Little Padub stood between her mother and Robert. She wrinkled her brow and nose and pointed directly at Robert, again exclaiming in Russian, "My mommy!"

"Yes, well, I'm not going to take away your mommy, Padub." He looked back at Dzhoanna with a half-smile. "She sure is a cute little thing," he said. Looks like she eats a few too many Russian pancakes and piroshki, though, he thought.

They all three walked out to the Aston Martin together. Padub was careful to keep herself wedged between Robert and her mother.

Robert hit the unlock button and opened the trunk. He offered to take Dzhoanna's backpack, which was stuffed with warm ski clothing, and set it next to his own pack. "Hold on just a second," he said as he frantically shuffled through the small rear compartment.

"The president of the United States must have raised the CIA's budget," observed Dzhoanna. "This is quite an amazing car compared to what I am used to seeing their agents drive."

"Yeah, well, I guess they want me to blend in to my affluent surroundings," Robert said, emerging from the trunk with his hands full of American Dental Association publications. He opened the passenger side door and pulled the seat forward. Then he spread the magazines across the very tiny backseat, thinking he would protect the upholstery from little Padub. Robert figured the seats were likely engineered to be so small and uncomfortable to discourage bringing along child passengers who could possibly stain the interior. "There we go," he said. "I've got it all made up for her back here."

"That is cute. You have made a barrier to separate little Padub from your leather seats," Dzhoanna said, snickering. "I do not think she leaks, Doctor,"

Embarrassed and turning a bit red, Robert thought, Then why was she wearing a diaper when I arrived at your apartment? He replied, "I think the CIA charges me if I get any stains on the seats."

He wanted to change the subject and get her buckled in, but something crossed his mind, causing him to pause for a second. "Oh, wait a minute. Doesn't she need a car seat?"

"What do you mean?" asked Dzhoanna

"You know, like a child safety seat."

"We do not really use them much in Russia. I think it will be OK."

Robert was getting nervous. What if there are safety-seat laws in Dubai, and we get stopped by the police? he thought. If we get pulled over, I could be arrested. This could blow my cover. Crap! This is why you don't haul kids along on black op assassination missions! the voice in Robert's head screamed. "All right," he said. "I guess…Hand the little gal to me, and I'll strap her in the best I can."

Robert tried to pick up the little girl to situate her in the tiny back seat. "*Nyet! Nyet! Nyet!*" cried little Padub in protest.

"I will get her buckled in," said Dzhoanna. She took her chubby child and fastened her into the shoulder harness.

"Be careful not to get her feet on the seats," said Robert nervously, looking over Dzhoanna's shoulder.

"This car is beautiful, Doctor," said Dzhoanna.

"Yeah, it really is, isn't it? What a great assignment." The two colleagues got in and discussed particulars of the mission on the way to the Mall of the Emirates, where the indoor ski complex was located.

By the time Robert pulled into an underground parking garage next to Ski Dubai, it was 11:15 a.m. He left his keys with the valet attendant and then walked up to the front gate of Ski Dubai with his date and her daughter. Robert spoke in Arabic to the sales assistant at the ticket window, while Dzhoanna and Padub stood close by. He tried to explain that they had missed their start time of ten, and now they had an additional skier.

"No small children without a lesson to certify that she is safe to ski," said the attendant

"That's fine," Robert replied. "I guess we'll go ahead and get her signed up for a lesson and reserve a spot for two adults in the next session then."

"OK. I can get two adults into the next session, and I have an opening for the child with one of our instructors on Tuesday morning."

"Tuesday? No, you don't understand. We were wanting to ski today."

"We don't have a lesson available until Tuesday."

"I could definitely just show her how to ski myself," countered Robert. "I grew up skiing at Telluride. I'm *from* Colorado."

"I'm sorry, sir. They may do things that way in Telluride, but in Dubai we are all about safety. She must have a lesson and be certified by one of our instructors."

"Look, lady, the slope here is nearly flat. In Colorado kids her age ski down runs that look like cliffs."

"Well, you are *not* in Colorado, sir. You are in Dubai, and our children are taught by professionals."

Robert was getting agitated. "Professionals? I've skied The Plunge in Telluride. This is like a medium-sized indoor sledding hill. I'm sure I am at *least* as qualified to teach her as one of your instructors."

The attendant's phone rang. She picked it up and talked while Robert continued to wait impatiently. After a brief conversation, she hung up the phone. "Sorry, sir, I just booked our only Tuesday lesson. The next available lesson for a three-year-old will be on Thursday."

"Forget it. I'm not jumping through a bunch of hoops to ski on an indoor bunny hill. This wouldn't even be a beginner slope in Colorado."

"Then I suggest you go back to Colorado, sir." She pulled a shade down over her window, displaying an Arabic sign that translated, "Next Window Please."

Shit, he thought. Robert knew that this wouldn't have stacked up to the mountains he'd grown up with, but he'd looked forward to the novelty of skiing in the desert. He turned and walked back over to Dzhoanna and Padub. "Sorry, guys, it looks like we won't be able to ski today."

Padub positioned herself between Robert and Dzhoanna, wrinkled her brow and nose, and pointed at Robert, exclaiming, "My mommy!"

All right, Gretel. Looks like that little finger is fat enough to feed to the witch now, Robert thought. "You sure are a cutie," he said.

"Mommy, I am hungry," said little Padub, looking up to her mother.

"You mentioned that there were lots of great places to eat in Dubai, Doctor. Maybe we should just have lunch and talk about what we want to do next."

Robert *was* getting a little hungry. He'd gone on a five-mile run in the morning and ended up missing breakfast to make sure he picked up Dzhoanna on time. "Yeah, I sure could eat if you two are ready. There are supposed to be some amazing restaurants in the city. What are you in the mood for?" he asked. "Middle Eastern, Italian, Chinese?"

Dzhoanna turned away from Robert and looked down at her daughter. "What are you in the mood for, Padub?"

The little girl motioned for her mother to lean down. Then Padub whispered something in her ear.

Dzhoanna stood up, laughing.

"What did she say?" asked Robert

"Oh, little Padub ate at a Taco Bell once in Moscow. She was not excited about coming to Dubai, but after I promised her that there was a Taco Bell in the city, she agreed to come."

"Yeah, that's cute," Robert said. "So are you thinking Mexican then? I suppose they might have a few nice Mexican restaurants here."

"What do you want then, Padub?" she asked the little girl.

"Taco Bell."

"Well, I guess it is Taco Bell then," Dzhoanna said.

Are you freaking kidding me? Robert thought. You're really going to let the kid pick Taco Bell with all the amazing restaurants out here?

Robert had nearly survived eating from the dollar menu in college. Before he'd signed on with the CIA, Taco Bell was the only place besides the school cafeteria he could afford. But now he could eat wherever he wanted. Besides, there was a Taco Bell right across the street from his Dallas dental clinic back in the states. This kid is ruining the entire date, he thought.

"Do you mind?" Dzhoanna asked.

Robert was trying not to look angry, but he was becoming visibly agitated when he replied, "No, no. Taco Bell is great." Then he paused for a second and thought about it. I have to admit that a Nachos Bell Grande and Doritos Loco Tacos sound pretty good right now. "I'll just look it up on my cell phone," he said.

Sure enough, there was a new Taco Bell just opening on the other side of the giant shopping complex in the food court. The trio made their way across the fabulous Mall of the Emirates, passing through irresistible aromas from restaurants operated by world-renowned chefs. As they neared their destination, they strolled through a mini amusement park located right in the mall.

"Padub, maybe you would like to ride on some of these rides after we finish eating," said Dzhoanna while they walked in front of a carousel.

Just as the bell from the Taco Bell sign came into view, little Padub stopped in her tracks.

"Let's go, sweetie. We're almost there," urged Robert, pointing to the sign. After walking past so many nice restaurants, he was getting even hungrier. He was actually a bit thankful that the little porker had derailed the original plan and redirected to Taco Bell. At least you knew what you were getting there. Fancy restaurants could be a bit of a crap shoot. You might end up ordering something that looked like a piece of art but lacked flavor and the capacity to satisfy hunger. Besides, what could be more artistic than the orange-powder-dusted Doritos Loco Taco shell? He was starting to get excited just thinking about it.

Padub stood firm with her feet anchored to the marble floor in front of the carousel ride and pointed up at a candy vendor's display of giant-sized bags of bright-blue cotton candy. "Cotton candy," she said.

"Oh, little Padub loves cotton candy," said Dzhoanna.

Robert quickly pulled a gold tenth Baraah coin from his pocket and made the purchase. "Here you go, sweetie," he said, handing over the bag, which was almost as large as the little girl.

Padub looked up to her mother, waiting for approval. Dzhoanna nodded, and Padub smiled and eagerly grabbed the bag out of Robert's hands. "*Spacibo*," she said, thanking him. "No problem, honey," Robert said while patting her on the head. "But you might want to wait until after we eat lunch."

The little girl ignored Robert and immediately tore into the bag. Dzhoanna didn't seem concerned, so Robert figured he shouldn't be either. The beautiful mother was more interested in the Baby Gap store located across the hall. "Baby Gap. That is cute. We do not have these in Russia," she said.

The three resumed their walk and entered Taco Bell, while round, little Padub stuffed large fists of cotton candy into her mouth. As with all small children, she became more blue and sticky with each cycle of hand to bag, hand to mouth, and then back to bag.

Dzhoanna and Padub took a seat, while Robert took their order and went to the counter. Boy, Dzhoanna sure can eat for being such a fit-looking little thing, Robert thought as he placed their order. "Four Doritos Loco Tacos with large Nachos Bell Grande for the two girls to share." Robert ordered a couple tacos and an order of nachos for himself as well.

He returned with the tray and divvied up the food before sitting down on the plastic-molded seating. "Dubai certainly is known for its five-star dining establishments, isn't it?" he joked.

Dzhoanna took one of the tacos for herself. Then she laid the nacho platter and the other three tacos in front of her daughter. Padub grunted in disappointment.

"You only get three tacos, my darling baby. When you turn four next year, you can have four tacos," her mother reassured.

Rolls on rolls on rolls, thought Robert as he looked at Padub's portly arms. She determinedly alternated between tacos, cotton candy, and nachos.

The orange powder from Padub's Doritos Loco Taco shells, the blue dye from the cotton candy, and clumps of stark-white sour cream from the Nachos Bell Grande accumulated in the corners of her mouth and cheeks, not to mention on her hands and halfway up her arms. Robert watched the little girl crunch through the lightly seasoned, crispy corn tortilla taco shells, and he began to wish he hadn't ordered virtually the same lunch, as the sight of her smorgasbord was starting to make him feel a little nauseated. In fact, Robert had to opt out of his second taco, putting it back in the to-go bag for eventual disposal.

"Uuh, uuh, uuh." Padub's eating pace didn't falter in the slightest while she grunted and pointed at Robert's rejected taco.

"Are you not going to eat that, Doctor?" Dzhoanna asked.

"No, I guess I wasn't as hungry as I thought I was," he replied.

"Little Padub wonders if we could save your taco for her to eat later. Do you mind?"

"No, no that's great," he said. This kid certainly couldn't afford to miss a meal, he thought. "Be my guest."

Robert handed over the wrapped taco. Dzhoanna tucked it neatly into a counterfeit Coach bag she had purchased a year ago on a trip to Manhattan. Wow, that's nice he thought. She's going to smell like a taco for the rest of the day, while that thing stews in her purse.

Padub licked her black, plastic Nachos Bell Grande tray, making sure to leave not a speck of the nacho goodness behind. Then she pointed her orange-and-blue sausage of a finger back out at the carousel in the mall. "*Konskiy. Konskiy,*" she said.

"Oh little Padub, do you want to ride the horsey?" her doting mother asked.

The little girl nodded happily.

"Would you ride the carousel with us, Doctor?" asked Dzhoanna.

"Sure," he said. "But please, just call me Robert when we aren't at the dental office." He figured that if she hadn't dropped the "Doctor" on her own by now, she never would.

"Great, Robert. Let's go then." Dzhoanna grabbed her daughter's fleshy blue-and-orange hand, while Padub reached up to Robert with the other, having significantly warmed up to him since he bought her the cotton candy and gave her his taco.

Oh my God. I can't touch that germy, little paw, he thought. He patted her gently on the head, and there his hand remained as they walked out of Taco Bell toward the carousel.

"You hold on to little Padub while she rides the horse, and I will take a picture," said Dzhoanna.

"Uhhh…, why don't you two ride, and I'll take a picture of you?" countered Robert.

"Why would I want a picture of myself, silly? Please take her."

Robert laid down his backpack of ski clothing at the feet of Dzhoanna and lifted the little girl up onto a lime-green carousel horse. She wrapped her sticky fingers around the brass pole that rose up from the saddle.

The ride began to rotate slowly, while carousel music blasted. Round and round they went. Robert held onto Padub, while she went up and down on the horse and looked out at Mommy, Baby Gap, cotton candy stand. Mommy, Baby Gap, cotton candy stand. Mommy, Baby Gap, cotton candy stand.

Dzhoanna hollered, "Smile and wave, Padub," as she took a picture.

Mommy, Baby Gap, cotton candy stand. Mommy, Baby Gap, cotton candy stand. The carousel music played on, and Padub started to cry.

"You smile and wave too, Doctor!"

Mommy, Baby Gap, cotton candy stand.

"I think she wants off!" shouted Robert down to Dzhoanna as he rotated by.

Mommy, Baby Gap, cotton candy stand.

Suddenly through streaming tears and in near-perfect English, Padub looked up at Robert and declared, "I don't feel good."

Before he could react, Robert was sodden in a noxious mixture of blue-and-orange liquid loaded with chunks of poorly chewed taco meat and softened corn-tortilla clumps. Without thinking he grabbed little Padub, who was also covered in puke. With arms fully extended to keep maximum distance, he jumped off the moving carousel. He passed the crying child to her mother and violently ripped off his vomit covered shirt.

Dzhoanna scurried off to the restroom to clean up her hysterical daughter.

Compared to most areas in the Middle East, Dubai was a relatively liberal Muslim city when it came to dress, but Robert quickly gained the attention of a group of women cloaked from head to toe in black niqab coverings. Even though some passed by with more modern clothing, Robert was certainly the only person standing in the grand hallway of the Mall of the Emirates not wearing a shirt.

A nearby mall-security guard drew his Taser while radioing an occurrence of indecent exposure to city police. Just then Robert remembered that in his backpack there was a heavy llama-fiber sweater that Dr. Ritchey, his chemistry professor from college, had given him as a graduation present. The sweater was green and ugly, but he'd planned to wear it to keep warm while skiing before plans had changed. Quickly, Robert shuffled through his bag and grabbed the sweater to get himself covered.

Once the security guard saw that the situation had been rectified, he canceled his call for backup and holstered his Taser.

Robert wadded up his vomit-covered shirt and stuffed it into a trash receptacle, but he was still contaminated. His reluctance to enter public restrooms would have to be set aside. He certainly dreaded the germs he would encounter in the men's room, but at this point he needed to get cleaned up quick.

While rushing toward the restrooms, Robert noticed splatter marks all over his jeans. He decided he would just throw them away and put on his ski pants from his back pack. The defiled agent took four quick deep breaths to build his oxygen and held the last one before he blasted into the lavatory. He quickly washed his arms and hands in one of the sinks. Still holding his breath, he bent down to untie his shoes but was startled after noticing a few half-chewed pieces of undigested cheddar cheese pasted to his shoestrings.

Unbelievable, he thought as a shiver went up his spine. The combination of being puked on, seeing the cheese bits, and the mere thought of being in a public restroom made him start to gag. His lungs burned for air, but he continued to hold his breath long enough to rip off his shoes and pants, and throw them all in the garbage dispenser.

Robert was turning a little purple, and the survival urge to breathe was overtaking his stubborn commitment not to. He quickly slid into his ski pants and frantically washed his hands again before running back out of the lavatory in his socks. After getting a safe distance away from the men's room, he let out his breath with one final gag, and then panted rapidly for a minute before finally resuming normal breathing.

Robert went to sit down on a bench across the grand hallway from the carousel. There was now a sign printed in Arabic in front of the ride that read, CLOSED FOR MAINTENANCE. He was being made to feel uncomfortable by the ride operator who continually shot him dirty looks while mopping puke from the attraction.

"That wasn't my kid," lipped Robert in Arabic while shaking his head, pointing to the carousel, and shrugging.

The looks didn't subside, so Robert moved to a bench behind the cotton candy stand, which now partially shielded him from eye contact with the carousel operator. It turned out to be a better seat anyway, because the obstruction also shielded him from being able to see the wet blue-and-orange mop head.

Just then Dzhoanna emerged from the ladies' room, carrying little Padub, who was wearing a green llama-fiber sweater with black ski pants. The carousel operator went out of his way to curl his neck around the cotton candy stand. He shot one more seething glare at Robert and the little girl, who was now dressed just like him.

Robert shrugged and gave a defeated look back to the carousel operator.

"Oh, look at the two of you. You are dressed just alike," observed Dzhoanna. "How cute."

How cute indeed, thought Robert, with a growing well of sarcasm and disgust. "Hmm," he said. "Looks like you didn't get all of the orange-and-blue stuff off your hands." Robert pointed to the cotton candy and taco powder still stuck to Padub.

"She is such a messy eater," said Dzhoanna with a chuckle. "Little Padub always has something stuck to her hands."

Robert was becoming seriously concerned that if the child's hands still had blue-and-orange crap all over them, Mom probably hadn't done a real thorough job of puke removal either. "Well, I probably ought to go ahead and take you two home now since she doesn't feel good," he said in a disappointed voice while at the same time being relieved to end the date.

"Oh no, she is fine," Dzhoanna insisted. "Padub always gets motion sickness when she spins."

Robert tried not to look stunned, but he was stunned. Then why the hell did you let her eat like a potbelly pig and put me on a carousel ride with her? he thought.

"I think she is ready to go swimming. She has been so excited ever since I told her about your pool."

"You know, if she's not OK, you guys could always come over and swim another time," Robert said.

Not getting the hint, Dzhoanna bent down to her daughter and asked, "You are feeling OK, right, Padub?"

The little girl nodded briefly, but was then side-tracked by something that caught her eye. "Ooh!" she grunted and pointed up over her mother's shoulder.

Dzhoanna turned around to the cotton candy stand behind her and looked straight up at an eight-inch-diameter, candy ribbon-swirl lollipop. "Oh, doesn't your tummy still hurt a little, baby?"

Padub continued to point at the giant "Whirly Pop" while she puckered her lips and puffed up her chubby cheeks, frowning up at her mother.

"OK, you little cutie." Dzhoanna affectionately rubbed her hand across her daughter's thin, blond hair momentarily, pushing her short, straight bangs to the side before they immediately fell back into place.

Robert stood with dropped jaw while he watched Dzhoanna purchase the giant lollipop. She handed it down to Padub and cautioned,

"OK, Mommy says do not eat this right now, baby. We will want to save it for later."

The tubby little girl smiled and thanked her mother. Then she immediately removed the plastic wrapping and aggressively licked the enormous treat.

"Should we head out to swim now?" asked Dzhoanna.

"Yeah...sure...Let's head out," said Robert, exasperated.

As the three walked back through the mall toward the parking garage, Padub happily ran her tongue over all parts of her lollipop. Dzhoanna started shuffling through the contents of her bag and then turned back to Robert. "If you want, I can take the messy clothing from your backpack and put it in here with Padub's. I could wash your things for you and bring them back to work Monday."

Oh, dear heavens no, he thought. She's keeping the kid's carousel clothes. "Uh..., no thanks. I should be good."

Robert kind of had a rule about anything that got puked on: it was most definitely ruined and required disposal. He didn't like the idea of putting that kind of thing in a washing machine with chunks swirling around in the water. Unless a washing machine was also equipped with a garbage disposal and an autoclave, it would be insufficient to refurbish clothing that had been doused with vomit. Furthermore, Robert figured that a washing machine used for this sort of mess would be forever contaminated, passing on its defilement to every future load of laundry.

The valet attendant pulled the Aston Martin up to the date trio and handed Robert the keys. Robert tipped him with a new quarter Baraah coin and thanked him.

Robert quickly opened the trunk. "Let me put your things back here for you," he said, taking Dzhoanna's purse and backpack. At least the rest of the car won't smell like puke and a taco, he thought. "Why don't I take the lollipop and wrap it up to put back here also," Robert suggested.

It was too late. Dzhoanna already had her daughter strapped into the small backseat.

Shit! Robert thought. He slammed the trunk, while Padub worked her sucker.

The original plan for the date had included unleashing the Aston Martin for a long drive on E95 Highway through the Rub' al Khali Dunes. Fortunately, Robert hadn't mentioned this to Dzhoanna. Instead he now sped home, looking nervously back and forth between the road and the rearview mirror. He hoped an abbreviated drive back to the condo would minimize damage to his immaculate roadster. But he could see that Whirly Pop drippings were rolling off Padub's meaty arm and onto the rear upholstery.

Clearly preoccupied, Robert said few words to Dzhoanna as he roared down the highway. Not wanting to wait for the valet attendant, he tucked himself into an empty visitors' spot in the parking garage at Millennium Tower. Robert leaped out of the car and quickly unbuckled Padub. Surprisingly, it appeared that she hadn't made too much of a mess. "Good girl," he said.

As he lifted Padub out of the luxury roadster, she lost grip of the moist, white stick that anchored her sugary treat. The giant, wet sucker hit the back of Robert's hand, sticking momentarily. Robert quickly jerked and practically threw the little girl to her mother, disgusted at the thought of the exhaustively licked candy touching his skin. The sudden movement caused the candy to release. It fell again before finally coming to a rest in the middle of his leather driver's seat. He immediately looked back into the car with disappointment and pealed the lollipop off the soft, light-gray leather upholstery. A perfect seven-and-three-fourths-inch circular color swirl embossing of the candy sucker was left behind. Son of a bitch, he thought, clenching his teeth tightly, trying to hold back an outburst of swearing. What kind of spy has a big, freaking Whirly Pop stain on the driver's side seat of his Aston Martin?

Padub began to cry and kick in her mother's arms. "Candy, candy." She stretched and contorted so much that Dzhoanna almost dropped her before regaining her hold. The agitated child pointed toward Robert, crying, "Candy, candy."

Robert reluctantly held the moist sucker stick, noticing fibers from the leather seat now stuck to the lollipop. "She's not really going to want to eat this *now*, is she?" he asked.

"I think it will be OK. I will just rinse it off in your apartment," said Dzhoanna.

Robert tried to pass the giant lollipop to the Russian agent, but Padub quickly intercepted it and immediately resumed a furious licking pattern.

Dzhoanna asked Robert to pop the trunk, and she grabbed her things, including Padub's messed clothing. Then the dysfunctional date participants got on the high-speed elevator and headed up to the forty-second floor.

Security in Millennium Tower's residential suites was second to none. Robert looked into the retinal scanner mounted on his door for only a second before the lock disengaged and the door swung open.

They walked into the open-concept apartment with rich granite floors and faux-paint walls. The living room was spacious, and the ceiling was high. An interior decorator had gone to great expense, creating a living space that was a comfortable and inviting work of modern art.

Dzhoanna immediately recognized the contrast between the apartment she was in and Robert's luxury skyscraper condominium. "You are taken care of better than any CIA agent I have ever seen, Robert. You must be a very special man."

Unimpressed by the beautiful suite, Padub continued to lick her sucker. She looked at Robert's couch, thinking it would make an excellent trampoline until something caught her eye. "Kitty!" The word in Russian sounds the same in English. She pointed at Kitty Witty, who was taking a literal catnap on the couch.

"Oh, what a beautiful cat, Robert," said Dzhoanna. "What is its name?"

"Uh…, Kitty Witty," he replied, embarrassed by the unimaginative name. "But I just call him K-Dub for short."

"Little Padub adores cats. I would love to get her one, but she is very allergic."

Eager to keep the date moving, in hope that it would reach an eventual conclusion, Robert changed the subject. "Hey, I'm going to run into the other room and get into my swim trunks. Just make yourself at home. There's a guest room right down the hall that you two can use to change." Robert walked out of the living room, went into his bedroom, and closed the door.

Chubby little Padub hadn't taken her eyes off Kitty Witty since she'd first spotted him. She quietly tiptoed over to the couch and peered over the cushion that was just at her eye level. She stood very still, watching him sleep.

Dzhoanna walked down the hall and called back over her shoulder to her daughter. "Do not touch the kitty, Padub. Remember your allergies." Then she disappeared with her things into the guest room.

Ignoring her mother, Padub laid her Whirly Pop down on the Italian leather couch and climbed up next to Kitty Witty. Then she picked up the sucker with her left hand and resumed licking it, while she used her right hand to aggressively pet the cat.

K-Dub was immediately startled awake. He jerked and hissed while glaring up at the little girl. "Meow!" he howled.

"Kitty!" exclaimed Padub. She giggled and said, "You're a pretty kitty." She used both hands to pick up the cat by his neck while still holding the lollipop.

"Meow, Meow!" Kitty Witty moaned as he batted at the child's face with a useless, declawed paw.

Padub giggled. "That tickles. I love you, kitty." She tucked Robert's unwilling pet under one arm so she could attempt to free a hand and remove her lollipop that was now stuck to his fur.

"Reeer!" screeched Kitty Witty, who made a quick escape maneuver and bolted out of Padub's arms. The Whirly Pop, now only seven-and-one-half inches in diameter, was still firmly imbedded in his fur as he ran across the living room floor. He skidded to a stop in front of Robert's bedroom, where he pawed frantically at the closed door.

Padub placed her sticky, cat-fur-covered hands on the couch to spin herself around before sliding down to the floor. She slowly walked toward K-Dub while trying to lick the sticky off her fingers. "Kitty," she said. She took a few more steps. "Kitty, Kitty."

"Meow!" Kitty Witty moaned for help like a nervous competitor at a midnight catfight.

Padub took a few more steps until she stood hovering over the petrified cat. She giggled and leaned over to pick him up. Kitty Witty curled his nose and hissed, causing the little girl to cautiously step back for a moment. Then she giggled and said, "Bad kitty." She reached down toward him just as Robert opened the bedroom door.

"What happened, K-Dub?" asked Robert as he bent down and picked up his cat. "I see you have become acquainted with Padub, and it looks like she's wreaking havoc as always."

Robert carried the cat over to the kitchen, while Padub waddled closely behind. He turned the water on, filled the polished copper sink, and placed Kitty Witty inside. K-Dub twisted and thrashed, reminding Robert of his professor Dr. Ritchey after he'd caught on fire a few years ago in chemistry lab.

"It's all right, K-Dub. We've got to get the sucker out of your fur. This won't kill you."

Padub, standing below Robert, giggled and pointed as Kitty Witty whipped and jerked through his entire bath.

Finally, when K-Dub's fur was thoroughly soaked, the lollipop floated free.

"Candy, candy." Padub pointed up to the sink. "Candy, candy."

You're not getting this damn sucker back, kid, thought Robert as he laid it up on the counter out of her reach.

Dzhoanna came out of the spare bedroom and walked into the kitchen, wearing a cover-up over her swimsuit. "Oh, you are giving the kitty a bath. How cute," she said.

Robert figured it wasn't worth trying to explain. "Yeah, he gets a little dirty sometimes."

"While you are doing that Robert, would you mind if I throw Padub's clothes in your washing machine? I do not have a washer and dryer in my apartment. We have only two machines in a laundry room back at my complex, but they get so filthy from the oil workers."

Filthy? And you want to put puke clothes in *my* machine? Robert thought. He was horrified at the idea of the chunks of partially digested taco meat swirling around in his washer. He frantically searched his mind for a way out but could think of nothing. "Yeah...sure..., no problem," he said unenthusiastically. "The laundry room is right through those doors." He pointed across the kitchen. "Soap's on a shelf over the machine." Shit, he thought.

Dzhoanna grabbed her bag and disappeared into the laundry room.

Kitty Witty glared up at Robert and shot him a look with angry eyes that said, This is just wonderful. You let that freak kid ruin my soft pelt. "Meow!"

"Yeah, you've got it easy, K-Dub," said Robert, pulling the uncooperative cat out of the sink and placing him on a towel to dry him off.

"Can I dry, Kitty?" asked Padub while looking up at Robert.

"Meow!" K-Dub hissed from the counter above and batted his paw down at the little girl's face.

"No, honey. Your mommy says you're allergic. Maybe you should follow her into the laundry room and have her give you some Ritalin," Robert said.

Just then Dzhoanna walked back into the kitchen, where she stripped Padub's clothing and put her into a swim diaper.

Uhh. Swim diaper? Robert thought. That just doesn't seem like a good invention at all. He imagined that after Padub loaded her swim diaper in the pool, he would never swim there again. He had already decided that he would no longer be using his washing machine. He certainly knew that he would never be wearing his shirt, pants, or shoes ever again, as they were sitting securely in the trash bins at Mall of the Emirates. It had only been a short time since he'd met Padub, but the kid was systematically destroying everything around him.

Robert started walking toward the front door and said, "I suppose we can head up to the pool now." Dzhoanna followed him out of the kitchen.

Padub wasn't quite ready to swim. She stood on the very tip of her toes and fully extended her arm to maximize every inch of her short, round stature. With one final stretch and a small grunt, she managed to grab hold of her Whirly Pop and pull it off the counter. She resumed licking and ran to catch up with Robert and Dzhoanna.

All three got in the elevator that climbed to the pinnacle of Millennium Tower. Only in Dubai could you be on the rooftop of a sixty-story building and look up at another building towering another hundred floors above. The Burj Khalifa rose over Millennium Tower and everything else in Dubai. This was the first time Robert had been on the roof to see the pool. It was a perfectly designed infinity pool, appearing to simply drop over the edge of the roof with the mighty Burj Khalifa standing tall in the background.

"Amazing," said Dzhoanna. "It is just like a fairy tale. I cannot wait to get in."

But as soon as the trio got ready to enter the pool, a Tower security guard stopped them and spoke calmly in Arabic. "I'm sorry. No children under twelve, sir."

What a relief, thought Robert. But he figured he'd better put up somewhat of a fight, just for appearances. "Really, is there any way you could make an exception?" he asked.

The security guard paused and thought for a moment.

Oh no. No. It's OK. Never mind, thought Robert. Please, please don't let this kid in the pool.

"I'm sorry, sir. I could lose my job at the Tower. Can't you understand why we wouldn't want children swimming in this immaculate pool in a swim diaper?"

Oh, hell yeah, Robert thought. "No I can't," he said. "This is very disappointing, but I respect your decision. Thank you, sir."

Just then little Padub sneezed, and sneezed again.

"That is a terrible sneeze," said Dzhoanna with a frightened gasp while bending down to look at her daughter. She hadn't seemed to pay much attention to any of Padub's shenanigans up to this point, but now she was clearly beginning to overreact. The concerned mother held her hand up to her own mouth in a panic. "Oh, my little angel. You touched the kitty, didn't you?"

Dzhoanna looked away from Padub and up to Robert. "She is very allergic to cats. I will need her inhaler right now." she picked up Padub, and they all three hurried to the elevator.

The trio quickly returned to the apartment. Kitty Witty noticed them enter and immediately scrammed for cover under Robert's black, contemporary coffee table, which was artistically designed to contain a built-in gas fireplace.

Dzhoanna frantically looked through her purse and began crying. "This cannot be. I left the inhaler at home. She could stop breathing. I am so sorry, Robert, but we are going to have to leave."

"Achoo!" Little Padub sneezed again while she continued to calmly lick her sucker.

"I will have to get her clothes out of the washer and hang them to dry back at my apartment."

Well, at least my dryer won't be ruined, Robert thought. "Are you sure you can't stay?" he asked.

"Robert, I know you are disappointed, but I have got a sick little girl here." Dzhoanna rushed into the guest room to change out of her swim clothes, while Padub carelessly walked around the apartment, licking her sucker and looking for the cat. "Kitty. Kitty," she called. "Achoo!"

"Padub! I'm coming, Padub!" Dzhoanna hurried back out and grabbed her baby. Robert also tried to hurry in case she suddenly quit sneezing. They headed for the door.

Kitty Witty checked to make sure the coast was clear and appeared from under the coffee table, but he saw little Padub waving back to him from her mother's arms at the front door. K-Dub immediately hissed and darted across the granite floor before skidding to safety under an overstuffed chair.

After rushing to the elevator and down to the Aston Martin, Robert placed Dzhoanna's things in the trunk and then helped strap sticky, little Padub into her seat. He desperately wanted to lay down some more American Dental Association magazines to protect the interior, but he figured it was bad form, since Dzhoanna believed her child was having a medical emergency.

The trio flew down the highway, while Padub continued to lick her sucker in the backseat. She sneezed, and Robert immediately felt a syrupy spray hit the back of his neck. He jumped, causing the car to swerve a bit. Oh, what the hell? Yuck, he thought. Robert kept his composure, being comforted by the idea that a Kitty Witty-induced, lollipop squirt sneeze was quite a bit less nasty than the projectile hot dog meat burp that Agent Mercer had hit him with in Mexico.

Robert pulled into the Russian neighborhood and right up to the apartment where Dzhoanna was staying. He jumped out and opened the trunk to grab the girl's things. The temperature outside had reached 110 degrees, causing the aroma from the taco in Dzhoanna's purse to stew into the trunk's carpet.

Dzhoanna came around to the back of the car with her exhausted child asleep in her arms. "I am so sorry, Robert, but it looks like she fell asleep, and the sucker fell out of her mouth. I think it might be stuck behind the backseat."

Yeah, well, not a big shocker, he thought. "That's OK. I'll get it later," he said.

"Thank you, Robert. You are such a gentleman. You were very kind to little Padub. I can tell she adores you." Dzhoanna held the child in one arm and stood up on the tips of her toes while lightly touching Robert's shoulder. She looked at him with her ice-blue eyes and kissed him slowly and softly on the lips.

Robert's assessment of the date was suddenly tempered. Dzhoanna was beautiful and smelled almost as good as Padub smelled bad. His legs momentarily became a little weak, and he had to take a small step back to make sure he wouldn't lose his balance.

"I had a wonderful time, Robert," Dzhoanna said. "I will see you on Monday." She turned away with her sleeping child, walked up to her front door, and disappeared into her apartment.

22

GHALI

I t was Tuesday afternoon, and Robert was working in the Millennium Tower dental office, performing one of the more relaxing procedures for dentists: a root canal. He methodically used a series of small hand files to clean and shape the inner walls of the lateral incisor nerve canal. His patient was Umair Aalim, a graduate school professor of mathematics at Heriot Watt University Dubai.

Robert carefully pulled away diseased nerve, artery, and vein tissue from the pulp chamber, while Dzhoanna passed him each instrument he needed before he even had to ask for it. Scrape, scrape, scrape. In and out, in and out. If a dentist didn't really focus, he could almost put himself to sleep doing a root canal. In and out, in and out. Scrape, scrape, scrape. The root canal was only halfway done, but another busy day was almost over.

"So, what do you do for fun in Dubai when you're not teaching, professor?" Robert asked.

Umair attempted a muffled answer in Arabic through the rubber dam that Robert had stretched over his mouth to isolate the infected tooth.

Robert was a master of languages, and he was usually able to understand patients with his hands in their mouths, but the rubber-dam/foreign-language combination was exponentially hindering his ability to decipher Umair's responses.

Umair pleaded in Arabic, "*Lemathetis ahloni ahsila?*" (Why do you keep asking me questions while your hands are in my mouth?). The patient was clearly not as relaxed about the procedure as his dentist.

Hmm, I think I understood that one, Robert thought. "Yes, professor, that will be fine," He said. "I'll give you a break for a drink of water if you can hold on for just a few minutes more"

Scrape, scrape, scrape. In and out, in and out.

The patient sighed and waited for the next question that he'd be unable to answer. Despite being frustrated with the unilateral conversation, Umair was grateful that there hadn't been even a hint of pain through the entire procedure. He only winced and crinkled his nose from time to time due to the scraping sound that amplified from his tooth, through the bones of his skull, and into his eardrums. The noise for the patient was nearly thirty times more intense than the sound Robert and Dzhoanna could hear.

Scrape, scrape, scrape…Scrape, scrape, scrape…Crash! The sound of breaking glass blasted from the waiting room startling Robert, Dzhoanna, and the patient. A shrill scream called out amid advancing waves of pounding.

Robert stood up from his operating chair, but before he could take a step, frenzied Arabic orders were being barked from what sounded like ten or more men engaging in a minor battle just outside the operatory. Splintering wood cracked and more glass shattered, while tables and chairs were overturned. The only discernible words heard through the commotion were, "No! No! No! No!" shouted desperately by Umiar's wife, who had been waiting for her husband.

Suddenly, the crying voice of a hysterical child rose above the clamor.

Robert abruptly excused himself from the root canal. His patient struggled to sit up without the assistance of the automatic chair in an attempt to look out and see what was going on in the waiting room.

Robert darted out of the operatory and into pandemonium. He was immediately overtaken by two men who were unmistakably dressed in the red bisht cloaks and black ghutra head scarfs of Caliphate Guard officers. The powerful men slammed Robert up against the polished, black counter of his reception area. He saw flashes of more red cloaks dashing all around, while he was violently flung from the counter to the floor. Robert's cheek pressed unforgivingly against the cool, clean, black granite surface, while the barrel of an AK-47 dug into his temple.

"*Letah taharahki! Letah taharahki!*"

Robert clearly understood the command not to move, shouted wildly by the massive Caliphate Guard agent, whose right knee was bearing down onto his spine.

The shiny, black army boot of the Caliphate Guard officer stomped firmly in front of Robert's face, while the tail of his red bisht cloak draped over the powerless dentist's forehead, blocking all but a sliver of his vision. The scent of freshly polished boot leather replaced the sterile antiseptic dental-office smell Robert had grown accustom to. He could see only flashes of light and undiscernible glimpses of the mayhem whirling around him. All the office workers and patients in the waiting room were being overpowered and put to the ground at gunpoint just like him.

The increasingly hysterical voice of the screaming child called out, "Ghali! Ghali!"

The child's voice sounded familiar, but Robert didn't recognize the language, or the meaning of the word *Ghali*.

Another officer shouted to the guardsman who was restraining Robert, "Check and make sure he does not have a weapon! Check everyone!"

Robert's patient, Umair, peeked out of the operatory and into the hallway. His rubber dam was still intact, stretched over his tooth and across his face. He dropped like a stone after a Caliphate Guard agent hit him in the side of the head with the butt of his assault rifle

As the Caliphate Guard battalion took control of the office, Robert could hear Dzhoanna crying just a few feet away, but he couldn't see her.

"Hey, take it easy there!" Robert shouted while the guard's knee pressed ruthlessly into his back during an aggressive body search for firearms.

The Caliphate Guard commander shouted out, "Do not make another mistake, or another will lose his head!" Then a cracking crash pierced Robert's eardrum as the clank of metal resonated through the granite floor below him. A flash of tempered, shiny steel with red smears came into focus through the small opening in the robe draped over Robert's eyes. The blade of a blood-splattered sword now rested inches from his face.

Still rising above the commotion of some twenty Caliphate Guard officers taking siege of the office was the screaming of the little girl. "Ghali, Ghali," the voice screeched over and over.

Dzhoanna continued to cry and gasp just a few feet away.

Why can't she keep it together? Robert thought. She's the only other person in the office that has training for these circumstances. But then it hit him. Everything was starting to make sense. The crying child…It's Padub. Oh my God. They know our plan. They've rounded up little Padub, and they're going to execute her, Dzhoanna, and me right here. For that matter they're probably going to behead everyone in the office.

"Ghali, Ghali, Ghali!"

That's definitely Padub, thought Robert. He made an unsuccessful attempt to lift his head and see from beneath the robe, but the guardsman held him tight against the floor, digging the barrel of his gun deeper into Robert's scalp. The shackled agent grimaced with pain as blood trickled from his temple down into his eye, blurring what little view he had through the robe covering his face. Ghali? What does this mean?

Robert blinked rapidly, clearing his eye. The bloodied blade of the sword that would undoubtedly be used on him next came back into focus.

Then the door to the lobby opened and slammed back shut. The smell of the polished combat boot next to Robert's face was gradually overtaken by smoldering English Dunhill tobacco smoke.

"Is the area clear? Where is Dr. Cline? We need to get this taken care of immediately!"

Robert recognized the voice. He'd heard it many times on the news and on his Dubai operation intel video clips. It was Mudir Al-Shaitan.

The pipe smoke grew thicker, causing Robert to cough. He was startled when right in front of the opening in the Caliphate Guard officer's robe he saw a hand pass slowly by and then pick up the sword.

Oh shit. Robert thought. This can't end well. The actual guy is here, and he's getting his sword ready. Robert tried to mentally prepare himself to be tortured. They'll make a video of me pleading for rescue just before they saw off my head. He cringed at the thought of his parents seeing their son's execution play out over and over on the web.

"Ghali! Ghali!" The little girl continued to scream frantically.

Robert's mind raced to arrive at a plan that would save himself and the others in the office. But it was useless. He was heavily outnumbered. There was no way out.

Then, all of the sudden it hit him. Wait. The mission is obviously lost, but I can still save little Padub, Dzhoanna, and the entire staff. He had a plan that would work. At least it would be worth a shot.

Maybe if I claim to be an anti-Islamic extremist working on my own initiative to assassinate the Persian-Arab Union president...Maybe, just maybe, they'll let everyone else go.

Robert struggled again to move, trying to see through the red cloak still draped over most of his face. But with even the slightest flinch, the Caliphate Guard officer pressed his knee more forcefully into Robert's spine and dug the barrel of his machine gun deeper into his scalp.

"Get this done now! How many more heads need to fall? Get this done now!" Mudir Al-Shaitan screamed at his men like a rabid dog, while spit flew from his mouth and landed on Roberts arm. "The child must come first!"

That sick freak. He's going to kill Padub first. Robert tried to think of another way out, but nothing came to him.

The little girl screamed uncontrollably and continued to cry, "Ghali, Ghali, Ghali!" Her voice grew louder as someone carried her across the room and now held her over Robert. "Ghali! Ghali!"

Two drops of blood fell and hit the floor, passing through Robert's narrow field of vision on the way down.

What the hell have they done to her? Robert thought. All his training demanded that an agent was never permitted to give up, but he would deny any ties to the CIA or any US government agency. He made a quick decision.

"Hold on! Please just listen!" Robert prepared to breathe his last words and profess that he had plotted to single-handedly turn the Persian-Arab Union upside down. "The little girl didn't do anything. She's innocent!"

"Of course she is innocent. Who are you to speak of my child in this way?" said the United Caliphate president while hovering over Robert. Then Al-Shaitan waved his hand at his security agent and barked, "*Ahdefolka dhee matckee,*" ordering the guard to lift his knee from Robert's back.

"I presume you are Dr. Cline," Mudir said. "You need to get up, right now. My princess has broken her tooth, and you are going to fix it immediately. She is bleeding. We must stop the bleeding."

Once the Caliphate Guard agent stepped away, Robert was finally able to look up from the floor. Mudir Al-Shaitan stood over him, holding the bloodied sword. Next to the president stood a Caliphate Guard officer named Waqas, who held the screaming Malikah Al-Shaitan. Waqas's face was splattered with blood. His gloves, normally white, were covered in more dried blood.

Malikah cried hysterically, while a tiny drizzle of blood mixed with saliva dripped from her mouth and onto her hand. Her clothing was also completely covered with dried blood. It had been Malikah who was crying the entire time. It hadn't been Padub at all.

Robert stood up and tried to take charge of the situation. "We need to call an ambulance right now. It's a miracle this little girl is still alive! There has to be two pints of blood just on her clothing alone."

"Don't worry about the blood on her clothing, Dr. Cline. Most of it is not hers," said the Caliphate president. "But you do need to stop the bleeding in her mouth and fix her tooth."

"Ghali! Ghali," Malikah screamed.

Needing to quickly assess the little girl's condition, Robert probed, "What do you mean, the blood isn't hers? If you're wrong, then we have a medical emergency, not a dental emergency."

"I told you the blood is not hers!" shouted Al-Shaitan. "Do you think I am a fool? Now I am losing my patience with you, Dr. Cline. Fix my baby girl now!"

Robert couldn't believe he had nearly blown his assignment when they were never here to execute him at all. But what the hell was going on with all the blood and the sword, and what was up with destroying the office? he thought. Robert had been advised that when he was finally in the presence of Mudir Al-Shaitan, security was of the "scorched earth" variety. His guards had been known to turn restaurants and theaters upside down in preparation for a visit by the supreme leader of the Persian-Arab Union. Caliphate Guardsmen were ruthless in looking for anyone who might be a threat. But this seemed to be on a scale far exceeding anything the rookie agent had been warned of.

Robert looked around the office at the brigade of Caliphate Guardsmen, who were holding each member of his staff at gunpoint. What the hell? he thought. Are you freaking kidding me? He looked at Mudir and tried to conceal the anger in his voice. "So what's going on with terrorizing my staff and ransacking my office?"

Quickly, one of the Caliphate Guard agents who had been at the office with the First Lady, and who only moments ago had had his knee in Robert's back, stepped between the dentist and the president of the United Persian-Arab Caliphate. "Lower your tone, Doctor! The supreme leader has many enemies! We make certain there will be no threats when he is present!"

Robert snapped back at the guardsman. "His family has already been here! You've been here! You know that we're no threat." Robert shook his head in disgust. "Well, I'm going to need my assistants. Is there any way we can lower the machine guns so they can set up a room for Malikah?"

Al-Shaitan nodded, and the guardsmen released Robert's staff.

"I'm going to need to check on Umair real quick." His root canal patient was still unconscious and bleeding from the blow to the head.

"No. He will be fine," growled Mudir. "See my daughter now!"

"Operatory one is clean, Doctor," said Evie. "I can seat her right away."

Evie rushed down the hall toward operatory one with Al-Shaitan and a contingent of Caliphate Guard officers close behind. Guardsman

Waqas carried Malikah into the treatment room and set the sobbing child down on the dental chair.

Robert motioned for Dzhoanna to check on Umair before following the group into the operatory.

"You will not hurt her, Dr. Cline," barked Mudir.

"I won't hurt her." Robert lowered back the dental chair and patted the crying child gently on the arm, trying to calm her, but she wouldn't be consoled. "So what happened?" Robert asked her father.

Mudir stood at the foot of the dental chair, holding the bloodied sword. "When I am not working, Malikah is always with me. Today I put her in the care of her personal guards for only five minutes while she played on her trampoline. They let her fall off, and now her beautiful, little tooth is fractured. She is a princess. She is perfect, and perfect she must stay."

"Ghali! Ghali!" cried little Malikah.

"I'm sorry, but what is *Ghali?*" Robert asked. "I don't know that word. Is she trying to tell me something? Is she in pain? What does it mean?"

Aside from Malikah's crying, there was a sudden silence in the room. All the Caliphate Guardsmen stood perfectly still, looking at one another through the small slits in their ghutra scarves.

Mudir took a deep draw from his pipe and blew it straight into the air above the dental chair. He growled, "Ghali was her personal bodyguard who had no job other than to ensure that my princess was safe and happy. It is Ghali's blood on this sword. It is Ghali's blood on my baby's clothing. It is Ghali's blood on the face of Malikah's new guardian, Waqas."

Mudir Al-Shaitan laughed with a sinister snarl. "Waqas is very good at removing heads. He will remember that I ordered him to saw through his friend Ghali's neck every time he takes his eyes off my princess. The memory will help keep him focused as the new agent in charge of my baby's safety. I believe that Waqas is ready to protect Malikah, and he knows firsthand what happens when there is failure."

Waqas stood close to Malikah and stared back and forth from Robert to the crying child. He was clearly agitated that the little girl was in distress, and he knew her discomfort put him at risk. Though Caliphate Guardsmen's faces were almost completely covered with a black scarf, Robert could clearly see the fear in Waqas's eyes.

"My wife tells me you are very good, Dr. Cline" said Mudir. "I hope for *your* sake she is right."

Robert needed to get the out-of-control situation under control. He kneeled down and handed a small, stuffed elephant toy to Malikah. "Hold on to his trunk, and he will help you be brave," said Robert.

Malikah sniffled and calmed down enough to say, "Thank you, Doctor." Then her lower lip curled, and she began to sob more quietly. "But I miss my Ghali," she said.

"I know. It's going to be OK, sweetie. Let's take a look at your little tooth." Robert gently examined his tiny patient. Just inside Malikah's top lip there was a quarter-inch laceration that was oozing a slow trickle of blood. The chip on her upper front baby tooth was certainly noticeable but fairly small.

As he began to realize just how minor his patient's injuries were, Robert's blood began to boil with anger, and his face turned beet red. His thoughts screamed for no one to hear: You've got to be freaking kidding me. Someone was beheaded over this? Then he took a deep breath and regained his composure.

"Looks like we'll need to place one suture for her little lip," Robert said calmly. "And the tooth will be very simple to fix, honey. You're going to be just fine."

Mudir Al-Shaitan seemed to be irritated with Robert's assessment. "She is bleeding, Doctor. That is not fine. And that tooth makes her look like a freak, not a princess."

"I promise you that she'll be perfect when we're finished," reassured Robert, veiling his mounting disdain for the United Caliphate president.

Then Al-Shaitan reached over to grab his daughter's hand and warned, "Good. But if she needs a shot, it had better not hurt."

Here we go, thought Robert. "Mr. President, you need to trust me. And please try not to talk about the procedure so much. It really upsets children to hear details." Robert turned to Waqas. "Please tell your boss what I discussed with the Caliphate Guard officers at the children's last visit." Then he looked back at Mudir and said, "I am very good at taking care of children if their parents don't get them alarmed."

A nefarious grin spread across Mudir's face. While he angrily clenched his teeth, the afternoon sun shined through the operatory window and reflected off the gold crown that covered Mudir's lower-left first molar. He growled back at Robert, "Don't tell me how to handle my children, Dr. Cline! She is bleeding, and her smile is a wreck. Fix her tooth now!" He threw his pipe against the wall and cracked his sword on the floor, fracturing the black polished granite.

Waqas quickly pulled his machine gun up to Robert's head, and Malikah began to scream and cry more desperately than before.

Then Evie leaned over from her dental assistant's chair and took the little girl's hand. "It's OK, baby." She used a tissue to gently wipe away their patient's tears, but nothing could wipe away the scar on her broken heart. Malikah had been with Ghali from the time she was born. He'd watched her every move. He took care of her. He protected her. Ghali loved Malikah like she was his own child, and Malikah loved Ghali. But now Ghali was dead, beheaded in front of the little girl who adored him.

"Hold my hand, sweetie," said Evie. "I can tell you that Ghali is OK, and he loves you very much, but now he is with Jesus. Our precious God will make him well. Ghali would be sad if he knew you were crying."

Robert was stunned by what he was hearing. He shot his assistant a sharp stare of disapproval, hoping she could read his thoughts. *What in the hell are you doing? You don't tell the caliph of the Muslim world's daughter that Jesus will heal her bodyguard. This cannot be happening!*

"Evie! Please be quiet," Robert demanded. His heart pounded with anger. He was simply blown away by her lack of common sense. *We haven't been beheaded yet, but it looks like she's throwing us back up on the chopping block,* he thought. "Why don't you go on out of here and call Dzhoanna to help me finish up?" he said.

Malikah looked up at Evie. "Ghali is OK?" she asked.

Evie smiled and nodded while gently moving the child's hair away from her face.

Suddenly little Malikah quit crying. "Thank you. I love my Ghali," she said.

"Evie, please." Robert glared at his assistant.

"Don't worry, Dr. Cline," said Mudir. "If a fairy tale makes my princess feel better, then let it be so." Most radical Muslims would have flipped over Evie's statements, but Mudir wasn't a radical Muslim. He wasn't Muslim at all. He used his religion only to manipulate people. It really didn't matter if someone prayed to Allah, Buddha, or Jesus Christ, as long as Al-Shaitan got what he wanted. "Malikah is comfortable with her now. Let her stay."

Mudir Al-Shaitan walked over to his pipe and picked it up off the floor. He lit up and slowly began to fill the room with smoke, while Robert went to work. The Caliphate president lost interest in the procedure and walked past the foot of the dental chair. He stared out the window at his magnificent Burj Khalifa and the capital city, while Waqas and five other red-robed Caliphate Guardsmen watched to make sure Robert didn't hurt Malikah.

Robert brilliantly distracted his patient as he injected her with anesthetic. He carefully sutured her lip, stopping the bleeding completely. Then he meticulously repaired the small chip in her tooth, matching shape and color to perfection.

"There. You look beautiful again, little princess," said Robert while sitting up the chair and handing Malikah a mirror. "You are all better now, and this will be good practice for your filling appointment coming up this week." Then he used sleight of hand to give the illusion that he had magically pulled a small, bouncy ball from her ear. "This is for you. I think you're going to have a lot of our toys by the time we're all through with you."

Little Malikah stood up on the patient chair and hugged Robert with all her strength. "Thank you, Doctor," she said.

"Let's go home, my darling," said Mudir. "We have a party to get ready for." The Caliphate president took his daughter's hand and helped her slide off the side of the dental chair.

As soon as her feet hit the floor, the little girl pulled her hand away from her father and ran over to Evie. Looking up, she said, "Thank you. Thank you for telling me about Ghali. Does he know I miss him?"

Evie bent down and smiled. "Yes, sweetie. And you will see him again someday."

"Come on, Malikah," grunted Mudir. The entourage started to clear from the office. Al-Shaitan turned over his shoulder as he walked down the hall toward the exit. "My wife says she invited you to this evening's party, Dr. Cline. Please bring Miss Evie with you. I am sure Malikah would love to see her."

The Caliphate president, his daughter, and the entire security team walked out of the office, leaving only quiet wreckage behind.

Immediately, one of the dental hygienists walked up to Robert and handed him an envelope with a resignation letter she had jotted down while he was working on Malikah. "I just can't put up with the stress here," she said. "I'm sorry." Then she turned and made her way through the destroyed waiting room and out the exit.

Dzhoanna hurried over to Robert and said, "I have got Umair back in the dental chair. He has regained consciousness. Do you want to finish the root canal?"

"I'll be right in Dzhoanna, but you're going to have to give me a minute."

Robert stomped toward his office, and without saying a word, he motioned for Evie to follow. He angrily pushed through the door and sat down in the black leather chair in front of his desk, where he waited for her to enter. When Evie walked in, he motioned for her to close the door, which she did.

"Evie, I'm happy that your religion gives you some kind of comfort, but please understand that we are working in an Islamic nation, and I'm here to serve predominantly Islamic people. Do you realize that your carelessness could have gotten us all killed today? There will be no more talk to my patients about your religion, or you *will* be fired. Besides, telling children things that aren't true just turns them into confused adults."

"But everything I told her *was* true. I knew Ghali. He went to my Christian church on the west side of Dubai."

Robert snapped back with unapologetic sarcasm, "One of the bodyguards of the leader of the Muslim world went to your church? Hmm...Are you kidding me?"

"No, I am not. He was a wonderful man. He knew he was taking a risk by practicing his faith, but he loved God, and God loves him."

"Well, yeah, *clearly*, and it looks like God was *really* watching out for him today. Just listen closely to what I'm about to say, Evie. No more talk of your religion at the dental office, e*specially* around the Al-Shaitan family! Do you understand?"

"I promise." She paused for a moment, looking down at her feet. Then she looked back up at Robert with her dark, brown eyes. "But is it OK if I talk about it to you away from work?"

Give it up, lady, he thought. He hoped to quickly squelch any idea she had about discussing religion once and for all. "Well, I'm pretty busy, and you definitely won't be getting me into a church, but if we're ever alone, then sure; go ahead and talk all you want. In fact, you can talk until you're blue in the face. I love science, which explains everything about this world. If you ever felt the need to talk to me about religion, I would simply extinguish your fantasy with fact. Science wins every time. Now I've got a root canal to finish." He stood up and walked toward the door.

Evie started talking again before he reached the exit. "I don't know a lot about science, Doctor, but I do know that God will forgive you for the things that make you run from him."

"This is the dental office, Evie. Zip it!"

"OK Doctor. So, it sounds like the president of the United Caliphate would like me to come to the party with you tonight. Will you be picking me up, or should I catch a cab?"

Robert didn't answer, but instead he walked out of his office and down the hall to check on his root canal patient.

23

SHAHZAD

A warm evening breeze blew gently through the open windows of the Aston Martin DB9 as it glided down the long, brick drive leading to the grand entryway of the fabulous Jumeirah Al Qasr Hotel. Robert had just cleared a relatively painless vehicle-security checkpoint search by the Caliphate Guard. He was pleased that the inspection, though extensive, wasn't on the destructive scale of that afternoon's siege of his dental office.

Even after Robert had driven well beyond the first check station, there was no mistaking the Caliphate Guard presence. Red-robed guardsmen blanketed walkways alongside the roads and Venetian-style canals that connected the luxury hotel's three hundred guest rooms. The Al-Shaitan family had rented the entire resort, including its ballroom, convention center, and all forty-four restaurants and bars. The hotel was heavily shielded for the event of the season; the sixth birthday party of Shahzad Al-Shaitan.

The party's guest list included former leaders and dignitaries of Middle Eastern countries, who had been in favor of incorporation into the United Persian-Arab Caliphate. Most of the leaders of annexed regions who supported unification now held subordinate gubernatorial or figurehead positions in their home territories that were now union states. Nonsupporters of the unification were not in attendance, because most had been tried by the Caliphate for terrorist activities and were subsequently executed in public.

Also present at the party were representatives of all major oil and gas companies from around the globe. In addition there were CEOs invited from large construction, technology, and service corporations. All were seeking hefty government contracts from the newest and most prosperous nation in the world.

The Aston Martin pulled up to the valet station, where a parking attendant opened the driver's-side door. Robert stepped out of the car, looking tall, dark, and dignified. He was certainly fit for an event of this magnitude, wearing a new black Giorgio Armani tuxedo he'd purchased with the assistance of his Millennium Tower concierge.

Robert noticed that most of the women walking into the party were clothed in traditional, conservative Muslim dress. But a significant number had taken advantage of the liberating influence of Mrs. Gasol-Al-Shaitan and had dressed in high-priced, Western-vogue evening gowns.

Evie Garcia stepped out of the DB9's passenger door in a basic off-white, chiffon dress she had purchased off the rack for only eighty euros at Primark of Spain. She was breathtaking in her simplicity. Her full-length dress gently adorned her soft curves and olive-colored skin. The hotel lights reflected brilliantly off Evie's long, jet-black hair as she swung it to drape softly over one shoulder. She removed a scarf from her purse and carefully covered her hair in respect of the more conservative Islamic party guests.

Towering over the Aston Martin stood a three-story statue of an Arabian stallion plated in bronze. The meticulously crafted steed rose above a magnificent water fountain and guarded the hotel lobby entrance. The parking attendant directed Robert and Evie to walk around the massive statue, where they would find an entryway checkpoint.

All party guests went through TSA-type x-ray body scanners just after walking inside the hotel. They were then hand searched by Caliphate Guard officers. After Robert and Evie passed through the scan, the guardsman in charge of the checkpoint motioned for them to step around the hand search. They were allowed to pass dozens of people, including the former president, and now governor, of Libya. The guardsman pulled the black scarf away from his face and smiled. It was Nasir, one of the officers who'd been in the dental office with the Al-Shaitan family. "We know you are OK, Doctor. Enjoy your evening."

Robert and Evie walked side by side beneath a two-ton chandelier hanging from the ceiling of the hotel's grand ballroom as a harp quartet serenaded them and hundreds of other dignitaries. While the who's who in the Middle East were pampered with fine food, their children were extravagantly entertained in the adjacent conference room, which was visible through large, soundproof glass windows.

Robert wasn't naturally drawn to big gatherings of this sort. He spent most of his days practicing dentistry while talking continually to keep his patients entertained and distracted from their dental work. As a result he usually didn't look to spend a lot of time talking during his off-hours. He especially didn't like to converse about dentistry when he wasn't at the office, but that was exactly what most people he encountered wanted to discuss.

Maybe I won't have to talk about teeth tonight, he thought. Nobody at the party even knows I'm a dentist except the Al-Shaitan family, and they'll be busy entertaining their more important guests.

Suddenly from behind, Robert felt a tug on the calf of his tuxedo trousers. He turned to see what was grabbing him. There, looking up at him with her big, green eyes, was little Malikah Al-Shaitan. She was sucking her thumb on her right hand and holding onto the stuffed elephant Robert had given her in her left hand. She didn't say a word, but held up the toy as if to show him how special it was to her.

Robert was touched. He kneeled down and said, "Wow, you still have your prize from the dental office."

Just then Linda Gasol-Al-Shaitan approached with Malikah's bodyguard, Waqas. "Hello, Dr. Cline. I'm glad you could attend." She looked down at her daughter. "Malikah has not put that toy down since she left your office. Mudir is the most powerful and wealthy man in the world. He gives his children whatever they desire, yet she cherishes the cheap gift you gave her. You have made quite an impression on my children, Dr. Cline."

A high-pitched shout from the doorway leading to the children's area interrupted the First Lady. "*Dobiib ehsnahn, dobiib ehsnahn!*"

Everyone in the ballroom stopped what they were doing and turned to see what was going on. The shouts were coming from Shahzad Al-Shaitan, who was now running across the regal ballroom, followed closely by two armed Caliphate Guard officers. He continued shouting, "*Dobiib ehsnahn,*" Arabic for "my dentist."

Well, I guess my cover as a nondentist party guest has been blown, thought Robert. He was flattered that Shahzad had noticed him, but he was also frustrated, knowing the rest of the evening would undoubtedly be spent discussing people's dental problems.

"*Dobiib ehsnahn!*" shouted Shahzad as he ran up to Robert and gave him a big hug. "Please come do a magic trick for my friends," he begged.

"That I *can* do," said Robert. "*¿Esta bien?*" he asked, looking over at Mrs. Al-Shaitan.

"*Claro que si,*" she said with a smile of approval.

Shahzad and Malikah each took one of Robert's hands and led him into the adjoining children's area. The party planners had gone all out, hiring clowns and actors dressed like popular cartoon characters to interact with and entertain the child guests. There were multiple giant-screen televisions playing 3-D movies, a full-blown video arcade, and even a trampoline obstacle course.

Hopefully there are only broken arms tonight and no broken teeth. Hate to see another Caliphate Guard officer lose his head, thought Robert as he passed by the trampolines.

Before long Robert had managed to draw the attention of nearly one hundred children and staff members away from the organized entertainment. His young audience cheered as he performed some of the magic tricks he used on kids in the dental office.

While Robert put on a show for the children, Evie and Mrs. Gasol-Al-Shaitan stayed in the ballroom and talked in their native language about their love for Spain. They had just agreed that their favorite beach was *playa la concha* in San Sebastián when they were interrupted by a thundering voice.

"Dr. Gasol, you are serving the best baklava!"

Mrs. Gasol-Al-Shaitan turned to see her former boss and ex-Saudi prince Aahil Naqvi. He now held a post-unification position as the United Persian-Arab Caliphate ambassador to the United States. The first lady joyfully spread her arms to hug the massive man, but she managed to reach around only one-half his girth. "I think you need to lay *off* the baklava, good prince," she said. "How have you been, my friend?"

"Good, good, but I was better when you were my personal physician. I have lost three more toes since I lost you to Mudir."

"Well, you know that you are supposed to keep your diabetes under control," she scolded.

"Yes, but it's so hard to remember to take my pills and constantly check my blood sugar. Besides, who can keep track of insulin injections day and night?"

"Oh, I know how you are with insulin." Dr. Gasol-Al-Shaitan gave him a stern, accusatory look. "You didn't load up before the party, did you?"

Naqvi laughed and replied sarcastically, "No, no, I wouldn't do *that.*"

"You need to take better care of yourself, Ambassador. Mudir constantly tells me how important you have become in dealing with the United States. He really needs you alive. *I* need you alive, my old friend."

Naqvi looked around to make sure nobody would hear what he was about to say. Then he whispered, "To tell you the truth, I think your husband is trying to kill me."

Horrified, the First Lady turned ghost white. She quickly excused herself from Evie before pulling her friend aside to the foot of the ballroom's grand staircase. Mrs. Al-Shaitan shooed a few guests and servants away before sitting with the ambassador on the second stair. She leaned in close and whispered, "What do you mean—Mudir is trying to kill you?" She knew her husband was ruthless. Mudir Al-Shaitan had already killed hundreds of men who'd been faithful servants to the Union, not excluding Ghali earlier that day.

Naqvi had a grave expression as he continued to speak softly so no one else could hear. "Mudir knows I am a diabetic, and I think he is trying to poison me. He built our new embassy in Washington, DC, two blocks away from…a Krispy Kreme doughnut shop. Those little doughnuts are so sugary and delicious. They make even your baklava seem like health food. I just can't stop eating them." He let out a thundering laugh.

Linda Al-Shaitan was relieved but didn't appreciate the humor. She tried not to laugh but cracked a smile as she slapped her former boss across his turban. "You are terrible," she said.

"No, but honestly, my health has declined since you stopped caring for me." Naqvi's tone became very serious again. "I'm concerned that I may have cancer."

Mrs. Gasol-Al-Shaitan raised a skeptical eyebrow and rebuked her former boss. "I just don't think I have any more time for your twisted sense of humor, Ambassador. Go make jokes about your health to someone who doesn't care so much for you."

"I only wish I were joking," Naqvi replied somberly. "Look." The ambassador set down his plate of baklava. Then he reached his powerful hand up to his face and opened his mouth. He inserted his index finger and thumb, and started moving one of his molars from side to side. "See? They *all* wiggle. My teeth are loose. Do you think its leukemia, Dr. Gasol?"

The First Lady gasped and put her hand to her mouth. "Oh, dear," she said, looking like she might start to cry. Then she stood up and grabbed the ambassador by the arm. She hurried him across the marble floor, past hundreds of party guests, and back to where Evie was standing. "Please, can you go get Dr. Cline and have him come over quickly," she pleaded to the dental assistant. "It's an emergency."

Evie ran out of the ballroom and into the kids' play area, where she found Robert shoeless, jumping through the trampoline obstacle course with the Al-Shaitan children and a battalion of their friends. The dentist appeared to be thoroughly enjoying himself, and the little guests were obviously enjoying him. The clowns and other hired entertainers also appreciated that Robert was keeping the children busy.

Several of them took advantage of the break and moved off to a quiet corner to smoke.

"Dr. Cline, the First Lady would like to speak with you right away," hollered Evie up to her boss.

Oh great, thought Robert. He felt at ease being the only twenty-six-year-old playing in the kids' room. He dreaded returning to mingle with the adults at the real party. Robert did a backflip off the trampoline, invoking cheers from the children. Then he put on his shoes and followed Evie toward the exit, where he turned and waved good-bye.

"No, no. Don't leave, Doctor!" shouted Shahzad.

Malikah called out like her brother. "Don't leave, Doctor."

"Sorry, kids. It looks like the adults want me for a while. I'll come back as soon as I can." The children waved as Robert disappeared through the exit.

The second Robert and Evie entered the ballroom, they were met by a panicked Gasol-Al-Shaitan and Ambassador Naqvi. "Please, Dr. Cline; I need you to look at my friend. All of his teeth are loose. I fear he may have cancer. Can you tell me what you think?"

Naqvi stuffed another large piece of baklava into his mouth while the First Lady was speaking.

"Prince Naqvi!" scolded Gasol-Al-Shaitan. "Am I going to have to leave my family just to travel with you and make sure you take better care of yourself?"

The prince stopped chewing momentarily and smiled with a full mouth. Then he quickly swallowed and cleared his throat. "I'm sorry, Doctor Gasol," he said ashamedly.

"This is our family dentist," the First Lady said. "His name is Dr. Cline. Show him what you can do with your teeth."

Here we go, thought Robert.

Naqvi demonstrated for Robert that he could wiggle multiple teeth.

"Do you think its leukemia, Doctor?" the First Lady quizzed.

"Well, you never really can say without blood tests and a full medical workup. A ballroom is not my favorite setting for making any kind of diagnosis." He tried not to sound irritated or sarcastic, but Robert feared he was coming across that way. He tried to adjust his attitude. "You know, any number of things can cause teeth to become loose." Robert looked the prince over from head to toe and estimated that he may weigh close to five hundred pounds. "You aren't by chance a diabetic, are you?" Robert asked.

Naqvi responded, "They have said that I could be hitting the early stages of diabetes, but if I watch what I eat—"

Gasol-Al-Shaitan interrupted, scolding, "Oh, you are absolutely *not* in the early stages of anything, Prince. You have been a full-blown, insulin-dependent diabetic for quite some time, and you know it."

Ambassador Naqvi flashed a nervous grin. Then he noticed a server passing by with a silver serving platter loaded with plates of lumet il adi pastries. Naqvi grabbed two servings.

Gasol-Al-Shaitan quickly slapped the plate out of his hand just as he was getting ready to take a bite. The sticky pastries skidded down the ambassador's robe, and the serving dish shattered on the floor.

Robert was feeling a little awkward about getting into the middle of the tussle for Middle Eastern desserts, but he continued to speak anyway. "Well, again, it's hard to make a diagnosis at a party without x-rays and blood tests, but I would be willing to bet that your teeth are loose due to periodontal disease exacerbated by uncontrolled diabetes."

"But I do keep it pretty well under control," replied Naqvi innocently.

"Oh no, you do *not* control your diabetes, Ambassador!" snapped the First Lady. Then she turned to Robert. "So if it isn't cancer, can his teeth be saved, Doctor?"

She doesn't seem to be listening, does she? Robert thought. "Again, it's very hard to determine without doing a full workup in the office, but I *will* say that teeth with this degree of mobility normally don't have the best of prognoses. At the same time, if some teeth are lost and if the supporting bone hasn't completely deteriorated, we have some great options for tooth replacement nowadays. I guess the bigger concern is what the uncontrolled diabetes is doing to the rest of your body Ambassador. As you know, Dr. Gasol, uncontrolled diabetics have a much higher risk of heart attack and blindness. They can even lose toes due to gangrene."

"Yes, he has lost many toes."

Naqvi tried to lighten the conversation. "Did she ever tell you that she amputated one of my toes with a butter knife in a hotel room in Spain?"

"That's enough, Prince! Your damn toe was so bad, it was about to fall off on its own," scolded the First Lady. "Now how long will you be in Dubai, Ambassador?"

"Probably until Saturday."

"Do you think you can see him in your office before then, Dr. Cline?" Gasol-Al-Shaitan asked.

"I don't have my schedule in front of me, but I'm sure we can find a spot for him. Just call in the morning, and we'll set up an exam."

Clearly relieved, the First Lady said, "I will talk to Zasu tomorrow when we bring in little Malikah for her filling appointment."

"Perfect," said Robert. "Hey, I hate to set a bad example for the ambassador, but I think I'm going to go get ahold of some of those pastries real quick." He was anxious to get out of the party dental-consultation mode as soon as possible.

"Yes, of course, Doctor. Oh, and thank you again for being so kind to my children."

"No problem. They're great kids," he said. "Nice to meet you, Mr. Ambassador. We'll make sure to take a look at you this week." Robert excused himself and escaped quickly. Leaving Evie standing with the others, he hurried over to the serving table and started filling a plate with Middle Eastern delicacies.

"Hey, Doc, can I ask you a question?" a familiar sounding voice called out from behind.

The accent was unmistakably Texan, like he was used to hearing at the Dallas public dental clinic. But when Robert turned to see who was talking, he had no idea who stood before him. "Were you talking to me, sir?" Robert asked the middle-aged man who was wiping crumbs from his handlebar moustache. The mystery person was wearing a light-gray, three-piece Western suit with a matching cowboy hat and shiny, black cowboy boots.

"Absolutely, Doc. Didn't I hear those kids say you were a dentist?"

Oh no, Robert thought. Here we go again. He was starved. He could almost taste the food that sat uneaten on his plate but Robert politely postponed his snack and asked. "Yeah, what's up?"

"Hey, well, my name's Austin Ward. I'm from Texas—"

No kidding, Robert thought.

"—and I'm here working in Dubai. I've got a dentist and all, but I'm stuck here for a few more weeks. My guy is real good. Maybe you know him. His name is Dr. Pete Erickson, DDS."

First of all, why the hell does everybody think all dentists know each other? Second of all, it's either Dr. Pete Erickson or Pete Erickson, DDS. You don't say both, thought Robert. "No, I can't say that I've heard of him," he said. "But I'm sure he's a great dentist."

"Amen that, brother...Oh, I mean, Doctor."

Robert looked down at his food as it cooled on the plate; then he looked back up at his new cowboy friend. "It was sure nice to meet you, Austin. I guess I'm going to go ahead and eat now."

The man continued, "Hey Doc, I hate to bother you—"

Then don't, Robert thought.

"—but I've got a little problem with my partial plate." Austin reached up to his mouth and pulled out a partial denture, which clipped onto his two remaining lower canine teeth. He turned the denture over in his hand and pointed at it. The pink resin base of the denture was packed thick with some of the hummus dip he'd just finished eating.

Robert immediately felt a gag welling up in his throat, but he managed to swallow and hold it back.

"Right across this plastic part, it looks to me like I've got a hairline crack, and I'm worried it's going to give while I'm out here. I'd sure hate to have people see me without these things."

Then why on earth would you take the teeth out in the middle of a party like this? Robert thought. "You know, the lighting in here is pretty bad, and I just can't really see a crack. Why don't I give you my card, and maybe you can set up an appointment for me to look it over in my office?"

"Oh, no, no. The crack is very visible. I drink tons of coffee and smoke a lot, so the crack is almost black."

Robert's appetite was quickly escaping. "I'm sorry, sir," he said. "It looks like there's some food or something covering the denture and I really can't see the crack."

Austin looked down at his false teeth. "Oh, I'm sorry. I was eating some pita chips and hummus. There must be a little stuck on there. That stuff's the closest thing I've found out here to Tex-Mex bean dip." He lifted the denture up to his lips and extended his tongue, licking the thick accumulation of hummus away from the denture flange.

Robert finally let out a gag. As a dentist, he was used to things most people would consider disgusting, but this ranked up there with one of the nastiest things he'd ever witnessed.

A little denture hummus stuck to Austin's moustache, but otherwise his false teeth had now been licked relatively clean. Robert tried to look at Austin's eyes, then at his western suit, then at his boots. No matter where he focused, Robert could still see the little glob of hummus in Austin's moustache. He gagged a couple more times.

"You all right, Doc?" asked Austin.

"I don't know. I think I'm getting a little bit of a stomach bug actually."

Then Austin grabbed a handkerchief and sneezed.

Good, he got the hummus with the handkerchief, thought Robert with relief.

"Well, I don't want to take up too much of your time with you trying to eat and all," said Austin.

"No, no, that's OK. I'm thinking I might wait on dinner until my stomach settles. But I really can probably give you better information in my dental office." Robert handed his full plate of uneaten food to a busboy that was passing by. He needed to make a power move to get out of the conversation. "You know what? I'm going to give you my card. It's so refreshing to see someone from the US. I'll repair your partial at no charge if you come by my office. We're located in

Millennium Tower just a few blocks away from the Burj Khalifa capitol building."

Delighted, Austin took the card. "Well all right. I sure appreciate the gesture. By the way, how did you end up practicing in Dubai?" he asked.

Changing the subject only to continue the conversation wasn't exactly what Robert had in mind. But, he was glad to at least be steering away from discussing the hummus-filled denture. "I just wanted to work in an exotic location where taxes were low. Can't beat Dubai for exotic and can't beat zero percent for income taxes in the United Caliphate."

"You're right there, buddy. When I retire, I'll probably be living over here with you." Austin leaned in close to Robert and spoke softly. "So did you ever wonder why there weren't any taxes in the Persian-Arab Union, Doc?"

No. I don't really care, Tex or Dallas or whatever your name is, Robert thought. "I guess I never really thought about it," he said.

Austin continued. "I work for North America Oil and Gas. Mudir Al-Shaitan disperses a percentage of American Healed Earth money through me to my company. We use part of the money to build new oil refineries in the United Caliphate. We use the rest to finance a super PAC that supported President Dunham and now endorses Bo Jaden."

This sounded like the kind of information George had warned Robert to stay away from. But he couldn't help but ask, "That seems a little fishy, but what does it have to do with the zero percent tax rate in the caliphate?"

"You see, that super PAC money is the kickback the president of the United States requires to continue providing five billion dollars a year per Persian-Arab Union State. Bo Jaden knows the massive super PAC checks help make sure he gets reelected. In return, when you add up all the Middle Eastern states, the United Persian-Arab Caliphate gets close to one hundred billion dollars per year in US aid."

This wasn't making sense to Robert. "I thought the Healed Earth money was supposed to be for reduction of oil production. So what's up with the new refineries?"

"Now you're getting it, buddy." Austin chuckled. "Oil keeps flowing, and we keep refining. The United Persian-Arab Caliphate and all US oil companies in the Middle East still produce as much gas as ever. We just sell a lot more to China. We still sell petroleum to the United States but a lot less and at a much higher price. Everybody in gas and oil is getting rich, the cooperating presidents of the United States keep getting reelected, and the Persian-Arab Caliphate is becoming the wealthiest, most powerful country in the world. So when the United Caliphate keeps bringing in all that oil money and all that Healed Earth money, they don't really need to tax their citizens."

"Hmm. Then if what you say is true, the American taxpayer seems to be getting screwed by the Persian-Arab Caliphate *and* the president of the United States," observed Robert.

Austin slapped Robert on the shoulder, laughing. "And that's why the smart guys like you move to Dubai."

Just then Evie walked up next to Robert.

"Well, I'll be. There's a lot of money in oil and gas, but you doctors still have the upper hand with the ladies." Austin winked at Robert and looked Evie up and down, undressing her with his eyes. "I will *definitely* see you in the dental office this week, Dr. Cline," he said with another wink, this time directed at Evie.

Evie smiled uncomfortably.

"You dentists are sure a chatty bunch," said Austin. "You'd probably talk my ear off if I let you, but I'm going to have to break away and get me some more of them pita chips and that hummus dip." He excused himself and vanished into the crowd.

"Who was that?" asked Evie.

"I don't know. Just some guy with a broken partial denture. I guess you'll see him again this week."

"You're really good at marketing yourself, Robert," Evie said. "You already attracted two new patients in the short time we've been here."

"Yeah, I guess so," Robert replied. "For some reason this is just how it works out when you're a dentist at a party." Then he looked up at the ceiling and all around the ballroom. "Hey, does it seem like it's getting darker in here?"

The lights were definitely dimming. A giant, retractable screen lowered behind a podium just ten feet away from the table where Evie and Robert had planned on sitting. Suddenly, the United Persian-Arab Caliphate national anthem thundered from speakers mounted on the ceiling. A double row of at least forty Caliphate Guardsmen marched in, passing right in front of Robert and Evie. They were surrounding Mudir Al-Shaitan.

Most of the children in the adjoining conference center walked away from their entertainment to see what was causing all the commotion next door. They pressed their tiny hands and faces against the glass that separated them from their parents in the ballroom.

Mudir Al-Shaitan stepped through the Caliphate Guard escort and walked up to the podium. He wore a black tuxedo with a red bow tie and a matching red turban. A video of the Persian-Arab Union flag blowing in the wind played on the giant screen behind him. Everyone in the room rose to their feet and cheered.

Mudir smiled and waved. "Thank you. Thanks to each of you for coming." The cheers continued so that the president of the Persian-Arab Union was unable to speak. He simply waved and grinned, getting in only an occasional "Thank you."

Then in unison the Caliphate Guardsmen stomped one boot onto the floor and saluted their president, signaling quiet. The five hundred party guests quickly sat down and allowed Al-Shaitan to speak.

"Thank you for joining me tonight to celebrate the birthday of my son, Shahzad Al-Shaitan, who on this day turns six years old." Again the room erupted in applause. After the guests sat back down, Mudir continued. "In addition to the birthday of my son, I have a surprise announcement for all of you. I will be brief so you can continue to enjoy the wonderful food and good friends. As you know, the United Persian-Arab Caliphate has become the most prosperous and respected nation in the world in just a short time."

The crowd stood again, united in applause.

"Many nations are envious of our great wealth and resources. We have received requests from countless countries to join our union, but not just any territory can earn the right to be a state in the United

Caliphate. Any petitioning country must bring a wealth of resources, educated minds, and culture to the table if they are to join our union."

"Tonight I am pleased to announce that the French parliament, with overwhelming support of the citizens of France, has pleaded with me to allow them to join our great nation."

Surprised guests gasped, while others cheered.

"Yes, my friends; on this day France will become the first European addition to the United Persian-Arab Caliphate."

A still shot of a map of France played on the giant video screen behind President Al-Shaitan.

"I regret to announce that despite the insistence of France's people and Parliament, the French premier brings only resistance to the annexation table. However, because the French people currently pay over seventy percent tax, and because income tax is illegal in the United Caliphate, we are sending in a contingent force to arrest the uncooperative premier as we speak."

The map of France quickly transitioned to a video feed of the French premier and his wife being ripped from their bed and taken into custody by red-robed, black-cloaked Caliphate Guard officers.

Playing out live on the giant ballroom screen to now completely silent party guests, the French premier and his wife initially gave themselves up without a struggle. But then a skirmish broke out as French secret service loyalists, also known as the *Direction Centrale du Renseignement Intérieur*, or DCRI, made an attempt to fend off the Caliphate Guard.

The DCRI loyalists were quickly overpowered while a Caliphate Guard agent held a pistol up to the head of the French leader. The premier's wife screamed and begged for her husband's release, as the trembling premier raised his hands in surrender. The Caliphate Guardsman didn't lower his pistol but instead shouted repeatedly in Arabic, *"Des hod auleruhk betehkah! Des hod auleruhk betehkah!"* (Drop to your knees! Drop to your knees!).

The French premier shouted back, "Please! Do not shoot! I don't understand what you're saying!"

Again, more frantically than before, the Caliphate Guardsman shouted, *"Des hod auleruhk betehkah!"*

The premier pleaded with tears streaming down his face. "I don't understand. Please, I'll do whatever you want, but I don't understand!"

Then a second Caliphate Guardsman hit the premier in the face with his pistol and shouted that this would be the final warning. *"Des hod auleruhk betehkah!"*

There was no way out. The defeated premier looked up to the ceiling and crossed himself. Then he looked over to his crying wife and whispered, *"Je t'aime,"* telling her he loved her.

Then the lead Caliphate Guard officer placed the barrel of his gun on the forehead of the French premier and emptied his cartridge, while life emptied from the conquered leader's body.

The younger children who watched the giant screen through the glass from the play area next door were fortunate, not fully understanding what they were seeing. The older children, however, looked on in horror, witnessing the murder telecast before their very eyes.

The video feed quickly transitioned to a live shot of the Eifel Tower, while Mudir Al-Shaitan resumed his speech. "Regrettably the penalty for treason is enormous, but on a lighter note, tonight I also announce that we are renaming Paris, France. The capital city of the French state of the United Persian-Arab Caliphate will now be named Shahzad, France, in honor of my son on his birthday. We will also be renaming the Eifel Tower. Let it be known that from this day forward, the Eifel Tower will be known only as the Burj Malikah, after my lovely daughter."

Just then a massive fireworks display erupted behind the Eifel Tower or Burj Malikah. In 2013 the United States had given a fleet of F-16 fighter jets to the Egyptian government. Now part of the United Caliphate Air Force, they flew in victory formation over the Burj Malikah.

The live video panned to the streets of Paris, or Shahzad, where citizens burned the French flag while waving Persian-Arab Caliphate flags and chanting the name of their caliph. "Mudir Al-Shaitan! Mudir Al-Shaitan!"

The ballroom guests were seated in complete silence. The weight of the event loomed heavily over the room.

"Do you have no response, United Caliphate?" shouted Mudir Al-Shaitan as he pounded his fist on the podium.

Immediately, everyone at the party rose to their feet and erupted in applause. They chanted in unison, "Mudir Al-Shaitan! Mudir Al-Shaitan!"

Robert and Evie stood as well, looking quietly at each other in fear and disbelief. They were watching history unfold, as Mudir Al-Shaitan had just made a bold move to expand his empire beyond the Middle East.

What wasn't announced at the party was that earlier in the week, there had been secret negotiations between the European Union and the Persian-Arab Union to ensure the peaceful annexation of France. Initially, when negotiations had broken down, Mudir Al-Shaitan informed the European Union president that the nuclear missiles he'd acquired with the appropriation of Pakistan and Iran were now pointed at Germany and England. Mudir had promised a large-scale nuclear attack if there was any European interference.

"Thank you all for coming," said Mudir. He stepped away from the podium and grabbed a glass of water before briefly disappearing behind a curtain. Within minutes the United Caliphate president triumphantly reappeared to mingle with his guests. He was swarmed with people congratulating him and shaking his hand. He walked right next to Robert, who had no choice but to shake his hand.

Words escaped Robert, but he followed along with the others in the crowd. "Congratulations, sir," he said.

Mudir smiled. "Thank you. I hope the food is to your satisfaction this evening," he said. Then he moved on to the next table.

Robert looked puzzled. He leaned over and whispered to Evie, "The man who just shook my hand is not Al-Shaitan."

"What do you mean? Of course he is," she whispered back. "His eyes are pure evil."

"No, it's a body double. Look again." They both looked over at the United Caliphate president, who was already two tables away. "Wow, he really does look exactly like him, but when Al-Shaitan was in the office today, I noticed that he had a gold crown on tooth number nineteen, his lower-left first molar. I saw the crown again when he gave his speech, before he walked behind the curtain, but this guy has no crown."

"Are you sure?" Evie asked. "I don't remember seeing a crown."

Dentists always noticed dental work, and CIA agents were trained to look for distinguishing characteristics. Robert was certain that this was a body double. The practice of using doubles was widespread among Middle Eastern leaders. It was thought that Saddam Hussein had once had as many as four body doubles. In fact, there had been controversy after his execution, with some CIA agents insisting that it wasn't actually Saddam who'd been killed.

"Not that it really matters right now, but that's definitely not him," said Robert.

Evie whispered in his ear, "We have to go, Doctor."

"We can't leave now," he said. "It would look like we disapprove of what we just saw."

"We *don't* approve of what we just saw..." Evie looked at Robert with a surprised frown. "Or do you? Anyway, we should not be here, Robert."

"Good or bad, Evie, we're right in the middle of a monumental, world-changing event. I think we should stay, at least for a few more minutes so it doesn't look like we're leaving because we're against the annexation. Otherwise we might end up in the same predicament as the French premier."

Robert could see Evie was scared, but he was just starting to regain his appetite after the hummus-filled denture encounter. "Just let me grab a little snack, and as soon as I'm done eating, we'll head out."

"I can't believe you could eat *anything* after witnessing what we just saw."

"Unfortunately, I've seen worse," said Robert just before he left to go to the serving table. He grabbed a couple small finger sandwiches made of some kind of grayish-colored meat he feared was lamb. He pretended the meat was beef, and the sandwiches went down pretty smoothly. Tasty, he thought.

After his snack, Robert returned to Evie and took her by the arm. "Are you ready to go?" he asked.

"Yes. Thank you."

As they headed for the exit, Robert and Evie caught the eyes of Shahzad and Malikah Al-Shaitan, who stood waiting across the ballroom at the entryway to the play area. The two children jumped up and down and screamed to get their dentist's attention.

Robert was amazed that the kids had been watching closely enough to notice that they were leaving. Malikah held up her little stuffed elephant to show that she still had it. Robert and Evie both smiled and waved good-bye just before quietly ducking out of the grand ballroom.

24

THE FOUNTAIN

Robert and Evie walked out of the Jumeirah Al Qasr Hotel entryway and into the warm, starlit night. They strolled around the extravagant fountain that was guarded from above by the majestic Arabian Stallion statue.

Evie looked over at Robert and asked, "What did you mean back in the ballroom when you said you've seen worse?"

Robert had been thinking of the night he helped torture and kill Pablo Alva. He wasn't sure if the haunting image of Pablo being disintegrated by a long-range missile would ever fade from his thoughts or dreams. Of course, Evie was a civilian working in the Dubai dental office, and she had no knowledge of his involvement with the CIA. Robert certainly wouldn't reveal what he really meant, so he began to steer her off-track.

"Well, Evie, when you're a dentist, you see a lot of things that have the potential to turn your stomach."

"Oh, really? Like what?" she asked.

"Like, for example, tonight when that Texan showed me his denture jammed with hummus. I thought I was going to blow chunks when he licked the wad of dip out from beneath his false teeth."

Evie was still upset from Mudir Al-Shaitan's shocking presentation, but she surprised even herself when she let out a tiny, involuntary giggle. "So a *dentist* gags when he looks at a food-filled denture, but he can watch someone be killed without the slightest loss of appetite?"

"Yeah, something like that," Robert said, smiling.

They walked next to the hotel's brick drive, circling around the spectacular fountain, while soothing streams of water hummed gently above the night silence. Across the driveway and on the other side of a narrow Venetian canal, there was a picturesque coffee shop. In front of the shop, there were a few tables and chairs neatly arranged on the veranda that overlooked the canal and fountain.

"Do you mind stopping at the café?" Evie asked.

"Look who's getting her appetite back," Robert razzed. "I thought you were too traumatized for food."

"No, I actually was hoping to get a little herbal tea to help me sleep tonight," she said.

They both turned to cross the hotel's grand drive but had to wait for a perfectly restored 1927 Rolls-Royce Phantom 1 to pass slowly in front of them. "Must be a Kuwaiti oil man," noted Robert as he stared in amazement at the $300,000 car.

The pair crossed the drive, and then strolled over a small bridge. They paused to watch below, while a gondolier slowly rowed two party attendants to their guest room. After stepping into the coffee shop just long enough to order some tea, Robert and Evie returned to sit at a patio table, lit by hanging copper lanterns. Water from the fountain across the way rolled softly in the background, interrupted only occasionally by the sound of tires from a luxury vehicle tottering along the brick drive.

Evie removed her head scarf, allowing her glistening, black hair to fall softly down over her shoulders. "I'm really glad we got away from the party, Robert. I've so looked forward to being able to talk to you alone," she said.

"Yeah, it was kind of noisy in there." Robert figured Evie would try to hit him up again to do dental work at the orphanage. He'd considered this possibility before the party and had already thought up several excuses that would get him out of even the most aggressive pitch. He was ready to have that discussion and was well prepared to fend her off. "So what did you want to talk about?"

"You know: God," she answered.

He wasn't ready for *that* discussion. "Uh…Well, I don't think I'm really in the mood to talk with you about religion, Evie."

"I don't want to talk about religion, Robert."

"I thought you just said you want to talk about God."

"Yes, God, not religion."

Robert became agitated. "OK, go ahead and call it whatever you want. Bible thumpers are all alike. You mince words and try to push your religion or belief in some delusion of a god on everyone else. I'm here to tell you that there is no such thing as God. And that's pretty much the end of the discussion."

"But you said we could talk away from the office, and we *are* away from the office. Didn't you mean what you said?"

Robert thought for a second. "Actually, no. I think what I really meant was that I definitely would not permit you to talk about God at the office, but that doesn't mean I want to talk about religion away from the office. I don't want to talk about God with you at all, Evie."

She continued as if he hadn't said a word. "You are a great man, Robert, but I can sense an emptiness and sadness in you that the Lord can fill."

"Kind of like he filled Ghali?" said Robert sarcastically.

Evie pulled her hand up to her chest. It was as if Robert's comment had knocked the wind out of her. She paused and took a deep breath in an attempt to hold back tears. She was shocked that Robert would be so insensitive about her friend, who had just that day been brutally beheaded at the order of Mudir Al-Shaitan. "Actually, Ghali was filled with God's spirit, and he is in heaven with his savior as we speak," she said.

Robert felt cornered in the discussion, but he knew his comment was extremely insensitive, and he could tell he'd crossed the line. "I'm sorry, Evie. I don't mean to talk about Ghali that way, but it's really just one more example of how this so-called God, who is supposed to be so great, just seems to have no control over this chaotic world. If God is so good, why does he let so many bad things happen? And it's not just Ghali." He was thinking of his own part in the brutal torture and killing of Pablo Alva but used another example instead. "What about when President Dunham was innocently watching a basketball game just before he was assassinated? What about the thirty thousand people who were killed with him in the Madison Square Garden bombing? What about the little girl, whom we all saw on television after the bombing. Do you remember watching, as she walked hopelessly down Thirty-Fourth Street in New York City, crying for her parents, who had been killed in the blast? If God exists, why on earth does he let so many horrible things happen?"

Evie didn't miss a beat and responded, "I once heard a preacher named Max Lucado interviewed after a horrific school shooting where many small children were killed. Someone asked Lucado why God would allow such a tragedy to happen. He answered that it was simply a violation of one of God's greatest gifts to us; our free will. He said the shooter chose darkness instead of light, hate instead of love. But in order for us to have the gift of choice, we at times must suffer the consequences."

"Well," said Robert, "then I guess I've chosen to do enough bad things in my life that I've abused the gift, so God wouldn't be interested in Robert Cline anyway."

"It doesn't matter what you've done wrong, Robert, and it also doesn't matter what you do to try to earn your atonement. We have all sinned, but Christ paid the ultimate price and sacrifice for our sins. You haven't sinned enough to nullify his amazing grace. At the same time, you couldn't do enough good on your own to redeem your own self. You can't pay the price of your salvation. The price has already been paid."

Robert was starting to feel more uncomfortable, and he was losing footing in the debate. Pushed further into a corner, he shot back, "So then why do the people who supposedly choose the love and light of God still behave so badly so often? It seems to me that some of the nastiest, most hypocritical people I've known have been so-called Christians." He was thinking of his Sunday school teacher, who'd given him the brown Easter egg when he was only in third grade.

"That's the saddest thing of all, Robert. People judge God by the actions of his followers. But we are all sinners, while only God himself is free of sin. Even though we are forgiven, we still stumble into bad behavior. So sadly, when someone sees a Christian sin, they say, 'If that's what God is all about, then I'm not interested.' Again, believers still misbehave, and they can no more work their way to heaven than a nonbeliever. Only Christ's gift provides their salvation. I'm not saying that you can't see God in his people, but unfortunately you *can* still see evil in them sometimes."

Robert was growing more and more uneasy with the conversation as he reflected on the fact that he'd been running from the idea of God his entire life. He definitely didn't like that some of what Evie said was starting to make sense. But then again it was all just a little too simple. He still couldn't reconcile between two separate realities: the Sunday morning reality, where God created life; or the Monday-through-Saturday reality, where life came from nothing but science and time.

Just then, out of the darkness, a majestic Arabian stallion appeared, walking along the brick roadway in front of them. It didn't notice Robert or Evie watching.

What in the world is a horse doing here? Robert thought. There was no rider, and there were no stables nearby. It was completely out of place. The powerful creature walked slowly up to the hotel entryway fountain and lowered its head to take a drink.

Robert looked up at the stately bronze stallion statue that towered over the fountain. He'd never seen the artist, but he knew the statue was beautifully hand crafted by the sculptor. Then he looked back at the beautiful, black horse drinking from the fountain. He was certain that the horse, which walked over to the fountain with its own power, had come from nothing but environmental pressure, evolutionary time, and chance. Robert also knew without a doubt that no quantity of time, environmental pressures, or chemical accidents could have created the statue that stood still, watching forever motionless over the fountain. In contrast, he understood that the horse, which was drinking life-giving water, was made from DNA that had simply assembled itself through trillions of chemical accidents and mutations. Those mutations had somehow loaded the horse's DNA with blueprint information that had come from nothing.

Then Robert remembered he had rejected his college chemistry professor, who pointed out that DNA cannot and does not spontaneously appear from the attractions of raw chemicals. Dr. Ritchey had explained that DNA is constructed only from protein but that protein is constructed only from DNA. One couldn't exist without the other, and one couldn't be constructed without the other. The fact that DNA and its assembling proteins had to be created at the same time was what his professor liked to call "biochemical proof" of the existence of God.

There was a storm of information raging in Robert's head, and he didn't like the way it was all starting to piece together. Everything he'd ever believed was suddenly in question. Could his college chemistry professor have been right? As a nonbeliever, Robert's only hope in God was that God didn't exist. He closed his eyes, blocking his view of the horse that had come from nothing and the statue that had a creator. He squeezed his eyelids even more tightly so not even a little light could pass through. He hoped to reboot and purge the ignorant thoughts spinning through his mind. But suddenly, the darkness was replaced by the image of Pablo Alva, whom he'd helped tie to the catamaran mast. Alva hung motionless, glowing in the light of the missile right before it struck him.

Robert gasped and opened his eyes.

Then Evie spoke softly with compassion. "I don't know what haunts you, Robert Cline, but God can forgive whatever it is. We have all sinned and done our part in helping hang Christ on the cross. But the beautiful and ironic truth is that he died there so we would be forgiven for the very things we did to put him there. We have *all* been offered this gift of forgiveness, but we each must choose whether or not we accept that gift."

Evie touched Robert gently on the forearm and stood up. She wrapped her hair neatly back into the scarf. Then she walked away.

Robert sat alone and began to weep silently while looking at the mighty stallion just as it stopped drinking from the fountain. It raised its head and stared straight into Robert's eyes, while the statue looked on motionlessly, guarding the fountain and the entrance to the hotel. Then the jet-black Arabian horse turned away and galloped off into the shadows from where it had come.

Robert raised his tear-filled eyes and gazed into the starry sky for a few moments. Then he bowed his head and whispered, "Forgive me, Lord."

25

EXECUTIVE ORDER

Robert entered his Millennium Tower apartment. He walked straight to his bedroom and pulled an unpacked suitcase out of his closet. He threw it on the bed and opened it before reaching into a small side compartment. Then he pulled out a Bible that was given to him by the same church that had also given him the atheist Easter egg. He'd never actually opened the book and didn't even know why he'd kept it all these years. Maybe it was because of the simulated leather cover or the gold, sparkly stuff on the edges of the pages. He definitely didn't know why he'd brought the Bible to Dubai. He certainly hadn't planned on reading it, at least not until now.

As Robert cracked open his Bible for the first time, Kitty Witty jumped up on the bed and into his lap.

"Hey, K-Dub, I think we're going to be making a few changes. You know, maybe a little less swearing and things."

With a loud, rattling purr, Kitty Witty rubbed his chin against the corner of the Bible cover. After thoroughly scratching his itch, he looked up at Robert and let out a long "Meow," which Robert interpreted as, Speak for yourself, Cline.

Suddenly, a blinking red light and a series of high-pitched beeps came from the desk in the corner of the bedroom. It was Robert's satellite video phone, indicating that Case Officer Harpole was trying to make contact.

Robert rushed over to the desk and pulled open the cover. The screen illuminated with George's image.

"Hello, Cline. We've got a bit of a situation." George normally spoke in a light, carefree manner no matter what the topic, but Robert could tell right away that his tone was different than usual.

"What's up, George?" Robert asked.

"You may or may not have heard, but Mudir Al-Shaitan just announced to the world that he's annexed France as the newest member of the United Persian-Arab Caliphate. He's even changed the name of Paris to Shahzat or some nonsense."

"Shahzad," Robert said.

"What?"

"It's Shahzad. He changed the name of Paris to Shahzad in honor of his son."

"How do you know this?" asked George.

"I was there tonight at his son's birthday party when he made the announcement."

"Yes, we heard through your office wiretap that you'd been invited, which brings me back to my warning for you to try to keep yourself insulated from getting too much information."

"I'm the dentist of the first family of the United Persian-Arab Caliphate. It would be kind of impossible not to hear some of this stuff, George."

"OK, I'll give you that, but why in the world were you at his son's birthday party?" George asked. "You know what?...Never mind. We have a change in plans that we need to get implemented by tomorrow morning."

"What do you mean?" Robert asked.

"Well, in light of the unfolding events with the French annexation and with a couple more European Union countries in line to follow, there's a new urgency surrounding the proposed assassination of Mudir Al-Shaitan. We need to have our missile strike the United Caliphate president as soon as humanly possible. Our sources tell us that the French premier is scheduled to be arrested tomorrow and go on trial on Friday. He'll likely be executed before next week."

"Yeah, well, I just *now* watched a live video feed of the French premier being pulled out of his bed and executed by the Caliphate Guard, George."

"What the hell are you talking about, Cline?"

"They showed it to all of the guests at the party. You don't know about this yet?"

"No, I don't know about this! It's almost impossible to gather intelligence in the Persian-Arab Union."

"So why doesn't the agency let me do a little more snooping around while I'm here. I'm learning a lot without even trying."

"Again, you were told to do nothing of the sort, Robert. Straying from protocol won't do anything but put you in danger and the mission in jeopardy." George took a deep, disgusted breath and rubbed his forehead, as if trying to scrub away a headache before continuing. "So if what you're telling me about the premier is true, this exponentially advances the deadline for our assassination. Mudir Al-Shaitan needs to be taken out immediately."

"Deadline?" Robert asked skeptically. "OK, so I've worked on both of his kids, but he hasn't even made an appointment yet. I'm really developing trust with the family, as is indicated with my invite to Shahzad's birthday party, but I can't implant the device until I have Mudir in the chair."

"As you know, Robert, we're linked into your office appointment software so we can clearly see that he isn't scheduled. That said, we do get a little intelligence from time to time, indicating Al-Shaitan's location. We've looked at the possibility of sidestepping the original plan and using this intelligence as the foundation of a location-based missile strike, but we're still concerned about the likely possibility that Mudir has body doubles. An unguided strike has the potential to accidently kill one of these imposters instead of Al-Shaitan and then spiral into World War III."

"I knew it," said Robert. "The man who shook my hand after Mudir Al-Shaitan gave his speech tonight didn't have a crown on his lower-left first molar, but when Al Shaitan was in my office, he definitely had a gold crown on that tooth."

"Way to confirm that for us, Cline. Maybe your intelligence gathering *will* pay off in the end," George said. "Anyway, according to your appointment book, you have Malikah Al-Shaitan scheduled in your office tomorrow for a filling."

"Yeah. So maybe we press the First Lady harder to get Mudir scheduled for an appointment."

"Not exactly. When we analyzed the office wiretap from a few days ago, we learned that Malikah sleeps every night between Linda and Mudir Al-Shaitan. Is that the way you understand it?"

Robert paused. His heart seemed to stop beating for a moment. He didn't answer.

"Have we lost our connection, Cline?"

"No, sir. I can hear you."

"Good. I asked if it is your understanding that Malikah sleeps in the bed with Mudir Al-Shaitan every night."

Robert clearly remembered the conversation with Mrs. Gasol-Al-Shaitan about Mudir giving his daughter milk each night after she got scared and climbed into bed with them. "I guess I remember something like that he said."

"You guess? Well, our audio was very clear. You seem to remember everything else that we don't want you to remember, but you're telling me that you don't remember this?"

Robert did not like the implications but responded, "I do remember, sir."

"It's the agency's position that Malikah Al-Shaitan would most certainly be climbing into bed with her real father every night. She would never sleep with his body double. If we follow our primary plan, we could end up waiting on Mudir Al-Shaitan for months, and then you could accidentally place the missile-guidance device in the tooth of one of his body doubles. But thanks to your conversation with the family, we know with certainty that Malikah sleeps next to the real deal. Don't you agree?"

Robert quickly came up with a way out of what he thought was coming. "Yes, sir, that would be a certainty, but you see, I *know* the real Mudir Al-Shaitan. I know that he has a gold crown on tooth number nineteen, and the body double doesn't. I can identify the real United Caliphate president, and there will be no mistake when I place the device in his tooth. I'll press his wife to get him an appointment as soon as possible. The family will listen to me. They love me, George. They invited me to their kids' birthday party, for heaven's sake."

"I'm afraid we just don't have time for that scenario anymore, Robert."

"What are you suggesting, George?" Robert knew the answer but asked anyway.

"The new operation calls for you to implant the missile-guidance device in the tooth of Malikah Al-Shaitan when she visit's your office tomorrow."

"Wow. That's horrible. How could you come up with this?"

"It isn't coming from me or the agency. We simply don't have that kind of authority." George paused. "It's coming from higher up."

"We don't have a problem, do we?" It wasn't George asking. There was another voice coming over the satellite phone's speaker. "You probably haven't even seen all of the body doubles, Agent Cline. Come on, you're a dentist. Don't you think Mudir could get one of those gold crowns placed on the tooth of any of his stand-ins for about a thousand bucks or so?"

"Excuse me," said Robert. "Who am I talking to?"

"I'll *tell* you who you're talking to. This is Bo Jaden, the president of the United damn States of America! That's who you're talking to, and yes, these orders are coming from higher up. They're coming all the way from the top!"

The president pushed his face in front of George's. "We're talking to you from the White House situation room, and that means there's a son of a bitching situation!"

"OK," said Robert.

"Listen up, Robbie." Robert hadn't been called Robbie since the fifth grade. "We know that Malikah Al-Shaitan has an appointment in your office at ten a.m. tomorrow. So you need to have the stones to put the missile-guidance device into the kid's tooth. Is that perfectly clear, Doc?"

"Well, yes, Mr. President, but—"

"But nothing. You need to get this done, Agent Cline!"

"With all due respect, sir, the device is designed to fit inside the molar of an adult. Malikah is three years old. She doesn't have any teeth large enough to properly house the device. I'd have to drill all the way into the nerve chamber of one of her baby molars to even come close to having enough space. I'd have to do a pulpotomy—kind of like a root canal for kids—and the treatment estimate I gave Linda Gasol-Al-Shaitan doesn't call for anything like that."

"So then do the damn root canal," demanded President Jaden.

"Yeah, well, the problem I see with that is that her mother and all of their bodyguards hover over me and watch every move I make. They've made it clear in no uncertain terms that if I ever hurt one of their kids, they will kill me, and they have machine guns aimed at me the entire time I work."

"So are you saying that you can't do a root canal without hurting someone, Agent Cline?" The president turned back to Harpole and chided, "I thought we had the best, George. I had a root canal last month, and it didn't hurt at all. It sounds like maybe we got the wrong guy for the job."

Robert explained, "No, sir. I'm not saying that at all. But I will tell you that when you drill into the nerve chamber of a healthy baby tooth, the tooth bleeds…a lot. With everyone watching me, there's no way that I'll be able to keep them from seeing blood. If they do see blood, I'll likely be shot dead on the spot."

"Hell, I thought you were supposed to be some kind of magician, pulling teeth out of little kids' ears and what not," Jaden challenged. "Sounds to me like you're just going to have to figure out how to get this done without the guards or the mother seeing blood." He looked back at Agent Harpole, shook his head in disgust, and then turned back into the screen. "Get the device in the kid's tooth tomorrow morning at oh ten hundred. Do I make myself clear, Robbie?"

Robert didn't know what to say.

"Do I make myself clear?"

"Yes, sir, Mr. President," said Robert sheepishly.

"Good!" President Jaden's scowl turned to a big, insincere grin, exposing a mouthful of large teeth with bathroom sink-white porcelain crown and bridgework. "You're a hell of an American, Robbie. Oh, and don't let this get to you. We'll initiate the launch code tomorrow in the middle of the night. That little girl will be sleeping peacefully. She won't feel a thing." His fake grin was immediately replaced with a deep frown. "War is hell, but remember the old saying: you have to crack a few eggs to make an omelet."

Jaden's bathtub-white smile reappeared. He laughed boisterously and turned over his shoulder, looking back at Agent Harpole. "Isn't that right, George?"

George didn't answer the president but shrugged instead.

"Now report back when you've implanted the device so we can get you the hell out of Dubai," ordered Jaden. He stood up and walked just out of view of the satellite phone video monitor.

Agent Harpole moved back toward the screen and asked, "You OK with this, Robert?"

Still out of view, Jaden interjected angrily, "He damn well better be OK with this, George! Otherwise, we'll just leak a tweet that he's some kind of French spy, and he'll be captured and beheaded by the Caliphate Guard by noon tomorrow!"

The video screen went black.

26

THE APPOINTMENT

9:50 a.m., the next day

Robert sat motionless, staring out the window of his dental laboratory. There was no view of the Burj Khalifa today. Instead, an apocalyptic, thick-brown cloud hung heavy and low over the city of Dubai. The Millennium Tower was normally well insulated from the sounds that encircled it, but today the howling cry of an unforgiving gale moaned like a distant air-raid siren. A dirty sand blizzard was raging in from the Rub' al Khali Dunes, blasting and pitting everything in its path that wasn't covered or indoors.

Most of the normal activity in Dubai had been ground to a halt, and the morning's first three patients had already canceled. As Robert sat looking out at the angry storm, he hoped for the news that the Al-Shaitan family would be canceling Malikah's appointment as well.

The smothering fog of sand kept coming, but instead of a cancelation notice, Dzhoanna entered the lab and said, "She is here, and *he* came with her. Are you ready, Doctor?"

Robert looked up at her, took a deep breath, rubbed his forehead, and then slowly ran his fingers back through his dark-brown hair. He knew what he had to do, but now it was time to get his mind right with it. "Yep, I guess so, just like we were briefed last night. We put the device into one of Malikah's teeth."

"Are you OK with this?" she asked, concerned.

"Sure. Why wouldn't I be? Aren't you?" He turned his attention back to the sandstorm outside the window.

"Well, Doctor, I was expecting that we would be doing this to Mudir. The little girl is so innocent and cute." She walked up next to Robert and looked out the window with him. "My director at the SVR says we will be saving hundreds of thousands of lives in the future if the mission is a success."

"Yeah, I know all that, but this isn't a slam dunk. Remember, we're going to have to drill down into the nerve chamber to make enough space for the transmitter. So you're going to have to stay on top of the suction. I'm pretty sure if anybody sees any blood, we'll be done for, and when I say 'fill,' you need to very discretely hand me the device." Robert stood up and turned to the lab door. "Let's go get our scorched-earth security check."

Robert opened the door for Dzhoanna, and she led the way down the long hallway toward operatory one, where Malikah was already waiting. Robert felt detached from the situation, almost like he was watching from above. His breaths were fast and heavy, filling his own ears and competing with the sound of the howling wind. He could feel every beat of his own heart pounding in his chest. Each step down the hallway seemed to take an eternity. .

Robert was met just outside the operatory by three Caliphate Guard agents, who painstakingly but gently searched every inch of his body. Three more agents searched Dzhoanna. The guards were considerably more restrained than before, knowing that Dr. Cline and his staff were people they could trust. Robert had really become a family friend.

Four guards stood by the front desk, and four more stood by the main entryway of the office. The Al-Shaitan family was always pro-tected by ample security, but the disproportionately high number of Caliphate Guard agents in the office and the full security pat down confirmed one thing: Mudir Al-Shaitan himself was here with his daughter.

"*Kienh tahtaubihb mohreifehk,*" said a Caliphate Guardsman, giving Robert the OK to enter the operatory.

Mudir Al-Shaitan was pacing at the foot of the dental chair in front of the sandstorm-darkened window, barking orders in Egyptian to someone over his cell phone. Mudir didn't even notice that the dentist had entered the room.

Robert was immediately greeted with an enthusiastic "Hello, Doctor." Malikah was sitting up straight in the dental chair, ready to be cared for by her family dentist. She held up the toy elephant he had given her just the day before."

"Oh, you still have the elephant. You sure are taking good care of him."

She nodded and smiled. Then she raised her little hand and motioned for Robert to come closer. He bent down next to her, and she motioned for him to come closer still. Robert leaned in over the little girl. She stood up on the chair, cupped her hand up to his ear, and began to whisper. "Can you fix his tooth?" she asked, pointing out that one of the plush tusks was missing from the elephant. "My brother broke it," she said with a pouty face, and tears starting to well up in her eyes.

Up to this point in the morning, Robert had mainly frowned. He'd only managed to muster up an indifferent look before entering the room, but now an involuntary smile spread across his face. "Do you have the tooth, my princess?" he asked as he took the stuffed animal to assess the damage.

Malikah turned back in the dental chair and grabbed her little purse, which hung on one of the armrests. She quickly shuffled through its contents and pulled out the detached tusk. She handed it to Robert with full confidence he could fix it.

"Oh, this will not be a problem at all," he reassured her. "I think we can fix the tusk just like we fixed your front tooth."

Robert turned to Dzhoanna and said, "Grab me a silk suture kit, please, Ms. Olen."

She quickly opened a drawer in her assistant cabinet and pulled out a suture kit and hemostat.

"I would love it if you would be my dental assistant, Miss Malikah," Robert said. "Can you please get her some gloves and a mask, Ms. Olen?"

Little Malikah quickly climbed out of the dental chair and stood up on the floor, holding out her hands for the gloving procedure. The extra small gloves that Robert's assistants used were enormous for the three-year-old. Dzhoanna struggled to get each one of the little girl's fingers properly positioned in the gloves. Waqas and Nasir, Malikah's Caliphate Guard agents, looked at each other with machine guns resting by their sides and laughed at the little girl, who was completely absorbed in the role-play game.

Mudir Al-Shaitan was oblivious to what was happening in the room as he continued to bark angrily into his cell phone.

Robert pulled the operating mask gently over Malikah's nose and mouth, careful not to disturb one hair on her head. "OK, Miss Malikah, you hold the suction and the tusk, while I place the sutures."

Malikah's large mask gradually slid down her face and came to a rest just under her chin, while she sharply focused on the procedure. Robert carefully and quickly reattached the tusk in just the right spot with a few strategically placed stitches. He handed Malikah the scissors and showed her where to cut away the extra suture thread.

The little girl squinted her left eye and held the right wide open. She stuck her tongue out of the corner of her mouth and concentrated to make the cut in just the right spot. With a little assistance from her dentist to ensure the cut didn't take any fingers, the procedure was completed.

Dzhoanna took the scissors, and Robert held up the elephant, inspecting his work. "The operation was a success, princess. Thank you for your wonderful assistance."

Malikah smiled and clapped her hands, causing one glove to fall loosely to the floor. She quickly bent over to pick it up and placed it back on her hand.

"OK, it's your turn next," proclaimed Robert. "Jump back up into the chair for me."

"I'll keep your gloves and mask safe for you until after we are done with your filling," said Dzhoanna as she carefully removed them from the little girl. "That way you can take them home with you."

Just then Mudir Al-Shaitan put away his phone and demanded, "I'd like to know what we have going on here, Doctor. I do not have all day to stand in your dental office while you play. We need to start getting something done."

"Absolutely, sir," Robert replied. He began lowering his little patient back down in the chair. As it slowly reclined, the enormity of the moment overtook him, slowing time to a near standstill. The operatory darkened as the storm outside the window intensified. The wind moaned like a mortally wounded animal, waiting for death to prevail.

All eyes were on Dr. Cline. He would have to be perfect. Robert carefully followed his routine. It was always easier to work on children the second time, once they had a good experience to look back on.

After applying the topical, Robert asked for two carpules of anesthetic. "One plain Mepivacaine three percent and one lidocaine with 1:50,000 epinephrine please," he said to Dzhoanna.

She handed Robert the cartridges, and he assembled his syringe behind his patient's chair, loading the Mepivacaine and mounting a 27 gauge long shaft, surgical, steel needle for a mandibular block.

"I don't like to watch this part," said Mudir to his guards, briefly flashing his gold crown as he chuckled and turned away.

Well, that certainly doesn't send the signal that something bad is about to happen, thought Robert.

Fortunately Malikah didn't hear her father and opened wide at her dentist's request.

Robert cautiously shielded his little patient's eyes with his left hand, while he evaded her line of sight and situated the needle in her mouth in the ready position.

"Please adjust the light, Miss Olen," said Robert. Then he directed the conversation back to Malikah.

"OK, remember, just like last time. Raise your left hand if I make a bad spot, and it will only take me five seconds to fix it. Robert breathed heavily, while Malikah's guards and two of Mudir's guards leaned in to watch.

Robert slowly and masterfully began injecting the anesthetic into the mandibular block region without causing pain. "Are you doing OK?" he asked his little patient.

Malikah attempted a smile, while her mouth was wide open. She nodded, indicating that all was well. She knew that her dentist was her friend and that he always took special care of her.

"Almost finished," Robert said as he carefully repositioned the needle after getting a small aspiration of blood, indicating that he was in a vascular area. Once there was no more aspiration, he deposited the remaining anesthetic. "There we are. All finished. You're such a good patient."

Malikah offered a droopy grin, while Robert turned and hid the syringe from her. He resheathed the needle, unloaded the empty Mepivacaine carpule, and inserted the lidocaine with 1:50,000 epinephrine for later.

Mudir laughed. "I don't know how you give her a shot without her even noticing," he said.

Yeah, and thanks to you, she knows now, idiot, thought Robert.

Dzhoanna could tell Robert was irritated with the shot comment but supposed it really didn't matter at this point, since this would be Malikah's last dental appointment and her last day to live. From the time the mission plan had changed, Miss Olen understood that Robert would have to keep his patient comfortable enough to complete the procedure and plant the missile-guidance device. However, she was especially touched that Robert was going out of his way to make the little girl's last day as enjoyable as possible.

After waiting for the anesthetic to take full effect, Robert explained the procedure to his patient. "OK, we're going to remove the yucky cavity from your tooth and replace it with a beautiful, strong filling." A game he used with younger children was to tell them he was carving a picture or special shape into their tooth. He would normally let them pick the design, and then pretend to create the artwork while he was actually removing decay. "What shape would you like me to use for your filling today? I can do a kitty, a flower, a butterfly—anything you want," he said.

The little girl didn't hesitate. She knew the image she wanted on her tooth. "Batal," she said.

"What was that, honey?" Robert asked.

"Batal," she said again with a smile.

"I'm sorry. I guess I don't know that word. What is *Batal?*" he asked, looking up to the Caliphate Guard officers.

"Batal; it is the name of her champion Arabian stallion," interrupted Mudir in an irritated tone. "When will we be finished, Dr. Cline?" he grumbled.

Robert lost his breath for a second. He took a swallow and looked back down at Malikah. "OK, we will make a picture of Batal on your tooth," he said.

Robert went to work, while Dzhoanna suctioned. Mudir got another call on his cell phone and went about the business of running the United Persian-Arab Caliphate. Not one of the Caliphate Guard agents had their machine guns drawn. They all trusted that Dr. Cline would take good care of Malikah. They all knew she was in good hands. They all knew she was safe.

"OK, now I'm making the stallion nose," said Robert as he applied pressure to the whistling high-speed drill and penetrated the pulp chamber. Blood erupted from the tooth, but Dzhoanna continually rinsed and suctioned to keep it from showing.

"Does Batal have a big tail?" asked Robert.

Malikah nodded and smiled with her mouth wide open.

"Oh, now I'm shaping his tail then," said Robert as he used his slow-speed handpiece to remove all the vascular and nerve tissue from the tooth. The bleeding slowed significantly. Then Robert placed a layer of calcium hydroxide paste over the tooth's canals and stopped the bleeding altogether.

A sudden, powerful gust of wind caused thousands of tiny pellets of sand to ping against the window as the sky turned from dark brown to black. Mudir paced in front of the window at the foot of the dental chair and gave orders through his phone, speaking in French to his newest governor.

Robert painted a layer of adhesive in the cavity prep. Then he said, "Let's fill," signaling Dzhoanna to give him the missile-guidance device. She handed the tiny metal apparatus to Robert, being careful that no one in the room could see. He took the device, and then asked for composite to cover it.

Dzhoanna gave Robert a concerned look. "Did you get the fill, Doctor?" she asked.

"Yes, I did. I'm ready for the composite, Miss Olen."

Dzhoanna leaned her head over Malikah's mouth and attempted to look in her tooth.

Robert placed his thumb over the cavity prep. "We're going to have saliva contamination here in a second, Miss Olen. Composite," he demanded while raising his eyebrow and shooting a piercing look across at her.

Dzhoanna turned to grab the white filling material, while Robert reached for his anesthetic syringe. In a split second that seemed to last an eternity, Robert jumped up and lunged past the Caliphate Guard agents and across the operatory. He gripped the syringe tightly in his right hand.

In unison, Waqas and Nasir pulled their AK-47s up to their shoulders.

Robert drove the 27 gauge long shaft, surgical steel needle into Mudir Al-Shaitan's chest between the fourth and fifth rib, and slightly left of the sternum, causing aspirated blood to rush into the cartridge of lidocaine with epinephrine. Agent Robert Cline quickly injected the entire carpule into the United Caliphate president's right ventricle, causing his cardiac muscle to violently seize and release into a tachycardia arrhythmia.

The wind outside howled like a suffering beast pleading for its life as Mudir Al-Shaitan dropped motionlessly to the ground.

Out of the corner of Robert's eye, he saw a flash of red from the cloak of one of the advancing Caliphate Guard agents. Then he heard the sound of the butt of an AK-47 cracking against his skull.

The room went black.

THE FINAL CHAPTER

Blackness and nothingness prevailed. No thoughts, no feelings, no happiness, no sadness, no pain. There was only blackness.

———

Then there was a sense of light breaking through the darkness. Next there was feeling. Robert could feel the warmth of the light on his face. He couldn't move. Not an inch. Robert Cline opened his eyes and saw only the light with darkness all around. The light was beautiful.

———

Then a throbbing pain started to pulsate through the side of Robert's head. "Pelton & Crane?" he asked just under his breath. The center of the light above was broken by a small emblem that read "Pelton & Crane," one of the dental supply companies that made operatory lights and other dental equipment. Robert still couldn't move. He heard mumbling in the background, but he could only see the light.

"Where am I?" Robert asked.

A familiar voice coming from just outside his field of vision ordered, "We've got to find out what he knows. Give him a shot, Crow."

A gloved hand, holding a 27 gauge long shaft needle attached to a surgical steel syringe, passed just over Robert's face. Then it hovered above, relatively still with only a slight tremor. A drop of bright-orange liquid slowly formed at the beveled tip of the needle and came sharply into focus.

Robert smelled strong smoker's breath with a distinctively enchilada accent.

Then Dr. Crow leaned in closer with the 27 gauge long shaft in one hand and a Jennings Gag in the other. He sneered, "Hello, Robert. Long time no see."

The End?

Certainly not. Robert Cline returns in the second book of the series, "Escape from Dubai."

GLOSSARY OF NAMES

Rais: Captain

Rasil: Messenger

Turhan: Of Mercy

Aaquib: Follower

Baraah: Innocence

Atikah: Purity

Hafaza: The guardian angel

Shahzad: Son of a king

Malikah: Queen

Hami and Nasir: Shahzad's bodyguards (both names mean "protector" in Arabic)

Ghali: Valuable, dear, beloved

Umair: Intelligent.

Waqas: Warrior.

Batal: Champion.

Mudir Al-Shaitan: Like "27 Gauge Long Shaft" on Facebook, and ask author Craig Droskin the meaning or significance of this or any name that appears in the book. Also submit any questions about 27 Gauge Long Shaft or future books in the Robert Cline series. Follow on Twitter @27GaugeLong.

"Muslim Boy Names." Names 4 Muslims. Copyright 2014 Names4Muslims. com Accessed June 1, 2013, from http://www.names4muslims.com/names/baby-boy-names.html

Made in the USA
Columbia, SC
08 July 2020